TALES OF THE

Frog Princess

E.D. BAKER

BLOOMSBURY

LONDON BERLIN NEW YORK SYDNEY

Bloomsbury Publishing, London, Berlin, New York and Sydney

This omnibus edition published in Great Britain in 2007 by
Bloomsbury Publishing Plc
50 Bedford Square, London, WC1B 3DP

The Frog Princess first published in Great Britain by
Bloomsbury Publishing Plc in 2002

Dragon's Breath first published in Great Britain by
Bloomsbury Publishing Plc in 2003

Once Upon a Curse first published in Great Britain by
Bloomsbury Publishing Plc in 2004

A CIP catalogue record for this book is available from the British Library

ISBN 978 0 7475 8946 4

FSC
www.fsc.org
MIX
Paper from
responsible sources
FSC® C018072

Typeset by Dorchester Typesetting Group Ltd
Printed in Great Britain by Clays Ltd, St Ives Plc

3 5 7 9 10 8 6 4 2

www.bloomsbury.com

This book is dedicated to Ellie for being my first reader; to Kimmy, Nate, Emiko, Sophie, and Andy for their love and support; to Victoria for her insight; and to all my wonderful fans for being so encouraging

Contents

The Frog Princess 1

Dragon's Breath 219

Once Upon a Curse 515

The Frog Princess

One

Even as a little girl, I had thought that the swamp was a magical place where new lives began and old ones ended, where enemies and heroes weren't always what one expected, and where anything could happen, even to a clumsy princess. Although I'd believed this for most of my life, I had no proof until Prince Jorge came to visit and I met the frog of my dreams.

I had gone to the swamp to avoid the prince, a favorite of my mother's but never of mine. My escape hadn't been planned, yet the moment I heard that Jorge was coming, I knew I couldn't stay. Normally, few people in the castle ever seemed to notice me, so it was easy to sneak away undetected and flee to the swamp. It was only after I was secure in my escape that I began to worry about how my mother would react. I could almost see the disdain in her eyes as she gave me her usual speech about the proper behavior of a princess. Although I saw her as infrequently as we both could manage, I'd long since grown accustomed to that look.

Thinking more about my mother than I was about my surroundings, I almost stepped on a snake that had slithered onto the path from the tall grass. I shrieked and jumped back, catching my heel on the root of an old willow tree. With my arms flung wide, I tried to keep my balance, but my long, heavy skirts and usual clumsiness overwhelmed me and I landed hard on the rain-soaked earth. Grasshoppers exploded up from the ground as I floundered about, struggling to get to my feet, my gown soaking in the pungent odor of the swamp. Unfortunately, being born a princess doesn't automatically make a girl graceful or confident, a fact I've lamented for most of my fourteen years.

When I'd finally gathered my skirts and pushed myself off the ground, the snake had disappeared into the tall swamp grass. I edged away, searching for something that I could use to defend myself should the snake reappear.

"Thanks a lot!" said a throaty voice.

I looked around, but there was no one in sight. "Who said that?" I asked. Aside from my aunt Grassina, I was the only one from the castle who ever visited the swamp.

"It's me, over here. You aren't very observant, are you?"

I turned toward the voice and looked high and low, but all I could see was the pond, its murky water partially rimmed with a halo of algae, and a stand of cattails at the far end. Aside from the dragonflies, mosquitoes, and water striders, the only other living creature was a frog glaring at me from the edge of the pond. I jumped when he spoke again, although it wasn't so much his words that surprised me as seeing his lips move. I'm used to magic, for my aunt Grassina is a witch, but no animal had ever spoken to me before.

"I was going to eat those grasshoppers for lunch, but because of you I'll never catch them now!" The frog scowled, shaking his webbed finger in my direction. "A big, galumphing girl like you should be more careful where she puts her feet!"

"I'm sorry," I said, offended. "I didn't mean to. It was an accident."

"Hah!" said the frog. "Apologies won't bring back my lunch! But then, it wouldn't matter to you, would it? I bet you've never gone hungry a day in your life!"

The frog annoyed me. It was enough that I had to watch my tongue around my mother. I wasn't about to do it around a frog as well. "For your information," I said, frowning at the little creature, "I haven't eaten a thing all day. My mother invited Prince Jorge to visit and I left home before he arrived. I couldn't bear the thought of spending an entire day with him."

"What is wrong with you?" demanded the frog, curling his lip. "Missing a meal because you don't like someone! You would never catch me doing that! I know Jorge and even he isn't …" The frog blinked and his eyes opened wide. He leaned closer, scrutinizing me from head to toe as if seeing me for the first time. "Wait a minute … If your mother invited a prince to visit, does that mean that you're a princess?"

"Maybe," I said.

The frog grinned from eardrum to eardrum. Straightening his smooth green shoulders, he bowed from where his waist would have been if he'd had one. "I do apologize, Your Highness! If I had realized that you were such an exalted personage, I would never have made such churlish comments."

I groaned and rolled my eyes. "Give me a break. I hate it when people talk that way. I liked you better before you knew I was a princess."

"Ah-hah!" said the frog. He hopped toward me, his eyes never leaving my face. "I'm delighted to hear that you like me! In that case, would you be so kind as to do me the eensy-weensiest little favor?"

"And what might that be?" I asked, regretting my question even before the words were out of my mouth.

"Would you do me the honor of giving me a kiss?"

I couldn't help but laugh. I guffawed, I chortled, I wheezed. I laughed like I always do. Startled blackbirds took to the air as if hurled from a little boy's slingshot. A turtle basking in the sun scuttled off his rock and plopped into the water. The frog stared at me through narrowed eyes. "Are you sure you're a princess? You don't laugh like one."

"I know," I said, wiping away tears. "My mother tells me that all the time. According to her, a princess's laughter should sound like the tinkling of a bell, not the bray of a donkey. I've told her that I can't help it. My laugh is not something I can control, not if it's sincere. I don't think about it. It just happens."

"Whatever you say," said the frog. "So how about that kiss?" Puckering his lips, he rose up on his toes and raised his face in my direction.

I shook my head. "Sorry, I'm not interested in kissing a frog."

"I've been told that kissing a frog is good for the complexion," he said, sidling toward me.

"I doubt it. Anyway, my complexion is fine."

"What about the old saying, kissing a frog would bring you luck?"

"I've never heard that saying. It can't be too old. I think you just made it up. All kissing a frog would bring me is slimy lips." I shuddered and backed away. "The answer is no, so quit asking!"

The frog sighed and scratched the side of his head with his toe. "Maybe you would feel otherwise if you knew that I was a prince turned into a frog by an evil witch. I had the misfortune to criticize her fashion sense.

She didn't take kindly to my comments."

"What does that have to do with a kiss?"

"If I can get a princess to kiss me, I'll turn back into a prince!"

"That's not very flattering to me, now, is it? All you need is a kiss from any old princess. A girl likes to think that her very first kiss will be something special. Well, I'm not going to kiss you! I have no idea where you've been. I could catch some awful disease. Besides, considering what you must eat, I bet you have awful breath."

"Well!" said the frog. He drew himself up to his full froggy height. "Now you're being rude. I simply asked you for the courtesy of a small favor and instead you insult me."

"That was a big favor and you know it. I kiss only people I like, and I just met you!"

"But this is important. It's a matter of life or froghood!"

"I'm sorry. I'm not in the habit of kissing strangers, regardless of their species. Can't you get someone else to kiss you? There must be another princess you could ask. Someone petite who doesn't trip over her own feet." Although I wasn't about to admit it to the frog, his comment about my size still rankled. I had heard the same kind of remark from my mother many times, but it never stopped bothering me.

"Sure! I'll ask one of the hundreds of other

princesses who are hanging around the swamp, begging to be kissed!"

I'd had enough. Gathering my skirts in one hand, I turned to go. "If that's the way you're going to be, I'm leaving. I left the castle today so I wouldn't have to visit with an obnoxious prince. Now here I am, talking to an obnoxious frog who says he's a prince."

"No! Wait! Come back!" called the frog. "You can't go now! This is an emergency! Where's your compassion? Where's your sympathy? Where's my kiss?"

I stopped at the edge of the path and tried to speak in a calm voice. It wasn't easy, and I'm afraid my words came out sounding short and sharp. "I don't care if it's the end of the world as we know it," I said between gritted teeth. "I have better things to do with my time than listen to unreasonable requests from a frog. Good day, Frog."

The last thing I saw before I turned to leave was the hopeless look in the frog's eyes. It was the look of someone in terrible trouble. It was a look that would haunt me for the rest of the day.

Two

I spent the rest of the afternoon visiting my favorite places in the swamp. Following hidden pathways, I skirted the treacherous, boggy ground until I reached solid footing. After searching the thicket where I'd stumbled across twin fawns earlier that spring, I lounged by the deep pool that mirrored the drifting, puffball clouds. As the day grew warmer, I took off my shoes and stockings and waded through a shallow stream to a tiny island whose smooth, water-tumbled pebbles felt good under my bare feet.

It was late by the time I returned to the castle. Rather than going straight to my bedchamber, I climbed the long, narrow tower steps to my aunt Grassina's apartments. The Green Witch, as she is called, is my mother's sister and has lived in the castle since before I was born. She has taught me more than anyone else ever has, and not just about how to be a princess. And unlike the rest of my family, she doesn't criticize me at every opportunity.

Reaching the top of the stairs, I knocked softly on the door and waited for her to answer. Somehow, she always knew who was knocking. She'd told me how useful a skill that was, because she wouldn't have to answer the door if it were someone she didn't want to see. After only a few seconds the door flew open, but instead of my aunt's familiar features I saw a yellow duckling drop a gnawed stick and rush out of the room to snap at my ankles.

"Come back here, Bowser!" my aunt called from inside the room. "I'm not finished with you yet!"

The duckling darted back and forth, quacking loudly as it herded me over the threshold.

"Shut the door, Emeralda!" shouted my aunt from her seat by her workbench. "That stupid dog won't hold still long enough for me to finish the spell!"

"This is Bowser?" I asked, trying to fend off the ball of fluff that was viciously attacking the toe of my shoe. "Father won't be happy that you turned his favorite hound into a duck."

"Duck, dog, what's the difference? Bowser will be his miserable self again faster than you can say the Greek alphabet backward. Now, where was I? Oh, yes. Here, sprinkle some of this on him while I find the spell again."

"What, me? I can't!" I backed away from her outstretched hand. "I'll make a mess of it! Remember that time with the crab apple dumplings?" After I used that spell to make them, they grew claws and ran away. It took us weeks to find the crabby little things, and by then they were stale and their claws had pinched us black and blue.

"Phooey," said Aunt Grassina. "Everybody makes mistakes."

"But not the kind I make! I used that cleaning spell you told me about nearly four months ago and it's still as strong as ever! Every time I drop anything on the floor in my chamber, a little breeze whisks it away and dumps it on the dung heap behind the stables. You wouldn't believe how many stockings and hairpins I've lost that way! I can't do magic anymore. I just make things worse when I do."

"How do you ever think you'll learn to be a witch if you don't try?"

"I don't want to be a witch!" I said for the hundredth time. "I know you think I should, but I'd be terrible at it. If I could mess up such simple cooking and cleaning spells, imagine what I could do with something really important. We could all end up with three left feet or stuck head-down in some desert!"

"Oh, Emma! Of course you want to be a witch! You just don't know it yet. Give yourself some time and a little more practice. I'm sure you'll be very good at it once you decide to apply yourself. Now, where is that parchment? I know I put it around here somewhere."

I left my aunt shuffling through a stack of old, musty parchments and headed toward my favorite chair in front of the fireplace. The truth was, I used to dream about being a witch like Grassina, but to try so hard for so long and never have anything go quite right … I slumped into the chair and closed my eyes, letting my bad day melt away in the peace of Grassina's room.

The difference between my aunt's room and the rest of the castle was wonderful. Whereas the castle itself was cold and damp and generally gloomy, Grassina's room was warm and inviting. A small fire always burned behind the decorated iron grate, heating the entire room, yet never needing new logs. Gleaming balls of witches' light bumped against the ceiling, bathing the white-washed walls and brightly colored tapestries with a rosy glow. The cold stone floors were covered with thick, woven rugs of various shades of green, giving it the appearance of a forest floor dappled with sunlight. Sometimes the room smelled of freshly crushed mint leaves, or pine boughs like the ones used to decorate the Great Hall during the winter celebrations, or sun-warmed clover on a summer's day.

Two chairs cushioned for comfort and separated by a small table waited in front of the hearth. A fragrant bouquet of crystalline flowers bloomed in an etched bowl atop the table. A gift from the fairies, the bouquet was the home to glass butterflies whose delicate wings clicked softly as they flitted from one blossom to another. I'd spent many hours curled up in one of the chairs while my aunt occupied the other, regaling me with stories of far-off lands and times long ago.

There were many wonders to be found in my aunt's room. One of her tapestries depicted a miniature town in perfect detail with a lion and a unicorn fighting each other in the streets. Once, when I touched the lion with my fingertip, it bit me, taking a small sliver of skin from my finger. I howled as tears streamed down my face. My mother cuffed me for lying, but Grassina winked and wrapped my wound in spider's silk.

A sea witch named Coral had given Grassina a large bowl filled with salt water and the tiny replica of a castle, spires and all. The castle was perfect in every detail, and occasionally I'd see schools of miniature fish swimming by.

Sometimes, when I'd visit after the sun had set, I saw lights glowing in the tiny windows of the castle. Even so, I never would have thought it more than an interesting curiosity if I hadn't come to visit my aunt one winter's afternoon when I was nine or so. Having taken longer than usual to answer my knock, she came to the door with dripping hair and a cloth she was using to dry it. The entire room smelled strongly of fish, but when I asked what she'd been doing, she smiled and left the room to change her clothes. As I moved to warm my hands by the fireplace, I stepped in a damp patch on the floor and thought that the salt water in the bowl had overflowed. Glancing at the bowl, I saw a flash of silver and blue. I hurried closer to peer into the water, just as the diminutive figure of a mermaid reached one of the tiny doors. Jerking the door open, she turned to look over her shoulder and saw me. Her eyes grew wide in alarm and she darted through the opening, slamming the door behind her. I began to think that the bowl might contain more than it appeared.

The duckling quacked, a surprising sound in the quiet room. I opened my eyes and sat up, turning toward my aunt Grassina. She was perched on a tall stool facing a massive wooden table, ignoring the duckling as it gnawed on the table leg. An old quill pen stuck out of Grassina's thick chestnut hair, the same color as mine.

I've been told that Grassina and I look much alike, but whereas her nose is thin and refined, mine is prominent like my father's. Her eyes are green, a shade or two lighter than my own. Grassina's smile is beautiful on the rare occasion when she treats us to one. However, her smile never seems to reach her eyes. My old nanny, long since retired, told me that Grassina was quite cheerful in her youth but that time and my grandmother had taken their toll.

Grassina always wore green and her gown on this day was the color of summer moss. Shapeless and loose, it had no certain style, hanging limply from her tall frame. My aunt always dressed as she pleased, never worrying about what others might think. I was not so fortunate; my mother never let me forget that a princess is always on display.

I watched as Grassina, caught up in her work, used both hands to hold a partially unrolled parchment. Other parchments littered the table and spilled onto the floor. The last rays of the setting sun slanted through the window to pool on the surface of the table and turn her farseeing ball, just like the one she'd given me, into a dazzling sphere of light. A small apple-green snake lay coiled among the parchments, soaking up the sun's warmth.

"What are those for?" I asked. I hopped out of my chair and crossed the room to stand beside my aunt. The snake raised its head and flicked its tongue in my direction. Shuddering, I stepped back a pace or two. Although the creature had lived with my aunt for many years, I had never grown used to its presence. There were few things I feared in the world more than snakes, regardless of the temperament or type.

"I was cataloging my parchments when I came across the spell for ducklings. I thought I'd try it out and Bowser just happened to be handy. Now, where is that spell? I know it was in one of these. . . .

"So," she said, turning around in her seat and raising

an eyebrow. "I have a feeling you have a question for me. You do have a question, don't you?"

"Have you ever turned anyone into something like, say, a frog?"

"Certainly. Human-to-frog is a simple spell and easy to remember. I've used it many times myself. Why do you ask?"

"I've met a frog who claims to be a prince, and I was wondering if he might be telling the truth."

"Now, that would be hard to say. He could be a prince, but then again he could simply be a talking frog. Some witches have strange senses of humor. I should know."

"Say he is a prince. What would he have to do to go back to being human?"

"That depends on the witch who cast the spell. But whatever it takes, she would have had to tell him. The spell won't work if there is no remedy or if she doesn't tell him what it is. However, the usual method involves asking a maiden, preferably a princess, for a kiss. I'm surprised you didn't know that. When I was young, kissing a frog was the only way some girls got dates. I myself spent too much time searching ponds and marshes for frogs to kiss. Of course, I was looking for one in particular at the time."

"You mean Haywood, your old beau?"

"You remember that story, do you? Yes, it's true.

After I brought him home to meet your grandmother, she took a dislike to him and he disappeared for good. I was convinced that she'd turned him into a frog. Your grandmother was never a very imaginative person. But try as I did, I never found my darling Haywood. I'd given up eating and sleeping and spent all of my time searching the swamp, kissing every frog I could catch. My mother finally made me stop by threatening to lock me in an abandoned tower in the middle of nowhere unless I returned to my studies. He wasn't just my beau, you know. We were engaged to be married. He was the only man I've ever loved."

"So to turn a frog back into a prince . . . ," I said, trying to get the conversation back on track.

"Oh, yes, well, it doesn't have to be a kiss. It could be anything, within limits. If a spell were too easy to break, it wouldn't be strong enough to last. If breaking it were impossible, it would go against the natural laws of magic and also wouldn't last. There is a certain degree of fairness involved, you know. Speaking of fairness, do you think that you were being fair when you took off this morning, leaving me to deal with your mother? Chartreuse was madder than a wet peacock when no one could find you. I told her I had sent you on an errand, so now she's angry with me again."

"Sorry about that," I said, avoiding her eyes. "And thank you for covering for me. Mother had invited

Prince Jorge to visit. Jorge spends all of his time bragging and acting as if I don't exist. I didn't see why I needed to be there. Jorge never talks to me anyway. As far as he's concerned, I might as well be a piece of furniture."

Bowser was scratching at my aunt's skirts with his webbed foot while making an odd whining sound. When she ignored him, he wandered off and attacked the table leg, his little bill clacking against the wood.

"Well, I don't mind this time," Grassina told me, brushing a stray lock of hair from her eyes, "but you'll have to face her one of these days. I won't always be around to cover for you like I was today. It's getting late and I doubt you've had a thing to eat. You'd better go get yourself something from the kitchen. I don't have time to cook for you and I'll never get anything done with you here distracting me. Now, where did I put that parchment?"

Three

The next morning I was out of bed and dressed long before the rest of the household was stirring. Wearing my dark blue gown with my pale blue kirtle, and carrying my third-best shoes in my hand, I tiptoed down the stairs, shivering at the icy chill of the stone. According to her maid, my mother had gone to bed with a headache the previous night. I had yet to see her. Coward that I was, I was determined to be out of the castle and away from the grounds before she could corner me about the previous day's disappearance.

The sun was peeking over the distant hills when I reached the edge of the swamp. A lone mosquito circled my head, whining in its high-pitched, irritating way. Tripping on my own feet, I stumbled into the underbrush and stirred up a cloud of its relatives. The blackflies swarmed as I neared the pond, but because I'd used a bitter-smelling salve that Grassina had made to repel them, none of the insects landed on me. Even so, the persistent whining began to get on my nerves. I flapped my hand to swat them away, and to my surprise, I connected with a large fly, knocking it over the water.

Thwip! A long, froggy tongue flicked out and snagged the fly. "Thanks!" said a familiar voice. "I needed that!"

"I wasn't trying to feed you," I said. "I just hate these obnoxious bugs."

"Really?" said the frog. "I think they're delightful, although some are a little too salty. So tell me, did you sleep well last night or did your conscience bother you for abandoning me in my hour of need?"

"No, I didn't sleep well. . . ."

"Ah-hah!"

"But it had nothing to do with my conscience. It was curiosity more than anything. I was wondering—exactly who is it you claim to be?"

"I am His Royal Highness, Prince Eadric of Upper Montevista." Bowing, the frog fluttered his hand in a noble gesture. "So what do you say?" he asked, looking up. "How about that kiss?"

"Just because you say you're Prince Eadric doesn't mean you really are. Traveling minstrels are awful gossips, and I would have heard if a prince had been turned into a frog."

"Only if people knew what had happened. I doubt my family has any knowledge of the calamity that befell me. Then again," he said under his breath, "they might know what happened and are trying to cover it up. That happens a lot in my family."

"Mine, too," I said. "You should see how fast my mother can make an embarrassing situation disappear. You'd almost think that she was the witch instead of Aunt Grassina."

"You have an aunt who's a witch?" the frog asked, becoming agitated. "Is she ... Is she really ugly with hair like a thistle? Is she mean and nasty and cruel to innocent fashion critics?"

"No, nothing like that. My aunt Grassina is wonderful! She's the best relative anybody could have. Grassina is the only one in my family who doesn't ridicule me for being clumsy. She doesn't expect me to be the perfect little lady every minute of the day, and she's taught me a lot of useful things that no one else would ever have thought of teaching me. And her presents! My parents always give me boring presents like clothes on my birthdays, but aunt Grassina gives me much more interesting things, like my farseeing ball and a bottomless bottle of perfume and this beautiful charm bracelet." I shook my wrist for emphasis, making my bracelet jingle merrily. "Grassina told me what the symbols mean, but I was only a little girl then, so I don't really remember. I love it, though. It glows in the dark and I wear it all the time, even at night."

Mosquitoes tickled my scalp, the one place I hadn't

put any salve. When I tried to brush them away with my hand, one of my combs fell out and landed in the mud. I reached for it and it came out with a squelch, splattering my sleeve with muddy droplets. "Listen, I'd better go now. If you're Eadric, you're going to have to prove it."

"How?"

"I don't know. Think of something. I'll come back when I can."

I hurried off with the insects pursuing me all the way home. It didn't seem to matter where I was—it just wasn't going to be an easy morning. I knew I couldn't put off facing my mother any longer, and my stomach was already tying itself in knots. I tried to distract myself by thinking of the frog's request. If he really was Prince Eadric, he was in big trouble and needed my help. I couldn't stand to see any animal suffer, whether he was an enchanted prince or not. And if it was all a trick, well, I needed to know that, too. I already made a fool of myself too often without someone else doing it for me.

My mother must have alerted all the servants to watch for me: as soon as I set foot on the castle grounds the head gardener intercepted me and hustled me off to my mother's chamber. For someone who had been anxious to see me, my mother didn't seem very pleased.

"So there you are!" she said, looking me over from head to toe just as she always did. "Stand up straight, Emeralda! Don't slouch! Look at you! Your hair is a mess, your dress is soiled, and you have mud on your shoes." My mother lifted her chin and sniffed daintily, her delicate nostrils flaring only the tiniest bit, the barely discernable wrinkles around her eyes deepening only slightly.

"Good morning, Mother. I'm sorry I displease you."

"You've been off to that dreadful swamp again, I see." Mother curled her lip in disgust.

"Yes, Mother," I said, focusing on one of Mother's carefully crafted curls. She spent hours on her appearance each morning, and I had never seen her without her honey-gold hair looking perfect.

"It's a pity you weren't around yesterday. I had a lovely visit with Prince Jorge. He really is quite charming."

"Yes, Mother," I said, barely able to force the words past my lips. Although I'd seen him be charming to other people, he'd never acted that way toward me. The first time I met him I tripped entering the room. Instead of helping me up, he laughed, making me feel even more like an idiot. Our relationship had only gone downhill from there.

"I've done something wonderful for you, child, and you will, of course, thank me for it."

"Thank you, Mother," I said, wondering what it could be. The last time I'd had to thank her without knowing what I was thanking her for, I'd been ill and she'd invited a bloodletter to put leeches on me. I hoped there were no leeches involved this time, although with my mother, anything was possible.

Mother smiled smugly as she adjusted the lace on her sleeve. "I've begun engagement negotiations. We've tentatively scheduled the wedding for the end of the summer."

My heart sank. Marry Prince Jorge? I couldn't believe that anyone might think that we were suitable for each other. I was clumsy in social situations and terrified of talking in public, never knowing quite what to say. Jorge was poised and handsome and so full of himself that even his horse had to kneel when his master entered the stable. I began to think that the arrival of the bloodletter and his leeches might have been better news.

"But I can't marry Jorge! We don't love each other!"

My mother gave me a look so cold that I stepped back a pace. "What does that have to do with anything?" she asked. "Husbands and wives who love each other are the exception, not the rule. Stop whining and be happy that he wants your hand at all. Not many princes would be willing to marry someone as awkward as you. Despite all my efforts, you have few social graces. If only you'd been born a boy as your father and I had wanted! Maybe then I could have made something of you. As it is, this match is the best that you can hope for, so I expect you to be gracious about it. Now see what you've done! I can feel my headache returning."

Marrying Jorge would be a terrible mistake. I was beginning to feel so desperate that I was unable to let the subject drop. "Mother," I said, "Jorge is a fool! I can't marry him!"

"Many women have married fools and been perfectly happy. Negotiations have begun and despite what you may think, they do not require your approval. You should be glad that I care enough to arrange a marriage for you at all. Now, hurry and fetch my maid. My head is pounding."

I was devastated. To think that my mother wanted me to leave my beautiful swamp and marry that horrid Prince Jorge! After sending my mother's maid to her, I went in search of my aunt Grassina, but the door to her tower room was locked. A dripping sign written in red berry juice had been nailed to the thick wood.

> Beware, all ye who would trespass here. Those who set foot beyond this portal uninvited shall have their hearts ripped out by dragons and their brains eaten by maggots. Deliverymen, please leave all packages by the door. Emeralda, I've been called away for a few days. I'll let you know when I get back. We'll make your favorite fruit tarts.
>
> Grassina, the Green Witch

I had to talk to someone about my mother's dreadful plans. I went in search of a friend who wasn't too busy to talk to me, but I didn't have much luck. Fortunata, the daughter of mother's favorite lady-in-waiting, was sick in bed with a cold and couldn't be disturbed, which was just as well, for she was a terrible snob herself and probably would have considered Prince Jorge a great catch. Violet, the scullery maid, was scrubbing the kitchen floor for the second time that day and was not in a good mood. Bernard, the undergardener, was being scolded for failing to rid the garden of slugs. Chloe, the second-best seamstress, was helping the head seamstress sew yet another gown for my mother. I tried to think of someone else I could talk to, someone who wouldn't be too busy or impatient for a real conversation. Somehow, I kept thinking about the obnoxious little frog in the swamp. He was rude and sarcastic, but at least he wanted to talk to me.

Hurrying back to the swamp, I was surprised at how eager I was to see the frog again. When I saw him sitting on his lily pad, I smiled for the first time that day.

"Couldn't stay away, huh?" he said as soon as he saw me. "Sorry, I haven't thought of any proof yet, although I could tell you about some of my exploits. I'm sure the minstrels are singing about them already. For instance, there was the time that I—"

"Never mind that now. I just have to talk to someone! You'll never guess what awful thing my mother has done!"

"She nailed all of your shoes to the floor."

"Of course not! Why would she do that?"

"She had a servant wash all of your whites with red stockings!"

"Whatever are you talking about? You aren't even close!"

"She ordered you to kiss the first frog you met!" the frog said, batting his eyelids at me.

"Not in a million years! I told you you'd never guess it. She's arranging for me to marry Prince Jorge!"

"You're kidding! I can't imagine anyone marrying Jorge. He's so in love with himself that there's no room for anyone else in the relationship. Have you ever seen the way he looks at his own reflection in a looking glass? It's enough to make a dog sick! And confidentially," whispered the frog after looking around to make sure that no one else was listening, "I've heard that Jorge has a fondness for ladies' shoes. He has a whole trunk of them that he keeps locked in his bedchamber!"

"I don't know about that, but I do know that I can't marry him. He's a rude idiot who barely acknowledges my existence. I could never be happy married to someone like that! Besides, he makes me so nervous I get all tongue-tied and can't think of what to say."

"You don't seem to have any problem talking to me," said the frog.

"You're different. It's easy to talk to you. You're just a frog."

"I'm a prince, too!"

"Maybe, but you don't look like one. You don't act like one, either, so it's easy to forget. But Jorge is something else. He never lets you forget that he's a prince."

"Maybe if you talk to your mother …"

"It wouldn't make a bit of difference if I did. Appearance is everything to my mother. I know she won't change her mind. And my father will do whatever she says just so he doesn't have to argue with her. How could my mother do this to me? Why, I'd rather marry you than Prince Jorge, whether you're a prince or not. You wouldn't ignore me or laugh at me, would you?"

The frog blinked in surprise. "No, of course not."

"See? And at least if I married you, I wouldn't have to leave the swamp!"

"Gee," said the frog, looking flustered. "I don't know. All I asked for was a kiss."

"You want a kiss? Fine! I'll give you a kiss. I'd rather kiss you than Prince Jorge any day!"

I knelt on the ground at the edge of the pond. With a mighty leap, the frog landed on the ground beside me and puckered his lips.

"Wait just a minute," I said, drawing back.

The frog looked distressed. "You haven't changed your mind, have you?"

"No, no, it's just that … well, here." Fumbling in the small pouch attached to the waist of my gown, I found an embroidered handkerchief. I reached out and gently patted the frog's mouth clean. "You had dried fly feet stuck to your lips," I said, shuddering. "All right, let's try again."

This time the kiss went without a hitch. I leaned down, puckered my lips, and closed my eyes. Violet, who had had far more experience than I, had told me you should always do that when kissing a boy. I assumed it was the same when kissing a boy frog. The frog's lips felt cool and smooth against mine. The sensation wasn't too unpleasant. It was what happened next that took me by surprise.

The tingling began in my fingers and toes, then spread up my arms and legs. A shiver ran up my spine, chased by a golden, fuzzy feeling. Suddenly, my head felt light and full of bubbles. A tremendous wind rushed past me, knocking me to the ground. I covered my face with my arms, but my arms no longer felt real. When I tried to stand, my whole body shook, and a gray cloud filled my head.

Four

I opened my eyes and blinked. My head felt woozy; nothing would come into focus. Gradually my vision sharpened, but everything looked different somehow. The colors seemed brighter and there were more of them. An enormous butterfly flew past, its wings see-sawing up and down through the air. It wore beautiful reds and shades of purple that I'd never seen before.

"Oh!" I said aloud, and flinched at the timbre of my own voice. It sounded strange in my ears and talking made my throat feel funny.

My nostrils flared at the sour smell of decaying vegetation and swamp muck. The leaves in the trees rattled loudly in the wind while the hum of a million insects nearly deafened me. *Thump!* Something heavy hit the damp soil by the edge of the pond. *Thump!* It came again, louder and closer. Heavy breathing filled the air.

I tried to stand, but my legs wouldn't cooperate. Still dazed, I looked down. The ground was much closer than it had been only a few moments ago; the clumps of dirt were larger as well. A pair of webbed feet and long, muscular legs stretched out in front of me. Puzzled, I squeezed my eyes shut, then opened them to look again. The legs were attached to a short, plump body covered with mottled, green skin. My brain refused to acknowledge what my eyes told me. I lifted my hand and wiggled my fingers. Four green, crooked fingers twitched. Suddenly, I understood: I wasn't looking at some other creature. I was looking at myself!

"What's this? What's happened? How did this—" I babbled. My heart raced as panic set in. "I'm dreaming, that's it! I'm home in bed and I'm dreaming!"

Thump! Whatever I'd heard before was coming closer. I squeezed my eyes shut and pressed my body to the ground. "I'm imagining this. If I ignore it, it'll go away," I said aloud. My mother had often derided me for having a vivid imagination, but this was too much even for me!

Thump! Thump! Thump! Something large and wet pressed against my back, snuffling hot, smelly air from my head to my feet. *It's so real,* I thought, and opened first one eye, then the other. An enormous white dog with short, dirty fur loomed over me, studying me intently with its huge, red-rimmed eyes. My father's dogs were all brown or black or gray. This dog was a stranger to me and therefore all the more frightening. I shuddered as it pushed me with its nose, tumbling me over onto my side. It snuffled me once more, then opened its cavernous mouth wide. My stomach churned from the smell of the dog's breath. A big drop of hot, stinky slobber dripped onto my head.

This is not a dream, I thought. With a convulsive twitch, I rolled to my feet and leaped as far and as fast as I could. My movements were clumsy and uncoordinated, but I leaped again and again, each time putting more and more distance between the dog and myself. One final leap, a half twist, and a flop, and I landed in the water with a splash.

"Frog!" said the dog as it belly-flopped into the water after me. "Come back! I need to talk to you!"

Too frightened to answer the dog, I flailed my arms and tried to get away. Although I'd grown up near the water, I had never learned how to swim. As clumsy as I was, I was sure that if I ever stepped in water that went higher than my ankles I would drown. I floundered, thrashing my arms and legs and going nowhere. The dog lunged for me again, creating a wave that washed me toward the middle of the pond. Drawing up my legs, I kicked hard and shot through the water, away from the dog and its crushing jaws. *It worked!* I thought, surprised at myself. I did it again. The water rushed past as I hurtled forward, barely missing a tiny sunfish. I twisted around and rose to the surface to look for the dog.

Dashing back and forth in the shallow water at the edge of the pond, the beast was no longer a threat.

A wave of relief washed over me. *I did it!* I thought. *I got away from that giant dog all on my own! I can do anything!* Gleefully, I twirled around in the water. I splashed from one side of the pond to the other, and when I grew tired of kicking, I ducked my head and blew bubbles. Floating on my stomach, I watched the minnows dart past in frenzied formation. I enjoyed every minute of it, delighting in the sensation of the warm water coursing against my skin. As a princess, I had never been able to go outside unencumbered by heavy fabric and long skirts. The new feeling of freedom was exhilarating!

Eventually, I rolled onto my back and gazed up at the wispy clouds high in the clear blue sky. I wondered what had happened to Frog. I hadn't seen him since my transformation. It occurred to me that maybe it was a trick. Maybe we had switched places and he was now a human. But how could that have happened without my seeing it? Besides, although he might be obnoxious, I didn't think he was sneaky.

I climbed onto a partially submerged log, and thought about all that had happened that day. In the excitement of my escape from the dog and the discovery of my newfound abilities, I hadn't really thought about what I would do next. I was alone in the swamp with no one to turn to. What was I going to *do?*

Distraught, I hunched down and began to cry. I hated crying and almost never did. My mother had told me many times that a princess should never cry in public, but I knew that sometimes a person just couldn't help it. Large tears rolled down my cheeks and plopped onto the rough bark of the log. I was so miserable that I didn't notice Frog climb up beside me.

Five

"What's wrong?" Frog asked. He had to ask me twice before the question pierced my bubble of misery.

"Oh," I said, peering at him through tear-filled eyes. "It's you."

"I'm glad you're so thrilled to see me," Frog said. "But you still haven't answered my question. What's wrong? Why are you crying?"

"Isn't it obvious?" I asked. "I'm a frog and it's your fault! This wasn't supposed to happen. You said you would turn back into a prince. You never said I could turn into a frog!"

"What do I look like, a gypsy fortune-teller? No one ever told me this might happen. I'm sorry. I can't imagine why it did. But it's not so bad, you know. Being a frog, that is. I've been a frog for quite a while. It really does have its advantages."

"Oh?" I sniffled. "Like what?"

Frog shrugged. "You won't have to marry Jorge, for one. Life is less complicated as a frog. Why, I can do whatever I want to, like stay up all night or sleep all day. I don't have all the responsibilities or the worries that I used to have, either. You can't imagine how much of a relief it is not to be asked to slay a dragon or behead an ogre or shut down the troll extortion rings under the bridges, although I must admit that I was very good at all three. Now I only have to worry about finding enough food and being eaten."

"Those sound like pretty serious worries to me," I said.

"Not if you keep your wits about you and pay attention to what's going on. Which is something you need to learn to do."

"I guess I have been a little preoccupied."

"Do you think so? Come on! A dozen dragons could have landed here and toasted you for lunch and you wouldn't have noticed. You're lucky that I'm the one who climbed onto this log! But don't worry. I got you into this, so I'll teach you what you need to know."

"You don't have to teach me anything! Just undo whatever you did and turn me back into a princess!"

"I wish I could," said Frog. "Except I have no idea how to do it."

"Then you'll have to help me find out! I may not have been the happiest princess, but I don't want to spend the rest of my life as a frog! I can't believe this happened! At first I thought it was all a dream, but … Say, where did you go, anyway? I didn't see you around when that dog came."

Frog shrugged his smooth green shoulders. "When you kissed me and I didn't become my handsome, princely self again, I admit I was a little upset. It took a while before I noticed that you weren't around anymore, at least as a human. By the time I realized what must have happened, that dog was there and you were hopping around like a lunatic. You disappeared, but it was easy to find you since everyone in the swamp was gossiping about the crazy talking female frog who couldn't swim any better than a newly hatched tadpole."

"I thought I swam quite well!" I said, remembering my pride in my newly learned skill.

"Maybe for a rank beginner."

I couldn't help it. My lip began to quiver.

"Don't do that!" he said. "This is fresh water and you're going to make it salty!"

Two big tears rolled down my cheeks. I sniffled louder.

"Now what's wrong?" Frog asked impatiently.

"Everything!" I wailed. "I've been trying so hard and I thought I was a good swimmer and now you tell me that I'm not and I'm a frog and I don't want to be and I'm scared and now on top of everything else I'm hungry!"

"Maybe if you kissed me again, you'd feel better,"

said Frog, leaning toward me.

"What?" I said, so surprised that I stopped crying. "Why would I want to do that?"

"It might cheer you up."

"I don't think so!"

"Well, then, maybe we'd be lucky and it would reverse the spell."

"And maybe we'd be unlucky and something worse would happen, although I can't imagine anything worse than being turned into a frog." I began to sniffle again.

"So!" Frog said quickly. "You said you're hungry. Now, that's something we can fix."

"What do you eat?" I asked, rubbing my eyelids with my fingers.

"Whatever comes along. Just watch me. You'll get the idea."

Frog hopped to the tip of the log and sat motionless. He sat still for so long that by the time he finally made his move, I'd become bored and fidgety and almost missed seeing what he did. A dragonfly about the length of a grown man's thumb zigzagged past the end of the log. Without warning, Frog leaped, opened his mouth, and flicked out his tongue. Before he hit the water, Frog had curled his tongue back into his mouth, dragging the dragonfly with it.

"You expect me to do that?" I asked incredulously when Frog rejoined me on the log.

"Only if you want to eat," Frog replied, licking his lips. "Look," he said, holding up the dragonfly's wings. "Aren't they beauties? If we were near my pad, I'd add them to my collection."

"You collect those things?"

"Are you kidding? I'm becoming quite an expert, if I do say so myself. My collection is probably the largest and most comprehensive in the world. Now look over there. See that big, juicy fly headed this way? Go ahead, I'll let you have it."

"I'm not eating a fly!" My stomach churned at the thought.

"You will when you get hungry enough. Watch me. I'll show you one more time."

"You can show me a million times, but that doesn't mean I'm going to do it. Isn't there anything else to eat besides bugs?"

"Hmm," said Frog. "I'll tell you what. I know a spot where there's lots to eat, but we're going to have to swim to get there."

"Fine with me," I said. "As long as I don't have to eat flies."

Frog grinned. "Stay near me and do what I do." He hopped to the edge of the log and plopped into the water. I followed close behind, worried that I might lose sight of him.

With Frog leading the way, we headed back

downstream. Swimming with the current was much easier, and I was surprised at how quickly we reached the pond. Suddenly, Frog motioned for me to stop, and even though I couldn't understand why, I remembered my promise to follow his lead. Sneaking a look past him, I saw what he had already noticed. A hungry heron stood at the edge of the water, searching the reeds for a likely meal. The bird towered over us, with its long, sticklike legs going on forever. Placing his finger to his lips, Frog signaled me to be silent. I nodded and followed him around the opposite edge of the pond.

We dove deep, staying out of sight near the bottom, skirting the water weeds that grew thickly on the sunny side. We were still hiding from the heron when a shadow blocked the sun. I looked up to see a large dark shape gliding through the water over our heads. A golden circle dangled from its mouth, glistening in the morning light. Suspended from the circle, little shapes twinkled in a familiar way.... It was my bracelet! I lurched forward, determined to retrieve my property, but Frog grabbed my arm and held me still until the shape had passed out of sight.

Pent-up anger and frustration propelled me to the surface when Frog finally let me go. "Did you see that?" I asked after taking a quick breath of fresh air. "That big animal—what was it?"

"An otter," replied Frog.

"It had my bracelet—the one my aunt gave me! We have to find that otter! I need that bracelet and I have to get it back!"

"No, you don't. Don't you know anything about otters?"

"Of course I do. My aunt Grassina told me all about them; where they live, how they play …"

"How they eat frogs …"

"They eat frogs?" I squeaked.

"We're their favorite food."

Suddenly, our swim didn't seem quite so carefree. I looked around, half expecting to see hungry eyes watching us from the muddy bank. "There are lots of animals that like to eat frogs, aren't there?" I asked.

Frog nodded. "We're on nearly everyone's list of favorite foods. That's why you have to be on the lookout all the time."

"And my bracelet …"

"Gone for good, which is probably just as well. You wouldn't be able to carry it now anyway. Come on, we don't have much farther to go."

A short distance later, Frog led the way up the bank and across marshy ground to a small hill. A wild plum tree grew at the top; the ground around it was littered with rotting fruit. Green and black flies zipped from one overripe plum to another.

"This is the food you were talking about?"

"Sure is. Help yourself."

Although the plums didn't look very appetizing, I was convinced that they had to taste better than the flies. I hopped to the nearest plum and tried to find a spot that wasn't too rotten.

"There's a part at the top that doesn't look bad," said Frog.

"How do I reach it from here?"

"You're a frog. Use your tongue," suggested Frog.

"My tongue? I can't do that! Are you sure I can't use my hands?"

"Not if you really want to eat. You're a frog now and frogs use their tongues."

"I don't know. I'm not very coordinated ..."

"Don't be a tadpole! You can do it!"

"I'll try," I said doubtfully. I opened my mouth and uncoiled my tongue, flicking it toward the top of the fruit. The first time I did it, I didn't put enough energy into it and my tongue flopped onto the ground.

"Nice try!" said Frog, snickering behind his hand.

I glared at him as I tried to brush the dirt and grass off my tongue. Although I was very careful, I didn't get it all off, and it felt prickly when I pulled my tongue back into my mouth. Refusing to be discouraged, I tried again with all my strength. Unfortunately, I was too enthusiastic. My tongue hit the soft skin of the rotting fruit and continued on into the center of the pulp. When I tried to pull my tongue out, it wouldn't come. I jerked my head back, hoping to yank my tongue out that way, but it just made my mouth hurt. Frog was no help at all, standing off to one side, his stomach jiggling as he laughed at me. Finally, I grabbed hold of my tongue with both hands and pulled, jerking it out so fast that it flew back and hit me in the eye. I staggered, rubbing my head while Frog rolled on the ground, holding his sides and howling.

"Thanks for the encouragement!" I said once I had my tongue back in my mouth. "I thought you said you would never laugh at me. Now what do I do?"

"Try again!" he said. "I haven't laughed this hard in a long time!"

I thought about sticking my tongue out at him, something I'd seen Violet do to one of the pageboys, but because I seemed to have so little control over it, I was afraid I might actually hit him with it by mistake. "Turn around!" I said instead. "I can't do this while you're watching me."

Frog was still chortling when he turned to face the other way. When I knew he wasn't looking, I sidled over to another piece of fruit, not liking the taste of the first plum. This one was bigger and glistened with juice. It was also covered with flies. I flicked out my tongue again, and this time I did it just right, hitting close to where I was aiming. The fruit was squishy and tasted sour, although not as bad as the first one I'd tried, but when I pulled my tongue in, a fly was stuck to the tip. It was the most disgusting thing I had ever done.

"Yuck!" I shouted. "Ged dis ding oth my tongue!" The fly wriggled and buzzed, trying to get free. Frog was there in an instant, but all he did was poke my tongue with his finger. I gagged and my tongue snapped back into place. The fly buzzed loudly, tickling the roof of my mouth.

"Mmph!" I said, pleading for help from Frog.

"Blink!" he ordered.

"Mmph?" I said again.

"Don't think, just blink!"

I couldn't imagine what blinking had to do with the fly in my mouth, but I tried it anyway. I blinked. When my eyelids closed, my eyeballs pushed down on my throat, and I swallowed the fly. I shuddered when I realized what I'd done.

"Gross! Yuck!" I said, then spit until my mouth was dry.

"Good, huh?" asked Frog.

"Good? It was disgusting!" I wiped my tongue with my fingers, trying to get rid of the taste.

"Be honest, now. What did it taste like?"

"Horrible!"

"Really?"

"Well," I said reluctantly, "the plum was sour, but the fly was kind of sweet."

"Ah-hah!" said Frog. "I knew you'd like it! You may

still be a princess at heart, but you're living in a frog's body, and frogs like flies!"

"I said it was sweet. I didn't say I liked it. Hey," I said, suddenly suspicious, "was this a trick? Did you bring me here so I couldn't help but catch a fly?"

"Would I do such a thing?" he asked. "Don't you know me better than that?"

"I hardly know you," I said, thinking that he might actually be a little sneaky after all.

Frog shrugged. "You couldn't go around acting all prissy and never trying anything new. You needed to see that eating a fly isn't so bad. You're going to have to get used to it if you're going to survive."

"Don't frogs eat anything other than flies?"

"Sure, lots of things. Gnats, mosquitoes, dragonflies. You name it—if it's an insect, it's on our menu."

"I'm doomed!" I moaned, but I remembered how the fly had tasted. It really hadn't been bad. Tilting my head to the side, I gave the flies an appraising look.

Frog smiled. "You ate one and it didn't kill you. Try another. It's an acquired taste, and the sooner you acquire it, the better off you'll be."

I certainly didn't intend to remain a frog my entire life, but I needed to live until I could figure out how to go back to my old self. I gagged again and swallowed hard. *Maybe,* I thought, *it would be better if I didn't think about it. Just do it and get it over with.*

"How did you learn what to do?" I asked Frog. "You couldn't have known what a frog does the instant you became one."

"I watched other frogs," Frog said, shrugging. "It's amazing what you can pick up when you're as intelligent and observant as I am. Go ahead, see if you can catch another one."

"Then go away," I told him. "It really is easier if you're not here."

Frog wandered off to catch his own meal while I looked for the juiciest plum. When I found it, I focused on the biggest fly and flicked my tongue again. It uncurled with a soundless snap, missing the fly by inches. I coiled my tongue back into my mouth while the lucky insect buzzed angrily and flew off to another, less dangerous plum. I kept trying, but I didn't catch many flies. My eye-tongue coordination wasn't very good.

Frog's stomach was full long before mine, so he came over to give me tips on improving my aim. He also came over to brag. "You should have seen what I just did!" he said. "I found a really rotten plum so covered with flies that I couldn't see the fruit. It took a while, but I lined it up just right and caught eight flies with one flick of my tongue. Eight at once! Imagine that!"

His bragging was getting on my nerves. "I have a question for you," I said, wanting to change the subject. "It was all right to call you 'Frog' when you were the only frog I knew, but now I'm a frog, too, and it no longer seems right. What should I call you?"

"You could try calling me Eadric."

"You mean you really are Prince Eadric? That wasn't something you said just to get a kiss?"

"I really was Prince Eadric, back when I was human. I'm surprised you hadn't heard of me. I was quite famous, you know. However, now that I'm a frog, I'm just plain Eadric."

"In that case, I'm Emma. Princess Emeralda is much too formal for a frog."

"Huh!" grunted Eadric. "Okay, Emma, then how about trying for that fly over there?" He pointed to an insect buzzing angrily on the ground. "Even you can catch him. I think his wing is damaged."

I ignored his suggestion, as I wanted to tell him about my idea, one I'd come up with while I stalked my flies. "I've figured out how we can get out of this mess. All we have to do is go to my castle and wait for my aunt Grassina to get home. I don't know how long she'll be gone, so we may have to wait a while, but I'm sure she'll help us as soon as she gets back."

"It's not that easy," he said as if he were talking to a simpleton.

I tried not to let him provoke me, not after he'd been trying so hard to be helpful. "Sure it is," I said. "She's a very knowledgeable witch. I'm sure she'll know what to do."

"That's not what I mean. In the first place, waiting around a castle would be an invitation for disaster. Frogs aren't exactly welcome on castle grounds. Don't you think I would have gone home if I could have? I've seen too many frogs tortured by dogs, cats, and bored under-gardeners. It's something I'd rather not experience, thank you very much! And although I don't really know all that much about magic, even I understand that one witch can't undo spells cast by another. In fact, adding a second witch's magic would only make the spell that much harder to undo. Your aunt wouldn't be the one to see. We'd have to go to the witch who cast the spell in the first place. In cases like this, it's always best to go to the source."

"Then let's go see her!"

"I don't know where she lives."

"You aren't very encouraging," I said, trying not to show how discouraged I actually felt. "Maybe Grassina could help us find her—"

"Hold it right there. Didn't you hear a word I just said? I don't want to sit around your castle waiting for your aunt to show up! Anyway, I *am not* going to go talk to any strange witch. How do I know she won't cast another spell on me?"

"My aunt wouldn't do anything like that."

"Really? Then tell me, has she ever turned anyone into a frog? Be honest now."

"Well, yes, but—"

"Ah-hah! And you wanted me to go see her! It'll be a cold day in the swamp before I go see another spell-casting witch!"

"But she's not—"

"Forget it!" Eadric said, turning his back to me. "There's nothing you can say that would change my mind."

I sighed. I'd met stubborn people before, but none of them had been as aggravating as this frog!

"So what do we do now?" I asked, thinking fondly of my aunt Grassina's rooms, where I often headed at the end of the day.

"Let's go back to my pad," said Eadric. "I want to show you my collection."

"Your collection?" I wondered what a frog could possibly collect.

"My dragonfly wings, remember?"

"Oh, right," I said. He was the strangest prince I'd ever met. Of course, if I were to remain a frog for as long as he had, I might seem awfully strange, too. The thought was depressing, considering how many people already regarded me as odd. There was only one solution: I was going to have to get myself turned back as quickly as possible.

Six

Daylight was fading as Eadric escorted me to his lily pad, which was tucked in a quiet backwater of the stream. It was a large, smooth pad, floating near the overhanging branches of a weeping willow. I tried to climb onto it, but it kept sagging under me, dumping me back into the water. After I'd tried three or four times, Eadric got impatient and shoved me onto it from behind. He pushed me so hard that I skidded across the pad, nearly sliding off the other side. When I tried to climb to my feet, the lousy thing dipped and swayed and I slipped helplessly.

"Isn't it great!" enthused Eadric as he strode to the middle of his pad. "That willow is so close that some days I don't even have to go anywhere to eat. It's almost always full of bugs and I can catch them without even trying. I can even do it lying down. See that spider dangling from the end of that leaf? Watch this!" Stretching out on his side, Eadric rested his chin in his hand and flicked out his tongue, plucking the spider from the leaf like an expert.

"How convenient," I said, certain that he couldn't get any lazier.

Nee deep! Nee deep! We were interrupted by deep voices sounding from the undergrowth lining the stream bank. *Pa reep! Pa reep!* Higher-pitched voices from among the trees joined in the chorus.

"What is that?" I asked.

"Just some of my friends. They have concerts every night this time of year, as long as the weather is nice."

"You have friends among the common frogs? I'm happy to hear that you're not a snob like Jorge!"

Eadric scowled at me and shook his head. "There is no royalty in the animal kingdom. All frogs are created equal. My friends are a great bunch of guys. I'll introduce you to them after the concert. Let's go. I know where we can get good seats if we hurry."

We slipped off the lily pad into the water and swam side by side to the soft mud of the stream bank. Frogs of every size had already begun to gather at the edge of the water. "That's Bassey over there," Eadric said, pointing to a large frog whose deep voice resonated throughout the crowd. "And that little guy is Peepers. He's a soprano." The little frog saw Eadric and waved from his vantage point on a tree.

Eadric led me to a soft patch of grass, picking his

way between the frogs who had already taken their seats. A few frogs greeted us while others smiled their welcome, making me feel comfortable from the start.

"This is nice," I said, settling down beside Eadric.

He bent down and spoke directly into my eardrum. "I'm glad you like it. So how about a kiss now?"

"Eadric!" I said so loudly that everyone turned to stare. There'd been a pause in the music, making my voice sound that much louder. Embarrassed, I waited until the music resumed. "I can't kiss you now! All your friends are watching!"

"It's all right," he said. "We'll close our eyes."

"No, thank you. I don't want to take any chances. No more kisses until we know why the first one went wrong!" I was too loud again, and the frogs seated closest to us turned around to shush me. Covering my face with my hands, I shrank into my seat, almost wishing we hadn't come.

More frogs arrived, joining in the chorus. I was surprised when Eadric began to sing, too. I liked his voice, which wasn't as deep as Bassey's or as high as Peeper's. *I could listen to this all night,* I thought, closing my eyes. The warm evening breeze felt good on my skin. The music was so beautiful that it gave me chills down my spine and frog bumps on my arms.

Nee deep, nee deep! sang the big frogs like Bassey. *Pa reep, pa reep!* sang the tiny frogs like Peepers. *Barbidy,*

barbidy! sang Eadric. I was nodding my head in time to the music when suddenly the night grew silent and I opened my eyes to see why. A grass snake as long as a human man's arm slithered out of the weeds edging the stream. Before anyone could move, the snake struck, sinking its fangs into a member of the audience. The poor frog was halfway down the snake's gullet in an instant. Its twitching legs stuck out of the snake's mouth, kicking and jerking as if the frog could still hop away and escape. It was horrible! I screamed and the snake swiveled its head to look directly into my eyes.

"Come on!" urged Eadric, squeezing my arm to get my attention. Mesmerized by the snake's eyes, I couldn't move. "I said, come on!" Eadric shouted again, yanking my arm until I turned away. "Jump!" he yelled as the snake slithered toward me.

I jumped, landing on the back of an old frog crawling through the shallow water. "Sorry!" I said. "I didn't mean—"

"Hurry up!" shouted Eadric, from the middle of the stream. "You don't have time to apologize!"

"Sorry!" I said again, and pushed off from a slippery rock, sailing into the air and landing far out in the stream. "I can't do this!" I screamed, spluttering as I got a mouthful of water. "I can't live this way!"

"Don't think, swim!" he shouted, pulling me.

With Eadric at my side, I scissor-kicked as fast as I

could until I was too tired to kick any longer. Eadric found a place to hide in a mud bank far downstream. Guiding me to the hole, he helped me climb inside.

I was terrified and couldn't stop shaking. Eadric patted my back consolingly. "It's all right," he said. "That snake can't find us here."

"But there are other snakes!" I whispered, my throat tight with fear. "Sooner or later one is going to get us! I can't live like this, Eadric. I was never afraid that I would be eaten when I was a princess. You must know someone who can help us!"

"There is one possibility," Eadric said reluctantly. "It's sort of a last resort, but we can try it if you really want to."

"What are you talking about?"

"We can go see the old witch who turned me into a frog. I don't know where she lives, but each month on the night of the full moon she goes to a certain spot to collect plants—or at least she used to. The full moon is only two nights away. We can reach it in time if we leave in the morning."

"Do you really think she'd help us?"

"She might. She said I just needed to be kissed by a princess to become a prince again. You're a princess and you kissed me, so why am I still a frog? The old witch cast the spell, so she's responsible for making sure it works. She should know how to fix it."

"Why didn't you tell me about this before? You knew I didn't want to be a frog!"

"Because it's risky. There's no telling if she'll help or not or even if she'll be there. Besides," he said, blushing a dark green, "if I have to remain a frog, it's kind of nice having another frog around who once was a human. I enjoy your company. But," he added briskly, "we'll do it if you really want to."

"Oh, believe me, I do! I don't think I could stand being a frog for much longer!"

I didn't know what to think of Eadric's confession. He could be rude and obnoxious, but underneath it all he was a nice frog and I liked him. Even so … I went to sleep that night thinking about Eadric. Considerate and helpful, he treated me as if I were an important person worthy of his attention. And it was much more pleasant to think about him than it was to think about that horrid snake and the poor little frog that had been eaten.

I'd been asleep only a short time when something woke me. I looked around, but nothing had changed inside the hole and Eadric was snoring peacefully beside me. Then it came again, the mournful sound of a dog howling in the distance. Instead of frightening me, I felt sorry for the beast, since I felt like howling myself. *But it's luckier than I am,* I thought. *At least it doesn't have to worry about being eaten.* I shivered and moved closer to Eadric, safe for the moment in our muddy sanctuary.

Seven

Eadric and I woke long before the sun was up the next morning. Even though I wasn't hungry, Eadric insisted that we have our breakfast before setting out. It was still dark and there were plenty of mosquitoes around. I was surprised when I tasted my first one. It was salty, but extremely filling for such a skinny insect.

"We'll be traveling over land for the first part of our trip," explained Eadric between mosquitoes. "We'll be safe enough as long as we follow some rules. One, don't make any unnecessary noise. Two, eat while you hop—we're on a tight schedule. Three, keep your eyes and eardrums open at all times. If you hear anything suspicious, don't talk. Just signal me like this." Eadric flapped his arm and patted his head. "That should get my attention."

"Yours and that of every other creature around," I said. "What if I tap you on the shoulder instead?"

"Fine," Eadric said, nodding. "That should work, too."

Our trip began over swampy ground, but as the sun rose overhead, we reached higher, drier land. I stopped to admire a bedraggled patch of dandelions, having had little contact with flowers other than the crystalline blossoms in Grassina's room. Ordinary flowers were banned from the castle because both my mother and my aunt were allergic to them.

I continued on when Eadric harrumphed impatiently, and we soon found ourselves hopping across pebbled earth where little seemed to grow. It made us both nervous, for the rocky soil and occasional scraggly weeds gave us nothing to hide behind if a predator should come along. Eadric and I hurried across the open ground, anxious to reach the tall grass beyond it. Suddenly, a ladybug zipped past my nose and flew toward a short, squat rock. I remembered Eadric's advice to eat while we hopped and tried to do just that. I jumped, flicking out my tongue at the same time, but the target was smaller than I was used to and I missed, my tongue coming back empty. Since I'd been concentrating on my tongue, I hadn't been paying attention to my feet, so I tripped and fell flat on my face. *Thppt!* Someone else's tongue flicked out and caught the ladybug.

"Better luck next time," said a gravelly voice. I stared

in disbelief. What looked like a rock blinked and shifted a lumpy foot.

"You're a toad!" I exclaimed, startled.

"And you're a lousy jumper!" replied the toad. "Just how old are you, anyway?"

"What does that have to do with anything?" I asked.

"I haven't seen such lousy jumping since my tadpoles first got their legs!" replied the toad. "You're going to have to work on your coordination if you're going to catch anything."

"She's been a frog only for a few days," said Eadric.

"What was she before that?" asked the toad.

"I can speak for myself, thank you." I said. "I was a princess!"

"That explains it. Never have seen a princess who could jump worth grasshopper spit. Whoa!" said the toad, looking behind me. "Look out, little lady. Here comes a big one."

I turned around, expecting to see a large insect. Instead, the same huge white dog that had once tried to eat me was trotting straight toward us. I couldn't take my eyes off it.

"You might want to sidle on out of the way," suggested the toad. "I can handle this one."

I scurried behind a scraggly clump of grass while the toad hopped boldly into the open. After one look at my face, the toad laughed. "Don't worry, little lady, I know how to take care of myself. Watch this!"

Three more hops set the toad directly in the dog's path. The dog's eyes lit up. "Hmmm!" it said, snuffling the toad from front to back before closing its great jaws around the lumpy, gray body. A strange look came over the dog's face and it dropped the toad as if it were hot. White foam dripped from between the dog's jaws. Whimpering pitifully, it pawed at its mouth.

"Yuck!" said the dog. "What *is* this stuff?" It shook its head and great flecks of foam splattered the dry soil. With a pained yelp, the dog ran back the way it had come.

"You poor thing! Are you all right?" I asked the toad.

"Fine as frog's hair. Thanks for asking."

"What did you do?" I asked. "I thought it had you!"

"Not me! Mother Nature gave us toads a little secret weapon." The toad lowered his voice to a conspiratorial whisper. "You frogs think you're so superior with your smooth skin and your pretty faces, but you don't have anything like this. You see back here behind my head? This gooey stuff isn't dog spit, no sirree! I make my own poison and I've been told it tastes downright nasty. Heh, heh, heh! That dog didn't stand a chance."

"That poison ... He isn't seriously hurt, is he?"

"Nah, nothing time won't cure. Might have learned a lesson, though, if he's lucky."

"I never would have guessed that you could do that."

"That's what makes it a secret weapon!" the toad

said. He beamed at me before turning to Eadric. Eadric scowled back.

"We'd better be going," I said. "Thanks for your help!"

"My pleasure, little lady. Good luck with your hopping! Keep on practicing and you'll do just fine."

Eadric and I continued on, neither of us saying another word until we were concealed by a tall, rippling sea of grass. Once we were in its shade, I breathed a sigh of relief. "Now what was that all about?" I asked Eadric. "I think this was the first time I've seen you looking angry."

"He didn't have to do that!" grumbled Eadric.

"What do you mean?" I asked. "Who didn't have to do what?"

"That old toad. He didn't have to show off like that! Who does he think he is, your knight in warty armor? If anybody is going to rescue you, it will be me! We didn't need him! If he hadn't interfered, I would have done something about that dog."

"Like what?"

"I don't know. Something would have occurred to me, I'm sure. But I didn't need some old toad to protect you like that. Interfering old busybody!"

"Eadric, he was just trying to be helpful."

"We didn't need his help! Look at me! I'm big! I'm strong! I'm a superior example of froghood and capable of protecting us both!"

I gave up. From the furious scowl on Eadric's face, I was better off not saying anything.

Intent on maneuvering through the dense grass, I ignored my companion. Because there were few clear areas that allowed straightforward hopping, I had to develop my own crawl-hop-wiggle style that got me through the grass but left my muscles aching.

The stars were twinkling overhead when Eadric and I finally reached the edge of the grassy field and took shelter under a flowering thornbush.

The next morning, we entered a trembling copse of young saplings and heard the distant murmur of rushing water. With the sound as our guide, we detoured around boulders and old stumps, breathing a sigh of relief when the tangled underbrush bordering the stream came into sight. We had been out of the water for so long that my throat was parched and my skin was beginning to feel like old leather. Working my way through the maze of stems and branches, I leaped into the clear, sun-sparkled water only seconds ahead of Eadric.

The swim was easy and relaxing, because we were heading downstream. I swam beside Eadric, kicking now and then but mostly letting the current do the work. Around midday, fat black clouds gathered overhead. Rain peppered the water, landing on my head in oversized, heavy drops. *A little more water won't hurt us,* I thought, but at the first crack of thunder, I began to feel uneasy.

"How much farther is it?" I asked Eadric, who had been single-mindedly looking for landmarks.

"We're closer than I thought. Do you see that old oak over there?" Eadric pointed to a tree on the far side of the stream. "I tied my horse to the lowest branch the night I was turned into a frog. I wonder what became of him. His name was Bright Country and he was the best horse I'd ever had. I'd hate to think that something bad happened to the old fellow."

"I'm sure someone found him or he got himself loose. I don't see any old horse bones lying there. But why did you come here? You've never told me the story."

"It was no epic tale, believe me. I thought I was in love with a princess and hoped to win her favor by giving her some meadwort. I'd heard that if you picked it at midnight on the night of the full moon, then boiled the leaves, you could see your true love's face in the bottom of your cup. I was convinced that I was her true love and that it was my face she'd see."

"I've never heard so much garbage! Meadwort doesn't do anything like that. Who told you that it did?"

"My little brother," Eadric admitted.

"And you believed him? I don't know much about little brothers, but from what I've heard they are not the most reliable sources of information. It sounds like he pulled one over on you."

"I guess so."

Eadric's face looked so forlorn that I took pity on him. "I'm sure he wouldn't have done it if he'd known how it would end."

"Probably not," admitted Eadric. "He isn't a bad sort."

"I didn't know you were a romantic at heart."

"Romantic! Is that what you call it? I thought I was just having a run of bad luck. The really sad part is that a few months after I became a frog, I saw the princess. Her coach almost ran over me when I was crossing the road. It was decorated for a wedding, so it must have been her wedding day. My rival won by default, I guess. She'd been seeing a lot of him while I'd still been a human. That's why I'd even considered my brother's advice. I was getting desperate."

"You didn't finish your story. What happened when you came looking for the meadwort?"

"I never found it, but I did come across the old witch. She was out looking for plants that night, too. I stumbled across her in the dark, which was pretty unpleasant, believe me. She was wearing a filthy gown and smelled terrible. That's when I made a comment about her clothes and hygiene. She took offense and wham! The prince became a frog!"

"So how much farther is it?"

"It's right there," said Eadric. "We can wait under that blackberry bush. That's where I spent my first night as a frog. If there are any rotten berries on the ground, we should find plenty of insects."

Eadric and I climbed out of the water and made ourselves comfortable under the blackberry bush. To our disappointment, we found neither berries nor insects, although the leaves kept the cold rain off us. It had been a long, tiring trip and we hadn't slept well in days. With the soothing patter of rain on the leaves, it wasn't long before we were both asleep.

Eight

When we woke, the rain had stopped and the air felt clean and cool. The full moon peered through a gap in the clouds, casting an otherworldly light on the landscape. We spoke in soft whispers, not wishing to disturb the silence that comes after a heavy rain.

"Is it almost midnight?" I asked.

"I don't know," said Eadric, "but it must be getting close."

"Thank you."

"What for?"

"For bringing me here when you really didn't want to. I know how you feel about seeing the old witch again, but you said you'd help me and you have. Thank you."

"You're welcome. You know, of course, that my motives are not completely unselfish. I want to be turned back into a human, too. Even so, I know of a way you could thank me."

"And what's that?" I asked, certain I already knew the answer.

"You could kiss me." He puckered his lips and stretched his neck to bring his head close to mine.

"At a time like this? The witch could be here any moment!"

"But I don't want to kiss her!" said Eadric.

"I didn't—"

"Listen," said Eadric. "I think I hear something."

It came again. Someone was approaching and making no effort to be quiet.

"Look! That must be her," whispered Eadric. A light bobbed across the uneven ground. The sound of footsteps slogging through the muck could be clearly heard in the still night air.

As the witch approached, the full moon outlined her silhouette, yet did little to illuminate her face. The light of the lantern she carried had been focused toward the ground by the use of movable shutters, leaving her face in relative darkness. Indistinctly seen in the moonlight, the woman resembled a ghostly apparition. Her wild, uncombed hair hung loosely about her shoulders. She wore long, dark garments that dragged on the ground, snagging twigs and muck as she walked.

Trying to get up the courage to approach her, Eadric and I cowered under the berry bush. The witch drew near, intent on her midnight search.

"Hurry," I told him. "She'll be gone and we'll have lost our chance."

"I'm not sure I should," said Eadric. "I have a bad feeling about this. Our last meeting didn't end very well."

"Please go. It's why we're here," I said. "I'll go with you. Just be nice and discreet this time. Remember, no sarcastic comments!"

"Fine, if you'll stop making up rules—it'll be hard enough as it is." Together we hopped into the witch's path. When the light of the lantern reached us, we covered our eyes against the glare.

"Ma'am," called Eadric. "We need to talk to you. It's urgent!"

The witch stopped short and set the lantern on the ground.

"You might remember me. I'm Prince Eadric," he said warily, trying to see the witch past the brilliance of the light. "We met here one night and had a short conversation. I said something about your sense of style and you turned me into a frog."

"Go on," said the witch.

"You said I'd stay a frog until a princess kissed me, but I did and nothing happened. You have to do something!"

"What do you mean nothing happened?" I exclaimed. "I turned into a frog, too! I think that's a pretty big something!"

"This is Princess Emeralda. She's the one who kissed me."

"This wasn't supposed to happen!" I said. "You must

have done something wrong when you cast the spell."

"Shh! Emma!" whispered Eadric. "Don't make her mad! And you told me to be discreet!"

"But I—"

Eadric cleared his throat and turned back to the witch. "We didn't come to accuse anyone of anything. We just need your help fixing it."

"Really? And how would I do that?" the witch asked in a friendly voice.

Encouraged, I couldn't keep the words from tumbling out. "Just turn us back into humans and I'll see that you're handsomely rewarded. My parents will do anything to get me back."

"Is that so? And I'm the lucky witch you chose to talk to! My, oh, my," she said, her voice losing its sweet tone. "You picked the wrong one tonight, froggies! Or should I call you Your Royal Highnesses?" In one swift motion, the woman dropped the sack she'd been carrying and swooped down on us, snatching us off the ground and raising us to eye level. She studied us intently, turning us over and examining us from top to bottom. "Such nice, strong specimens! You two will do just fine."

For the first time we could see the woman's face. She was young. Her long, frizzy hair had been dyed black and showed mouse-brown roots. Her eyes were dark and sunken, her cheeks gaunt, and her skin pale. Everything she wore was black, from her long, threadbare dress and ratty shawl to her worn leather shoes.

"Emma," Eadric whispered in a horrified voice, "it's not her! This isn't the witch who did it!"

"You are a smart froggy, aren't you, Prince? I've never turned anyone into a frog, but I've been looking for two frogs like you. Your bad luck is my good fortune! Two talking frogs in one night. My luck has finally changed." The witch hummed happily as she opened the sack and dropped us in.

I landed on my back. Wiggling and twisting, I tried to turn myself over. It was dark inside the sack, with an overwhelming musty smell. I scrabbled for a handhold on the coarse cloth, wishing I had my bracelet with me. Even the small amount of light it gave off would have been helpful. A moment later the woman lifted the sack and we tumbled to the bottom, where we lay in a tangled heap.

"Ow!" moaned Eadric, rubbing the side of his head. "Watch your elbow, will you?"

"Sorry," I said, "but I didn't hit you on purpose. Maybe if we sat up …"

I kicked the sack, the weight of our bodies making the fabric taut, but my leg bounced off and caught Eadric squarely in the stomach.

"Oof," he said, doubling over.

"Sorry," I said again. "Are you all right?"

I'd knocked the breath out of him, so it took a moment for him to answer. When he did, he was wheezing and I felt awful. "I'll be just fine … if you'll hold still!" he said.

I inched away, trying to put some space between us, but being inside a sack didn't make it easy.

The sack began to move, swaying like a pendulum with each of the witch's steps. As she walked, she muttered to herself in a voice too low for me to understand. Suddenly, she stopped and set the sack roughly on the ground. Eadric and I could hear her trudge away, although she didn't go far.

"Quick!" I said. "See if you can open the top of the bag. Maybe we can get out while she's gone."

Eadric shifted his weight beside me. I tensed, trying to keep out of his way while he reached toward the top of the sack. "It's no use," he said a moment later. "She's tied the top shut."

"Never mind. The way our luck has been running, she'll probably be back soon anyway. Can you believe that witch? She doesn't care who we are. It looks like we're more valuable to her as talking frogs than we are as royalty. What are we going to do, Eadric?"

"I really am sorry about this," began Eadric. "If I hadn't tried to get you to kiss me …"

"I never would have met the best friend I've ever had. You're not the only one responsible for this. No one made me kiss you. And if it weren't for me, we wouldn't have come out here to talk with the witch. So stop feeling guilty and help me figure out a way to get through this."

"Maybe if we move to the opposite sides of the bag …"

"We'll roll together again like we did last time. At least if we start out near each other we won't bump together as hard when she picks up the sack."

"I have an even better idea," said Eadric. "If I hold on to you, we won't roll into each other at all."

"Fine," I said. "We could try that."

"And while I'm there, you might as well give me a kiss."

"What?"

"Who knows what that witch has in mind? She might toss us in a cauldron of boiling water or feed us to a pet dragon. This may be our last chance to show how we feel about each other."

"Show how we … Are you crazy? Kissing you is the last thing I want to do right now!"

"Hey, it sounded like a good idea to me."

"I told you," I said, getting exasperated, "I don't want to take any chances!"

I could feel the ground vibrate as the witch returned. She opened the sack suddenly and the moonlight poured in.

"Do you think we could make a run for it?" I whispered in Eadric's eardrum. "Because if she—"

A small, thorn-covered plant fell on us. The wet mud encasing the roots dripped in sour-smelling globs onto our heads. Sputtering, I covered my face with my hands.

"Ow!" wailed Eadric. "Those thorns are sharp!"

I spit out a mouthful of mud. "Try not to talk. That stuff tastes terrible!"

The witch jerked the sack off the ground and carried it a few yards. She opened the top again, but only long enough to drop in a handful of leaves. I cringed, having recognized the shape of the poison oak leaf at once, but it was too late and I knew it. *I'm in for it now,* I thought. Even the briefest contact with poison oak gave me a rash, and now my back was covered with the leaves.

When the witch picked up the sack, Eadric and I tensed our muscles, waiting for the next impact with the ground. But the sack continued to sway in the witch's hands as she slogged across the marshy ground. After a while, Eadric began to groan.

"What's wrong?" I asked. "Is it the thorns?"

"No," whispered Eadric.

"Is it the mud?"

"No," whispered Eadric.

"Then what is it?"

"It's this swaying back and forth," he said. "I don't feel very well."

"Take a deep breath and think of something else. And please face the other way if you're going to be sick."

If the witch's house had been any farther, we might not have made it. As it was, Eadric was groaning loudly long before the witch opened her cottage door and I was worried that he wasn't going to survive the trip: he was groaning so much that if he didn't die of bag-sickness first, I was going to strangle him to put him out of his misery. I wondered if all male frogs were such babies when they were sick, or only the ones who used to be princes.

I was still trying to block out Eadric's moans by covering my eardrums with my hands when the witch set her lantern down with a clang. Reaching into the sack, she grabbed us and shoved us into a small wicker cage. My head spinning, I lay on the cage floor while she slammed the door shut and fastened a complicated latch.

"There," she said. "That should hold you until I'm ready."

"Ready for what?" I asked the witch as my head cleared. The woman ignored me and emptied her sack onto a rickety table in the middle of the room.

"Yoo-hoo, Witchy! Ready for what?" Eadric echoed me in a shaky voice. The witch turned her back on our cage and took off her shawl.

"Has anyone ever told you that you're very rude?" Eadric asked, his voice getting stronger. "You kidnap us, lock us in a cage without an explanation, and expect us to be nice, well-behaved frogs. Obviously, you don't know me. I don't take anything quietly!"

"Eadric! Shh!" I hissed at him. "You'll make things worse!"

"How can it get worse than this? We were better off as free frogs happily living in the swamp. Now we're stuck here with Rudella the witch and we don't even know why. Hey, Witchy! Answer me! What do you want with us?"

When the witch continued to ignore him, Eadric got a funny look in his eyes. "No witch is going to ignore me for long," he whispered in my eardrum. "Watch this!" He thought for a minute, then planted his hands firmly on his middle and called out, "Hey, Witchy! You're so ugly that you don't have to dye your clothes! One look at you and they die on their own!"

I could see the witch's back stiffen, but that wasn't enough for Eadric. He winked at me, then shouted, "I know why you don't have any mirrors in this place. You got tired of cleaning up the broken glass!"

With a cry of rage, the witch whirled around, scowling ferociously. "Listen, Your Royal Lowness, I don't like frogs and I like princes even less! I suggest you keep your rubbery little lips shut if you ever want to see the light of day again. Now lock those lips, sit down, and don't move. I'll be right back!" Taking a small vial from a shelf, the witch stomped out the door.

"You couldn't be quiet, could you?" I asked. "If that was the kind of thing you said to the other witch, it's no wonder she turned you into a frog! And now you've gotten a second witch mad at you. Who knows what she's going to do."

"She doesn't care what I say. What can we do? We're in a cage, for frog's sake! If we annoy her enough, maybe she'll let us go."

"Or kill us so she doesn't have to listen to you," I said.

Eadric and I were glowering at each other when the witch returned with a freshly unearthed nightcrawler in her hand. With a gleam in her eye, she dropped the dirt-flecked worm through the bars of our cage and set the vial back on the shelf.

"There you go!" she said in a syrupy voice. "Have a bedtime snack. Get some sleep and don't worry so much. Too much stress can make you sick and we don't want that, now, do we?" With that, the witch blew out the lantern and shuffled across the room.

Tiptoeing to the side of the cage, I listened as the witch kicked off her shoes and settled back on an old straw-filled mattress. Seconds later her breathing evened out in sleep.

"Do you want some?" Eadric said through a mouthful of worm.

I spun around in surprise. "What are you doing? I thought you were sick to your stomach. You shouldn't eat any of that—it might be poisoned! Spit it out! Spit it out right now!"

"Are you kidding? This is delicious. It's not poisoned. Here, try some."

"Great," I said. "I'm stuck in a cage with an idiot who eats food given to him by a witch and will probably be dead by morning."

"Hey, I'm not the one who's going to bed hungry. You are such a worrier! I've eaten half of this worm already and I still feel fine. If you're sure you don't want any, I'm going to finish the worm and get some sleep. We'll think of a way to get out of this in the morning. Now, leave me alone and let me enjoy my worm in peace. Unlike someone else around here, I know how to appreciate the finer things in life."

Furious, I went to the back of the cage, as far from Eadric as I could get, and tried to shut out the sound of munching. Although Eadric was soon asleep, I was too restless to lie down. I paced the width of the cage, the gritty floor crunching beneath my feet, but I couldn't sleep and I couldn't come up with an escape plan, either.

After a while I stopped talking to myself and listened to the sounds of the night. I'd heard something stirring at the other end of the room, a dry rustle that could have been caused by just about anything. Then something else moved overhead until it seemed to be right above me. Whatever else was in the room, I wasn't the only one who was awake. Suddenly, I had something else to make me nervous. Not knowing who or what might be there, I hunched down in the middle of the cage, hoping that the bars were as effective at keeping creatures out as they were at keeping us in. When I finally drifted off to sleep, it was to dreams of my family's dungeon and large, frog-eating worms that made me itch when they touched me.

Nine

It was the itching that woke me the next morning. The rash that I'd predicted the night before covered my back, and no matter how I twisted or turned, I couldn't reach all the itchy spots. I was getting desperate when I finally found that if I twisted around a certain way and rubbed against a bar of the cage, I could relieve some of the worst itching.

"You look like an old bear when you do that," said a voice from above. "Not that I've seen many old bears."

A bright shaft of sunlight came through a hole high on the wall, in the general direction from which the voice had come. At first I thought I might be having a divine visitation, but the voice had been high and squeaky, not at all the sort of voice I thought would belong to a divine being. *Maybe it's a trick,* I thought. But it couldn't be Eadric. He was still sound asleep. It wasn't the witch, either. I could see her lying on her back with her head turned to the side. Her mouth was open, drool trickling onto the thin mattress with the stained gray cover.

"Where are you?" I asked, squinting through the shaft of sunlight and the dancing dust motes. Other than the cracks in the shutters covering the two windows, the hole in the wall was the only source of light in the room.

"I'm up here," squeaked the voice. "By the rafters."

I looked toward the ceiling. A tiny patch of darkness seemed to shift, but I couldn't be sure. "Sorry," I said. "I can't really make you out from here. . . ."

"But I'm right . . . oh, forget it. Here, is this better?"

A bit of shadow detached itself from the rafter and flapped down into the dimly lit room. "Oh, my," I said, taken by surprise. It was a bat. As a rule, I didn't like bats, although I'd never encountered one in person before. It was just that I'd heard so many bad things about them.

"Are you satisfied yet? Can I go back to my rafter now?" the bat asked.

"Of course!" I said, embarrassed by my bad manners. "I didn't mean to inconvenience you."

"Inconvenience! My, aren't you a nice little frog! None of the other idiots around here would ever think about what is or isn't convenient for me. Take that nasty little witch on the bed, for instance."

I turned toward the witch in the back of the room, afraid that she might be awake and listening. "Don't worry," said the bat. "Vannabe's still asleep. I always know when she's awake, believe me. Anyway, she never thinks about what's convenient for me. It's always 'Go away, ya stupid bat!' or 'Get that bug, ya stupid bat!' If I didn't know better, I'd think my name was Stupid Bat. It isn't, of course. It's Li'l Stinker. That's what my first mistress named me when I was a youngster. Now, that woman was far more considerate. She used to say, 'Li'l Stinker, you'd better get that fat, juicy bug or you won't have any dinner tonight.' See what I mean? She was a much more thoughtful person."

I was beginning to feel overwhelmed. I had always thought that bats were quiet creatures, but this bat could talk more than anyone I'd ever met.

I rubbed my back against the bar again. The rash was itching more now and was spreading to my chest.

"I couldn't help but hear you talking to Vannabe last night," said Li'l. "You can talk to humans, huh? That's too bad. The only humans I can talk to are witches with the talent and that's the way I like it. So, did your friend eat the worm?"

"He sure did. He ate the whole thing. I was afraid that he'd be poisoned, but he's fine."

"I wouldn't say that exactly. He's still asleep, isn't he?'

"Well, yes, but neither of us has gotten much sleep lately. He's really tired."

"Is that it? Go shake him and wake him up."

"I was going to let him sleep for a while. He needs his rest."

"Go shake him now and see what he does."

"I'd rather not."

"Just do it! It's for your own good!"

It was obvious that the bossy little bat was going to pester me until I did what she'd said. Reluctantly, I hopped to Eadric's side and gently shook his shoulder. He continued to snore. I shook him harder. He snorted and rolled over.

"I can't seem to wake him," I said, frowning.

"Of course not. You won't be able to if he ate that worm! Didn't you see that vial Vannabe had in her hand? It was sleeping potion. A tiny drop and you'll sleep for days. What do you think those witches used to help Sleeping Beauty and Snow White get all that beauty rest? A full vial can knock you out for a hundred years or more. Now, unless you want to take a very long nap, I suggest that you don't let the witch know that you're still awake. Go curl up somewhere and pretend that you're asleep or she'll find another way to give you that potion. She has her reasons for wanting you two to stay quiet. Now watch out!" Li'l Stinker said softly. "She's waking up."

I scurried to the back of the cage and pretended to be asleep, just in case the bat was right. With my eyes half closed, I watched Vannabe yawn, sit up, and scratch her ribs. Drool shone wetly on her cheek, but she didn't seem to notice. Kicking off the grimy blanket, she swung her feet to the floor.

"What are you looking at?" Vannabe said grumpily, looking up at the bat. Li'l Stinker didn't give her an answer, but the witch obviously didn't expect one, for she stood up and shuffled across the room without another word.

Still in her bare feet, Vannabe went out the door, leaving it open. I thought the fresh air would be a relief, but instead it stirred up the dust in the room and recirculated the odor of unwashed clothes, filthy cages, bat droppings, and old grease. I was almost happy to see the witch come back inside and close the door behind her.

Still scratching her ribs, Vannabe shuffled to the fireplace, where she bent over the fire, her back to our cage. She lifted a wooden spoon from a hook on the wall and stirred something in a greasy black pot. Then she took it to the table in the middle of the room and sat down to eat. When she was finished, she scraped the bottom of the pot with her wooden spoon.

"Here now, can't have anyone go hungry with all this good food around, can we?" said the witch as she walked toward our side of the room. "Don't eat it all at once, 'cause you won't be getting any more today."

My view was blocked by a stack of books on one side and a collection of bottles on the other, but I could hear other creatures moving about in their cages as the witch gave each of them their own dollop of food.

When the witch came near our cage, I kept my eyes closed and made my breath come slowly and evenly, trying to make it sound like Eadric's. Vannabe opened the cage door and I thought my heart would beat its way out of my chest, but I willed myself to hold still. Even when a long fingernail poked me in the ribs, I kept my eyes closed and stayed as limp as I could. "Princess, huh?" Vannabe's voice was harsh and mocking. "What's it like being a frog, Miss High and Mighty?"

The hand moved away and I refused to look, picturing Eadric receiving the same treatment. "As for you, Prince ... slain any dragons lately, or is it dragonflies now?" Vannabe laughed, the shrill sound grating on my eardrums. *And people say that I have a strange laugh,* I thought.

When the cage door had shut with a soft click and I was sure that the witch had moved away, I opened my eyes to slits and was relieved to see her pick up her sack from the floor and head out the door. "Behave yourselves, vermin!" she told the animals. "No wild parties while I'm gone!" Laughing, the witch slammed the door behind her.

With the witch gone, I could finally relax. I bent my leg and scratched my back with my toe, but I still couldn't reach the really itchy spots.

For the first time I was able to take a better look at my surroundings. The cottage was small, with the witch's bed against the wall opposite the only door. Li'l Stinker hung from a rough-hewn rafter near the front of the cottage and appeared to be asleep. Birds' bones suspended from a frayed cord clattered together. Our cage rested on a dust-covered shelf next to a stack of books. The skull of an unborn baby dragon sat on top of the books, the dust so thick that the eye sockets were nearly filled.

A collection of jars and bottles stood on the other side of the cage. They were all labeled, although some of the labels were turned so that I couldn't read them. Rabbits' ears, cats' tails, and wild boars' tusks filled some of the larger jars, and crystals and dried compounds filled others. One jar was filled with dark blue, fuzzy clumps and was labeled *Troll Navel Lint.* Another contained smooth white balls suspended in a clear liquid. When one bobbed about, turning to stare at me, I gasped: they were eyeballs, obviously alive, from the way they jostled for position. I quickly realized that there were other jars with living contents, like the squirming, puckering pieces of green flesh in a jar labeled *Lizard Lip*s and the wrinkled, snuffling *Pig Snouts.* The contents of one slim vial may not have been alive, but the colored gases swirled, mixing and separating in intricate, never-repeating patterns.

Something thumped by the fireplace and I scurried across my cage to look. There was nothing there but an old stick used for poking logs and two crudely constructed barrels, one labeled *Trash Can,* the other *Trash Can't.* The Trash Can was uncovered. When I listened carefully, I thought I could hear something gurgling inside. A wooden lid covered the Trash Can't and as I watched, I could see the whole thing shake and thump. To my surprise, I could also hear creatures calling from other cages.

"Who are they?" squeaked one voice.

"I don't know, but I heard one of them talking to Li'l Stinker." The speaker's voice was so faint and breathy that I had to strain to hear it.

"Do you think she'll introduce us?"

"I don't know. Ask Miss Bossy. You know she always has to be in charge."

"I'd be happy to," interrupted the bat. "But I don't know their names yet. Hey there, Frog!"

Because I'd heard the entire conversation, I was ready when Li'l called to me. "I'm Emma and this is Eadric," I began. "We're both enchanted frogs. I'm a princess and Eadric is really a prince."

I had never heard animals howl with laughter before. It would have made me feel defensive if they hadn't sounded so funny. I began to laugh, too, and suddenly I felt the best I had in days.

Li'l shifted around on her perch until she faced me again and waited until my laughter grew weak enough that I could hear her. "That's some laugh you have there,

Princess!" Li'l declared as I hiccuped my way to silence. "Did you get that when you became a frog or have you had it all along?"

"It's my laugh no matter who or what I am. My real name is Princess Emeralda, and his is Prince Eadric. I'm the only child of King Limelyn and Queen Chartreuse of the Kingdom of Greater Greensward. Eadric is the eldest son of the rulers of Upper Montevista." Proud of my royal heritage, I was sure that these creatures couldn't help but respect me now, so I was stunned by the reception my news received.

"Yeah, right," squeaked a voice.

"Then I'm King Mouseworthy!" squeaked another.

The creatures acted as if they'd heard the funniest thing in the world. Li'l Stinker laughed so hard that she tumbled off her rafter and flapped wildly, trying to regain her balance.

Indignant, I tried to shout over their laughter. "But I really am a princess! I can play the lute and embroider and sing and dance and do all the other things that princesses are supposed to do, although not as well as my mother would like. I can also do some other things that most princesses can't do. I can count and read and—"

"Did you say read?" asked Li'l, suddenly becoming serious.

"Why, yes," I said. "And I can swim, although I

couldn't do that before I became a frog. I can—"

"All right! I believe you! That's quite a list of accomplishments," said Li'l.

"It sure is!" chimed in a breathy voice. "I wish I could count. It would probably help me with some of my patterns."

My legs were beginning to itch. The rash was spreading. "Now it's your turn," I said, feeling moderately appeased. "I want to hear everyone else's names."

"That's easy enough," said the bat. "I'm Li'l, as you know, and in the cage below you are the spiders, Eenie, Meenie, and Moe. They used to live by the broom in the corner, but Vannabe found them and stuck them in a cage."

"We had another brother named Miney," whispered a tiny voice, "but the witch stepped on him when she caught us."

"I'm so sorry!" I said, furiously scratching behind my eardrum.

"It's one of the hazards of being a spider," said the voice sadly.

"Clifford and Louise live in the cage next to the spiders," continued Li'l. "Clifford and Louise are the mice who used to live under the bed. They've been together for a long time, so they tend to finish each other's sentences."

"Vannabe said she got tired—"

"—of hearing us scurry around."

"She put us in the cage—"

"—and we don't have anywhere to go."

"It's so boring!"

"We used to have the best adventures!"

"You wouldn't believe—"

"—what we found in the walls!"

"Some things are better left alone," said Li'l. "And that brings us to Fang. Fang has lived here since Vannabe moved in. She found him in the yard and put him in a cage her very first day. Fang doesn't talk much, so I'll tell you a bit about him. His cage is on the floor in the corner. It's the biggest cage in the cottage, but it's not nearly big enough for Fang. He was a large snake when he got here and he's grown since then."

A snake, I thought. Even if it was in a cage, the thought of a snake in the room made my heart beat faster and my skin feel cold and clammy.

"It's our turn!" breathed one of the spiders. "I want to hear how the two frogs were enchanted."

"Go ahead, princess!" squeaked a mouse.

"Tell us how—"

"—you became a frog!"

With a snake in the room, all I wanted to do was hide, but it seemed only fair that I answer. I swallowed hard and tried to speak normally. "Actually," I began, "it was Eadric who became a frog first. He said something to a witch that she didn't like and she turned him into a frog. Then when I kissed him so he would turn back into a prince, I turned into a frog, too. When we first saw Vannabe, we thought she was the witch who did it, but it wasn't her at all."

"Are you kidding?" said Li'l. "Vannabe couldn't turn a cabbage into coleslaw. She's trying to be a witch, but she doesn't have the knack for it."

"If she's not a witch, what does she want with Eadric and me? What is she going to do with those plants she found?"

"I'll tell you if you really want to know," said the bat.

"She'd be the one to tell," whispered one of the spiders in a voice so soft I might have imagined it. "Li'l Stinker has lived here most of her life. She's tied to that rafter with a piece of twine. It's too short to reach any of the cages, or one of us would have helped her untie it long ago. I've seen her try many a time, but that knot lasts like iron. I wish I could get up there to see what kind of knot the old witch used."

"Moe's very interested in knots. Eenie and I like to try different designs in our webs, but our brother has made knots his life study. You can see some of our handiwork on the broom against the back wall. Eenie, Miney, Moe, and I did it before the witch caught us."

"I'm sure you're very talented," I said.

"If you all are finished talking, I'll tell her about

Vannabe now. I refuse to try to speak over your cackling!" Li'l glared at each of the cages before swinging around to face me. "I'm going to have to give you a little history first. Vannabe has lived here for about a year. I'm the only one who's been here longer than that. I used to live here with the old witch, Mudine. She was a nice old lady, although kind of crazy toward the end. Hardly anybody came by because she didn't like company and she made people feel uncomfortable. She had me live with her only because she didn't like the bugs. The old woman thought cleaning was a waste of her time, so there were always plenty of bugs and I was here to eat them."

Li'l sighed and rearranged her wings. "Those were the good old days. That witch could do real magic and some days this place was hopping! But Mudine was old even when I first came to live with her, and her health wasn't good. Then she got sick and she couldn't take care of the animals anymore, so she let them all out of their cages. By then she was too weak to undo my twine, so I was still here when she lay down on her bed and disappeared in a puff of smoke.

"We'd known that a young woman from one of the farms had been snooping around for some time. We didn't let on, but we knew. The day the old witch vanished, Vannabe took the place over. The puff of smoke was still fogging up the room when that woman barged in and made herself at home. As far as I can tell, she hasn't even a hint of magic in her. Her only claim to fame is that she can read, which, I admit, is an accomplishment in itself. Why, these days the best witches are the ones with the talent who can also read. You have to read the old spells, you see. Passing them down by word of mouth can be a bit shaky. People forget things, mispronounce a word or two... Who knows what can happen then?

"Anyway, Vannabe really wants to be a witch, but it takes more than just wanting. You have to have some talent or you can do only the simplest spells, the kind you just read from the book. Vannabe's not interested in the basic spells. She's got it in her head that to be a real witch she has to do big, showy magic, the kind that would impress lots of people. She doesn't realize that the little magic is powerful, too."

"But if she doesn't have the ability to do the magic, why is she here?"

"I can't answer that one. Maybe she doesn't realize she can't do it yet, maybe she's too stubborn to give up, or maybe her life on the farm was so bad, she'd rather be here."

"What is she looking for now?" I asked.

"She has some idea about trying one of Mudine's fancier spells," said Li'l. "The spell requires some unusual ingredients like that dragon's breath on the shelf next to you. See it there—it's the pretty bottle with the swirly colors. It was part of Mudine's collection. Vannabe would never have gotten it on her own."

"What is the spell for?"

"Nothing unusual. She thinks it will give her everlasting youth and beauty. These things usually backfire, but there's no telling her that."

"Tell the frog about the rest of the ingredients." The voice was dry and raspy. Just hearing it made my skin crawl. *The snake,* I thought, shuddering.

"Oh, yeah," said Li'l. "Aside from some rare plants, all she needed were the tongues and toes of talking frogs. She has plans for you and your friend. Your fate was sealed as soon as she heard you talk. That's why she wanted to keep you calm. She wouldn't want you to damage those precious tongues and toes right when she was about to use them."

"Our tongues and toes! She wouldn't listen when we tried to tell her that we aren't really frogs! I even told her that my parents would reward her, but it didn't make any difference."

"Of course not. If you were humans, you wouldn't be of any use to her. She needs talking frogs to make her spell work. No gold or jewels would get her what she wants. Only the right ingredients could do that, and that includes you, or at least parts of you."

"What are we going to do?"

"Hope that she doesn't find the plants she's looking for. She can't do the spell without them."

"You really do know everything that goes on around here," I said.

"I should. I've been here the longest and can see just about everything from my rafter," Li'l said proudly.

Wind blew through the cracks in the shutters, sending dust and scraps of litter swirling around the cottage. The room grew dark and rain pattered on the roof. It lasted only a few seconds, then abruptly stopped. The wind blew again and I coughed at the swirling dust. When the rain came in earnest, it was heavier and louder than before. A steady drizzle fell through a dozen holes in the roof, leaving damp spots on the table and floor. Li'l edged along her rafter, avoiding the worst of the leaks.

Everyone had grown quiet when the rain began, lulled by the steady drumming. Although the sound was soothing, I was unable to relax, for I'd begun to feel a prickling down my spine as if someone was watching me. Certain that I would have noticed Vannabe's return, I glanced over my shoulder. At first I thought that no one was there, but then I noticed the jar of eyeballs. Every one was focused on me. It made me feel the way I had on the rare occasion that my father had me sit beside him on the raised dais of the throne room while he received petitioners. Courtiers and commoners alike had stared at me as if hoping I'd make a fool of myself so they'd have something to talk about later. I'd hated the feeling then and I hated it even more now; these eyes were unsettling even when they weren't looking at me. I tried to ignore them, but it was nearly impossible.

In a way, it was almost a relief when the door squealed on its ancient hinges and Vannabe stalked into the room: all the eyes turned to watch her. Tossing her dripping sack on the table, she hurried to light the lantern. I crouched down and pretended to be asleep, but my heart began to race when the witch walked toward my shelf. *This is it*, I thought. If anyone had ever told me that I'd end up as a frog used in a witch's spell, I would have sworn he was crazy. But now . . .! The witch stopped beside my cage and I held my breath. I was positive that I was about to lose some of my favorite body parts until I realized that Vannabe was looking through the pile of books and not at me.

"It's somewhere in one of these," Vannabe muttered to herself. "The old woman kept good records. I'm sure she wrote about the plants I need." She took the dragon's skull from the pile of books and set it aside, then selected some books and carried them to the table. A few minutes later she was back, shuffling through the books again.

Each time the witch approached our cage, I pretended to be asleep. I opened my eyes only when I was sure she was looking the other way, and then I opened them only a little. I was glad of this the next time she passed by, for she paused by our cage to look at us. Even with my eyes closed, I could feel the woman's eyes boring into me.

"The frogs' tongues and toes can wait until I'm about to start," Vannabe decided after a long silence. "They'll be more potent if they're nice and fresh."

I heard her move on to the books and look them over one more time. A chill crept through me and I fought to keep it from showing. Vannabe selected a book and returned to the table. The room grew quiet, and although I knew she was lost in her studies, I was too scared to open my eyes.

Tongues and toes, I thought. *She's going to take our tongues and toes. Even if she doesn't kill us, we'll be maimed for the rest of our lives. What are we going to do?*

It was late by the time Vannabe found the book that she needed. Musty and yellowing with age, it contained notes written years before by the old witch. Vannabe pored over the pictures, looking for the plants named in the spell. "Found it!" she said at last. "But according to this I need the stems, not the leaves. Good," she said, yawning. "I'll get them first thing in the morning. Tomorrow is the big day!" Still studying the drawing, the witch fell asleep with the book clutched in her hands.

When I was sure that Vannabe was asleep, I hurried

to Eadric's side and shook him as hard as I could. "Eadric!" I whispered in his eardrum. "We have to think of something. We have to get out of here tonight. She's going to cut out your tongue tomorrow! She's going to cut off your toes! Please, Eadric! You have to wake up!"

Eadric groaned and raised his head to look at me through heavily lidded eyes. "Leave me alone, Emma," he said. "I'm too tired to talk."

"You're awake, Eadric! You're awake!" Eadric's head sank down onto his arm. I grabbed his shoulders in desperation and shook him. "We have to talk now, Eadric! We only have until tomorrow morning!"

Eadric began to snore. I sank to the floor of the cage in despair. *What am I going to do?* I thought for the hundredth time that day. Fat tears rolled down my cheeks and plopped onto the bottom of the cage.

"Hey, it's not that bad," Li'l said from her rafter. "If he woke up enough to talk, you'll probably be able to wake him completely in the morning. Leave him alone and get some rest yourself. You're going to need it tomorrow."

"I can't sleep, Li'l—I'm too scared," I protested. "And even if I could, this itchy rash is driving me crazy."

"A rash, huh? I can't keep you from being afraid, but I may know of a remedy for that rash. We'll need light for it, though, so we'll see about it tomorrow. Now relax and try to sleep. Nothing is hopeless, at least not yet."

Ten

"Psst!" The sound woke me from a restless sleep. "Psst! Emma, wake up!"

Still groggy, I lifted my head. At first I felt disoriented, the cage and the drafty room unfamiliar and threatening. Then I remembered where I was and what was supposed to happen and suddenly I was wide awake.

"Emma! Wake up! Vannabe's gone! Hurry—I thought of something!"

"I'm awake." I blinked and looked up.

"Finally!" said the bat, and she dropped like a stone from her perch to the stack of books on the shelf.

"Li'l!" I exclaimed. "What are you doing?"

"I have an idea," she panted. "I was thinking about your rash and I remembered this book." Stretching her tether as far as it would go, the bat tugged one of the books off the pile and dropped it onto the shelf. "There!" she said triumphantly. "I think that's the right one."

"What are you talking about?" I asked. "How is a book going to help anything?"

"Open it up and take a look. If I remember right, there should be a great spell for getting rid of rashes."

"The rash isn't my biggest worry now, Li'l."

"I know, but the book with the spell for rashes has a lot of other useful spells, too. I can't read, so I'm not sure if this is the right book. Go ahead, take a look."

"But I can't, Li'l! I can't do magic! I make a mess of it every time!"

"What are you talking about? All you have to do is read it! You can do that, can't you?"

"Yes, of course, but you don't know me! I can botch even the simplest spells! You should have seen what happened when I tried to clean my chamber using magic! My bed still makes itself whether I'm in it or not!"

"It's up to you. If you'd rather lose your tongue than try . . ."

"All right! I get your point! I guess it wouldn't hurt to try." I reached for the cover of the book, but my arms weren't long enough to touch it. Even turning sideways and shoving my leg between the bars of the cage wasn't enough.

"I can't reach it!" I said, stretching my leg as far as I could. Hoping to find something that I could use to extend my reach, I looked about my cage. There was nothing close enough to the cage that might be useful, and the only thing inside the cage was Eadric, lying on his back with his belly in the air and his limbs flopping at his sides in a most unfroglike position. His legs were long, longer than mine, and if I could wake him …

At first I was gentle, shaking his shoulder, whispering his name and poking him in the ribs, but when that didn't work, I tried more enthusiastic means. Shouting his name just made him twitch in his sleep. Pulling his leg made him roll over. Finally, I tried lightly slapping his cheeks.

"It wasn't me, Mother," Eadric mumbled, brushing away my hand. "I would never put a mouse in Nanny's ale, even if she did leave the room to use the privy."

I glanced up at the bat, who had returned to her rafter and was hanging upside down, watching me. "Li'l, you said he would probably wake up today, but look at him. What am I going to do?"

"I suppose you could try the remedy used on those nitwits Snow White and Sleeping Beauty. I told you they were given the same potion, remember?"

"Right, right, I remember now. They were both princesses and they were both woken by princes, if I remember correctly. And the princes both … aw, Li'l, I'm not going to have to kiss him, am I?"

"Only if you want him to wake up."

"But I told you what happened last time."

“I’d be real surprised if you turned into anything else now. But whatever you’re going to do, you’d better hurry. You don’t have much time here. Vannabe won’t be gone forever.”

“I know, but … oh, all right. I guess even if we did turn into something else, it couldn’t be worse than being a frog.” I squatted beside him and placed my hands on either side of his face. “It’s funny,” I said. “He’s finally getting his kiss and all he had to do for it was oversleep.” I was about to kiss him when something else occurred to me. “Li’l?” I tilted my head to look up at the bat. “If I kiss him and he does wake up, I’m not going to have to marry him, am I? I mean, both of those princes married the girls they woke this way.”

“Naw, you won’t have to marry him unless you want to.”

“Good! I want to keep my options open.” I kept my eyes open as well this time, thinking half seriously that that might keep me from turning into something else. His lips were cool and smooth, just like the first time, and I had barely taken my lips from his when his eyelids fluttered open and he gazed up into my eyes.

“Well, hello there, beautiful! Is there something you want to tell me?” Eadric said, leering froggishly.

“What do you mean? I was just—”

“Don’t get me wrong! I like being kissed by beautiful young ladies; I just wasn’t expecting it, that’s all.”

"I wasn't kissing you. I mean, I was, but it was only to wake you up!"

"And I liked it! You can wake me that way every morning, and put me to sleep that way, too." Eadric winked and reached for my shoulders.

Pushing his hands away, I hopped to the other side of the cage, giving me space and the time I needed to explain. "I was kissing you only because you've been asleep since the day before yesterday! I warned you about that worm! But no, you had to eat a worm doused in sleeping potion! You had to sleep when you should have been trying to help me find a way to escape! I've been scared to death while you've been dreaming the time away and it just wasn't fair!"

"Emma," Eadric began.

"Never mind. We don't have time to talk now. The witch is going to be back soon to chop off our toes and cut out our tongues. Now get up and come help me! We have to look through this book and I can't reach it. Do you think you can turn the pages?"

Eadric looked thoroughly confused, but he didn't question me. With a long-suffering sigh, he struggled to his feet and hopped to the side of the cage. Crouching down, he stuck his arm between the bars, but it wasn't quite long enough.

"Maybe your leg," I said.

I was overjoyed when his longer legs reached easily.

"What is it we're looking for?" he asked.

"Just turn the pages when I tell you to," I said. "I'll let you know when I find it."

"See if you can find the rash spell first," said Li'l. "Then we'll know if it's the right book."

Eadric turned around with a jerk, aware of Li'l for the first time. Trying to look nonchalant, he leaned over until his lips brushed my eardrum. "Who's the bat?" he whispered.

"She's a friend," I explained. "Her name is Li'l. Now be quiet and let me read this!"

I studied the book of spells, concentrating on some while skipping over others. At my direction, Eadric slowly turned one page after another until I saw what I wanted near the back of the book.

"Here it is!" I said, pointing to a spell. "Rash Rid—rid yourself of that itchy rash in those hard-to-reach places."

Li'l shifted nervously on her seat atop the stack of books. "Try it. It'll be good practice."

"Do I just read this out loud, Li'l?"

"Read it with feeling, Emma! And make big, dramatic gestures with your arms!"

"Anything special?"

"No, no! Just be dramatic!"

"All right, here goes!" I read the spell with as much emotion as I could, waving my arms and gesturing wildly.

Red blotches, rosy bumps,
Itchy spots, scaly lumps,
All you rashes here and there
Under shirts and underwear
On the legs and on the feet,
Don't look now, you're in retreat!
Begone, rash, and nevermore
Irritate my tender pore!

Despite the closed windows and doors, a blast of cold air blew through the cottage. For the briefest instant, I felt prickly all over. I looked down at my leg. It was the same smooth green it had been before I got the rash. I twisted around to look at my back. It, too, was smooth and green. All the itchy bumps had disappeared.

"Good job," said Li'l. "You know, that works for pimples and boils, too. If you were a human, you'd never have another blemish for the rest of your life!"

"That was amazing! If these spells really work, this book is incredible! Look at some of these other spells, Eadric. Here's one for skin softening. It says it will make your skin as soft as a baby's bottom. You can have the hair color you've always wanted with Hair So Nu. This one's called Body Beautiful. It says you can eat what you want without gaining a pound. I wonder if there's a spell that would make me graceful."

"They look like a lot of useless beauty tips to me,"

said Eadric. "How would any of these help us with this witch?"

"They're not all useless. Look, this could be a big help. Squeak Be Gone—squeaky hinges squeak no more. How about Grow Rite—grow the biggest vegetables in the marketplace! Easy Open—open any container without breaking a nail. Listen, they're so simple." Using my normal reading voice, I said,

Unlatch, unlock, undo, untie,
In the twinkling of an eye.
Open ye lock,
Lift ye latch,
Remove ye block,
Release ye catch.

A sound like thunder shook the cottage. A tiny whirlwind twirled debris around and around the room. Then, with a pop, every container in the cottage opened. Lids flew off boxes, corks flew out of bottles, shutters swung open, the door to the cottage slammed back with a crash, the bat's tether twitched loose, and every cage opened with a *whoosh!*

"Would you look at that!" exclaimed Li'l.

"Li'l, you're a genius. You were right about this book!"

"Ladies, the door is open! Don't just stand there

talking!" said Eadric. "Let's get out of here before the witch gets back! Look, there go some mice."

Clifford and Louise had wasted no time and were already crossing the threshold. "Watch out, Emma!" called Clifford.

"Fang is loose!" shouted Louise.

"I'd forgotten all about the snake!" I gasped. "Where do you suppose he is?"

"Snake? What snake?" said Eadric.

"There was a big snake in one of the cages. His name is Fang," I explained.

"Of course it is," muttered Eadric. "What else would it be?"

"He's probably long gone by now," said Li'l. "He never was very sociable, so I doubt he hung around. I have to tell you, though, Emma, I'm proud of you! I knew you could do it as soon as you said you could read."

"So why didn't you have me read that spell right away? What if I hadn't read it at all?"

"I wasn't sure which spells were in that book. I just knew that they were simple spells and that a couple might have worked one way or another. I've never read them myself. You're the first creature I've met who could read."

"What about the spiders?" I asked, remembering the smallest of Vannabe's captives. "Are they still in their cage?"

“They were the first ones out,” said Li’l. “I saw them going down a crack in the floorboards.”

“What’s that?” squeaked Eadric, pointing toward the fireplace, his eyes bulging even more than usual. Convinced that he was overreacting, I looked to where he was pointing. I must admit that if frogs could break out in a cold sweat, I would have done it then. Something still slopped around inside the barrel labeled *Trash Can,* but it didn’t look any different than it had before. However, the lid had popped off the barrel labeled *Trash Can’t,* leaving it open to the air. Three slimy tentacles writhed over the rim, probing the side of the barrel. I shrieked when another rose up and slapped the wall with a soggy squelch.

“Dang,” said Li’l, fluttering her wings in agitation. “Looks like Vannabe’s got herself two Trash Cans!”

I gulped and whispered hoarsely, “You mean one barrel was called a Trash Can’t …”

“Because the trash couldn’t get out of it. But it sure can now!”

“Which makes it a Trash Can!”

“Yup!” said Li’l.

“Another reason we should get out of here as fast as we can. Look at those things!” Eadric’s lips crinkled in disgust when an unattached tentacle slid to the floor and oozed toward the table, leaving a slime trail behind it. “Let’s go somewhere safe!”

"He's got a point," I said. "See you later, Li'l."

"Emma, before you go," called the bat, "take this with you." Li'l flapped down to the shelf beside Eadric and me. Wrapping a wing around the vial of dragon's breath, she dragged it to us. "Without this, she won't have any reason to look for other talking frogs."

"But won't she come after us if she thinks we took it?"

"She won't know we took it if she doesn't see us with it, now, will she? And she won't see us with it if we're gone when she gets back." Eadric grabbed the vial with both hands and dragged it to the edge of the shelf.

I waved good-bye to Li'l and followed Eadric. Together, we jumped to the floor, then quickly hopped to the threshold.

"Wait," I told Eadric. I turned back into the room and looked up at the shelf. The bat still stood where we had left her. Her head and wings drooped and she looked so forlorn that I felt like crying.

"Li'l, aren't you coming?" I asked.

"No," said Li'l. "I think I'm going to stay here. I've spent most of my life in this cottage and I don't have anywhere else to go."

"You could come with us," I suggested.

The bat's expression brightened momentarily; then she shook her head and frowned. "It's no good," she said. "I'm meant to be a witch's bat. It's what I've always been and it's what I'll always be."

"But she'll tie you up again!"

"Not in this cottage. Not after that spell. Nothing is going to stay closed or tied in here unless she finds another spell to reverse it. Now hurry and get out of here. I can hear her coming."

I hopped to the doorway and looked out. Although I could see all the way to the other side of the clearing, there was no sign of the witch. "I don't see her. How can you hear her all the way over here?"

"You're questioning a bat's hearing?" asked Eadric. "If the bat says the witch is coming, the witch is coming. Let's go. This thing is heavy."

But I still couldn't leave. "Li'l!" I called. "Vannabe isn't even a real witch. If you want to be a witch's bat, you can come live with my aunt. She's the Green Witch and she's much nicer than Vannabe. Come with us and I'll take you to meet her. I know you'd get along wonderfully!"

"I don't know, Emma. Are you sure about your aunt? Maybe she already has a bat."

"No, no bats, only a small green snake who's free to come and go as she pleases."

"Li'l, please come," said Eadric. "She's not going to move unless you do."

"All right, I'm coming!" said Li'l. "But you go on ahead. I have to get something."

"You heard her," said Eadric. "Let's go!"

With his arms still wrapped around the vial of dragon's breath, Eadric hopped out the door and into the clearing beyond. I hopped along at his side, turning around every so often to look for Li'l. We didn't stop to catch our breath until we reached the tall grass. "Do you see her yet?" I asked. "Do you see Li'l anywhere?"

"No, there's no sign of the bat, but look there! The witch is back!"

"Eadric, Li'l hasn't come out yet! If the witch catches her . . ."

Vannabe saw the open door the moment she entered the clearing. With a shout of rage, she hiked up her skirts and ran toward the cottage. Even though we knew she couldn't see us, Eadric and I crouched in the tall grass, our hearts pounding in terror.

We saw Vannabe drop her sack on the ground and dart into the cottage. A scream rang through the clearing. Moments later Li'l shot out of the cottage at full speed with the witch close behind. Waving her broom wildly, Vannabe cursed and tried to knock the bat to the ground. When Li'l pumped her wings and flew higher, Vannabe gave up and hurled her broom away in disgust.

"Then get out of here, stupid bat! I don't need you anyway!" she shrieked, her face twisted in anger. Clenching her fists, Vannabe glared at the peaceful clearing as if it might give her the answers. "Who did this?

Who freed my creatures and ruined my spell?"

"I guess she hasn't noticed that the dragon's breath is gone yet," I whispered.

Vannabe ran back into her cottage. A bloodcurdling scream rattled the window frames.

"I think she just noticed," said Eadric.

Movement in the cloudless sky made me look up. It was Li'l, zigzagging above the clearing as she searched for us.

"Li'l, over here!" I called softly.

Turning abruptly, the bat headed straight for Eadric and me.

"As soon as she gets here, do you mind if we get going?" asked Eadric. "I feel a little conspicuous lugging this thing around."

"Sorry," I said. "We can go now."

Li'l swooped overhead and fled into the forest. We tried to follow as quickly as we could, but the vial of dragon's breath slowed our progress. It was an awkward object to carry and made hopping difficult.

"Tell me again why I'm hauling this stuff around," Eadric said. "If we're just taking it so the witch can't use it, why can't I put it down now and leave it here?"

"Think of it this way," I said. "This is the only container in the whole cottage that didn't open. It must be pretty strong stuff. We don't want just anybody to find it.

And you never know, maybe we can use it ourselves someday."

"Now you sound like my mother. I don't think she's ever thrown anything away in her whole life. If we start keeping everything we might use someday, we're going to have to build a wagon to haul it around. All I can say is, this dragon's breath had better be worth it. And what's this about taking Li'l to see your aunt Grassina?"

"We have to go there anyway," I said. "I'm not going to fool around anymore. This time I'm going straight to her tower at the castle. If she still isn't there, why, we'll find someplace safe to wait until she comes back. We know that the witch who cast the spell is dead, so Grassina is the only one we can ask. If anyone can help us, it'll be my aunt."

"I don't think you realize how dangerous a trip to the castle would be. It's a long way from here and even if you did reach it, the guards wouldn't allow you within the castle walls. Then, if you could somehow make it inside, the dogs would get you or the servants would squash you on sight. Are you sure you want to do this?"

"I wish you'd have more faith in me. I got us out of that cage, didn't I?"

"Not because you'd planned it that way!"

"It doesn't matter," I said. "It won't be any more dangerous for me to go to the castle than it would be to stay here."

"For us, you mean," said Eadric.

I shook my head. "You don't have to go with me. You said you didn't want to talk to my aunt. She's a 'spell-casting witch,' remember?"

Eadric sighed. "If you're going, then I'm going, too. I think this is a foolish idea, but I can't let you go on your own. I'll do what I can to protect you. Don't forget, I have an interest in your welfare. If Grassina is your aunt, she can't be all bad, and if she turns you back into a human, I want to be there."

"So she can turn you back into a prince as well?"

Eadric gave me a lopsided grin. "If she can. Besides, maybe I'll get lucky and you'll give me another kiss."

Eleven

Because we had arrived at the witch's cottage shut inside a musty sack, I'd had no idea that Vannabe had carried us from the swamp into the forest until I saw the towering trees that ringed the clearing. As Eadric and I passed the first weathered trunks, I realized that I hadn't the faintest clue which way we should go. Tall trees blocked the sunlight, leaving the forest floor dark and gloomy. We passed beneath an old oak, hopping over its gnarled roots and the carpet of decaying leaves from years past.

"This place is spooky," I said, glancing over my shoulder.

"I like the dark," said a voice, and we looked up to see Li'l hanging from a branch, huddled against the trunk of the tree. "It makes me feel safer. I think I was born somewhere around here, although I don't remember it very well."

"I have no idea how to reach the castle from here," I

said. “Do you think you could fly above the trees and see if you can find it? That would help ever so much.”

“If you really want me to, I suppose I could go look. But it’s awfully bright up there …”

“If you don’t mind. It’s the only castle around with green pennants flying from the turrets. You can’t miss it.”

Li’l nodded. “I’ll be right back.”

We watched her flap her wings and fly between the branches in fits and starts.

“Does she seem nervous to you?” Eadric asked.

“Very,” I said, “but you can’t blame her. This is the first time she’s been outside since she was a baby. I think it would be frightening for her. So much of it will be new.”

“And her flying …”

“Give her some time. Don’t forget that she’s been tethered to a rafter most of her life. I doubt she’s been able to do much flying.”

“I have to set this down,” Eadric said, placing the vial on the ground and rolling his shoulders to work out the kinks in his muscles. “That vial is heavier than it looks. Of course, if you kissed me again, I might have enough energy to haul it around some more.”

I sighed and shook my head. “I don’t understand. Why do you keep asking for a kiss?”

Eadric shrugged. “Habit, I guess.”

"Well, I guess I'm in the habit of saying no!"

"Rejected again," he said, quirking up one corner of his mouth in a half smile. "I must admit, I'm getting used to it."

Leaves rustled as a squirrel darted along the branch of a tree. We both glanced up, and I, at least, felt very small, dwarfed by the immensity of the forest. The trees where we stood were ancient, their trunks so thick that I couldn't have put my arms around them even when I was a human. Broken branches littered the ground, and here and there we could see where one of the mature trees had fallen, exposing a patch of the forest floor to the sun. Young saplings were quick to grow in such spots, greedily seeking their share of the sunlight. With our backs to the meadow, the forest seemed to go on forever. It would be easy to get lost in such a place.

"You know," said Eadric, "it might be a real help to have your bat friend with us. If she can scout ahead, she should be able to keep us going in the right direction."

"Even if she weren't able to help us, I couldn't have left her behind. No one deserved to be left in that awful place."

"I am glad you think so," breathed a voice that sent a chill up my spine. I turned my head toward the sound. Dead leaves whispered beneath the biggest snake that I had ever seen. Four black stripes ran down his gray and white body. A streak of black accented each eye. I froze, unable to move as the snake stared into my eyes. "What is wrong?" breathed the snake. "Do you not recognize me?"

"Are you . . . Fang?" I asked through a throat tight with fear.

"At your service," the snake hissed, coiling his length under him. "You mentioned your destination. I believe that you could use my company."

"Why would we want you along?" Eadric asked, his voice quavering.

The snake swung his head around to face my friend, looking him up and down as if appraising his next meal. "Because I know what lives in this forest. Witches have lived here for centuries, and the spillover from their magic has changed even the trees themselves. But you need not fear the magical beings, for they will see you as an animal and therefore one who belongs. Still, you would not make it through without me, for your indiscretions will soon attract the attention of predators. Without my protection, your journey is doomed before you begin."

Great! I thought. *Even the snake is a critic!* I swallowed past the lump in my throat and tried my best to look brave. "So you're not going to eat us?"

"I do not eat creatures who have helped me. You freed me from a cage so small I feared I would soon go insane. I owe you far more than I can repay by a simple trip through the forest. No, I swear upon my honor as a snake that I shall not eat you." Fang dipped his head to me in a gesture both elegant and noble.

It was up to me to set an example. I resolved not to let anyone see either my fear or the revulsion I felt at being around a snake.

"Does that include my companions, too?"

"Of course. I will—"

"Snake! Snake!" shrieked Li'l, flitting back and forth just above our heads. "Look out, frogs! That's Fang and he's going to get you! What can I do? What can I do?"

The poor bat was frantic and I began to worry that she might injure herself in her frenzy. Apparently, I wasn't the only one concerned, but the snake was more disapproving of the commotion than he was worried about her well-being.

"Would you be so kind as to do something about Li'l?" Fang said in a voice that made my skin crawl. "She's drawing too much attention to us. If you don't stop her immediately, I shall."

I couldn't watch my friend risk her life, but trusting a snake went against all my instincts. Setting aside my misgivings, I waved my arms frantically above my head and shouted as loudly as I could. "Li'l! No! He's a friend!" I hoped it was the truth.

Li'l veered away in midflight and landed on the ground behind Eadric. "Has Emma lost her mind?" she whispered. "How could any snake be her friend?"

"Fang said he owes her a debt, so he's going with us. He promises not to eat us."

"Are you sure he can be trusted? He was always very polite, but he never seemed to want to be anyone's friend. How do we know this isn't a trick? From what I've heard, snakes are pretty sneaky characters."

"What do you suggest we do about it?" whispered Eadric. "He's bigger than the rest of us put together. I don't think it would do any good to tell him not to come."

"Maybe," said Li'l, "but we can keep an eye on him. We'll take turns watching him tonight. I'll take first watch."

"You won't need to wake me when it's my turn," said Eadric. "I won't be able to sleep with him around anyway."

"What are you two talking about?" I asked, although I'd already heard their conversation and feared that Fang had as well. I hopped closer to my friends while Fang raised his head and stared at them through slitted eyes.

"Nothing," said Li'l in a tiny voice as she noticed Fang watching her. She crouched down to hide behind Eadric until all I could see were the tips of her wings. "I was about to show Eadric my twine. It's my only possession and I couldn't leave it behind."

"You risked your life for a piece of twine?" I

exclaimed.

Li'l peeked out from behind Eadric. "That wasn't the only reason I stayed. I moved the book so Vannabe wouldn't know what we'd done. Anyway, the string will be really useful. We can tie the dragon's breath to someone's back with it. Here," she said, handing it to Eadric.

Eadric examined the coarse brown string, turning it over in his hands. "Fine. Tie it to my back. At least that way my arms won't get tired anymore."

"If you have finished your conversation, may I suggest that we move on?" hissed Fang. "You are wasting daylight hours."

At the sound of Fang's voice, Li'l ducked down behind Eadric again. "I saw the castle. I can show you how to get there," she whispered.

"That would be a big help," I said, trying to be encouraging.

"Uh, Fang," said Eadric, "I'd feel a lot more comfortable if you went in front of Emma and me."

"Excellent thinking," said the snake. "I'll scout ahead for trouble." Li'l took off, and the snake watched to see where she headed before slithering off into the leaf litter.

It was up to me to tie the vial to Eadric's back. Although frogs can do many things with their fingers, tying knots is not one of them. "You'd think four fingers would be enough to tie a knot," I said, fumbling with the twine. "But these things just don't work the same as human fingers do. I wish Moe were here. He was the one who knew all about knots."

"Who is Moe?" Eadric asked. "Not another friend of yours? You collect friends like black tunics collect dandruff."

I sighed. I'd forgotten that Eadric had slept through an entire day. "Never mind," I told him. "Someday I'll tell you all about everything you missed while you were asleep. But right now, you can tell me something. What are you and Li'l up to?"

"Li'l and I don't trust that snake and we want to keep an eye on him. I wouldn't want him behind us anyway. Who knows when he might get tired of watching such tempting morsels hopping along right under his nose? A promise is easy to forget when you're hungry."

"He was hungry when he left the cottage. If he wanted to eat us, wouldn't he have done it already?"

"My dear Princess Emeralda, you are awfully naïve, or perhaps I should say that you're too trusting. You think that everyone is going to be your friend until you learn otherwise."

"Look who's talking! You're the one who ate the witch's worm! But you're wrong, you know. I didn't trust you at first."

"Then you trust everyone but me."

"That's not true. I trust you now."

"Good! But you still shouldn't trust that snake. I don't think we need him, despite what he says."

"You don't think we're in danger in these woods?"

"I think the biggest danger we'll face just invited itself along."

"I don't know—these woods are awfully creepy. I can't wait to get through them and back into the sunlight." I looked up at the leafy canopy.

Li'l flew off periodically to check our progress, then returned to keep us headed in the right direction. However, we saw little of Fang for the rest of the day. He scouted ahead as he'd said he would, and if he came across anything dangerous, he didn't tell us about it.

We saw some strange sights as we traveled, things that could be attributed only to magic. Trees seemed to move in most untreelike ways, bending with a fluid grace to lean toward neighbors, the rustle of their leaves almost sounding like words. I swore I saw one pull up its roots and move into a patch of sunlight, but when we reached the spot the roots looked as if they'd been growing there for years.

We'd been traveling through the woods for a few hours when the ground began to shake and we heard the thudding footsteps of a large, heavy creature. Although the noise grew increasingly loud, distance and dense foliage kept the thing hidden from sight. Suddenly, there was a tremendous crash, followed by the shriek of splitting wood. The trees around us shuddered in sympathy, raining leaves like emerald teardrops. I jumped to avoid a falling twig, but the ground wasn't where I thought it would be and I landed in a depression nearly twice my height.

"Emma! What happened? Are you all right?" Eadric's shout made me cringe, for he had been loud and I knew the sound would carry.

"Shh!" I whispered. "Not so loud! I'm down here!"

Eadric's face appeared over the edge of the hole, peering down at me with a look of such concern that I immediately regretted scolding him. "Let me help you up," he said, extending his hand to take mine.

"You don't need to do that," I said, backing up a few steps. "I think I can make it. Watch out!" I tensed my legs and was about to leap when the ground shook with such force that the sides of the hole began to crumble, dropping clods of dirt onto my head and shoulders. A faint whimper came from above, and Eadric plopped into the hole beside me. The moment he landed, he shoved me back against the side of the depression and held me there, all the while looking as though he would like to disappear straight into the soil. There was a deafening thud, and something blew hot air reeking of brimstone into our hole.

"Frogs," grated a voice, sounding so disappointed that I almost spoke up. Eadric must have sensed this, for he clapped his hand over my mouth until the creature took off with a great flapping of leathery wings that sent leaves and other debris swirling down around us.

"What was that?" I whispered once the sound had grown too faint to hear.

"A dragon!" Eadric breathed. "I didn't know there were any around here! Why, if I had my sword …"

"You wouldn't be able to lift it! You're a frog, remember?"

"Oh, yeah. But as soon as I'm human again …"

"Uh-huh," I said, finding it hard to believe that Eadric would ever face a dragon in any form whether he had a sword or not. "Come on. We have to get out of here if we're going to get changed back."

Jumping out of the hole was easy, but we'd gotten turned around and it took us a few minutes to find our original heading. The trees seemed to have moved as well, but we finally found our footprints and determined which direction we'd been going before. We also figured out what had made the hole: it looked like a giant footprint.

"Giants and dragons!" Eadric said, grinning from eardrum to eardrum. "I really will have to come back here with my sword!"

"Right," I said. "Whatever you say."

I began to notice other prints after that, like the enormous marks of a griffin's talon and paw. We saw additional signs of the dragon as well, for some of the trees were singed, and the bark had been rubbed off others. Sensitive to the forest now, I saw shadows where there was sound but no substance, flickering lights where there should have been none, but nothing else came to bother us. If we had passed through this forest in the witch's bag, it was just as well that we had done it in ignorance.

We had both been complaining of thirst for some time when we finally came across a pool of water. Although sheltered by the canopy of ancient interlocking branches, the water sparkled invitingly as if lying in the direct rays of the brightly shining sun.

"What are you waiting for?" Eadric asked when I hesitated. "It looks clean enough."

"Maybe so, but what do we really know about it? It could be enchanted or even poisoned. I'm not sure—"

I gasped, for the face and dripping locks of a beautiful, ageless nymph had broken the surface of the water. She looked around eagerly, but when she failed to see whatever it was that she was looking for, her perfect mouth twisted in a sulky pout and her aqua-colored eyes clouded over. Sighing loudly, the nymph rose gracefully from the water and stepped onto the bank. Although her long green hair reached past her knees, it did little to cover her naked form. Ignoring us, she dropped down on one of the larger flat rocks and began to comb her hair, her gaze as unfocused as a daydream.

Eadric sighed and I glanced in his direction. To my disgust, he was gazing longingly at the nymph like some lovesick squire who'd just discovered his true love.

"Eadric!" I said, jabbing him with my elbow. "What's wrong with you? She's a nymph! You know she has only one thing on her mind."

"I know," he said, his eyes glazing over. "And I'm a handsome prince. . . ."

"Eadric, you're—" But my warning was too late, for Eadric had hopped onto the rock.

"You are the essence of beauty," he began, his eyes raised adoringly to the nymph's face. "You are my sun, my moon, my stars."

"You're a frog," she said, noticing him at last. "I don't talk to frogs."

"I'm not just a frog."

"You look like a frog to me," she said, the tiniest frown wrinkling her flawless brow.

"Yes, yes, of course I do, my sweet, but I'm really an enchanted prince!"

The nymph's eyes flickered with interest. "Prove it! Show me your crown or your jeweled sword!"

"I'm sorry, I don't have them with me."

"Oh," she said, her pout returning. "Then you'll have to leave. Someone important might come by at any moment."

"But I'm important! I'm—"

"You're a frog. Now go away. This is my pool and I don't allow frogs here. You lay those disgusting, gooey eggs and foul my nice clean water."

"But I'm a prince! I don't lay eggs! I won't—"

Tossing her hair over her shoulder with a dainty flip of her wrist, the nymph turned her back and pointedly ignored Eadric. He looked so crestfallen, I almost felt sorry for him. Almost, but not quite.

"But I *am* a prince!" he said when he joined me back on the bank.

"Not right now you're not, and it's a good thing, too! Nymphs drown princes, so be happy that she's not interested in you. It's the only reason you're still alive. The potion Vannabe put on that worm must have softened your brain. We'd better go before you make an even bigger fool of yourself."

I couldn't tell whether Eadric was upset by the nymph's rejection or because I'd called him a fool, but either way, he was in a sulky mood. It was probably just as well that he didn't feel like talking to me, since I was so irritated that I couldn't have said a pleasant word to him even if he'd paid me with all the mosquitoes in the forest.

Fuming silently at Eadric's foolishness, I was relieved to see a friendly face when Li'l found us on the forest floor. She'd come to tell us that we didn't have far to travel, but it was already getting too dark to see, though she seemed not to mind.

"I think we'd better stop now," I said, raising my hand and wiggling my fingers. "I can barely see my hand in front of my face."

"If you really want to," Li'l replied. "Although I think it's just getting nice out! But if you want to go to sleep, you should find a good place to hide. Who knows what comes out at night in these woods."

"I can think of one thing," Eadric said, spotting a sudden flash of light. "Fireflies! Ladies and gentlemen, I think dinner has arrived."

A firefly darted erratically through the gloom beneath the trees, its tiny light pinpointing its path. Despite the empty ache in my stomach, I was reluctant to try to catch one. I'd heard that fairies often flew about at night dressed in little more than twinkling lights. Because they were nasty when insulted, I shuddered to think what they might do if you tried to eat them. Eadric, however, had no such qualms and quickly set about catching his dinner. I laughed when I saw his throat lit up from inside. My guffaw was loud in the darkened night and sounded strange even in my own eardrums. I stopped abruptly. Frightened by the thought of the predators that might hear me, I no longer felt like laughing.

Eventually satisfied that they really were fireflies and not deceitful fairies, I flicked out my tongue, coiling it back with a tingle of anticipation. It wasn't bad.

While Eadric and I waited for another firefly to pass by, Li'l flew over to sit beside me. "How do they taste?" she asked.

"Delicious! And just think, a week ago you couldn't have paid me to eat a firefly!"

"A week ago I didn't know what they were," said Li'l. "I've never had one."

"Never?" I said. "Then you need to try them!"

Something rustled the leaves in the tree above us, prompting Li'l to look about nervously. Wrapping her wings around her body to make herself as small as she could, she shuffled toward me until we stood shoulder to wing.

Although the night sounds made me nervous as well, I was reluctant to let Li'l see it, as I was sure it would only add to her fear. "While you're here," I said, hoping to distract her, "there's something I've wanted to ask you. Back in the cottage, why did the 'open box' spell work even though I didn't gesture or use a dramatic voice like you told me to?"

Li'l shrugged her wings. "You don't have to do those things to make the spell work. I just like it better when it's done that way."

"You mean all that arm waving I did was just for show?"

"Yup."

"I thought it might be something special that Mudine did to make the spells more powerful."

"Nope."

"And what about the first spell? The one for rashes? It worked only on me, but when I did the spell to open boxes, it opened everything in the cottage."

"Actually, they both would have worked on everyone near you, but you were the only one with a rash. If you want a spell to be specific to one subject, you need to use something to focus it. You can point just about anything at your subject to aim the power."

"Like a magic wand?"

"Yup, although it doesn't have to be a wand. In fact, if a witch has had enough practice, pointing her finger works just fine."

I'd been watching Eadric while Li'l and I talked, amazed at how many insects he'd eaten. Neither our conversation nor the strangeness of the forest could distract him from the pursuit of food. "Will you look at that!" I said to Li'l. "If we don't stop talking and go catch some fireflies, Eadric'll eat them all himself!"

Li'l smiled halfheartedly and took to the air to chase her first firefly. Darting between the trees, she snatched insects from the air as if magnetically drawn to them. A day of flying had improved her rusty skills and she no longer seemed so hesitant.

We ate until we were full. Then Eadric and I made

ourselves cozy beds in the decomposing leaves while Li'l flew into the branches of the ancient maple above us. It didn't take Eadric long to fall asleep, but I lay awake far into the night. My thoughts bounced from one subject to another, and I found myself worrying about everything. What would happen to Eadric and me? Would Li'l like living with Grassina? How would I explain everything to my mother? Would the trees still be in the same place when we woke up in the morning? I wanted to go to sleep, but it seemed as if I'd forgotten how. Forcing myself to relax, I listened to the night sounds of the forest: Eadric snoring gently under his blanket of leaves; Li'l moving from one branch to another; a distant owl hooting softly; mice rustling the leaves in search of food; the creak of branches and the whispering of leaves. Eventually, the sounds grew fainter.

The next thing I knew I was in the Great Hall of my parents' castle. It was dark and deserted. Even the guards were nowhere in sight. Torches burned in the wall sconces, casting a feeble light that flickered and created shadows. A snorting, breathy sound came from a darkened corner of the room. The shadows swayed, dancing in a nonexistent breeze. Crossing the hall, I entered the corridor beyond. It was the corridor that led to my aunt's room, the corridor that had always led to safety.

Inside the doorway, I found myself in the cozy familiarity of my aunt's room. The fire burned brightly in the fireplace just as it always did. The drifting balls of witches' light cast their comforting glow just as they always did. But still, something didn't feel right.

I walked to the fireplace, my hands held toward the fire to warm the chill from my fingers. Then suddenly, everything was different. The room had changed. No longer in my aunt's safe, inviting room, I now stood by the fireplace in Vannabe's cottage. Bright, shiny objects lay on the table, drawing me to them. The air around me wavered as I moved across the floor. Reaching the table, I found knives made of brightly polished metal. The whisper of fabric came from behind me. I turned quickly.

Vannabe stood in the doorway, her heavy skirts swaying, a wide-bladed knife in her hand. "I won't keep you long," she said. "I only want your tongue and your toes. You know you'd do anything to help a friend. Think of me as your friend and let me have them. It's just a small favor. Tongue and toes, that's all I want." The whispering came again as Vannabe drew closer. "If you hold still, this won't hurt too much."

I woke with a start. My heart raced and my hands felt clammy. I felt disoriented and lost. My nest beneath the leaves was dark and confining. Panic-stricken, I pushed the leaves aside and scrambled into the open. I glanced around, trying to get my bearings. The back of my neck prickled the way it had when the eyeballs watched me. Vannabe was here! But when I looked up, it wasn't the witch who was swooping down on me, but an owl, its beak open in anticipation! Too scared to call out, too frightened to move, I pressed myself against the ground, convinced that I was about to die. Suddenly, a large, sinuous body whipped between us. Hissing, the snake lunged, barely missing the startled owl as it pulled up only inches from me. Its wings beating frantically, the owl fluttered away in distress, still alive.

"Are you all right?" hissed Fang, keeping his eyes on the departing owl.

"Yes," I breathed with a throat too dry from fear to say more.

"Go back to sleep," whispered Fang. "I will keep guard. You have nothing more to fear this night."

I surprised myself by believing him. If Fang had wanted to eat me, he wouldn't have waited this long. For the first time in days I began to feel secure. Burrowing under the leaves again, I thought of waking Eadric, of telling him how close I had come to being an owl's midnight snack. But the more I thought about it, the fewer reasons I could find for waking him, so I let him sleep undisturbed. *I'll tell him in the morning,* I thought. *There's no need to tell him now.*

Eadric was still asleep when I woke the next morning. I remembered my intention to tell him about the owl, but in the light of day I began to doubt that it had really happened. After eating a dozen salty mosquitoes, I went looking for a nice juicy beetle. When I returned, I found Eadric and Li'l in the midst of a heated discussion.

"Why didn't you wake me?" demanded Eadric. "I told you I would take the second watch."

"You told me you weren't going to sleep at all! I could hear you snoring all night long," Li'l said.

"Don't exaggerate! Frogs don't snore! Maybe your hearing isn't as good as I thought it was."

"Maybe not all frogs snore, but you do. I found myself a hidey-hole in the trunk of that tree and I could hear you even from there! It's a good thing nothing happened last night. If I could hear your snoring, other creatures could have as well. We're lucky no predators came to see what was making that awful racket."

"Good morning, Li'l, Eadric," I said, nodding to my friends. "Is everything all right?"

"Just fine and dandy," said Li'l, yawning broadly. "If you're ready, we should be off."

"I'll tell Fang," I said. "He's around here somewhere."

"Don't bother," said Li'l. "I already told him. Just follow this deer trail up the hill and over the other side. You'll be able to see the castle once you reach the road. I'm going to find myself a new hidey-hole at the edge of the forest so I can take a nap. I'll see you when you get there. Your voices will wake me up. I have excellent hearing, remember?" Spreading her wings wide, she glared at Eadric. "And Eadric, next time I will wake you up, whether you want me to or not."

Li'l took off, leaving me to adjust the vial on Eadric's back. I untied the knot and straightened the twisted twine. "What happened back there between you and Li'l? She seemed pretty upset."

"What can I say? She's a bat with an attitude problem. I am feeling out of sorts, though. I had a terrible nightmare last night."

"What happened in your nightmare?"

"An owl almost got you. Thank goodness it was just a dream, Emma. I'd never forgive myself if anything ever happened to you."

Eadric looked so sincere that I almost felt sorry for him, except his mistake had put a life on the line, and the life had been mine. I pulled the twine tighter, then tried to tie a better knot. "It wasn't a dream, Eadric. There really was an owl and it really did almost get me. And Li'l was right. You do snore! If it hadn't been for Fang, I'd be filling some owl's stomach right now!"

Twelve

Eadric and I hurried now; we could see the castle from the top of the hill and were eager to reach it. Farmland lay on both sides of the castle road almost as far as the gates. Behind the castle lay the swamp.

We had started down the hill and were passing one of the ancient oaks when we heard the angry buzzing of flies. Although we had both eaten before starting out that morning, Eadric was determined to investigate. I followed him, hoping that I could persuade him to come away. We found the flies along with a few scraps of fur and a scattering of grisly bones—all that was left of some unfortunate forest creature. The flies clustered on the remains, their black bodies glistening blue and green in the sunlight.

"Please don't stop now," I said to Eadric. "We've almost reached the road!"

Eadric smacked his lips, obviously more interested in catching flies than in anything I might have to say. "I'll only be a moment. Why don't you have some, too? There are plenty for both of us!"

"No, thank you," I said. "I'm not hungry." The thought of eating flies that had just crawled on carrion turned my stomach.

Unable to watch, I headed toward the road, hoping that Eadric would soon catch up. I had climbed halfway over a broken branch when something plucked me from the ground and flipped me over onto my back, squeezing the breath out of me. Screaming was impossible, for I didn't have enough air in my lungs to do more than grunt, but I kicked and thrashed about, frantically trying to free myself. Suddenly, I was flipped over again and found myself face-to-face with Fang. *Eadric was right!* I thought. *How could I have ever trusted a snake?*

Caught in the scaly coils, I was sure that I was looking at death itself when I noticed that the snake was no longer looking at me. Its eyes were fixed on something behind me, something that hissed and made the dead leaves rustle with its passing. The pressure on my body grew unbearable as the coils tightened. Then, in an instant, I was tossed aside like rubbish. I flew through the air and would have kept on going if I hadn't hit a tree, slid down the trunk, and landed on my back with my legs sticking up in the air. Partially stunned, I turned my head and looked back the way I'd come. Much to my surprise I realized that there were two Fangs, or at least two snakes that looked like Fang, coiled together in a silent battle. I tried to scoot backward, hoping that neither one would notice me. Writhing, the snakes twisted around until they were facing each other.

"Why, Fang, sweetie, is that you?" said a feminine voice. I noticed for the first time that the snake that spoke was smaller than the other, her body slimmer, her markings slightly different.

"Clarisse?" said the larger snake in a voice that I recognized as Fang's.

"Where have you been, lover boy? You've been gone an awfully long time."

"I was captured and imprisoned by a witch. We have only just escaped."

"We?"

"You attacked one of my companions. Emma," Fang said, raising his head to look at me, "this is Clarisse."

"Pleased to meet you, Emma," said the slimmer snake, delicately flicking her tongue in my direction. "Now, Fang, do you suppose you could let me go? I have a little unfinished business to attend to."

"As long as it doesn't include eating one of my friends."

"Any friend of yours is a friend of mine, and you know I never eat friends."

"Of course, Clarisse. My mistake." The snakes relaxed their coils and slid apart, although they didn't go far.

"Are you home to stay, Fang, or just passing through? The children are quite sizable now, and I know they would love to see their daddy."

"I have an obligation I must fulfill, but I shall return in a few days."

"Good!" said Clarisse. "It's almost that time of year again. Now, you make sure you come look me up as soon as you get back!"

"Rest assured, Clarisse, I intend to do just that."

"You take care now, Fang. I'll be seeing you later." She rubbed her head against Fang's in a gesture so tender that I felt embarrassed to be watching. Swiveling her head to look at me, she flicked her tongue in my direction once more. "It's been nice meeting you, Emma. Good luck with whatever it is you two are doing!"

Fang watched Clarisse slither off, his eyes glazing over as her tail disappeared in the leaf mold.

"Was that your wife?" I asked, wincing at the pain of bruised ribs.

He blinked and slowly turned to me as if he were coming out of a trance. "Unlike humans, snakes do not marry."

"Your girlfriend, then. Your mate, maybe."

"Perhaps one of those terms would apply."

"She's very pretty," I said. "For a snake."

"Actually, she is considered quite lovely."

"Hey, you two," called a voice, and Eadric appeared

from behind a tree. "I thought you would have reached the road by now. You should have stayed and tried the flies. They were delicious."

"Maybe I should have," I said, "considering what the alternative turned out to be."

It was already midmorning by the time we left the shade of the forest. Li'l was waiting for us just as she'd said she would, hanging upside down from the branch of a pear tree like an overripe piece of fruit. I could see the castle again from where I stood, the unmistakable towers rising above the countryside. With our destination seeming so close, I was determined to reach it before dark, although it would probably be a very long way to hop.

"You'll be leaving now, won't you?" Eadric asked Fang.

The snake shook his head ever so slightly. "Not yet. I shall go with you as far as the castle. When you have reached it safely, I shall return here to reclaim my territory and make my home."

"Have you ever been to the castle before?" I asked, proud of my own home and eager to hear some words of praise.

"No, although I know of some who have. You had best be careful when you get there. I hear the castle is a very dangerous place."

"Dangerous!" I said indignantly. "It's not dangerous at all! I've lived there all my life and I've never seen anything dangerous!"

"Of course not, for you were there as a human and a princess."

"Then you believed me when I told everyone at the cottage that I'm an enchanted princess and that Eadric is a prince? You all laughed, so I thought you doubted me."

"I do not know about the others, but I did not believe you until you read the spell. I do not know of any other frogs who can read."

"I believed her when she *said* she could read," Li'l said. "I've never met a creature who even claimed that before! Hey, everybody, see over there." She shaded her eyes with one wing and pointed with the other. "The road curves past those farms and ends at the castle gate. You're almost home, Emma."

"Thank goodness! And we'll be humans again as soon as we find my aunt!" I hopped onto the road, eager to leave. "I'll lead now. I know my way from here."

I was so excited that I couldn't hop the way I normally did. Instead, I jumped, leaped, and bounced down the road like a child's toy. My excitement must have been contagious, because Eadric tried to match his hops to mine while Fang slithered faster than we had ever seen him move before. Even Li'l was caught up in the excitement, flying loops in the sky above us until her wings began to tire. Panting at the unaccustomed exertion, she settled in an old apple tree by the side of the road and waited for us to catch up.

It wasn't long before Eadric discovered the anthills. He amused himself for an hour or so by taking samples from each one he found, but stopped after tasting a red ant. "They have too much bite," he told me, his mouth twisted in pain.

The road was warm and dry beneath our feet. Dust swirled around us as we hopped, coating our skin and making us cough. The air grew hotter as the day went on, and Eadric and I soon suffered the effects of the drying sun. After a while, feeling pinched and withered, we slowed to a halfhearted walk.

"I have to sit down," I finally told my friends. "I feel faint."

"Frogs aren't meant to be out of water for so long," panted Eadric. "We need to find a stream or a lake. Even a puddle will do."

"I shall ask Li'l to look around," said Fang, who never left our side for long.

I knew that talking to Fang made Li'l nervous, but she flew to us when he called to her and landed a good distance from him, listening to his request. After looking Eadric and me over and seeing the truth of Fang's words, she nodded and took off. I watched her circle and come back a short time later.

"I found a pond at the bottom of the hill," she said, landing beside me. She frowned when she saw Eadric sprawled on the dirt road. "What's wrong with him?"

"He's passed out," I told her, "and I don't feel well, either."

"We need your help, Li'l," said Fang. "I cannot carry him, so it is up to you."

"Me?" squeaked the bat. "I've never lifted anything that big before!"

"You lifted the books in Vannabe's cottage when you brought them to me," I said.

"It's more like I dropped them. Oh, all right. I'll try to carry him," said Li'l, "but I don't think I can for long. He's a big boy, isn't he?"

"Emma, are you well enough to walk?" asked Fang.

I tried to stand, but my legs buckled under me.

"Here," said Fang. "Climb onto my back. I can take you there if you can hold on."

"Ugh!" Li'l grunted, struggling to lift Eadric. "I'm going to get a hernia! This frog needs to start eating fat-free insects!"

Just beyond the next rise, the ground sloped away from the road. A pond lay at the bottom, a welcome sight for everyone. Li'l half carried, half dragged Eadric up the hill. When she reached the top, she lost her grip and his limp body slid down the other side.

"Look out below!" shouted Li'l. She took to the air

and flew after him, but he hit a bump and began to tumble head over heels over vial of dragon's breath. Finally, Eadric plopped into the water and Li'l flew off in search of a shady tree, her job done.

The pond was all we could have hoped for. It was close. It was cool. It was wet. I clung to Fang's back all the way down the hill, although I felt weak and nauseous and had a hard time concentrating. When he reached the bottom, Fang wriggled into the shallow water long enough for me to slide off. He stayed by the edge to make sure that I was all right, but as soon as I began to move around he slithered back up the hill and onto a large flat rock overlooking the pond.

I lay in the shallows until I started to feel like myself again. When I was able to, I swam toward Eadric, who still lay sprawled in the water where he had landed when he fell. I was concerned about him: his face looked pasty and his skin was too warm. He muttered when I laid my hand on his forehead, but his eyes remained closed. Taking his hand in mine, I waited until he twitched and opened his eyes before I turned and plunged into the depths of the pond. Eadric soon followed me, his feeble strokes becoming powerful scissor kicks as he regained his strength.

The water felt wonderful! We somersaulted and dove, we floated and twirled, and all the while our skin let water into our parched flesh. I thought of the day I had learned to swim and of how much else I had learned since then.

I was enjoying the water and the breeze that ruffled the surface of the pond when suddenly something grabbed my foot and pulled me under. Kicking hard, I shook Eadric's hand loose and popped to the surface like a cork. I was still laughing when Eadric followed me up, his face appearing only inches from mine.

"You know something?" he said, grinning. "You're a much better swimmer than you used to be. It won't be long before you're almost as good as I am."

"Is that so? And how do you think I'm doing in my other froggy skills?"

"Your hopping is good, but you still need to work on catching insects."

"Really? Well, I don't think I'll ever be able to eat as well as you can."

Eadric smiled smugly. I patted him on the shoulder, then did a flip in the water and swam away before he could see my own smile.

Thirteen

With Li'l leading the way and Fang guarding us from behind, we were soon back on the road to the castle. Mumbling her apologies, Li'l flew to the first tree she could find. When we reached the tree, Fang pointed out her darker shape amidst the leafy shade. "Li'l," he hissed loudly, "we are here."

"Go on without me," called back a tired voice. "I'll catch up later. I need to sleep a little longer."

"We'll meet you at the castle," I shouted. "Look for us by the drawbridge."

Li'l didn't answer. With a sleepy sigh, she'd already dozed off again.

"I hope she heard me," I said to Fang and Eadric as we continued down the road.

"She is a bat," said Fang. "I am sure she heard you. However, bats traditionally sleep during daylight hours and we have asked much of her today. She is also more timid than I expected now that she is out of her element, and I fear that she will be easily frightened for some time to come. I believe her bossy manner was a cover for her insecurities."

Late that afternoon, a farm wagon leaving the castle grounds rumbled down the road. Fang moved off into the grass while Eadric and I patiently waited for the wagon to pass. I was shielding my eyes from the cloud of dust when a young boy walking beside the wagon spotted us. "Look, Father," he called. "Frogs! I'm going to catch them!"

"Now, Robbie," said the farmer, "why don't you leave them where they are? You take them home and they'll die like the last ones."

"But I want to play with them," the boy insisted.

Eadric and I had heard the child and had no intention of letting him catch us. I hustled Eadric off the side of the road, following Fang into the tall grass. The boy, who had seen us go, ran over with a stick in his hand. "I know you're in there," he said, squatting on his heels. "Come out here where I can see you." The long stick jabbed the grass, narrowly missing us.

Eadric, trying to frighten the boy away by making himself look big and intimidating, straightened his legs and arms and put on his fiercest expression. Since his legs were longer than his arms, his back end stuck up higher in the air, forcing him to tilt his head back to look at the boy. With the vial of dragon's breath still strapped to him, Eadric looked like a bizarre multicolored hunchback, and I would have laughed if I hadn't been so frightened. Because he was in front of Fang, Eadric couldn't see the snake raise his head above the grass and glare at the boy through slitted eyes. Fang hissed softly and the boy nearly fell over his own feet trying to get back to his father's wagon.

"Did you see that?" said Eadric proudly. "I scared him off! He'll think twice before coming after a frog again, won't he!"

"I'm sure you're right," I said. "Especially one who travels with a snake. Next time he might even stay in the wagon."

With the farm wagon and the boy gone, we returned to the road. The rosy glow of the sunset outlined the castle and made it seem all the more inviting. However, we had gone only a short distance when we felt the vibration of approaching vehicles. Soon, two more farm wagons and a tinker's cart passed by. Petitioners from the village who had stayed late at court followed in a carriage. With so much traffic on the road, we decided that it was no longer safe and moved off into the fields.

Traveling across the uneven ground was slower than it had been on the hard-packed dirt, and night fell before we reached the castle. The drawbridge was already up. It wouldn't be lowered again until morning.

We were seated in the dust at the end of the road when Li'l flew down to land beside us. "There you are!" she said. "I've been looking all over for you! I don't like it out here. It's too open and there's too much going on. I think I saw a hawk, although I'm not real sure. So where are we going now, Emma? Do you have any good hidey-holes in that castle of yours?"

"I'm sure you'll find plenty of places to hide," I assured her, "but why don't you go see if you can find my aunt first? That's her tower, the tall one on the left. She said she would be away for a few days, but she should be back by now."

"What about you? Are you going straight there?"

"We have to get inside the castle," I explained, "and the drawbridge is up."

"Why's that a problem?" Li'l asked. "You're frogs. You can swim across the moat. I'll go up to the tower and take a peek inside. Now, you're sure your aunt won't mind?"

"She won't mind at all. Go on ahead. We'll be there as soon as we can." I watched Li'l become a dark speck as she flew over the moat. When I could no longer see her in the gloom, I turned and spoke to Fang. "And what about you, Fang? Are you coming with us?"

"No, I must return home now. I have much work to do to reestablish my territory."

"Thank you for being there all those times," I said,

throwing my arms around him. "You were right—we did need you."

"I know. And you are welcome." My hug made him uncomfortable, for he quickly backed away, eyeing me warily. "Emma," he said, "because of your emotional demonstration, I must tell you something that I would not otherwise have disclosed."

"You can tell me anything, Fang. If anyone has the right, it's you."

"I understand that humans whose lives have been saved may feel a certain … affection for their rescuers. If you are feeling such an affinity for me, you must know that my heart is engaged elsewhere."

If he thought that I had a crush on him … I tried not to laugh, and thought of a trick I'd learned when my mother caught me in a giddy mood and I knew she would disapprove if I laughed out loud. I had only to think of something sad, such as the death of my first puppy, to make myself lose the desire to laugh. I tried it now and it worked, allowing me to alter my expression to one more suitable to a jilted female.

"Is it Clarisse?" I asked, looking as mournful as I could.

"Yes," he said, nodding solemnly. "You are not too badly disappointed, are you?"

"I'll recover, but it won't be easy."

"Good luck in your endeavors. And the same goes

for you, Eadric."

"Thanks, Fang. It was ... an experience having you along."

I watched Fang slither down the road with mixed emotions. He was a snake and I had always been terrified of snakes. Because I was now a frog, he should have been one of my worst enemies, yet he had proven to be a friend, someone I could trust when I was in danger.

"What did you mean when you thanked Fang like that?" Eadric demanded. "He didn't do anything! And who is Clarisse?"

"And *you* accused *me* of being unobservant! Never mind, Eadric. Maybe I'll tell you about it one day. Let's just say that he was a much better companion than either of us thought he would be."

"I guess that's true," said Eadric. "At least he didn't eat us."

Fourteen

Following Eadric to the edge of the moat, I peered down into the water, thinking about how often I'd passed by without really looking at it. The moat had been a fixture, part of the castle fortifications that I knew we needed, but it had never seemed particularly important. I'd certainly never considered swimming in it before.

A breeze blew past, carrying the stench of decaying garbage. "Pew!" I said, wrinkling my nose. "Do you smell that? Is that the water?"

Eadric lowered his head and sniffed. "It sure is."

I stepped back from the edge, my stomach churning. Having grown up near the moat, I suppose I'd been used to the smell. Maybe it was because of my enhanced frog senses, or maybe the moat had gotten stinkier since I'd been gone, but for whatever reason, I now found the stench overwhelming. "I'm not swimming in anything that smells that bad!" I said.

"We don't have much of a choice, do we?"

"We could wait until morning when they lower the drawbridge."

"But then all the wagons and foot traffic will be going in," Eadric said, shaking his head. "Crossing the moat is probably the best idea. Just keep your mouth closed and swim as fast as you can."

I looked at the moonlight's reflection on the moat. The other bank suddenly seemed so far away, so high above the water. "I don't think I can do this!"

"Sure you can!" said Eadric. "You just need a positive attitude!"

"Fine! I'm positive I can't do this!"

Eadric sighed. "You're right. You can't do it if you don't believe you can. But don't imagine yourself failing—imagine yourself doing it. Picture yourself swimming across and climbing up the other side. I know you can do it if you really want to."

I closed my eyes and tried to picture myself swimming through cool, clear water, speeding to the opposite side of the moat and climbing the stones as if I'd done it every day of my life. Unfortunately, I could still smell the water, and the illusion was hard to maintain. It was easier to imagine Eadric swimming beside me, holding his nose with one hand and paddling with the other, saying, "Picture yourself as a bubble, floating across the water," his voice fading as he disappeared in a stinky green fog.

I giggled. "Now, *that* I can believe!" I said under my breath as I slipped into the moat.

I tried to breathe as little as possible, but it wasn't easy. The cold, greasy water made me gasp, and I gagged when it almost got in my mouth. Holding my head as high as I could, I tried to keep my face dry. A large glob of something soft and sticky bumped into me and I shuddered with disgust. *Thank goodness it's dark and I can't see what that was,* I thought.

"Emma, hurry up," said Eadric. "I think there's something in here with us."

"There sure is," I agreed. "There's all sorts of garbage floating in this water. This is disgusting!"

"No, I mean something alive. I just felt something swim past my feet."

A small wave nudged me forward, carrying me closer to the side of the moat. "Eadric," I whispered, suddenly afraid to talk out loud, "did you feel that? What could have made that wave?"

"Something bigger than a frog!" Eadric whispered back. "Here it comes again. Hurry, Emma, we're almost there!"

With the dry ground edging the moat only feet away, the castle loomed over us forbiddingly. Although I had always loved my home, I had never seen it from the moat before. Now I wished I never had. I kicked as hard as I could, arrowing through the water, and almost bumped into the fish. It was a small fish, only half as big as I was, but it startled me just the same. Its eyes were red and watery and swollen. It looked as though a third eye had begun to form between the first two, a shrunken eye that rattled loosely in its socket. Something brushed against my feet, but when I looked, the fish was still keeping pace with me. Evidently, the deformed little fish wasn't the only creature that lived in the moat.

When I finally bumped into the stone wall, I reached up and touched it with my hand. Eadric, who had already climbed out of the water, grasped my wrist and began to pull me up.

"Hurry!" said Eadric. "There's something in the water behind you!"

I looked down. Reflected in the light of the rising moon, a large silvery back arced above the water, heading toward me. Terror lent me the strength I needed. Digging my toes into the crumbling stone lining the moat, I fairly flew up the side and fell into Eadric's arms, knocking him off his feet. Something slapped the surface of the moat, splashing us with a wave of fetid water. Without looking back, we scrambled to safety as far from the moat as we could get.

"Now what?" I asked, wiping the moisture from my face with the back of my hand. Standing on the narrow stone ledge, I still felt exposed to whatever lived in the moat.

"Find a way in, I suppose. There has to be a hole or a missing stone or something we can use to get inside. We just have to look until we find it."

"And what if there isn't?"

"Then we wait until they open the door in the morning. Don't worry, I grew up in a castle, too, remember? Little boys explore everything. I found hundreds of chinks in the walls of my parents' castle, places too small for a little boy but certainly large enough for a couple of frogs. If anyone can find a way into your castle, it's me."

The moon was high overhead when we finally found an opening. Although it never grew any wider, it extended far back through the castle wall, forming a cramped, dark tunnel. Dried rodent droppings and beetle casings littered the floor, telling the tale of those who had passed that way before. The air was dank and smelled musty, but it was a way in and I was thrilled that we had found it.

The tunnel ended abruptly at a large open space. I was disoriented until I realized that we had reached the Great Hall, the heart of the castle and the most important room. A warren of corridors and lesser chambers led from the hall, making it the focal point of the entire building. The remains of a fire burned in the massive stone fireplace, and my father's dogs lay twitching in their sleep on the hearth, their bellies filled with table scraps.

"This is wonderful!" I whispered into Eadric's

eardrum. "We don't have far to go now. The stairs leading to my aunt's rooms are at the end of that corridor."

"What about the dogs?"

"We'll have to be careful not to wake them, that's all." Eadric looked skeptical, but I was insistent. "Eadric," I said, "we have to go now. It will be so busy here in the morning that it will be impossible to pass through then. If we don't go now, we might as well turn around and go back to the swamp."

"I can't help it—I don't like dogs. And look at the size of those monsters! Are you sure they're all asleep?"

"Of course I'm sure. Can't you hear them snoring? Here, I'll go first. Just stay close and be as quiet as you can."

I hopped once, but the slap of my feet on the stone floor echoed throughout the Great Hall. I froze and listened to the dogs. Their moans, whimpers, snores, and slow breathing assured me that they still slept. One dog growled in its sleep while another ran, its legs twitching, its body never leaving the floor. My father's biggest hound, Bowser, no longer a duckling, lay on his back with his legs in the air, flapping away as if he were trying to fly. I decided that Grassina must have finally found the right parchment to restore Bowser's dogness.

When there was no change in the rhythm of their breathing, I began to hop again, stopping every now and then to listen. We had reached the far wall and had only a little farther to go when I hopped into a puddle of dog pee, splashing myself with the smelly fluid from head to toe. "Oh, yuck!" I said, forgetting the need for silence.

My head whipped around when I heard one of the dogs begin to stir. It was Bowser. Blearily stumbling to his feet, the big hound lurched in our direction.

"Quick, in here!" said Eadric, pointing to a wooden bucket. Although the bucket was familiar, I couldn't remember what it was normally used for, but with Bowser on his way we didn't have time to be picky.

"One, two, three, jump!" I said and we both leaped over the edge and into tepid water. "Eadric!" I whispered as it dawned on me where we were. "This is the dogs' water! What if he's coming to get a drink?"

"Why didn't you tell me?"

"I just realized—"

"Shh! Here he comes!"

I shrank against the side of the bucket as Bowser's great head came into view. *The dog is half asleep,* I thought, *so maybe he won't notice.* I knew the moment that Bowser sensed us, for his ears pricked up. His rank breath washed over me as he looked into the bucket. When I saw Eadric swim to the bottom, I knew that it was up to me.

"Quack!" I said, sounding as much like a duck as I could. "Quack! Quack! Quack!"

"What the ..." Bowser jerked his head back in surprise.

"Quack! Quack! Quack!" I said again, bobbing up and down in the water like a duck.

"Oh, no, another one!" whined Bowser as he backed away.

Although I could no longer see him, I could hear his claws scrabbling on the stone floor as he scurried out of the hall. Eadric was still underwater when I decided that it was safe to go. Sighing, I reached down and pulled him to the surface. "The dog is gone," I said. "We can get out now."

"I guess it was too dark for him to see us under the water," Eadric said, boosting himself onto the rim of the bucket.

I slid over the edge and plopped onto the floor. "Or maybe he's afraid of ducks."

"Why would you keep ducks in your Great Hall?"

"I never said we did."

Turning to look behind us, Eadric scratched his head with his toe, and I heard him mumble softly, "But I thought you said ..."

After trying so hard to be quiet in the Great Hall, entering the corridor was a relief. "I'll race you!" I whispered, eager to stretch my muscles.

"You don't stand a chance, slowpoke!" Eadric whispered back.

We raced across the floor, extending our legs in long, bounding leaps. Arrow slits in the tower walls let in the moonlight, making the steps easy to see. We hopped up one pie-slice-shaped step after another, racing to see who would reach the top first. Eadric won even though he was still wearing the vial of dragon's breath, landing on the top step seconds before me.

When I reached the landing, I was panting and tired but happier than I'd been in a long time. "You won," I said, trying to catch my breath, "only because you have longer legs than I do."

"That's not it at all," he said, panting just as heavily. "I won because I'm a superior hopper and you are a slowpoke."

"It doesn't matter—we're here now!" I grinned so hard my face hurt. "With my aunt Grassina's help, we'll be humans again in no time!"

Fifteen

I had raised my hand to knock on Grassina's door when Eadric waved me back. "Before you get your aunt, there's something I've been wanting to say," he said, avoiding my eyes. "I know I'll be happy to be a prince again, but there's a lot about being a frog that I've really enjoyed, especially since you became one, too."

"What do you mean?" I asked.

"Just that … Oh, never mind. Go ahead, knock on the door." Eadric turned his face away, but not before I saw a frown creasing his forehead.

"In a minute. First tell me what you mean."

Eadric sighed. "I shouldn't have said anything. It's just that being a frog with you has been fun. Even the bad parts were better with you than when I was a frog by myself. As far as I'm concerned, it wouldn't be so awful if we had to stay frogs, not if we were together." Eadric finished in a rush, as if he wouldn't finish at all if he didn't hurry. He cleared his throat, then added, "And you'd never have to marry Jorge."

"I don't know what to say." I reached out to him, but he pulled away from me and turned to the door.

"You don't have to say anything," he said stiffly. "Go ahead and knock."

I'd seen the stubborn look on his face and knew that it was useless to try to question him. Not quite understanding what he meant, I could feel my excitement deflate. After all we'd gone through, did he want to remain a frog? Did he want me to remain a frog, too? I shrugged and lifted my hand to knock, determined to ask Eadric about it later. Before my hand touched the door, it was flung open and my aunt Grassina rushed onto the landing.

"Emma!" she called, her lips quirking at the corners. She turned her head, looking for some sign of me, but she never looked down to see two frogs waiting by her feet. Her smile faded, and she fumbled for the door behind her. "I could have sworn … ," she said to herself.

"Aunt Grassina, I'm down here!" I shouted, thrilled at finally seeing her again. *Now everything will work out,* I thought. *Aunt Grassina can take care of anything.* But my heart sank as Grassina looked down and, seeing only two frogs at her door, turned to go back inside. The sorrow in her eyes made my heart tighten. I couldn't stand to see her look so sad.

"It's me," I shouted, hopping up and down in

frustration. "It's me, it's me, it's me! It's your niece, Emma! I've been turned into a frog! Look at me, Aunt Grassina! Please look at me!"

When Grassina looked down, the stricken expression on her face almost made me cry. "It's not possible," she said. "I gave my niece a talisman to protect her from such spells. You can't be my Emma."

"But I am! I kissed an enchanted prince—Eadric, here—and turned into a frog!"

Grassina raised one eyebrow. "I suppose that could have happened if something went wrong with the talisman," she said slowly. "Emma did ask me about talking frogs and it would certainly explain her disappearance. Perhaps you two should come in."

We didn't need a second invitation. Eadric and I followed my aunt, nearly hopping on the hem of her gown in our hurry to enter the room. Even from a frog's point of view, the room was lovely. The rosy glow from the witches' lights made everything look warm and appealing. Sinking up to my knees in the soft rugs, I reveled in the way they cushioned my tired feet. I sank down on the rug in front of the fireplace and stretched out my legs. Eadric followed me to the rug without ever taking his eyes off Grassina.

"So that's your aunt, huh?" said Eadric under his breath. "She's quite a looker! She's a much better dresser than Vannabe or the old witch, too. She even smells better."

"Thank you," said Grassina, whose hearing had always been good. "I suppose I should take that as a compliment. Just who are Vannabe and the old witch?"

"The old witch was named Mudine," I said. "She lived in the forest, but she died a year ago. Vannabe wants to be a witch. She took over Mudine's house and books when Mudine died."

"I see," said Grassina. "That's too bad. Mudine was a talented witch in her day."

"Did you know her?" asked Eadric. "She was the one who turned me into a frog."

"Is that so?" said Grassina. "Then she can't really be dead, can she? If she had died, the spell would have been broken as well."

"So what do you think happened to her?" I asked. "We were told that she was sick. She lay down on her bed and disappeared in a puff of smoke."

"She may have gone somewhere for a rest. Or if she were very sick, she may have gone to see a witch doctor. Sometimes their cures take a long time to work."

"Maybe Grandmother knows what happened to her," I said. "The old witches sit around a bonfire and trade stories and recipes on Wednesday nights. She might have heard something about Mudine."

"Where does your grandmother live?" asked Eadric.

"In the Old Witches' Retirement Community. It's a very nice place where every witch gets to choose her own cottage. My grandmother's is made of gingerbread, but I think she's sorry she picked it. She's always complaining that children from the village are eating her out of house and home. I'm sorry she didn't get the one her neighbor has. It has chicken legs and can walk around."

"I've never heard of this place. Where is it?"

"Over the river and through the woods. It's easy to find. Even my horse knows the way."

"Well, Eadric," said Grassina, obviously becoming impatient, "regardless of what happened to Mudine, she did a good job when she transformed you. You are a very handsome frog."

Eadric beamed and ran his hand over his smooth green scalp as if brushing back nonexistent hair. I had never realized that a frog could look so vain.

"And what is that vial you're wearing on your back?" asked Grassina. "It looks like aged dragon's breath, if I'm not mistaken."

Reaching behind him, Eadric patted the vial and nodded. "It's a little something I picked up in Vannabe's cottage. Didn't want to leave it there for her to misuse."

"Very good thinking, Eadric. Leaving it for someone who doesn't know what she's doing would have been a terrible idea."

Eadric's smile was so smug it was sickening.

Grassina turned and looked me in the eye. "And as for you, you seem to know quite a bit about Emma's grandmother. You really want me to believe that you're my niece, Emma, don't you?"

"But I am Emma!"

"All right then, tell me why I should believe you. Let me hear your story so I can make up my mind." Grassina gently picked us up and carried us to a small table. Wings folded, the glass butterflies rested on the crystalline blossoms. I made myself comfortable beneath the nodding bloom of a large amethyst-colored rose. Eadric sat beside me, eyes wide as he realized that the flowers and butterflies were alive.

Sitting back in her chair, my aunt waited for me to begin.

"Where should I start?" I asked.

"Start with the day you became a frog."

"It's a long story," I warned.

"I'm in no hurry."

"Well," I began, "it was the day Prince Jorge came to visit...."

I have always been a thorough storyteller. I left out no details, including many that Grassina could have done without. Eadric fell asleep halfway through the story. Grassina, however, seemed to be captivated. She scowled when I told her about Vannabe's treatment of the animals, and she laughed when I told her about the way the fireflies lit up Eadric's throat. She interrupted me only once, when she got up to get herself a cup of tea and a saucer of water for me. My throat was sore by the time I finally finished talking.

"Wonderful story!" said Grassina. "Very entertaining! But anyone with a little imagination could have made it up. Tell me why I should believe that you are my niece. I need some sort of proof, something that you can't have overheard and is specific to Emma."

There was a rustling at the window and a black shape darted into the room. It flew behind Grassina's chair and cowered under the seat. "Tickle her!" said a voice. "Or tell her a really funny joke."

"What was that?" Grassina said, jumping to her feet.

"That's Li'l. I told you about her."

"Ah, yes, the witch's bat." Grassina crouched beside her chair and peered at the bat clinging to the underside of the seat. "So, Li'l, you think you might be interested in living here?"

"That depends. Are you a real witch or a pretender like Vannabe?"

"Oh, I'm a real witch all right. Just ask Emma's mother."

"Do you practice magic much?"

"I not only practice it, I do it! So, did I pass the test?"

"I guess, but there's still a problem. You don't have any rafters. Where's a bat to hang out without rafters?"

"Hmmm, rafters. I hadn't thought of that." Grassina tilted her head to look up at the ceiling. The witches' lights bobbed in the gentle breeze blowing through the window. "And I have all those lights, too. Don't worry, I'm sure we'll think of something. But what did you mean when you suggested that we tickle the frog?"

"Tickle her and you'll see."

Eadric had woken shortly before the end of the story. "I will!" he said, reaching for me.

"I don't know about this," I said, backing away from Eadric. "I don't like being tickled."

"It's for a good cause," he said, grabbing my arm with one hand and tickling me with the other. He tickled my neck. He tickled my sides. He tried to tickle under my arms, but I squirmed away, bumping into the vase. A pale pink rose quivered, dropping loose petals, which landed on the table with a *chink chink chink*.

Eadric grabbed my foot and sat down to tickle it.

"No!" I shouted. "Not that!" And that's when I began to laugh. I laughed until my sides hurt. I laughed until tears ran down my cheeks. I laughed until I was weak and gasping for breath. And my laughter didn't sound like the tinkling of bells. It was full-blown guffaws, belly laughs that started deep inside of me and erupted out of my mouth.

"Emma!" said the Green Witch, and she began to laugh, too. "Only my Emma laughs like that! It has to be true!"

"Stop! Stop!" I gasped, too weak to push Eadric away. Grinning, he let go of my foot and collapsed on the table.

"Tell me," he said, craning his neck to look at my aunt, "wouldn't there have been an easier way? Don't you have any magic powder or a spell to help you see who she really is?"

"Yes, I do, and I believe I'll use it now. There's something I want Emma to see. . . . Emma, you stand over here," she said, picking me up and setting me on the floor. "Eadric, you'd better step back. You don't want to be caught in the backwash."

Li'l peeked out from under the seat, her interest in magic greater than her fear of strangers. "Are you going to do magic now?"

"Yes, I am. Would you like to help me?"

"Oh, would I!" Li'l scurried across the floor to Grassina's side, gazing up at her with awe. "Mudine never let me do anything—except catch bugs, that is!"

Grassina nodded in understanding. "I see," she said. "But things will be different here." She turned and looked about, her eyes finally settling on an old candle stub resting in a congealed puddle of melted wax atop her worktable. With a whispered word and a flick of her finger, Grassina lit the candle. "Now, when I tell you, blow out that flame. But don't do it until I tell you to, understand?"

"Yes, ma'am," said Li'l. "I understand perfectly! Blow out that flame when you tell me to and not before! Yes, ma'am." Her eyes glittering with excitement, Li'l fluttered to the table, landing between a rolled parchment and the candle. Keeping her eyes on Grassina's face, Li'l puffed out her cheeks and held her breath.

"I do like enthusiasm," Grassina leaned down to whisper to me. "But we'd better hurry and get started before she passes out." Raising her arm, she pointed her finger at me and said, "Li'l, now!"

It took the little bat three puffs to blow out the candle, but when she finally did, the whole room suddenly went dark, darker than it had been before the candle was lit, since even the witches' lights had gone out. "How was that?" Li'l said, sounding pleased with herself.

Grassina spoke and her voice was sweet and clear.

Beyond the charm,
Beyond the spell,
Show us the truth
You know so well.

Discard the false
And let us see
Your real form
As it should be.

A shower of sparkles swept through the room, swirling around me like powdery snow caught in a sudden draft. They tickled my nose and I sneezed, squeezing my eyes shut. When I opened them, I could see myself standing above me, or at least that's the way it seemed. Where it had been dark only a moment before, the air now glowed with a diffuse light, showing my normal young-girl body standing with feet squarely planted where I still squatted on the floor. It was a bit disconcerting at first, until I realized that I could see through the image. Although no more solid than fine mist, my body looked natural except for the sparkles. At first I thought they were part of Grassina's spell, but they lingered, twinkling like a thousand fireflies around my image.

"What are those sparkles?" I asked.

Grassina turned to Li'l, who was hopping about on the table, her wings quivering with excitement. "I think Li'l can answer that, can't you, Li'l?"

Li'l bobbed up and down, too agitated to hold still. "She's got the touch, doesn't she? She's got the special flair that Mudine always talked about!"

"What does she mean, *flair?*" I asked.

"She means that you have a talent for magic," said Grassina. "It's a special gift and you have to be born with it. From what you've told me, Vannabe doesn't have it, but whether you want it or not, you do."

"I knew she did!" chimed in Li'l. "It took more than just being able to read to make those spells work so fast! You should have seen it. One minute those cages were locked tighter than a fat dog's collar, then she read that spell and wham! We were out of there! Mudine's spells never worked half that fast!"

Even after I'd worked the spells from Mudine's old books, I'd thought they had succeeded only because they were foolproof. I stood dumbly staring at my image with my mouth gaping like a dying fish. Maybe I really was meant to be a witch. Maybe, if I worked hard enough at it, I could come up with a spell that would rid me of my clumsiness. And maybe I could help other people as well! Grassina herself was always doing just that.

Grassina gestured broadly and the witches' lights glowed again, brightening the room and dissolving my already-thinning image. Her glance fell on me and her lips softened once more. "It's so good to have you back, Emma. I'd hug you, but I'm afraid I'd squash you flat."

"I'll wait," I said, relieved at her restraint.

"How do you like being a frog?"

"It has its moments. But that's what we want to talk to you about. We need you to turn us back into humans. Can you do it tonight or do you have to get ready first?"

"It's not that easy, I'm afraid. We have to determine why you became a frog. You say you kissed Eadric?"

I nodded. "It wasn't a very big kiss, either."

"Hmm," my aunt said, thinking hard. "Was there anyone else present when it happened?"

"No, we were alone."

"What were you wearing that day?"

"I had on my blue gown and my third-best shoes and my hair was—"

"No, I mean what jewelry did you have on? Do you remember?"

"Nothing, really, just the bracelet you gave me."

"Do you mean the charm reversal bracelet I gave you when you were five?"

"Charm *reversal* bracelet? So it wasn't just a pretty bracelet that glowed in the dark!"

"That bracelet had a special magic of its own. I gave it to you when you were just a little girl to protect you. Any witch who tried to cast a spell on you would find that same spell bouncing back onto her. But if you had that on when you kissed Eadric …"

"I did," I said, nodding.

"Then that may be the answer. You see, the spell wasn't being cast on you."

"So when Eadric and I kissed …"

"The bracelet reversed the charm. Kissing Eadric was supposed to turn him back into a human, but instead the reverse happened and you turned into a frog. That should be easy to fix. All you need to do is put on the bracelet and kiss Eadric again. If you do that, you'll both revert to your human forms."

I should have been happy that we knew what had caused my transformation, but I was disappointed that the solution wasn't going to be easier. When I noticed that my aunt was watching me, I frowned and began to fidget.

"You do know where the bracelet is, don't you, Emma?" asked Grassina.

"Sort of," I said reluctantly. "We saw an otter swim away with it. I guess we have to find him ... unless you can do something about it. Can't you undo the spell with one of your own?"

"Certainly, if I had cast the spell in the first place. But I didn't, so you are the only one who can reverse it. However, I might be able to help you find the otter.... Eadric, you look troubled. Is something wrong?"

"Not really," he said. "It's just that every time I think I'm going to become a prince again, something happens. Maybe I'm supposed to live out the rest of my life as a frog."

"You can if you want to, but then Emma will remain a frog as well. Your spells are linked now, so you either both remain frogs or you both turn back into humans."

"I vote for the human," I said, remembering how often my life had been in danger as a frog.

"Then I do, too," said Eadric. He sighed and scratched the back of his head with his toe. "I don't suppose you know anyone who is going toward the swamp tomorrow, do you?"

"I'll take you there myself. It isn't every day that I get to carry a prince and a princess in a basket!"

Sixteen

With dawn still hours away, we decided to get as much sleep as we could before heading for the swamp. Eadric was already snoring softly on a cushioned chair when Grassina bent down to say good night. "Sleep well, Emma. It may take longer than you expect to find the bracelet. I want you to have your wits about you so you'll come back in one piece. I don't know what I'm going to tell your parents about this."

"Don't tell them anything," I said. "I'll talk to them myself when we get back." I had no idea what I would tell them, but I knew that I had a lot to say. I was pleased when I realized that the thought of confronting my parents didn't make me nervous the way it would have before.

"Good!" Grassina said, sounding satisfied. "I knew that sooner or later you would handle these things yourself. But I must tell you that your mother misses you more than you might think. When she first realized you were gone, she had everyone in the castle out looking for you. She isn't a bad person, you know. In fact, when we were younger, she was rumored to be the nicer sister."

"That must have been hard on you."

Grassina chuckled. "But it was true! I was the one with the magic, you see, and I was always getting into trouble. We knew from our earliest childhood who had the gift and who didn't. It wasn't fair to your mother, of course. She was left out of so many things. But in the end it wasn't fair to me, either, for your grandmother favored me and rejected my only suitor for not being good enough, whereas Chartreuse was free to marry whomever she chose."

"You mean to say that she *chose* Father? I thought it was an arranged marriage."

"If it was arranged, she did it herself."

"Did my mother resent you?" I asked.

"Of course she did! I was the favorite child, after all. I think that's why she's been so hard on you. We're so much alike, you and I."

We took short naps and woke just before dawn. Grassina lined a wicker basket with soft cloths, placed a small fruit tart on the bottom, then set it on the floor. "I know fruit tart isn't normally part of a frog's diet, but I thought you might be hungry, and I'm out of insects."

Eadric promptly crawled into the basket and flicked his tongue toward the tart.

"This is wonderful!" he announced, settling down to devour the rest.

I followed him, too excited to eat. "Isn't this great, Eadric?" I said as Grassina lifted the basket. "We'll find the otter, get the bracelet, and I'll kiss you. We can be back in time for lunch, dinner at the latest."

"I'd be less worried if I were doing it as a human," grumbled Eadric.

Grassina carried the basket down the stairs and through the Great Hall. The dogs were awake, begging for scraps and getting under the servants' feet. Bowser took one look at my aunt and scurried under the table, but three other dogs came to investigate the basket, nudging it with their noses and whining to see inside. The wonderful smells of fruit tart and frog were more than they could resist. Grassina shooed them away, but they were persistent and followed her to the door. I crouched in the bottom of the basket with my eyes tightly shut, as if that would protect me from the dogs. Eadric was so engrossed in eating his fruit tart that he never noticed anything.

Once through the garden, I gave Grassina directions to the pond where I had met Eadric. While Eadric finished off the tart, I peered over the edge of the basket and watched the world go by. Little had changed since I last saw the pond. A wood duck had left its webbed footprints in the mud. A queen bee had started a new hive in the old hollow tree at the edge of the pond. Nothing looked as big and scary from up high. I began to feel as though I could handle anything.

"Now, where did this kiss take place?" Grassina asked. "We need to be fairly precise, so try to remember."

I pointed to a bare spot by the edge of the pond where nothing seemed to grow. "Right over there!"

"Are you sure?" said Eadric, leaning over the side of the basket for a better look.

"Of course I'm sure! It was my first kiss! I remember everything about it … at least until things went fuzzy."

"Fine!" said Grassina, catching Eadric as he started to tumble out of the basket, overbalanced by the vial he still wore. "Then you two sit right here and we'll see if we can find that otter."

After setting the basket on an old stump, Grassina took something shiny and black out of the pouch attached to her gown. Light glinted off its sharp angles and flat surfaces the same way it did off one of my father's highly polished swords.

"Where did you get that?" I asked. I had never seen it before and I thought I was familiar with most of the tools my aunt used for her magic.

"While I was on that trip last week, I did a small

favor for a dragon. He gave me one of his scales to show his appreciation. Dragons are known for having an unerring sense of direction, so I thought this might come in handy. Now watch this. . . ."

Holding the scale at arm's length, Grassina stepped to the spot I'd shown her and said,

A golden bracelet rich with charms
Fell to this soggy ground.
An otter chanced upon it here
And took what he had found.

The rightful owner wants it back,
She seeks the otter so
She can retrieve that which is hers.
Please tell her where to go.

Although the scale remained black as coal, colored lights began to shoot through it, red and blue, blue, then red. "Here," said Grassina walking over to set the scale in the basket, propping it against the side so I could see my reflection in its shiny surface. "As the bracelet's rightful owner, place your hand on the scale and determine which direction we must go."

My stomach flip-flopped when Grassina picked up the basket, and I grabbed the sides to keep my balance. I waited until my footing was secure before reaching for the scale. Black as the deepest night, it was as thick as my father's thumb and as wide across as the palm of his hand. The edge was serrated but for one smooth section and I was glad I didn't have to pick it up. With the surface so slick and the edges so sharp, I was sure I would have either cut myself or dropped it. "Now what do I do?" I asked Grassina, looking up at her.

"Just wait," she said. "Patience is a virtue and often vital when doing magic. The scale is seeking the otter for you. It will tell you the direction in a moment."

"You mean it's going to talk to us?" Eadric asked, pressing his eardrum against the center of the scale.

"No!" Grassina laughed. "Watch the color. Red means hot and you're going in the right direction. Blue stands for cold and will appear if you take any direction but the right one. Look, it's working."

The red lights were gone, leaving only blue to shoot about inside the scale. "It's cold, Aunt Grassina. This is the wrong direction. Turn around and we'll see what it does."

"Hot, cold, it sounds like a child's game," grumbled Eadric. "I thought the scale would tell us more than that."

Grassina smiled and shook her head. "I said it was a small favor! Besides, this will be sufficient. Now, Emma, how about this?"

My aunt began to turn in a circle, but the lights were

still blue. It wasn't until she had turned three-quarters of the way around that they began to flash red. "Now, Aunt Grassina! We have to go that way!"

"Very well! Then we'll be off." Gathering her skirts with one hand while holding the basket with the other, she started walking.

"Are you going to take us all the way to the otter?" asked Eadric, struggling to stay on his feet as the basket jiggled and bounced. "Because that's very kind if you are."

"I'm not trying to be kind. I'm just not about to let my niece go traipsing off into the swamp without me again. Not after what happened last time! Emma, keep your eye on the scale and tell me if I need to change direction."

"You're doing fine, Aunt Grassina. No, wait, you've lost it.... That's it, a little to the left..."

I never have been a good judge of distance, but it soon became apparent that the otter wasn't to be found close by. Grassina and I worked as a team, turning this way and that as the lights changed from red to blue. Sometimes the scale took us to an unpassable point and we had to turn around and find another way. Quagmires, ponds, even an apparently bottomless pit made it impossible to go straight. It didn't help that Grassina turned around and backtracked each time we encountered flowers, looking worried until we'd circumvented the plants by a large margin.

Having crossed swampy terrain myself, I knew how exhausting it could be, but Grassina never complained, remaining cheerful even when the mud tried to suck her shoes off her feet, branches whipped her cheek, or she had to retrace her steps yet again. It wasn't until I announced that my head ached from staring at the flickering lights that she suggested we stop to rest. I was grateful on my own account and pleased that I'd found an excuse to make her rest as well.

With nowhere to sit but the sodden ground, Grassina gestured at a small hummock and whispered softly. The ground rumbled and a large stone rose out of the mound, rotating to present a flat surface. Another word from Grassina and a puff of wind scoured the rock free of soil and insects. Sighing with pleasure, my aunt settled herself on the rock and set the basket on her lap.

"Can I ask a question?" asked Eadric.

Grassina smiled. "Yes, Eadric, of course, although I'm not sure that I can answer it."

"That spell that you said earlier, the one about finding the bracelet… Did you make that up as you went along or did you think of it ahead of time?"

"I made it up as I said it. That's how I do most of my spells."

"You're very good! I could never come up with something like that on the spur of the moment."

"It takes practice, that's all."

"Do all spells have to rhyme?" I asked.

"No. It depends on the witch, really. Rhyming works better for some, prose for others. Whatever she's comfortable with. I happen to prefer rhyming, but then I've always loved poems that rhyme. Haywood used to write the most beautiful poems for me. . . ."

"But coming up with the right words . . ."

"Comes with time and practice. It's best if novices use established spells, ones that are known to work."

"Hmm," I said. I had a lot to think about. My success with magic in Vannabe's cottage had made me look at the art in a different light. Sure, I had messed up every other time I'd tried it, but then I hadn't really believed that I could do it. But now that I knew that I could, and that I had the flair . . . I had an idea, vague at first, but the more I thought about it, the more I thought it would work.

And that was another thing. I appreciated Grassina's help and I knew that it had made finding the otter easier and faster, but I wanted to see what I could do.

"Aunt Grassina, I want to get the bracelet back myself," I blurted out, certain that if I didn't say it now, I might lose my nerve. "When we find the otter, I want to be the one to talk to him."

"Emma," said Eadric. "Are you crazy?"

Grassina frowned. "But why? I'll be there. The otter won't hurt me, but it's too dangerous for a frog."

"I've come up with a plan. I want to try some magic of my own. You said yourself that I have the flair, a natural talent for magic. If I really do have the gift . . ."

Eadric sputtered, trying to get the words out. "It's—it's out of the question! I told you that otters eat frogs!"

"But he won't see me as just a frog! I know what to do."

"Tell me about this plan of yours," said Grassina, looking as serious as I'd ever seen her.

"It's simple, really. I'll dress as the swamp fairy and tell the otter that the bracelet is mine and that he has to give it back. There isn't a real swamp fairy, is there, Aunt Grassina?"

"None that I know of, but I don't keep up with all the fairies in the area."

Eadric shook his head. "You're a frog, Emma! How do you think you can pass yourself off as a fairy?"

"That wouldn't be a problem," said Grassina. "Fairies are magical beings by their very nature and can easily take the form of an animal if they choose. I've met fairies who look like cats, so why not a frog?"

"What made you think of a swamp fairy, anyway?" Eadric asked.

"The otter isn't going to hand anything over to a frog, is he?" I said. "But I bet he would to a fairy. Everyone knows that fairies can be nasty if they're crossed."

Eadric snorted. "And what are you going to do if the otter doesn't laugh himself to death?"

"Use a little magic to convince him that I'm serious. I already have a few spells in mind."

"This may not be the best time to bring it up," said Grassina, "but you haven't had such wonderful results with some of your magic. . . ."

"This won't be the same at all. I remember some of the spells from Mudine's books. I'll use one of those, more than one if I have to."

"That's your plan?" said Eadric. "It'll never work! It's too simple."

Grassina shook her head. "I don't agree with you, Eadric. Sometimes the simplest plans are the best. Things get too complicated and there are too many things that could go wrong. But Emma, I can't agree with this idea of yours, either. It's just too dangerous! You're too inexperienced. Why, you haven't even been practicing magic the way you should have."

"I know, and I'm sorry about that, but I'm sure I can do this."

"Maybe so," said Grassina, "but this isn't the time to try out your magic. Even if you were proficient, the otter could be too fast for you. No, I'll have to handle this."

My aunt isn't the easiest person to argue with. Once she makes up her mind, she refuses to listen to other people's opinions. I was going to try anyway until I noticed a faraway look in her eyes and I knew that she was already thinking about what she was going to do.

Seventeen

By midafternoon we had reached the river, and it became obvious that we were getting close when we saw that the scale was filled with brilliant red lights exploding in a flurry of blazing sparks. Following the river, we came to an old willow growing halfway down the bank, its roots anchoring it to the crumbling mud that the river threatened to wash away. With the scale glowing a fiery, solid red, we knew that we'd found the otter's den.

Eadric and I peered over the side of the basket as Grassina took a step closer, and there, growing along the water's edge and completely surrounding the den, was a great swath of knee-high plants topped by clusters of clear blue blossoms. Grassina gasped, then turned and scrambled back upriver, away from the threat of the flowers.

"Oh, dear," she said, wiping a sheen of perspiration from her upper lip once she had gotten far enough away.

"That won't do at all."

"Are you all right?" I asked, not liking the way she had suddenly gone pale.

"Yes, yes, I am," she said, patting her face as if to make sure. "But I can't possibly go near the otter's den now. You saw that larkspur. If I were to touch it . . ."

"I don't understand," said Eadric. "Why would you be afraid of some plants?"

"Aunt Grassina is allergic to flowers."

"I'm afraid it's not an allergy, Emma. It's a curse, placed on our family generations ago. It began with Hazel, the first Green Witch."

"But I was told that you and Mother were allergic."

"We didn't want to frighten you, but this curse affects all the women in our family, starting on their sixteenth birthday. We thought we had a few years before we had to tell you."

"What does this curse do?" asked Eadric.

Grassina shuddered and a look of horror crossed her face. "It changes a witch, and she becomes hideous. Her hair becomes coarse; her nose lengthens, growing hooked and lumpy, nearly meeting her chin. Her face and body are covered with warts, her voice turns into an ugly cackle, and her personality—"

"That sounds just like Grandmother! Do you mean it was the curse that made her look that way?"

Grassina nodded. "She didn't believe in the curse

until it was too late."

Eadric scratched his head with his toe, the jerking of his leg making the basket shake. "Isn't there any way to break the curse? Surely a family of witches …"

"The curse is very old. According to the story I heard, Hazel was a lovely young woman and an already accomplished witch who threw a party to celebrate her sixteenth birthday, inviting all the local princes and princesses, witches, and fairies. Hazel had a green thumb and was known for growing the most beautiful flowers in the region. As the guests left at the end of the evening, she gave each one a bouquet that had been charmed to last a lifetime. However, some unexpected guests had arrived, so she ran short of bouquets. When the last fairy stood at the castle door having received nothing more than an apology, she cursed the witch Hazel and all her female descendents. Unfortunately, part of the curse involves an unpleasant disposition and Hazel became too surly to do anything about it. When she died, she took the solution to the curse with her. Fairies, however, live for a very long time, so the curse lives on in us. After our sixteenth birthday, we don't dare touch a flower for fear of falling victim to Hazel's fate."

"That's terrible!" said Eadric. "Don't worry, Emma. After you turn sixteen, I'll never bring you flowers."

"Gee, thanks," I said, certain he wouldn't have anyway.

Grassina wrung her hands in despair. "I'm sorry, Emma. I don't dare go near those flowers!"

"Can't you get rid of them with a spell?" asked Eadric.

"No. Even touching them with my magic would bring on the transformation!"

"It's all right," I said. "I wanted to do it myself anyway. But if you could help me get ready ..."

"Of course!" she said, but she still looked worried. "I feel very bad about this, you know. It's terribly dangerous. We'll just have to take every precaution." Grassina nodded, as if she'd come to a decision. "All right. What can I do to help?"

"First, we need to find a few things."

I would have preferred to use flower petals to make my skirt, but the curse made that impossible if Grassina was going to help. After finding velvety, heart-shaped leaves, we set about collecting the rest of my supplies. Aunt Grassina picked some broad leaves that I folded to make pouches, filling one with pine sap and another with bits of mica we chipped from a large rock. Pine needles and spiderwebs went into other pouches, and I found a straight twig that wasn't too long or too thick, one that felt just right in my hand.

I directed Grassina to a spot by the river where I had seen dragonflies zigzagging above the water on their own mysterious errands. We waited on the riverbank while Eadric caught a snack, bringing me an assortment of dragonfly wings on his return. I was just too excited to be hungry.

Once we were together again, we made our way to a sunny spot at the edge of a meadow with sun-warmed boulders to sit on and enough insects to keep Eadric happy. I tried to use the spiderweb thread to sew myself a leafy skirt, but frog fingers aren't made for holding needles, so Grassina had to do it. While she sewed, I made my magic wand, spreading pine sap on the end of the twig before dipping it into the pouch filled with bits of sparkling mica.

When I'd finished the wand, I sorted through the dragonfly wings Eadric had brought me, looking for the prettiest. After eliminating a few because they were either too big or too small, I chose a buttercup-yellow pair with pale green veining. Not only were they the right size, but they looked nice with my velvety emerald-green skirt.

Once I had the skirt on, I asked Grassina to glue the wings to my back with another dab of pine sap. They drooped a bit and we were trying to fix them when Eadric returned, his stomach bulging with all the insects he'd eaten.

"I'm ready!" I announced, although my wings still weren't quite right.

"Just a minute," said Grassina. Taking a chain from

around her neck, she showed me her farseeing ball, encased in golden filigree. She blew on it and the ball frosted over with her breath, turning milky and opaque. "Now tap it," she said, holding the sphere out to me.

I did as she ordered and my face appeared in the ball. "There," she said, making herself comfortable on the boulder. "It's focused on you now and will show me everything that goes on around you. I can watch from here. I'll know right away if you need me and I'll be there in an instant, curse or no curse."

"Grassina . . . ," I began.

"It's the only way I'll let you go without me."

"That's fine for you," said Eadric, "but I'm going with her."

"You can't!" I exclaimed. "It won't work if anyone else is there."

Eadric held up his hand as if that could stop any protest. "I won't go the whole way. The otter will never see me. I just want to make sure you're all right."

I was touched by his concern. He could be so obnoxious at times, so sweet at others. Sometimes I just didn't know what to make of Eadric.

After saying good-bye to Grassina and promising her that I'd be careful, I started back to the otter's den with Eadric at my side. He seemed cheerful enough at first, but as we neared the river, his expression became grim.

"I've been thinking," he said. "Why don't we just go

in the otter's den while he's out and find the bracelet ourselves?"

"And risk having him come back and find us there? We'd be trapped in his den just waiting for him to eat us!"

"That's true," he said. "But if one of us kept him away . . ."

"Eadric, we talked about this!"

"I know, but I don't think you should do it. You're not invincible, you know, and you're not as experienced as I am. You've never had to face the wrath of a charging dragon or a goblin gone berserk. I can't help it. I'm worried. If something happens to you, I'll end up a lonely old frog. Give me the swamp fairy stuff and I'll go instead."

I tried not to smile, but it wasn't easy. The thought of Eadric in the swamp fairy skirt was too funny for words, but the fact that he had offered to take my place meant a lot to me.

"That's an awfully nice offer, Eadric, but I'm afraid it wouldn't work. I don't think you'd make a very believable swamp fairy."

"I don't know. . . ."

"This is going to work, Eadric. I know what I'm doing." *I hope,* I thought, trying to look optimistic. What if the otter didn't believe me? What if Grassina couldn't get there in time? The consequences of failure would be far worse than my usual humiliation, for if I didn't do this just right, the otter would eat me. If I succeeded, however, Eadric and I would be humans again before the end of the day. Either way, what happened next would determine my future, or even whether I was going to have one.

The shadows were growing longer when Eadric and I approached the otter's den. With both of us caught up in what I was about to do, we forgot to pay attention to our surroundings. When we heard the thud of running paws, we barely had time to hop for cover before the huge white dog came into sight. It was the same beast that had tried to eat me, the same one the old toad had chased away. Although we hid in the tall grass, it was obvious from the way he was sniffing the air that the dog had caught our scent and would soon find us.

"What are we going to do?" I whispered to Eadric. "If I go in the water now, my costume will be ruined and I'll have to start all over again!"

"Don't worry." said Eadric. "I'll handle this. Look for the otter's den under the willow's roots. I'll meet you back here as soon as I get rid of the dog. Just make sure you get that bracelet back!"

Without telling me what he was going to do, Eadric crawled out of our hiding place and hopped directly into the dog's path. "Hey, doggie!" shouted Eadric. "I'm over here!"

The dog had been snuffling the ground, but at the

sound of Eadric's voice, its head jerked up. Eadric began to hop about erratically to get the dog's attention. I watched in horror as the beast spotted Eadric and bounded after him, its tail wagging so hard that it was just a blur.

"There you are! I've been looking all over for you!" said the dog.

Eadric took off, hopping faster than I would have thought possible.

"Hey!" yelped the dog. "Wait for me!"

They were well down the path before I knew what had happened, and although I wanted to go after them to stop Eadric from sacrificing himself, I realized that not only would it be useless, but it was already too late. Eadric was a much better hopper than I was and I could never catch up with them. The only thing I could do was follow my plan and get the bracelet back. With any luck, Eadric and I would both be successful and we really would meet back in the tall grass.

Worrying about Eadric made it harder to concentrate. I'd thought I'd gotten to know him during our travels, but I would never have expected him to be so brave. Eadric, of all people! For the first time I began to believe that his boasts might not have been unfounded after all.

Watching for some sign of either Eadric or the dog, I left my hiding place and hopped to the old willow tree, sitting down beside the half-concealed entrance to the otter's den. I hadn't been waiting long when the otter appeared, a fat fish flopping between his jaws. When the otter saw me, his eyes grew wide and his mouth dropped open. The fish he had been carrying fell to the ground, thrashing and gasping for air.

"Who in the name of all that's edible are you?" asked the otter.

"I am the swamp fairy!" I announced in what I hoped was a confident and convincing voice.

"You are, huh? You look like a frog, and to me that means supper. I do believe in big meals. There's always room for more."

"Don't be impertinent," I said, holding my head high. "It's never a good idea to insult a fairy. I'm here because you have something that belongs to me."

"Really?" said the otter. "And what's that?"

"My bracelet. You took it from the pond and I want it back!"

The otter laughed, a high, twittering chirp that ordinarily would have made me smile. "Sorry, you're not getting anything from me that way. Give me a reason I should think you're the swamp fairy and not the second course of supper."

"You asked for it," I said, flinging a handful of the sparkling mica dust into the air for an impressive effect. The otter drew back and winced, using his paw to wipe the dust from his eyes. I coughed and wiped my own eyes as well, for I'd neglected to take the breeze into account and half the dust had blown in my direction.

My eyes were watering as I pointed my magic wand at the otter. Thankful that I didn't have to read just then, I recited one of the spells I had read in Vannabe's cottage:

Be gone ye old and dingy hue,
Erase the old, bring on the new!
Bright and shiny, lustrous locks,
Make it look real, not from a box.

The spell, Hair So Nu, hadn't been intended for otters, so I decided to customize it.

Redo yon fur to shades of blue!
And make the color ever true!

With the sound of tiny cymbals and a flash of blue light, the otter's fur turned a nice shade of turquoise.

"Aagh!" screamed the otter. "What have you done to me?"

"I thought you needed a little convincing. Now do you believe that I'm the swamp fairy?"

The otter snorted. "I don't know if you're the swamp fairy or just some overdressed frog, but either way I'm not giving that bracelet to you! What would you do with it anyway? The thing is almost as big as you are! You can forget it!"

"What if I make all of your fur fall out?" I bluffed. "What will you do in the winter?"

The otter glanced down at his thick pelt and shivered. When he looked up, he seemed resigned, although none too happy. "You drive a hard bargain. Wait here, I'll get the bracelet. The light from the darn thing was keeping me awake at night anyway."

I was so excited, I hugged myself with glee as the otter trudged down the entrance to his den. The sound of thumping and scrabbling came from the tunnel, and then he reappeared, his blunt muzzle speckled with dirt. Frowning his displeasure, he shoved the bracelet into my hands. It was bigger than my head and would fit easily around my neck, but I was afraid it would choke me if I suddenly turned back into a human. Although I knew it was supposed to take a kiss to turn me back, just holding the bracelet made me nervous. After all, it had already done something unexpected once. I stared at it, trying to decide what to do.

"Well?" said the otter. "Did you want something else?"

"No, no, that was it," I said, backing away. "You may go about your business again, otter."

"Huh," said the otter, scratching his head. "Fairy or not, you sure are a strange one!"

Clutching the bracelet, I hopped back along the riverbank to the tall grass where I had last spoken with Eadric, but he was nowhere in sight. I started to call his name until I realized how dangerous that would be. If the dog was somewhere around, the last thing we wanted to do was attract its attention. We were still frogs, after all, and still needed to be careful. I waited in the tall grass for the longest time, getting more and more worried, until I heard the slap of something wet landing on the mud behind me, nearly making me jump out of my skin.

"So you got it! I knew you would!"

I whipped my head around and my knees went weak with relief. "Eadric! You got away from the dog! How did you do it?"

Eadric smiled smugly and tapped himself on the chest. "I'm a better swimmer, that's how. No dog can keep up with me!"

I grinned and threw my arms around his neck in a big froggy hug. "I was so worried!"

"Why?" he asked, frowning. "I told you I'd meet you here. Now put on that bracelet before we lose it again!"

"Is something wrong?" said a voice, and I looked up to see Grassina striding through the grass.

I shook my head and grinned up at her. "Not a thing! In fact, everything is perfect! Look, I got the bracelet!" I held it up to show her. It was so big it took both of my hands to lift it.

Grassina smiled back at me absentmindedly, as if she were thinking about something else. "I know. I saw. You did very well."

"I'd like to get a little farther from the otter before I put it on, though, just in case he changes his mind."

"Good idea," said Grassina. "Although I don't think he will. Excuse me, I'll be back in a few minutes. There's something about that otter…" She walked away in a daze, not noticing the prickers that caught at her skirts as she passed.

I would have followed her or tried to make her come with us, but Eadric grabbed my arm and tugged. "Come on," he said. "Let's get this over with."

"Fine, but as soon as we're back to normal, we have to find my aunt. She looks so odd…."

"Stop right there!" said an authoritative voice. A glimmering light descended from the sky and settled on the ground. The light swirled and shifted into the form of a fairy, her blue hair streaked with gray, her violet-colored eyes looking tired and slightly bored. Enormous, iridescent wings of violet and mauve fanned the air behind her. When she took a step toward us, her long blue flower-petal skirt, browned and curling at the edges, rustled around her ankles. Bending down, she stretched out her hand and said, "That bracelet belongs to me now!"

I gasped. "Who are you?"

The fairy glared at me. "I am the swamp fairy! The real, one and only, honest-to-goodness swamp fairy! I was told that someone was impersonating me! What is the world coming to? A fairy goes away on vacation for a couple of decades and suddenly everybody tries to take advantage.… Shame on you! I have to fine you for that! Hand over the bracelet!"

I took a step back. "What do you want with my bracelet?"

The fairy looked me over as if I might be hiding something. "It seems to be the only thing you have of any value, so that's how you'll pay your fine."

"No, wait! I can't give you this bracelet!" I said, clutching it to my chest. "We really need it! Isn't there anything else I can give you?"

"Nope, that's it. I don't need any firstborn tadpoles, if that's what you're thinking. So give me the bracelet and be on your way."

I couldn't do it, not when we were so close! Panicking, I turned to look at Eadric and my eyes fell on the vial of dragon's breath. "I know! Eadric, turn around!" I hurriedly untied the twine holding the vial on Eadric's back.

"I thought you said there wasn't any swamp fairy," Eadric whispered.

"I didn't think there was," I whispered back.

"But how do we know she's—"

"Eadric, don't say another word! You're going to get us in even more trouble!"

"I can hear you!" trilled the swamp fairy. "Hasn't anyone ever told you that it's not polite to whisper? Now I have to raise your fine!"

"Sorry," I said. "Here, would this do instead of the bracelet?" I held the vial in the sunlight so the fairy could see the beautiful swirling colors.

"What is it?" asked the swamp fairy, looking skeptical.

"It's a vial of dragon's breath. I understand it's very valuable."

"Dragon's breath? I haven't seen any of that in ages! Here, let me have it!"

I started to pass the vial to the swamp fairy, but I was fumble-fingered and it slipped out of my hand. My heart jumped into my throat when the vial landed with a thud on her foot.

"Ow! Ow! Ow! Ow!" she said, hopping on one foot while cradling the other in her hand. "You dropped it on me! Ow! Ow! Ow!"

Eadric and I backed behind a clump of grass, trying to stay out from under the hopping fairy. "I'm sorry!" I said, feeling like an idiot. "I didn't mean to!"

"Never mind that!" said Eadric. "Is the vial all right?"

The swamp fairy gave him a nasty look. Ignoring Eadric, I hurdled over the grass and bent down to pick up the vial. When I offered it to the fairy, she snatched it from my hand and gave me a nasty look as well.

The fairy uncorked the vial and sniffed it cautiously. Her face promptly turned a bright green. Coughing, she rammed the cork back into the opening. "Hoo-wee! Does that stuff ever stink! That's dragon's breath, all right. Sure, I'll take this as your fine. I have a good friend who's a dragon. He's getting old and fat and has been short of breath for years. This would make a great birthday present for him. But now you have another fine to pay. Two, come to think of it. One fine for whispering about me, and the other for hurting my foot! What else have you got that you can give me?"

"Why, nothing, other than the bracelet."

"Then I'd better take that as well. It is awfully pretty. . . ." Grabbing the bracelet, the fairy turned it over and shook it, smiling when the light danced on the little symbols.

"But we need it!" Eadric wailed. "Without that bracelet, we'll be stuck as frogs forever!"

"Really?" said the fairy. "What does this bracelet have to do with you being a frog?"

I didn't want to tell her, but Eadric had already said too much. I couldn't see any harm in telling her the rest. "I was a human until I kissed Eadric, but I was wearing the bracelet. . . ."

The fairy's eyes opened wide. "And the bracelet

turned you into a frog?"

I nodded. "Yes, it's a—"

"Here! Take it!" she said, thrusting the bracelet at me. "The last thing I want to do is turn into a frog! Imagine, me as a hairless, slimy—"

"Hey!" said Eadric, scowling at the fairy. Afraid of what he might say, I jabbed him in the stomach with my elbow.

"But that's all we have," I said.

The fairy took a step back. "Never mind. The dragon's breath will do just fine. If you promise never to impersonate me again, I'll forget your other offenses and we'll call it even."

"Oh, I promise!" I said.

Eadric and I hopped away from the river as if a dragon were after us. Faster than you can say "four fat frog feet" five times fast, we had jumped through a small copse of saplings and into a nearby meadow.

"Now can you put it on?" Eadric asked as soon as he'd caught his breath. "I hate to be pushy, but something else is bound to happen if you don't."

"Just a minute," I said, setting the bracelet on the ground. Since the bracelet seemed to remain the same size no matter what, I wasn't going to take any chances. I sat down, placed my wrist inside the bracelet, and patted the ground. "Eadric, have a seat over here."

Eadric hurried to sit beside me. "I'm ready," he said, puckering his lips.

"Let's hope this works!" I crossed my fingers and leaned over to kiss him.

I saw movement out of the corner of my eye and looked up to see the dirty white dog trotting into the meadow, its nose held high as it snuffled the air. A sparrow shot from the ground by the dog's feet, but the beast swung its head from side to side as if homing in on a scent, oblivious to everything else. I tried to ignore the dog as I kissed Eadric long and hard on the lips. When nothing happened right away, Eadric's face drooped in disappointment and I felt as though I was about to cry.

A breeze blew from behind us, carrying our scent directly toward the dog. With his ears pricked forward, he swung his head in our direction and trotted toward us, his tail wagging like a flag. Resigned to certain doom, I was watching the dog when my fingers and toes began to tingle. The feeling spread up my arms and down my legs. A shiver ran along my spine, chased by the golden, fuzzy feeling. Once again my head felt light and full of bubbles. Once again a tremendous wind rushed past me and I fell to the ground with a gray cloud filling my head, but not before I saw the dog collapse as well.

Eighteen

When I woke, my head felt woozy; nothing would come into focus. Gradually my vision sharpened, but everything looked different. The colors seemed duller and there were fewer of them. I shook my head, trying to get rid of the funny feeling in my ears, not liking the way the sounds were muffled. Glancing down, I saw that my clothes looked just the way they had on the day I had turned into a frog. My blue gown and kirtle were only slightly soiled, but no more than they had been when I kissed Eadric. My soft leather shoes were still damp, the mud on them fresh.

I heard a sound and turned to see Eadric struggling to sit up beside me. He was wearing a warm traveling cloak over his clothes, and his boots were splattered with muck. His tousled brown curls framed a strong jaw, laughing eyes, and a nose as prominent as my own. He was slightly pudgy and rather short. I thought that he was the most beautiful person I had ever seen.

Eadric looked at me and grinned. "We did it!" he said, laughing out loud.

"Finally!" I agreed. I had been convinced so often over the last few days that I was about to die that I felt giddy with relief now that I was a human again.

"You look beautiful, Emma."

"You do, too."

"But aren't you tired of wearing those wings?" He reached behind me and tugged something loose from the back of my dress. The dragonfly wings lay in his hand, limp and broken.

"Oh," I breathed, taking the wings from him. "I'll cherish them forever."

"Those old things!" said Eadric. "Why would you want to keep them?"

"Eadric, how can you say that? They made me look like a beautiful swamp fairy!"

When I tried to stand, my movements were stiff and awkward. I took a step and tripped over my own feet, landing in Eadric's arms. He held me with my head cradled on his shoulder so that I was looking up into his eyes.

"I was hoping I could get another kiss," he said, his eyes laughing.

"You never give up, do you? Well, I'm sorry! I'm not kissing anybody until I get this back to my aunt Grassina!" I raised my arm and jingled my bracelet next to his ear. "I don't want to—"

"—take any chances," Eadric finished for me.

"We'd better be careful or we're going to end up finishing each other's sentences like Clifford and Louise."

"Who?" Eadric asked.

"Never mind. I'll tell you all about it when we have the time."

Something snorted, sounding like the chuffing of an ancient dragon. Startled, Eadric and I looked up. A white horse with a silver mane lay on its side, trying to roll to its feet. Saddled for riding, it wore the trappings of royalty.

"Eadric! Why did you run away?" whinnied the horse.

"Brighty?" said Eadric, shading his eyes against the sun. "Is that you?"

"Who's Brighty?" I asked.

"My horse, Bright Country! I left him tied to a tree while I hunted for the meadwort and that's when I ran into Mudine. I was so worried about you, boy!"

With a lunge and a flurry of hooves, Brighty rolled to his feet and stood with his legs wobbling beneath him. "Dang, I'm sore!" he grumbled. He snorted again and looked toward Eadric, who dumped me on the ground and climbed painfully to his feet.

"Hey!" I said, struggling to sit up. "Why did you do that?"

"I've got to go. It's Brighty!"

I looked at his horse again. There was something about … "That's where the dog was standing when we kissed!" I said. "The big white dog that was chasing you!"

"You don't suppose that Mudine cast a spell on Brighty, too?"

"I guess it's possible! Then the reason the dog was chasing us …"

Eadric stumbled toward his horse. "Brighty! I always knew you were a good and faithful beast! You wanted to be with me, even when I was a frog!" With a happy sigh, Eadric flung his arms around the horse's neck and hugged him. Brighty leaned into his owner, making the prince stagger back.

The horse snorted, his breath ruffling Eadric's hair. "I've been looking for you everywhere! I saw that woman turn you into a frog; then she came after me. I was a dog, Eadric! You can't imagine what it was like. I had this urge to sniff everything! And some things were really disgusting and I didn't want to eat them, but I couldn't help myself. I'm so glad I found you. I knew if I did, everything would be all right. Don't ever leave me like that again!"

"Everything will be fine now, Brighty. I'm here," said Eadric, hugging his horse again.

I smiled and let out an unladylike snort of my own. "I bet your horse would kiss you if you let him."

"I wouldn't dare," said Eadric. "With all the magic that's been floating around here today, there's no telling what might happen."

"Speaking of magic, we'd better go see what happened to my aunt. That look on her face—it was almost like someone had cast a spell on her! And she was going toward those flowers …"

Leading Brighty by the reins, Eadric followed me through the meadow to the riverbank. Everything looked so much smaller than it had when we were frogs that I felt as though we'd entered a different world. The weeds that had shaded us from the heat of the sun now brushed against our ankles. I almost missed the clump of tall grass, for now it rose no higher than my knees. It was disconcerting to see the world so radically changed, and I know it bothered Eadric as much as it did me, because I caught him rubbing his eyes and staring at what we would once have considered an enormous butterfly, but now it seemed only average.

I heard voices talking as we neared the willow. I even thought I heard Grassina's laugh. After persuading Eadric to tie his horse's reins to a convenient branch, I hiked up the hem of my gown and clambered awkwardly over the uneven ground in search of my aunt Grassina. Still following the voices, we passed the den, and there, just beyond a jumble of rocks that jutted into the river, I found her with the otter curled at her feet. She glanced up at the sound of our approach, and I was stunned. Her smile was filled with so much joy that even her eyes sparkled with it.

"He wasn't a frog at all!" she said, taking the otter's paw in her hand. "That's why I couldn't find him. I kissed all those frogs for nothing! My mother turned him into an otter! Emma, Eadric, I'd like you to meet Haywood, my betrothed!"

Haywood tore his gaze from Grassina and looked up at me. "So you're Grassina's niece! The family resemblance is extraordinary! And you must be her beau, Eadric! Grassina has been telling me about you both."

"I'm not her beau, exactly," Eadric said, turning to look at me.

"I saw Haywood in the farseeing ball," said Grassina, "and I had a feeling that it was him. I felt the way I do when someone comes to the door and I know who it is before I open it. Then when I saw him up close … The spell changed his shape, but it couldn't change who he was inside."

"If it was that easy, why didn't you know it was us when we came to your door?" Eadric said, looking indignant. "You made Emma tell you the whole story and then you said you still weren't sure it was her!"

"Because my heart told me that it was Emma at the door, but my head said that she couldn't possibly be a frog. She wore the bracelet, so I didn't think it was possible. But I know to trust my heart now and my heart says that this is the same darling Haywood whom my mother sent away."

"I am a bit older, though, I'm afraid," the otter said, patting her hand with his other paw.

"Not so old, Haywood. No older than I."

The otter gazed into my aunt's eyes. "My darling Grassina, I wish we could go back to the way things were. That's all I've wanted for these many years. Do you think it's still possible?"

"Oh, Haywood," said Grassina, "I would like that more than anything in the world!"

"Kiss her," said Eadric, "and see what happens!" He grinned and turned to look at me. Seeing the surprised expression on my face, he added, "Well, it worked for us, didn't it?"

"Not at first! Aunt Grassina, you aren't wearing any charm reversal jewelry, are you? No bracelets or necklaces or anything like that?"

"No, Emma, I'm not. . . ."

"Then what are you waiting for?" Eadric asked, rocking back and forth on the balls of his feet as if he couldn't possibly hold still.

"Nothing," Grassina said, and bent down till her mouth was only inches from Haywood's. Her hair fell forward to hide their faces, but they both had dreamy looks in their eyes when they finally drew apart. We waited for a while, watching Haywood for any sign of change. As time dragged on and we realized that nothing was going to happen, Haywood's face fell and Grassina let out a heartfelt sigh.

"I didn't really expect it to work," said Haywood, "but I was hoping . . ."

Only a few weeks before, I probably would have thought it bizarre to see my aunt and an otter looking at each other with such adoration, but living as a frog had made me much more sympathetic.

"I know what we can do!" I said, too excited to keep quiet any longer. Everyone turned to look at me, but I plowed on, convinced that I was right. "Haywood, do you remember what my grandmother said you had to do to break the spell?"

The otter shook his head. "I'm sure she told me, but it's been so long. Something about dragon's breath and the lining of some seashell."

"Drat!" I said. "I knew we'd find a use for that vial! But that's all right, because the spell can still be undone by the witch who cast it in the first place. All you have to do is go see Grandmother."

"What makes you think she would do it?" asked Haywood. "She probably won't like me any better now than she did before."

"She'll do it, you'll see! You'll just have to explain things to her the right way. Every time we visit her, she complains that she has only one grandchild—me. But if she changed Haywood back and you two got married ..."

"Then she could have more grandchildren!" exclaimed Eadric. "Unless you're too old ..."

"Eadric! Please!" said Grassina, blushing a deep shade of pink, a color I'd never seen on my aunt.

"I think Emma's idea is wonderful!" Haywood declared. "And after Grassina and I are married, I'll return to my studies. Perhaps we can open a practice together, just as we'd planned!"

From the way Grassina and Haywood looked at each other, I knew that Eadric and I were in the way. But there was something I had to do before we left.

"Here," I said, removing the bracelet and handing it to Grassina. "Although it's a lovely bracelet, I don't think I'd ever be comfortable wearing it again."

"I don't blame you," my aunt said, taking her eyes off Haywood only long enough to drop the bracelet into the pouch attached to her gown.

"And if I were to kiss someone now ..."

"Hmm? Oh, you wouldn't turn into anything."

"Good!" I said. "Then it's finally over! I just have one other question. Why can Eadric and I still talk to animals even though we're human again?"

"Because you've been animals yourselves. Since you're a witch, Emma, you'll keep the ability, although

Eadric may lose it if he doesn't practice often. Is there anything else?" Grassina asked, flicking her eyes in my direction. I knew her well enough to take the hint.

"Not a thing! Come on, Eadric. Let's go!"

Although I would have liked to have left gracefully, Eadric and I were both so stiff that we had to help each other up the hill. When we reached the top, I saw an ancient oak whose graying bark bore a small carved heart surrounding the words *Grassina & Haywood forever.* It made me realize that Haywood had probably missed Grassina as much as she had missed him.

Now that I knew the truth about Haywood, things that I hadn't noticed before seemed obvious. Passing his den on our way to fetch Bright Country, I saw a patch of dry grass by the opening that looked remarkably like a doormat. A collection of roughly assembled twigs resembled a crude bench. Lavender, rosemary, and thyme grew in neat little rows on the side of the hill like a miniature herb garden. Haywood may have been turned into an otter, but he had gone to a lot of trouble to make his den into a vaguely human home.

After collecting Bright Country, we made our way back along the riverbank, too sore to move much faster than a slow shuffle. We hadn't gone far before Eadric and I stopped to stretch our aching muscles. "And what about us?" Eadric asked, trying to work the stiffness out of his shoulders.

"Well, now that that's settled, I can get started on all the other things I have to do."

"Such as?"

"Such as this," I said. Eadric's eyes grew wide when I slid my arms behind his neck and kissed him. It wasn't a quick kiss like the first one that had turned me into a frog, or the lip-crushing kind that was intended to turn us back, but a long, slow kiss that was soft and gentle and very sweet.

"Wow!" said Eadric, his eyes as big as fruit tarts. Somehow, his arms had found their way around me while we kissed, and it was a very pleasant feeling indeed.

"Oh, my!" I agreed, having enjoyed it as much as he had.

"And now what?" he asked, grinning boyishly.

"And now ... Now I have to have the moat cleaned out."

"And marry that jerk, Prince Jorge?"

"Of course not! I'll just tell my mother that I won't marry him. If she insists, I'll inform her that I can't wait to tell his parents all about my adventures as a frog. My mother would never live that one down. And if he's lucky, maybe Jorge'll find the perfect woman for him, one who wears the same size shoes he does."

"His feet are kind of small. It might take him a while to find her."

"I'm sure he'll manage. People like him always do."

"You know, I've been thinking. You could tell your mother that you met someone else you'd rather marry."

"Is that a marriage proposal, Prince Eadric?"

"Would you say yes if it were, Princess Emeralda?"

"Maybe, but I don't think I'll get married just yet. I have the potential to be a very good witch, and I think it's about time I began working at it. And even if I do decide to get married later on, being a witch could be very helpful."

My days as a frog had taught me many things, most of which I'd long suspected. The swamp was indeed a magical place where old lives could end and new lives could take the most unexpected turns, where friends and heroes could come in many forms, and where life could be wonderful, even for a clumsy princess.

Eadric reached out to tuck a loose curl behind my ear. "Fine. Just promise you'll never turn me into some loathsome creature if we happen to disagree."

"I promise I won't turn you into anything you don't deserve," I said. "Just don't ever try to stop me from visiting the swamp from time to time."

"Is that all it would take to keep you happy?"

"No, but it's a good start!"

Dragon's Breath

One

When I was a little girl, I dreamed about being a witch like my aunt Grassina. I imagined that the next time a page stuck out his tongue at me, I'd wiggle my fingers and turn him into a salamander. If my nurse nagged me about the dirt on my clothes, I'd say a magic word and her voice would become a sparrow's chirp. If my mother scolded me for being clumsy and sent me to my chamber, I'd wave my hand, banishing her to some far-off cave guarded by trolls. I never did these things, of course, but I comforted myself with the thought that someday everyone who had been mean to me would be sorry. Someday I would be a witch and no one would dare tell me that I wasn't as smart or pretty or graceful as a princess ought to be.

Lately, I had decided that those dreams were a waste of time. Although my grandmother and aunt were both witches, my mother hated magic and let everyone know it. According to her, no self-respecting princess would ever be interested in magic, not if she really wanted to make something of herself. She threatened to send me to a convent if she ever saw me try it. "They'll know how to keep you too busy for such nonsense," she told me more than once.

If it hadn't been for my aunt Grassina, I might have given up my dream entirely, but she said I had a talent that shouldn't be ignored. I resolved not to tell my mother I planned to study magic, and my attempts remained a secret between my aunt and me.

In a way, I owed all the excitement in my life to my mother. Because she never seemed to want me around, I'd often wandered off to the swamp or to my aunt's tower chamber. Then, when my mother had tried to get me to marry a prince I couldn't stand, I hid in the swamp, unwilling to meet with him. There I met Eadric, a prince who'd been turned into a frog. I'd ended up kissing Eadric, and that kiss had turned *me* into a frog as well.

The morning after I returned home as a human, I was eager to work on my magic, if only to gain more control over my suddenly crazy life. I had never learned how to cook, so I thought I'd use a spell to make breakfast for Grassina and my no-longer-a-frog-friend Prince Eadric. I chose a recipe from one of Grassina's books, *Wolanda's Big Book of Recipes, Potions and Cooking Spells for the Inexperienced Witch*—"time-tested, witch-approved." It was a simple spell, one that even I should have been able to handle.

After fetching some peacock eggs from the kitchen, I hurried up the tower stairs to my aunt's rooms. Since my aunt often cooked her own meals, she already had everything else I needed. According to the directions, all I had to do was assemble the ingredients and the cooking spell would do the rest.

Li'l Stinker, a bat who had become a friend in my days of being a frog, greeted me at the door. The room was quiet; my aunt was probably still sleeping.

I'd decided to use Grassina's magic pot. Made of iron and black with age, it heated itself until the food was cooked. I'd never known Grassina to burn anything when she used the pot, and I hoped the same would be true for me.

Glancing from the pot to the book and back again, I was careful to read the spell aloud exactly as it was written.

A pinch of this, a dash of that
A hint of lard, a dab of fat
A broken egg, no, make it three
One's not enough, as you can see.

Drop them in a cooking pot.
Add some spice, no, not a lot.
Chop an onion, put it in.
Stir it once, then stir again.

Heat the pot until it cooks,
Sniff, then see how good it looks.
Get the dishes, serve it all.
Don't let the portions be too small!

Cooking spells are fun to watch, but I enjoyed watching Li'l even more. She chortled when the eggs cracked themselves and plopped into the pot. I heard her gasp when the onions broke into small pieces, then spiraled into the mixture with the spices.

When I read *sniff*, the steam rising from the eggs wafted toward my nose, drifting past Li'l. "Smells good," she said, breathing deeply. "Now what do you do?"

"I'll taste them, just to be sure they're all right. Then we'll invite Grassina and Eadric to breakfast."

Although I'd used only three eggs, the magic recipe had doubled them, so there was more than enough for everyone. Wondering if it had doubled the spices as well, I nibbled a tiny morsel. It needed salt, so I glanced toward the shelves holding my aunt's supplies. A small salt cellar rested on a high shelf beside jars of dried herbs. Pleased by my success with the cooking spell, I pointed at it and said, "Salt cellar," expecting it to fly into my hands. Straightforward and simple—I didn't think anything could possibly go wrong.

Two

Whoosh! A damp breeze whisked me from the stool where I'd been sitting, twirled me until I was dizzy and plopped me down on a lumpy sack somewhere cold and dark. Dazed, I shook my head and looked around. It could have been worse. At least I knew where I was: my parents' dungeon. And the door was most certainly locked.

I'd visited the dungeon often, but always dressed warmly and carrying a torch. It wasn't safe to walk around the dungeon in the dark. Unseen hands moved barrels, holes appeared where none had been before and doors that were centuries old suddenly disappeared. Witches had lived in the castle for generations, and here, where the early witches had set up their workshops, the magic had permeated the walls and still floated about in currents and eddies that smelled like rotting vegetables.

My mother, who wasn't a witch, had ordered the

dungeon cleaned out and now used it just for storage. But the witches' ghosts remained to haunt the old dungeon, and not all of them were friendly. My mother didn't believe in ghosts and kept the salt in the room where I now found myself, a long, narrow room that had once been used as the torture chamber. Why had I wanted salt for the eggs?

The torture chamber had no windows; not even the faintest glimmer disturbed the inky dark. I thought about using magic to go back upstairs, but I didn't know any spells that would take me from one place to another. Though I wanted to practice my magic, I didn't think I was ready to try to come up with my own spells yet, especially since it was a simple spell that had brought me to the dungeon. To get out safely, I needed some sort of light. A tethered witches' light would have to do, even though it would be vulnerable to the old magic wafting through the dungeon.

One of the first spells my aunt had taught me was for creating such a light. I'd used it many times, but only when Grassina was around. I recited the spell, shaping my hands as if I was holding a ball.

Create a glow to chase the dark.
A light to help me see.
Let neither wind nor rain nor snow
Take it away from me.

The space between my hands began to glow a rosy shade of pink as a ball of gentle light took form. I released the ball, and it drifted above my head.

I'd started toward the door when a whisper of sound behind me made me turn to look. A swirling mist glowing a faint blue poured through a hole in the wall. As the mist filled the room, a young woman appeared only a few feet away, her long tresses lifting in a nonexistent breeze. She gazed at me through shadowed eyes, her lips moving, her hands reaching in a pleading sort of gesture. An aura as cold as a winter's night surrounded her, giving me goose bumps as she drew near. Her lips moved again, and I strained to hear her words.

"I'm sorry," I said, tilting my head so that I might hear her better. "Could you repeat that?"

The ghost sighed and dropped her arms to her sides. "Then listen carefully this time," she yelled. "I *hate* repeating myself. I said, 'Help, help, save me. The executioner is coming and I've done nothing wrong.'" She spoke in a matter-of-fact sort of way, as if reciting lines that she'd repeated too often.

"Too late!" said a voice by the far wall. "I'm already here!" A broad-chested ghost dressed all in black materialized before us. His eyes glowed crimson through holes in the hood covering his head. Silently, the executioner wielded an axe, its blade dark with blood. The young lady shrieked and started to run. I closed my eyes, and when

I opened them, her head lay on the floor, gazing up in silent reproach.

"That was pretty good," I said, "although it works better when you delay your entrance, Cranston. It's more effective when Margreth convinces me of her innocence first."

"Sorry," said the executioner. "We're both a bit off today. We've had so many visitors lately, stomping around in heavy boots and thrusting torches in dark corners."

"Why were they here?" I asked.

Cranston shrugged. "Looking for something, I suppose. We're much better with the torture scene. Would you like to see that one? It's more realistic."

"No, thanks," I said, never having cared for the gruesome historic reenactments that some of the ghosts enjoyed. "I have too much to do this morning."

The ghosts disappeared, leaving me alone once again. I was stepping into the next room when my witches' light dimmed so much that I could hardly see. Something scrabbled against the stone floor like scores of metal-hard claws. I took another step, hoping to take the light out of the drifting pool of magic that had muted its glow.

A large shape loomed out of the dark, its glowing red eyes unblinking. If I hadn't encountered the creature before, I would have been terrified, but Grassina had shown me how to deal with it on one of our early visits. It was a shadow monster left behind by one of my ancestors and could be deadly to anyone who didn't know its weakness. I took one more step into the room, and the creature charged. It was almost upon me when I danced aside, rapping it between the eyes with my clenched fist. As the eyes were its only vulnerable spot, the shadow beast whined and fled into the old torture chamber.

I took another tentative step, not caring to fall into a bottomless pit or tread on a magic serpent created by an old spell. My witches' light grew brighter, lighting the darkened niches. I was halfway across the floor when a pale glow played around the edge of a door, outlining it in an eerie blue light. The light pulsed and wavered, seeming to seep through the door itself. It grew stronger the closer it came, finally taking on the shape of a man, taller than most, with shoulder-length white hair and finely chiseled features. Although the image remained translucent, I recognized him right away.

"Grandfather, you're back! I thought you were still away on ghostly business." I smiled up at the holes where his eyes should have been.

Clammy fingers touched my hand; the scent of old leather grew strong. "My darling Emma!" he answered, a chilly puff of air caressing my cheek. "I'm sorry I was away for so long. The meeting of the Council of Ghosts seems to last longer every year. I hear that you were away as well. Grassina told me something about a frog and a prince. You remind me of your grandmother. She was always doing the unexpected, too. Still is, from what I hear. You even look like her in a way."

"What?" I was horrified at the thought of resembling my grandmother in even the smallest detail. Although I had my father's large nose, I'd been told that with my taller-than-average height, auburn hair and green eyes I looked like my aunt Grassina. This was the first time anyone had ever compared me to my grandmother. Her long hooked nose, pointed chin, beady eyes, warts and straggly white hair were enough to frighten me, so I couldn't imagine that *anyone* would want to look like her. At least no one had ever accused me of acting like my grandmother.

"Olivene wasn't always like she is now. She was quite lovely when I married her, and was the sweetest and gentlest woman. It wasn't until your mother and your aunt Grassina were nearly grown that your grandmother changed."

"You're talking about the family curse, aren't you?"

"So you've heard about how the first Green Witch, Hazel, insulted a fairy?"

I had. It was Hazel's sixteenth birthday, and she didn't have enough everlasting bouquets to give one to the fairy. The fairy got angry and cursed Hazel: if she ever touched a flower, she'd end up nasty, like my grandmother was now. Aunt Grassina told me that the curse was still strong and that any female in our family who touched a flower after she turned sixteen would become a nasty hag.

"Oh, yes," I said.

"And you believe it?"

"Yes, of course. Why wouldn't I?" I asked.

"Because your grandmother didn't, at least not until it happened. Her mother had avoided flowers her entire life, but Olivene thought her mother was crazy, so she didn't believe her stories about the curse. After the curse changed her, your grandmother didn't care enough to do anything about it except send me to the dungeons."

"Is that how you ended up down here?"

A ghostly sigh brushed my ear. "Before the change, Olivene complained that I never took her to tournaments or balls at neighboring kingdoms anymore. I didn't know she wanted to go! I thought she was happy raising our girls and running the castle. She was always so busy with her magic. When your grandmother said that if I loved her I'd be more attentive and bring her little gifts, I tried to please her."

"You mean you're the one who gave her the flowers that turned her into—"

"Yes, I was the one. I had never heard of the curse, but ignorance is no excuse. After I gave her the flowers and she changed, she used her magic to send me to the dungeon for a few days. I could have left anytime after that, but I liked the peace and quiet."

I could understand why he'd want to stay in the dungeon. I'd heard from my mother and my aunt how they had fought when they were young, and if my grandmother had been as nasty as she was now, the dungeon would have been the nicest place in the castle.

"I haven't seen your grandmother for years, but the funny thing is, I miss her. I saw your mother the other day, though. She stopped by to see if you were here. Chartreuse doesn't come down very often, I'm sorry to say. Why was she looking for you in the dungeon?"

"Maybe because she couldn't find me anywhere else. I kissed a frog named Eadric in the swamp. Then I became a frog, too. Until yesterday, that is. That's when I kissed him again with my charm reversal bracelet on and we both turned back into humans. Eadric is a prince and he wants to marry me, but I told him we had to wait and see."

"Do you love him? Your mother says that love isn't essential in a marriage, but it really is, you know. When we were young, I loved your grandmother so much."

"I guess I love him in a way," I said. I just didn't know if I loved him enough, not after seeing how much Grassina loved her betrothed, Haywood. He'd been missing for years; my grandmother had turned him into an otter. "But I'm not ready for marriage yet. I want to study magic first. Last night Aunt Grassina told me that if I work at it hard enough, I might be the Green Witch someday!"

"Just like her mother was before her."

"Grandmother was the Green Witch?"

"Before the curse took hold she was the nicest as well as the most powerful witch around. Those are both requirements for being the Green Witch." Grandfather floated beside me when I started toward the door. "Now, how did you get down here?" he asked.

"We're going to the Old Witches' Retirement Community this morning to see Grandmother and ask her to turn Haywood back into a human. She wants more grandchildren and my parents aren't about to have any more, so I think she'll do it. But I wanted to make a special breakfast first."

"Are you sure it's wise to ask your grandmother for help? She's a stubborn woman. You're going to have a difficult time changing her mind about Haywood."

"Even she has to see how much Grassina and Haywood love each other."

We were passing through a long corridor, and I could see the stairway leading out of the dungeon at the far end.

"OooOooOooO!" wailed a voice. "I smell a maiden with hair of flame—"

"Go on with you! You can't smell the color of her

hair!" said an older and less refined voice.

"I was being poetic!" said the first voice. "You should have let me finish!"

"Oh, go ahead, then. What else were you going to say?"

"I forget now! And it's a real shame because it was going to be beautiful!" The voice grew fainter.

At the approach of the ghosts, the temperature of the room had dropped even further. "I don't think I've met those ghosts before," I began. "They seem … ah … ah … ah-choo!" I knew right away that the sneeze wasn't an ordinary one. The tickling that had started in my nose filled my head, then rushed down my neck and into my entire body. I felt myself flash hot, then cold. My skin was suddenly sensitive to the air currents wafting through the dungeon, and I could clearly hear the sound of rats scurrying behind closed doors.

"Good gracious, child," said my grandfather. "What happened to you?"

"I don't know," I said, reaching for my tickling nose, but to my surprise, my nose wasn't there. "I think I …" I patted my face, then ran my hands over the top of my head, feeling the smooth, moist, hairless skin. "I can't believe this! I've turned back into a frog! What's wrong with me, Grandfather? Can't I do anything right? I … I … ah-choo!" I sneezed explosively, and suddenly I was back to my normal self.

"Are you all right, Emma?"

I patted my hair into place, glad that I had hair again. "Fine, I guess. But why did I change when I sneezed?"

"I can't help you there. I don't understand magic very well."

We had reached the end of the corridor and started to climb the stairs when I felt the tickling again. Not wanting to turn into a frog, I pinched my nose. When the urge to sneeze faded, I took my hand from my face and said, "I'd better go before … ah-choo!" I'd let go only briefly, but it had been enough. I was a frog once more.

"Perhaps if you sneeze again," said Grandfather, "you might turn yourself back."

It wasn't hard to do. I took a deep breath and felt the tickling sensation in my nose. The sneeze was coming, and it was going to be a big one! "*Ah-choo!*" I shot back up to my normal size and shape, but the tickling wasn't over. "*Ah-choo!*" My stomach lurched as I turned back into a frog. Too many changes too fast were more than it could take. "*Ah-choo!*" The instant I turned into a human again, I clapped my hand to my face and squeezed my nose so hard it hurt.

"Here!" said my grandfather, reaching through the door to unlock it. "Go before you change again! I love you no matter what shape you're in, but I'd much rather have a human granddaughter than one who's a frog!"

Three

As I hurried up the winding staircase to Grassina's turret, I tried to think of a way I could use magic to stop my froggy transformations. I was stepping onto the landing when I noticed that the door to my aunt's room was open. Inside, I saw Grassina and Haywood sitting on the window seat. It was obvious that their love was as strong as ever. For the first time I could remember, my aunt's eyes were as happy as her smile.

Grassina turned to look at me when I stepped into the room. "Wherever you went," she said, "it must have been awfully important to take you away before breakfast. It smells delicious. Thank you for making it."

"It needs salt," I said. "And I tried to use magic to get it. I pointed at the salt, said 'salt cellar,' and ended up in the dungeon."

Haywood winked at me and smiled. "These things happen," he said. "You just need to be more specific." Before turning into an otter, he had been a wizard in training and probably knew more about magic than I did.

"You're so wise, precious one," Grassina told the otter, stroking his ears.

"I saw Grandfather," I said before they could forget that I was there. "We had a nice visit, and he helped me find the way out. He said that Mother came down to look for me while I was away."

"Mm-hmm," murmured Grassina, leaning down to kiss Haywood's head.

Haywood turned to me. "Your mother must have been worried about you when you disappeared."

The door banged against the wall behind me, and Eadric rushed into the room. "There you are, Emma!" he said. "I've been looking for you everywhere. You wouldn't believe what happened while I was getting dressed. I was putting on my shoes when suddenly I turned back into a frog! It was so fast, too, not at all like the last time. I couldn't believe it at first, but it lasted only a little while, then suddenly I was back to being me. And then it happened again. What's going on? Yesterday when we turned back, I thought that everything would be all right."

"It wasn't only you, Eadric. I changed, too—every time I sneezed."

"Ah!" said Haywood. "You sneezed. That explains it!"

"I was afraid something like that might happen," Grassina said. "I was hoping you'd have more control of your magic before it did."

Eadric frowned. "I'm glad you understand. Now how about telling us?"

"It's simple, really," said my aunt. "Emma's magic is strong, and she has to learn how to control it. Until she does, whenever she stresses her body, that stress is going to snap her back to whatever form she was in last. That means that when she sneezed, which is an intense physical reaction, she became a frog. And remember that your spell was linked, so you both had to turn back into humans or you both had to remain frogs."

I couldn't believe my ears. I already had enough problems with my magic, and now this! "Why haven't I heard about this before?"

Haywood explained that it didn't happen often. Changing to another shape was generally discouraged among witches until they could exercise greater control, but in my case it wasn't a matter of choice.

"This could happen again?" I asked.

Grassina nodded. "I'm afraid so. You'll need to work on your magic as much as possible. It's controlling you now, and that's not a good way to live. I know you wanted to go with us to see your grandmother, but perhaps you should stay here."

I didn't like that idea at all. Sitting around the castle

worrying that I might turn back into a frog was the last thing I wanted to do. "I'd still like to go with you," I said. "I haven't visited Grandmother for a while, and Eadric wants to meet her before he returns to his parents' castle."

"What's that I smell?" Eadric asked. "Did someone make breakfast?"

"I did," I said. "Why don't you—"

Eadric hadn't waited to be asked. Grabbing a plate of eggs, he carried it to a bench by the wall. After popping a bite in his mouth, he said, "These eggs are delicious, but they could have used a little salt."

I rolled my eyes.

"I've met Emma's other relatives, and I've heard so much about her grandmother," Eadric said. "I'd like to meet her, too. Emma, you should have seen it!" he continued, turning to me. "Grassina sent a message to my parents saying that I'm all right. They can stop worrying now, and I can stay a while longer. I have to wait a few days for Bright Country, anyway. He still hasn't recovered from being turned back into a horse."

Haywood twitched his whiskers. "Do you know what you're getting into? Emma's grandmother has a nasty way with suitors."

"I'll tell her that we're friends," Eadric said. "She can't object to that. Hey!" he shouted, jumping to his feet. "Something pinched me!" Setting the plate on the bench, he rubbed his backside with one hand and thrust the other into the space between the bench and the wall, pulling out something small and golden brown. "Here's the culprit!" he said, waving it in the air.

"It looks like one of my crab-apple dumplings," I said. I had had enough experience with the nasty little things to recognize them even from across the room. Their flaky pastry had turned out well, but the claws they'd grown after my magic went awry could deliver a painful pinch. "I wouldn't eat it now. It's probably stale."

Freshness didn't matter to Eadric. After inspecting the golden brown crust and the squirmy, kicking legs, Eadric shoved the whole thing in his mouth and bit down. "Pretty good," he said through a mouthful of pastry. "Are there any more?"

"I hope not," I said, shaking my head. "But then, I thought we'd found them all weeks ago. Maybe the rest of us should have some eggs, too. Who knows when we'll get to eat again."

"I've already had my breakfast," said Haywood. "Fish, fresh from the pond. Best way I know to start the day."

It took less time to eat the eggs than it had to cook them. When she was finished, Grassina set her plate aside, and began to scratch Haywood behind his ears. Snuggling closer, he tilted his head from one side to the other. "That feels great," he murmured. "That's the spot!"

I grimaced and bit my lip. My normally calm, controlled aunt had not been herself since she found Haywood.

Grassina smiled and looked up at me. "Emma, you and Eadric are welcome to come with us if you want to, but there's no telling what might happen when your grandmother is involved. I'm not even sure if we should attempt this. Your grandmother can be quite hateful and—"

"Of course we should!" I said. "I'll talk to Grandmother. I'm sure she'll do it."

Grassina sighed. "No, I'll talk to her myself. She is my mother, after all. And perhaps she *will* turn him back. Even if she refuses, what more can she do? She's already turned him into an otter."

"I see the rumors are right, Grassina," said a voice from the doorway, and we all turned our heads at once. I was surprised to see my mother standing there. It had been years since she'd last visited her sister's chambers. Mother's lips were tight with disapproval as her gaze swept over us. "You do have an otter in your room. Why would you bring a creature like that into the castle?"

"He isn't a creature, Mother. At least that's not all he is," I said. "That's Haywood, the man that Grandmother didn't want Grassina to marry. Grassina discovered him by the river when she was helping us. Isn't it exciting that they finally found each other?"

"So, sister, our mother turned him into an otter and not a frog, as you believed. When I heard that an otter was up here, I was afraid that Emeralda had changed into another horrid animal since I last spoke with her. How are you, Haywood?"

"Just fine, Chartreuse. And I see you're still your same sweet self."

My mother frowned at the otter, then glanced at the wall behind him. A tapestry hung there, just as it had for years. It showed the image of a woman, her long auburn hair streaming behind her. She stood on the parapet of a castle with her arms upraised, and in each hand she held a glowing ball of green light. On the ground far below, the remnants of an army were in full retreat.

"Ah," said my mother. "The tapestry of the Green Witch. I remember the day you got this, Grassina. When we were little girls, who would have thought that you would end up with the title?"

"I know you thought it would be you, Chartreuse," Grassina said before turning to me. "When we were young, we'd often play at being witches, and your mother always insisted on being the Green Witch. She was devastated when we learned that I had the talent for magic and she didn't. But then, magic chooses its own, doesn't it, Chartreuse?"

My mother's eyes were cold, but she didn't say a word.

Haywood shoved his head into the palm of Grassina's hand, and my aunt bent down to scratch his ears. Mother groaned. "I have a bad feeling about this," she said to me in a quiet voice. "After they got engaged, Grassina couldn't think about anything but Haywood, whether he was around or not. It didn't matter so much then, but that was before she was the Green Witch. It isn't an empty title, you know, Emeralda. On the same day that Hazel, the first Green Witch, was given that tapestry, she received the ring Grassina wears now."

I glanced at my aunt, but I already knew which ring my mother meant. Carved from a single pale green gem, it looked like a band of tiny, overlapping leaves. She'd worn the ring for as long as I'd known her.

"Every Green Witch since Hazel has worn it. Both the ring and the tapestry symbolize the power wielded by the Green Witch. It's her power that protects this kingdom. Without a Green Witch in Greater Greensward, the kingdom would be vulnerable to attack."

Eadric had crossed the room to join us. "Are you talking about trolls and werewolves? Trolls invade my father's kingdom a couple of times a year, and the werewolves attack every winter."

"Really? We've never had any problems like that," I said.

"Most kingdoms aren't as fortunate as ours," said my mother. "Flocks of harpies, marauding goblins or packs of werewolves are drawn to kingdoms without a powerful witch or wizard to protect them. Just knowing that the Green Witch is here is enough of a deterrent for some, although she's forced to demonstrate her power occasionally."

"I've never seen Grassina fight anyone," I said.

"She hasn't had to for many years now. Her reputation is well known."

I didn't understand. I'd lived with my aunt my whole life, but this was all new to me. "I always thought it was Father and his knights who kept invaders away."

"Your father is a good man and terribly brave, but that means little to an army of trolls or a flock of harpies."

"Why didn't anyone ever tell me about this?"

"Because you never needed to know about it before," said my mother.

I heard a thud and turned in time to see Haywood scurry across a small table and peer into a bowl of water. A miniature castle rested in the bowl, but otherwise the water appeared to be empty. Licking his lips, Haywood stuck his muzzle in the water, then sat back on his haunches, making an awful face. "Ugh!" he said. "It's salty!"

"Oh, no, my heart's delight," exclaimed Grassina.

"You mustn't drink that!"

Mother crinkled her lip in disgust. " 'Heart's delight' is what she called him when they were young," she whispered. "We may have a problem if she's as besotted with Haywood as she used to be. She couldn't focus on anything that didn't concern him, and the rest of her life suffered from it. Our kingdom is in jeopardy if she's weak, no matter what the reason. Even now, trouble isn't far away. Your father should arrive home in a few hours, but he sent a courier on ahead. His men had discovered two spies at a local tavern. They escaped during the interrogation."

Eadric frowned. "Spies in Greater Greensward?"

Mother nodded. "We have to help Grassina come to her senses. She has to forget about Haywood and take care of her responsibilities here."

"No matter what form he's in, I don't think she'd ever forget about Haywood," I said. "But he may not be an otter for much longer. We're going to visit Grandmother today to ask her to turn him into a man."

"Grassina wants to ask her for help? Maybe my sister really is unbalanced."

"It was my idea," I said. "Grandmother turned him into an otter in the first place, so she's the one who has to turn him back."

Mother made a face as if she smelled something awful. "I've never known you to be so meddlesome before. Someone must have been a bad influence on you." She turned her glare on Eadric. "Whoever thought of it, the suggestion is ill-considered. My mother has never helped anyone except herself."

"If you can think of a better idea—" I began.

"Get rid of the otter. Haywood has complicated Grassina's life long enough."

"But she loves Haywood! She'd be miserable without him."

"Then get your grandmother to turn him back, but do it quickly." My mother shook her head when she glanced at Grassina and Haywood. "I have to prepare for your father's return. I must let him know what's happened here."

I walked with Mother to the door, hoping to hurry her out. "When I sent a message to your father telling him that you were home, I didn't mention your refusal to marry Prince Jorge," she said, pausing at the threshold. "I don't know how I'll break the news to him."

"I could tell him myself."

"Perhaps it isn't necessary. I've been considering the problem, and it's obvious to me that you haven't thought this through. If we keep your little frog-kissing adventure to ourselves, you can still marry Jorge." Mother's voice dropped to a whisper as she glanced at Eadric, who was eating again on the other side of the room. "No one need know that you've been a frog or disgraced yourself with that young man."

"What are you talking about, Mother?" I asked, trying to keep my voice down as well. "Prince Eadric is a gentleman! We didn't do anything wrong."

"They're all gentlemen, until they have you alone."

"We were frogs!" I said. "We were trying to turn back into humans. What could—"

"It doesn't matter what you actually did. You were alone with a young man who wasn't related to you. That's all people need to hear. You know, of course, that's the worst thing that could have happened. Without beauty or grace, all you really had was your good reputation, and if your story gets out, you will no longer have that. But all may not be lost yet. If I hurry the wedding plans and you don't say a word to Jorge—"

"I'm not going to lie to him, Mother." I was sure that Jorge would hear about it eventually. Everyone in our castle probably already knew what had happened. It was nearly impossible to keep a secret with so many ears around.

My mother pursed her lips. "Then tell your tale as often as you'd like, but you've made a grave mistake. I don't know what your father and I will do with you now. I doubt that even a convent will take you."

"I shouldn't have bothered to come back at all!" I said.

"Perhaps you shouldn't have," Mother answered.

As soon as my mother was gone, Haywood spoke up. "Don't let your mother upset you, Emma, although if you want, I could take care of her for you. I was only a beginning wizard when Olivene transformed me, and not a very good one at that, but I remember some basic spells. It would be easy to turn Chartreuse into a magpie or squirrel. They all like to hear themselves chatter."

I laughed and shook my head. "Your offer is tempting, but I'd better not accept."

"If we're going to talk to *my* mother, we should leave soon," said Grassina. "Emma, why don't you and Eadric get the carpet from the storage room? The day is too beautiful to spend cooped up in a carriage, and Haywood would have difficulty staying on a horse. Ask Li'l where you can find the carpet."

It was dark inside the storage room, the only light coming through a window as narrow as an arrow slit. Eadric followed me through the door, stopping just inside when he saw the clutter. Something rustled in the rafters overhead, and I looked up. Li'l was hanging by her feet amid dangling bunches of herbs.

"Li'l!" I said. "It's me, Emma!"

"It's about time," the little bat squeaked. "Where did you go? One minute you were making breakfast, the next you were gone—poof!"

"I had a problem with my magic. I went to the dungeon by mistake."

"Those things happen," said Li'l, "especially when you're new at it."

"Do you know where my aunt put the carpet?" I peered into the darkened corners, where I could only make out vague shapes.

"Sure do! I know where everything is. Your aunt's put me in charge of inventory. The carpet's over there, behind that old mirror. Move the mirror aside ... watch out, it tilts ... that's it! There's the carpet."

The carpet was rolled up into a long tube, set on end so that it leaned against the wall. Eadric took one end and I took the other. It was heavy and awkward, but we'd soon wrestled it through the door and back into Grassina's sun-filled room.

Although the carpet was grimy on the outside, the colors were brilliant when we finally spread it in front of the window. Threads of scarlet, gold, navy blue, dark green and cream shone in the sunlight in a repeating pattern of flowers and abstract designs. A wide rug, it would hold the four of us easily.

Eadric stepped back to look. "It's very nice, but what does it have to do with going to your grandmother's?"

"This isn't an ordinary rug, Eadric. It's a magic carpet," said Grassina. "It will carry us wherever we want to go. It's a very comfortable way to travel as long as the weather is good."

Eadric turned to me. "Have you ever ridden on a magic carpet?"

"Never," I said, "but it looks like fun!"

"I'm not sure I want to trust anything involving magic yet," he said.

"You just ate a magic breakfast," I said.

"Here, Emma," said my aunt, holding out her hand. "Put these in your pouch. You never know when you might need them."

I did as she directed, tucking away an odd assortment of objects: a length of string, a small square of cloth and a candle stub. When everyone was ready, Eadric and I took our places on the magic carpet behind Grassina and Haywood. With a few softly spoken words, Grassina made the rug rise into the air. It moved in fits and starts, as if it wasn't quite sure what to do.

"I haven't used it for a while," my aunt said over her shoulder. "The ride should improve once the rug gets a good airing. Just stay seated and hold on."

"What about the window?" asked Eadric, his eyes enormous as the rug jerked toward the narrow opening. We were only inches away when the sides of the window stretched like a smiling mouth, allowing us to slip through easily. Once we were through, the window snapped back into place with a loud twang.

Grassina chuckled. "Don't worry, Eadric. This isn't the first time I've done this."

Four

The carpet dipped and swayed as it flew above the moat, until I was sure we were about to fall in. I grabbed hold of Eadric's arm, wishing I could hold something more stable, since he was shaking even more than the carpet. Rounding the last of the towers, the carpet leveled out and shot over the training fields where my father and his knights often practiced with swords and lances. In only a few minutes we had passed over the swamp that Eadric and I had spent days crossing. Beyond the river, we flew over the tops of trees, some so tall that I could nearly reach out and touch them.

The Old Witches' Retirement Community was located deep in the woods, accessible only by enchanted paths or by air. The paths led directly to the individual cottages and were the surest although slowest way of getting there. From the air, the community was so well hidden it would be easy to miss.

I tried to observe everything at once, turning my

head back and forth like a confused weather vane. Eadric was just as excited as I was, and together we made the rug jiggle and bounce as we looked around.

A pink fog drifted over the forest, its wispy tendrils reaching into the trees. The faint odor of boiled cabbage reached us, and I wondered who was cooking it. We were over the fog when I noticed the Purple Mountains in the distance. When I looked again, they seemed to be much closer. A hawk flew by, drawing my attention with it. The next time I looked toward the mountains, they appeared to have moved farther away again.

"Are the mountains moving?" I asked my aunt as the rug dropped closer to the woods.

"Not at all, although it looks that way, doesn't it? It's just the effect of the magic miasma, that pink fog that passes over the woods now and then. It's pretty, but it makes the community harder to find. Wait, I think I see it!"

The cottages of the Old Witches' Retirement Community were scattered around a small clearing. A fire pit occupied the center, an added bonus for those witches who liked to cook outside. Wooden tables and benches surrounded the fire pit, seating for the witches and their guests. The clearing was the first thing we spotted from the air. As we drew closer, I began to see the cottages hidden among the trees.

There were four basic styles of cottages, but each

witch had decorated hers in her own way, so no two were exactly alike. Some of them were gingerbread houses like my grandmother's, some walked about on chicken legs and some had thatched roofs and were surrounded by bushes bearing red and white roses; others were made of stone and covered with ivy.

The community itself grew and shrank as witches came and went, the cottages lasting only as long as they were needed. Some, like the gingerbread houses, disintegrated over time if not maintained. The cottages with chicken legs walked away when their owners died.

The rug was skimming just above the tops of the trees when I spotted Grandmother's cottage. Made of gingerbread, it had been repaired so many times that it didn't look at all the way it had when it was new. Visitors had eaten most of the icing trim, and my grandmother had replaced it with spun sugar. The gumdrops decorating the shutters had gotten hard, so she'd set clear fruit-flavored lozenges in their place. She'd also had to replace the gingerbread doors and many of the more accessible sections of the walls. The newer pieces of gingerbread were darker in color than the older ones, giving it a patchwork kind of look.

Grassina landed the rug in the cottage's front yard, and I expected Grandmother to tear out of the house, waving her broom at us and screeching her usual greeting. When she didn't even peep out from behind her cotton-candy curtains, I became concerned. Scrambling to my feet, I hurried to her front door. The latch, made of licorice and bearing the teeth marks of some long-ago visitor, was so sticky that I didn't want to touch it, but I didn't have much choice.

Lifting the latch, I pushed the door open and peeked inside. "Grandmother! Are you there? It's me, Emma! Grassina's here, too!"

Aside from the normal creaking of a candy house, the cottage was silent. *That's strange,* I thought, stepping into the tiny entranceway. The cottage was small, so it didn't take me long to search it, but there was no sign of Grandmother in the kitchen, the parlor or either of the two guest bedrooms. I didn't really expect to find her in her bedroom at that time of day, but I glanced inside anyway. I was closing the door when I noticed a lump under her bedcovers. Tiptoeing into the room, I reached for the covers and yanked them back, but it was only her cat, Herald, taking a nap. An old orange tabby turning white around the mouth and eyes, Herald was the only animal I'd ever known my grandmother to like, and was one of the most disagreeable cats I'd ever met.

Blinking sleepy eyes at the sunlight flooding the room, Herald put his ears back and growled when he saw me. I was used to his temper, however, and knew enough to keep well away from his claws.

"I don't suppose you know where my grandmother

is," I said, not really expecting an answer.

The cat sneered, then sat up to lick the base of his tail. I turned to leave and was halfway out the door when Herald spoke up. "Even if I knew, I wouldn't tell you. You've never treated me the way I deserve to be treated. No self-respecting witch's cat wants to be cuddled and called baby names!"

"I'm sorry I offended you, but I know a lot of cats who like to be petted," I said.

Herald stretched out a leg and bent down to lick his thigh. "Well, I'm not one of them!" He glanced up at me and crinkled his nose in a half snarl. "At least you're working on your magic, although you're long overdue."

"How do you know what I'm doing?"

"You're talking to me, aren't you? Your grandmother will be pleased. She's been very disappointed in you lately. As for where you can find her, she disappeared a few nights ago. It's a good thing she put in that cat door or I might have gotten hungry by now."

I left the cat bathing himself and went outside to find Grassina. Hearing sounds in the backyard, I headed around the side of the cottage, passing Grandmother's rock candy sundial on the way. It was almost noon, Grandmother's normal lunchtime. She should have been there, setting the table for her midday meal.

When I found my aunt, she was kneeling beside the oversized oven that Grandmother used for baking large sheets of gingerbread. "What are you doing?" I asked.

"Checking to make sure she isn't in here," said Grassina. "She once had a neighbor who had some children visit for a few days. One of them shoved her in her own oven and slammed the door shut. All that was left of her were some charred bones."

"That's terrible! What happened to the children?"

"Not a thing. They said that she was going to eat them, and claimed it was self-defense."

I shuddered. "Was there anything in Grandmother's oven that shouldn't be there?"

Grassina shook her head.

Munching a piece of gingerbread he'd taken from someone's wall, Eadric came out of the forest with Haywood loping by his side.

"I think Grandmother's been gone for a few days," I said.

When Grassina raised a questioning eyebrow, I told her of my encounter with Herald the cat.

"I'm not surprised that you can't find her," said Eadric. "Haywood and I took a quick look around, but we didn't see a single witch."

"That's right," said Haywood. "I think this whole place is abandoned."

"Maybe we should check the other cottages," I said.

Grassina nodded. "We probably should. Just don't open any doors. These old witches don't take kindly to nosy people. Now be careful."

I joined Eadric outside the gate while Haywood accompanied Grassina. None of the cottages we found appeared to be occupied.

Once we had finished, Eadric and I headed for the clearing in the center of the community. We had reached the first of the tables encircling the fire pit when Eadric stopped and bent down to pick up something. "What's this for?" he asked, showing me a simple cloth bag.

I turned it over in my hands. "I don't know. Maybe we should show it to Grassina." I jumped when Haywood leaped onto the table beside me, landing with a thud.

"What do you want to show her? Here, let me see." The otter sniffed it, then weighed it with his paws before setting it on the table. "Seems harmless enough. Queen of my heart, come see this!"

Grassina stepped up to the table and passed her hand over the bag as if she was feeling for something. "There's nothing magical about it. Let's see what it holds." When her nimble fingers had untied the knot, she poured some of its contents onto her palm. Pure white sand the color of fresh snow formed a sparkling mound.

"It's sand!" said Eadric, sounding disappointed. "Why would anyone put sand in a little bag like that?"

"That's a good question, Eadric," said my aunt.

"Something is very wrong here. All of the witches seem to have left at once, although there were no fires, no threat of any kind and no obvious reason why they should leave. These witches wouldn't just abandon their homes or their animals, not with all the magic they have tied up in them. Keep looking and see what else you can find."

Once again, Eadric and I went in one direction, while Grassina and Haywood went in the other, inspecting the tables and the area around them. The fire in the fire pit had gone out, another sign that something was wrong, since the witches always kept it lit. Ashes from the pit had blown across the clearing, drifting all the way to the inner circle of tables. I was holding my skirts out of the ashes, nudging a lump with the toe of my shoe, when I noticed a mouse under the table.

Seeing that the mouse was running toward a small hole in the ground, I darted ahead and covered the hole with my foot. "Excuse me," I said, crouching down so that I was closer to its level. The mouse skidded to a stop, sitting back on its haunches in surprise. "I see that you're in a hurry, so I won't keep you long. I was wondering if you could tell me where the witches have gone."

The mouse looked over its shoulder as if expecting to see someone else standing behind it. When it realized that there was no one there, it turned back to stare up at me. "You're talking to me? No big people ever talk to me!"

"It's true, I am talking to you, but then I happen to know that mice can be very nice. My name is Emeralda. My grandmother lives in the retirement community, and her name is Olivene. I can't seem to find her or any of the other witches who live here. I was wondering if you might know where they went."

"I have no idea where the witches went, but the other evening they had a big meeting with lots of people talking. Then they all got excited and flew off with parchments in their hands that looked like that one." The mouse pointed at the ground.

Reaching under the table, I felt something beneath the ash. It was a parchment, so coated with ash that the writing was barely discernable. When I picked it up and shook it, I realized my mistake instantly. My nose began to tickle. I tried to hold the sneeze in, but it was too strong. My eyes began to water, feeling as if they might pop out of my head if I didn't sneeze. I looked around, wanting to warn Eadric … and then … "*ah-choo!*"

I've never been able to keep my eyes open when I sneeze, so I didn't see Eadric change. When I opened them, I was chest deep in the powdery ash, holding the edge of the parchment in my long green fingers. The mouse took one look at me and disappeared into its hole.

"Emma!" Eadric wailed.

"I'm over here," I said, waving my other hand in the air.

"Don't just sit there!" he said, his voice growing louder as he hopped toward me. "Turn us back!"

"I'll try," I said. If the ash made me sneeze once, it ought to do it again. Leaning toward the dust, I took a deep breath, but instead of sneezing, I started to cough, a loud hacking cough that reached deep into my lungs.

Eadric emerged from the ash like a small, lumpy ghost. He looked so funny that I would have laughed if I hadn't still been coughing. "How about a spell?" he asked. "Grassina said you'd have to learn to control the frog transformations through your magic."

"My magic! But I don't know any spells to turn us back."

"Then make one up. It can't be too hard. Witches make up spells all the time."

"I suppose I could try," I said, but my mind was already whirling. *Should I make it rhyme? What if I turn us into something horrible? What if the witches return and throw me in a cauldron before I can explain who I am? What if—*

"Are you going to make up a spell or not?" asked Eadric. "This ash is drying me out. We're going to have to find some water if you don't change us back soon."

"All right, all right. Just give me a minute!" *Frog, clog, dog, bog* … I tried to think of rhyming words that I could use. *Change, strange, range* … Although I had a good idea of what a spell could do, I had no idea how it worked.

"If you're not going to try a spell, I'm heading for those trees," said Eadric. "It's too hot here, and my skin is starting to shrivel."

"Fine, fine," I said. "I'll try this one."

I'm now a frog.
I was a girl,
Please turn me back
And make–

"No, wait!" shouted Eadric. "Think about what you're saying! You're still a girl, just not a human girl. Try again … something that doesn't involve gender. The last thing I want to do is turn into a girl."

"Okay," I said. "Then how about this?"

Frog isn't what
I want to be.
Please turn me in-
To my old me.

I could feel myself changing, although it wasn't at all like the other times. I grew bigger and taller, but I also felt weaker. I felt pains in my joints and my vision blurred. When I looked at my hands, they were human, but they were wrinkled and had brown spots on the back. I turned to look at Eadric and saw an old man with a potbelly and straggly white hair sitting in the ash.

"Here they are!" shouted a familiar voice, and Haywood came sliding on his stomach through the dust. "I found the old witches … but there's only two. And one looks like an old man."

"One *is* an old man," grumbled Eadric, his voice as creaky as rusty armor. "An old man who should be a young one. What's wrong with you, Emma? Can't you get anything right?"

"I told you I didn't have a spell ready, Eadric," I said, my own voice sounding shrill in my ears. "But you insisted that I—"

"Emma, Eadric, is that you?" Grassina stepped lightly through the ash. "Good gracious! What happened?" she said, glancing from Eadric to me.

Eadric scowled. "We were frogs, so Emma tried to use her magic to make us human again."

"I said I wanted to be turned into my old me. I guess I shouldn't have said *old*."

"No," said Grassina, "but at least this is one spell that's easily reversed." Taking a burnt piece of wood from the fire pit, Grassina scribbled something on a scrap of parchment she dug from her pouch, then handed it to me, saying, "Read this out loud, Emma."

I had to squint to read it, as my vision wasn't very

good, but she'd printed the letters large enough that it wasn't too hard.

From old to young,
Return us to
Our rightful age,
To each be true.

I sighed with relief when the aches and pains melted away. My scalp prickled when my hair turned from white to its normal auburn; my skin tingled as it grew firmer and the wrinkles disappeared. My eyesight improved as well, and everything that had been blurry came into focus. Although it didn't happen all at once, it was fast enough to be disorienting, and I had to grab Grassina's hand to keep my balance.

"Oh, my!" I said, closing my eyes until the world stopped spinning. "I'm glad that's over."

"Suddenly I feel sorry for the old witches," Eadric said. "Being old is terribly uncomfortable."

"How did it happen, Emma?" asked Grassina.

"Oh!" I said, glancing at the ground by my feet. "A mouse showed me a parchment. I picked it up and the dust made me sneeze. Here it is."

Careful to hold my breath, I retrieved the parchment from the ash and shook it clean. It was beautiful. Done in the style of the best illuminated manuscripts, a small picture depicted a dark and gloomy swamp where trees stood on stilted roots above a winding river. Toothy reptiles propelled themselves through the water with their long, ridged tails, while slender, beady-eyed snakes twined around branches. The text was handwritten in black ink with gold accents and looked very fancy.

Tired of retirement? Forget all your troubles and begin life anew in the Forgotten Swamp.

Eadric examined the creatures in the picture. "Look at the size of those things! Do you suppose they're real?"

"Maybe, but if they are, I wouldn't want to be a frog in that swamp!" I said.

Grassina, however, seemed even more impressed when I repeated what the mouse had told me. "Wonderful!" she said. "Now we have a good chance of finding the old witches."

Five

Grassina stuck two fingers in her mouth and whistled three distinct notes. She had scarcely finished when the magic carpet appeared over the tops of the trees. I tried to be careful stepping onto the carpet, but the ash I stirred up made my eyes water. Squeezing them shut, I wiped my eyelids with my handkerchief and held my nose so I wouldn't sneeze. When I could see again, I noticed that Grassina had taken her black dragon's scale out of the pouch on her belt.

"Is everyone ready?" she asked, settling her skirts around her.

Eadric took my hand and I glanced at his face. He was pale and his lips were pressed in a tight line. Realizing that he might be nervous about flying, I smiled at him in what I hoped was a reassuring manner and gave his hand a squeeze. "You don't have to go. We can drop you off at your parents' castle."

Eadric shook his head. "I'm going if you are. You

need me to keep you safe."

"I'll be fine—" I began, but from the set of his jaw, I knew he wasn't about to change his mind. "We're as ready as we'll ever be," I told Grassina.

Clutching the small bag of sand and the parchment in one hand, Grassina held the scale in the other and said,

Witches who around here sat
Suddenly decided that
They had someplace new to go,
As this picture seems to show.

Use these things to help us find them.
Let no one in secret bind them.
Be it near or be it far,
Show us where these witches are.

I peered over my aunt's shoulder to see the scale. A gift to Grassina from a dragon friend, the scale was an excellent direction finder, with sparks of light flashing red for hot when aimed in the right direction, and blue for cold when aimed the wrong way. My legs were beginning to cramp by the time the light flashed. It was blue at first, but my aunt tilted her head and the rug lifted a few inches off the ground, rotating slowly until the light changed to red.

Grassina muttered something under her breath and the rug rose into the air, its movement smoother than when we had left the castle. Rising above the treetops, the rug swayed in the air currents, settling down only after Grassina used a calming spell.

The lights sparking through the scale were faint, a good indication that we had far to travel. Before long, we were moving so fast that we had to squint against the wind. Although I tried to look at the scenery, I soon gave up and closed my eyes, clinging to Eadric's hand as the wind buffeted the carpet. I opened my eyes once and we had passed the Purple Mountains. I opened them again and we were flying over a vast plain where an army marched below us, so far away that they looked smaller than ants.

When daylight faded into night and the stars came out one by one, I closed my eyes and leaned against Eadric. I must have slept, for the next thing I knew it was daylight and we were flying over a body of water that seemed to go on forever. At one point, a group of enormous fishlike creatures passed below us, clearly visible despite the great distance that separated us. I wanted to share the sight with Eadric, but when I glanced at him, his face was pale, the skin around his mouth slightly green.

"Are you all right?" I asked.

Eadric moaned and shook his head, his lips pursed

shut as if speaking would take too much effort. I squeezed his hand. A moment later, he leaned toward the edge of the rug and emptied his stomach to the water below. I felt sorry for him when he finally sat up, pale and shaking, although I was grateful that the wind carried the smell away.

Most of our trip had been made in good weather, but as the hours passed, the sky grew cloudy and white-caps topped the waves. Eadric moaned more often now, and his hand felt cold and damp. *We need to set down soon,* I thought, and leaned forward to check the scale again. The lights were brighter, the red sparks flashing with such frenzy that I knew we were approaching our destination.

"Do you know where we are?" I asked, leaning close to my aunt's ear.

"I have a good idea. There's an island straight ahead. It's where we're headed if I'm not mistaken. Sit back and hold on tight. Our ride is about to get rough."

Despite the spell my aunt had used to keep us steady, the magic carpet jerked and shuddered as the wind increased. Now Grassina took us higher still. The clouds appeared dark and menacing, and I dreaded going through them. When we entered the first cloud, a chill enveloped us that made my breath catch in my throat. I shivered as the cold seeped into my bones. Eadric was only a vague shape beside me, though he was so close our hips touched.

The wind grew stronger, lashing us with rain. Looking up as lightning flashed, I saw the otter slipping toward the edge of the rug. “Haywood!” Grassina screamed, and lunged for him, grabbing his furry paw as he was about to go over. The otter scrabbled with his hind paws, dragging himself back onto the rug until he was huddled by my aunt, her arm pressing him to her side.

My stomach lurched when the carpet dropped and then shot up again just as quickly. Clutching the carpet’s edge on one side and Eadric’s hand on the other, I was truly frightened for the first time since our journey began. My heart thudded as the rug bucked and swooped. Damp and shivering, I bit my lip, trying not to cry out when I felt the tickling begin. Alarmed, I pressed my nose against my shoulder, but it wasn’t enough. The tickling became unbearable, and I squeezed Eadric’s hand in warning.

Of course I sneezed. The transformation was almost instantaneous. No longer a gradual tingling, it felt more like a shock that started in my fingers and toes, then coursed through my body until it reached my head, making it feel fizzy and light. When I glanced down, I saw smooth green legs jutting out before me. Looking up, I saw Eadric’s froggy mouth hanging open in dismay.

Unable to hold on to the rug with our small fingers,

we were helpless against the rushing wind. The next powerful gust blew us off the rug and we fell, tumbling through the air, our intertwined fingers all that kept us together.

I screamed, the sound carried away by the wind as we plummeted through the cloud, head over heels, twisting and turning until I wasn't sure which way was up. When I saw the terror on Eadric's face, I realized that I was the only one who could save us. With all the wind and rain, my aunt probably didn't even know that we had fallen.

The wind tried to tear us apart, but we held on, gripping each other's hand as hard as we could. Flipping over again, I found myself looking down at the water as it rushed up to meet us. My eyes were streaming from the wind, but even so, the waves looked far too close to me.

I forced myself to concentrate. There had to be something … I tried to remember all the spells I'd read, but none of them seemed appropriate. I had to come up with a spell of my own. What if some kind of creature could meet us partway and take us to the island? A bird, perhaps. I shouted the spell as I thought of it, although I doubt volume makes much difference when it comes to magic.

Winged creature flying near,
Save us from the death we fear.
Catch us now before we land
On the water or the sand!

I turned my head this way and that, hoping to spot a seabird braving the winds to rescue us. When nothing came, I closed my eyes and squeezed Eadric's hand, sorry that I'd gotten him into such a mess. Tumbling through the air, I expected to splat against the water at any moment, so I didn't know what to think when I hit something tough and leathery that gave beneath my body. I became even more confused when I opened my eyes. We had fallen onto a broad, black back, hurtling just above an enormous wave.

"Hang on!" shouted a voice, but there was nothing to hold on to except the rippling, leathery edge of the creature. Eadric and I grabbed hold just as the creature hit the water and plunged under the surface. I felt the pressure change when the wave roared over our heads.

What kind of bird is this? I wondered, peering through the churning water. We went deeper, gliding beneath the waves where the water was dark and murky. I studied the creature as best I could, but it didn't make any sense. It had neither feathers nor wings, yet it flapped like a bird. Its great, wedge-shaped body was smooth and black with a pair of curled horns, yet it had no head that I could see. There was no animal on dry land to compare it to, so I didn't know if we should be relieved at our rescue or terrified that this creature had found us.

"How are you doing?" the creature asked in a bubbly sort of voice. As I couldn't locate its face, I didn't know what part of the creature I should address.

"Who are you?" I asked, my own voice sounding strange underwater.

"They call me Manta. So, what are you two? I've never seen fish like you before, and you don't have fur like seals."

Eadric laughed. "We're not fish. We're frogs, or at least we are now."

"Frogs, huh?" Manta said. "Never heard of frogs before. You must be rare."

"As rare as enchanted royalty," Eadric said, puffing himself up.

"That's not rare. I wish I had a mouthful of plankton for every enchanted prince I've met. Speaking of plankton, do you mind if I have a snack?" Manta rose toward the surface while unfurling his horns, which I realized weren't really horns at all, but a way to funnel cloudy water into what had to be his mouth.

"You don't suppose he eats frogs, do you?" I whispered into Eadric's eardrum.

Eadric peered ahead to where the cloudy water was disappearing at an amazing speed. "I doubt it. From the looks of things, I think he prefers soup."

Another wave curled over our heads. I grabbed hold of the creature's smooth-skinned edge, gasping as he plunged into the heart of the wave. Flying beneath the violence of the surface, Manta's body rose and fell as his triangular wings propelled us through the water. His rhythmic movements were soothing and much more comfortable than the flying carpet. It would have been peaceful if it weren't for the muffled roar of the storm and the strange booms and wails that grew clearer as Manta dove.

"What's that sound?" I asked.

"Just the whales talking," Manta gurgled. "They say the storm is ending."

After a while, the voices of the whales died away, replaced by a series of high-pitched chirps and whistles. "Is that another whale?" I asked.

"That's a porpoise. Those guys are such comedians. They're always coming up with new jokes. Hey, have you heard this one? Why did the porpoise cross the ocean?"

"How would we know?" said Eadric. "We've never even met a porpoise!"

"You don't have to meet one. It's a joke! Come on, let's try it again. Why did the porpoise cross the ocean?"

"I don't know," I said. "Why?"

"To get to the other tide."

Eadric grunted and made a face.

"I'm sorry we don't understand your joke, Manta, but we're not familiar with the ocean. We've come a long way to find my grandmother," I said. "She's on an island near here and needs our help."

Manta dipped a wing and turned abruptly. "There's

only one island around this part of the sea. I'll have you there in three shakes of a mermaid's tail. Hold tight, I'm going up to look around."

Flapping his wings in long, powerful strokes, Manta sped to the surface, shooting straight into the air, and twisting before he fell. The sun had come out, and the clouds were disappearing on the horizon. Although the waves were still high, they were nothing like they'd been only a short time before.

An island stood off to our right. It was a beautiful place, with strange, frond-topped trees and a pure white shore. I caught a quick glimpse of huts and people in brightly colored clothes, but Manta flopped back into the water before I could see much more.

Circling the island, Manta brought us close to shore at a lonely spot well past the huts. I plopped into the shallows beside Eadric, who scrambled out of the water as quickly as he could. Holding on to Manta so that the waves wouldn't carry me away, I said, "Thank you for helping us. Most creatures wouldn't have bothered."

"It was my pleasure," he replied, his edges rippling. "I love meeting strange creatures, and you two are some of the strangest I've ever met!"

Six

Eadric had waited for me at the water's edge. He was frowning, and I knew he wasn't in a good mood. "Grassina was right when she said you should work on your spells. What were you thinking of with that last one? Winged creature? You could have called up anything from a gnat to a dragon!"

"I was trying to call a bird."

"Some bird!" he said.

"At least I tried! I didn't see you doing anything to save us."

"Huh!" said Eadric. He turned away and hopped stiffly up the beach. I followed only a few paces behind, tired, thirsty and with a terrible headache.

"We have to find fresh water," I said to Eadric's rigid back.

"That's where I'm going now," he grumbled. "I thought I saw sunlight reflecting off water behind these trees."

"I hope you're right," I muttered.

Although the rain had cooled the sand temporarily, it was already becoming hot beneath our feet. I tried to make long hops so that my feet didn't have to touch the scorching ground as often.

I was trying to keep up with Eadric when I bumped into a brown ball covered with coarse, thick hairs. The ball rolled aside, revealing a small green crab. I backed away when the crab clacked its claws in the air. A chorus of claws sprang up around me; I was surrounded by crabs even bigger and meaner than the first one.

"Eadric!" I shouted, hopping from one vacant patch of ground to another as more crabs threatened me with their claws.

"Over here, Emma!" Eadric had passed most of the crabs before they noticed us. I hopped again, but a crab scuttled forward unexpectedly and I landed on his back, flipping him over when I jumped again.

A dozen or so scurried to block my path. "This way!" Eadric shouted.

The crabs scuttled after him, leaving an opening. I knew I wouldn't stand a chance against the oversized claws of the larger crabs, so I hunched down, tensed my muscles and leaped as far as I could, flying over their heads. Although I made it past the crabs, I landed face first, getting a mouthful of sand.

We hopped away as fast as we could and didn't stop

until we landed in the freshwater pond Eadric had seen. While Eadric paddled across the pond, I rinsed the sand from my mouth, spitting until the grit no longer rasped my tongue.

The water was warmer than I was used to, and felt wonderful. Still, I couldn't wait to start looking for Grassina. Even if she'd landed safely, I was sure she'd be worried about me. But before we went anywhere, we needed to turn back into humans. There was no telling what other kinds of creatures we might meet on the island.

Not wanting to make myself prematurely old again, I was reluctant to try another spell, so I began to look around, wondering what I might use to make myself sneeze. I saw Eadric chasing insects at the water's edge and was about to call to him when I spotted the most beautiful crimson flowers. They didn't look real with their golden centers and long, curled petals, and I couldn't resist the urge to touch them.

I'd always been fascinated by flowers, perhaps because they were forbidden in my parents' castle. When I was younger, I'd been told that my mother and aunt were allergic to them, and I'd only recently learned the truth about the family curse. Since the curse didn't take effect until after one's sixteenth birthday and I had yet to turn fifteen, I was still immune.

I could smell the flowers' perfume even though I was

yards away. Climbing out of the water, I reached for a stem, pulling it down until I had the blossom cupped in my hands. The tingling began with my first sniff. I took another breath, deeper than the first.

"Eadric!" I shouted. "I'm going to … going to … *ah-choo!*"

The fizzy rush happened almost instantly. One moment I was a frog standing on tiptoe, sniffing a flower, the next I was a princess, crouched over a flower that I still cradled in my hands. I heard a shout and saw Eadric climbing from the pond, his clothes and hair streaming water. He wore the silliest grin, and I couldn't help but laugh. I guffawed, I chortled, I wheezed, just as I always do. Some unseen creature thrashed about in the foliage by the edge of the pond. A flock of shrill-voiced birds exploded from a nearby tree, scattering leaves and loose feathers. Eadric joined in, laughing so hard that he bent double, his arms wrapped around his stomach.

"Don't ever change your laugh, Emma," said a voice. "It's a wonderful way to find you." My aunt Grassina stepped into the sunlight surrounding the pond. Her hair hung down her back and was even more disheveled than usual. Bits of leaves peeped from the snarled curls, and wet sand smeared her clothes. Haywood scampered at her side, his drying fur ruffled and crusted with sand.

"Grassina!" I shouted. Scrambling to my feet, I ran to give my aunt a hug and to tell her the story of how we'd met Manta. "So what happened to you after we fell off?" I asked as we joined Eadric by the pond.

"It was a fight the whole way. I didn't notice you were missing until we had almost reached the island. When I saw that you were gone, I had the rug circle back. It never occurred to me that you might have turned into frogs again. No wonder we couldn't find you!"

"What did you do then?" I asked.

"We came to the island to wait out the storm," said Haywood, "but the wind had gotten stronger and we had a rough landing."

"Did you see the swamp from the sky? Did you see Grandmother or any of the other witches?"

Grassina shook her head. "We didn't see much of anything, but I don't think there's a swamp. The island isn't very big."

"The picture on the parchment—" Eadric began.

"Was a trick to get the witches here, if I'm not mistaken," said my aunt. "Knowing that group, a snake-infested swamp would be more of an attraction than a tropical beach."

"Do you suppose the witches might be on the beach? Eadric and I saw people and huts."

"Then that's where we should start looking. Come along, sugarplum," Grassina said, ruffling Haywood's fur. "Let's go see if we can find my mother."

I wasn't happy about walking beneath the trees since

I didn't want to encounter the crabs again, but there wasn't any way to avoid it. I didn't have to worry, however. The moment Haywood saw the crabs, he licked his lips and galumphed across the sand in pursuit of a large fat one, sending the rest into hiding. While Grassina waited for him to return, Eadric and I kept walking.

We were alone among the trees when Eadric said, "So how about a kiss? I haven't had one yet today." He took a step closer, backing me against one of the frond-topped trees, and leaned toward me with his hand braced against the trunk.

"A kiss? With all the things we have to do, is that all you can think about?"

Eadric grinned. "Sometimes. Other times I think about horses or improving my swordplay or what I'm going to have for dinner, but none of those things seem important when we're alone on this beautiful island."

"You mean I'm more important than horses right now?"

"And dinner. My stomach hasn't settled down yet, so I'm still not hungry. Do I get that kiss?"

I rolled my eyes. "After that romantic explanation it would be almost impossible to refuse, but I'll manage," I said, ducking under his arm.

"Hey!" said Eadric. "What's wrong? You kissed me the other day."

"You're right, I did. I must not have had anything

more important to think about then."

With Eadric trailing behind, I hurried between the last of the trees and stepped onto the beach. There were people there, scattered across the sand like brightly colored flowers. All elderly women, they were dressed in loose-fitting gowns made from vibrant fabrics. The sleeves were short, leaving the women's arms exposed. Although my mother would have been shocked, I thought it was practical for such a hot climate. I was already perspiring in my long-sleeved gown.

Small groups of women strolled along the water's edge, giggling when the waves wet their feet and legs. They'd stop now and then to pick up objects that the storm had washed ashore, exclaiming over their finds like children on a treasure hunt.

Other women were working on their own projects. The closest of these was an old woman in a yellow and orange gown kneeling beside a castle she was constructing out of sand. Since the castle was within the water's reach, she was constantly repairing walls and towers, scooping the sand with a large seashell.

"Hello!" she said, looking up as we drew near. "Come to see my castle? It's a beauty, isn't it? Watch what happens when the water fills the moat. See, it looks just like the real thing!" Water from one of the larger waves had run hissing up the sand, filling the moat and lapping at the castle walls. Clapping her hands, the old woman sat back on her heels and watched the wave retreat.

"You've done a beautiful job," said Grassina, coming through the copse of trees. "Did you build it all by yourself?"

"Of course. No one else can handle the sand so well. I'm the only one who can fashion a bridge or mold towers like these," she said, patting one tenderly.

"So you know everyone on the island?"

The old woman nodded. "There aren't that many of us. We all live right there," she said, pointing toward a nearby group of huts.

"I know that woman," Grassina muttered once we'd continued on our way. "But I'd swear she didn't recognize me. Her name is Hennah, and she isn't behaving like herself at all."

"She seemed nice," I said, glancing back over my shoulder.

"Yes, she does, which isn't like her. Normally, she hates people and goes out of her way to let them know it."

"All the witches from the retirement community must be here. We should have asked Hennah where we could find Grandmother."

"There's another witch," said Eadric, pointing farther down the beach. "Let's ask her."

An old woman with curling white hair so long that it brushed the sand was bent double, collecting seashells.

She looked up when our shadows crossed her path.

"Good day," said Grassina. "I was wondering if I might ask you a question. Do you know anyone named Olivene?"

The old woman straightened and brushed a strand of hair from her eyes. "I don't think so," she said in a husky sort of voice.

"Could you tell us your name?" I asked.

The old woman looked perplexed. "I can't seem to remember…."

"That's all right," I hurried to tell her. "Sorry to have troubled you."

The old woman held up her cupped hands, opening them to reveal an assortment of shells. "Would you like to see my seashells? I've found some lovely ones. Some of these must be the fairest in the sea!"

"Perhaps another time," said my aunt. "We have something we have to do first."

Since the witch was busy with her shells, it was easy to sneak away. I glanced at Grassina. The worried look on her face frightened me. "That was Cadmilla, one of the most devious witches around. Everyone knows that she tried to kill her stepdaughter."

"But she seemed nice, too!" I said.

Grassina shook her head. "It doesn't make any sense, does it? If even their personalities have changed—"

"They must have lost their memories altogether,"

said Eadric, digging the toe of his boot into the sand.

"Eadric!" I said, startled at his brilliance. "I bet that's it!"

"It makes sense, doesn't it? They can't even remember their own names, let alone who Grassina or Olivene are. If they can't remember that much, there's probably a lot they can't remember."

Shading my eyes with my hand, I glanced down the beach. "We'll just have to look for Grandmother. She must be around here somewhere."

We finally found my grandmother lying on a blanket, sound asleep. Her face was relaxed, without the cruel lines that usually etched her skin, and she looked kind of sweet lying there. I almost didn't recognize her.

"Do you think we should wake her?" I whispered to my aunt. "She looks so peaceful."

"What's all this noise about?" said my grandmother, turning her head to glare at us.

My aunt looked defiant, which was the way she usually acted around her mother. "We came to find you."

"Why? Do I know you? Doesn't matter. I'm taking a nap. Go bother someone else." My grandmother rolled onto her side, turning her back to us. Perhaps it was the curse, but even without her memory, Grandmother was the nastiest witch around.

Grassina shook her head and walked away, gesturing for me to follow. "This may take a while," she said once we were out of my grandmother's earshot. "Why don't you and Eadric see what else you can learn about the island? The more we know, the sooner we can get your grandmother's memory back and ask her to reverse the spell on Haywood."

"Will we take Grandmother with us when we go?" I asked.

"That depends on what we learn. Just be careful. There's more going on here than you might imagine."

Seven

Eadric and I headed down the beach in the only direction we had yet to explore. Although we didn't see anyone, we did spot a lone hut set off by itself. Larger than the others, it had the same cone-shaped thatched roof and stick-built walls, and it was situated on a small spit of land that overlooked the beach on one side and a tree-lined bay on the other.

As we got closer, we could tell that something was going on inside the hut. A shrill, scratchy voice was screaming, "Me too! Me too!" A deeper, less distinct voice answered.

Although it was broad daylight, with all the greenery we were able to sneak up and peek inside without anyone noticing. I saw only one person, a short old man with white hair, a rounded belly, a substantial mustache and a neat, trim beard. Dressed in a knee-length light blue robe, the old man wore a soft, four-cornered cap that threatened to slip off each time he turned his head. Both robe and cap were decorated with scattered silver stars, and a chain of larger stars twinkled around his neck. A large green and red bird with a well-developed beak sat on a perch beside him.

On a table against the wall, pink and white seashells held down the edges of a fresh piece of parchment. A quill pen lay on the table, dripping ink beside a small clay pot. From where I crouched, I could see that the parchment was clean except for a few written words and a splattering of ink.

"I'm sick and tired of this!" grumbled the old man.

"Me too!" squawked the bird, shuffling back and forth on its perch.

"I can't wait until we're finished and can go home."

"Me too!"

"I wish you'd think of something else to say!"

"Me too!"

The wizard's left eyelid twitched. "You know, it was funny at first, but now it's just annoying. Stop saying 'Me too,' Metoo!"

"*Thppt!*" The bird made a rude sound with its beak.

"Now cut that out! I don't know why I put up with you."

"Grack!" said the bird.

The old man shook a pudgy pink finger. "You stupid bird. If it weren't for you, we would have been finished and out of here already!"

"Awk!" squawked the bird. "Don't blame me, Olefat! I told you that lying to a bunch of old witches would get you in trouble, but you had to steal their memories—"

"It seemed like a good idea," said Olefat. "All those memories just waiting to be bottled up. Once I found the book, it was only a matter of time."

"You wouldn't have needed to do it if you could come up with your own spells."

Olefat shook his head. "That wasn't the point. Those witches were once the leaders in their field. By collecting their spells, I'm doing the world of magic a service."

"Then don't come crying to me when you don't like what you hear. Even you couldn't have expected those old memories to be pleasant." Sidling along his perch, the bird twisted his head to the side to stare at the old wizard.

"I never thought they'd be this bad," Olefat wailed. "I can't stand much more!"

Something rattled, and I peeked over the window ledge to see what it was. A row of bottles filled a shelf that had been pegged to the opposite wall. One bottle was a sickly yellow shot through with violet; another was gray with purple specks the color of a bruise. While some bottles were shaking, one that was the color of dried blood looked like it was about to rattle itself completely off the shelf.

"Are you through yet?" said a scratchy voice. "I'm sick of hearing you two yammer on. Close your mouths and listen before I turn you into a couple of cockroaches!"

"You're so full of hot air!" said another voice, shriller than the first. "You can't cast spells now. You're just a memory."

"Quiet, you old crones. It's my turn and I'm going to have my say. Ahem," said a husky voice clearing a nonexistent throat. "I married a widower king who doted on me for my beauty. I kept my splendor for years with a lotion I made from the dust of a thousand butterfly wings and the milk from two bushels of milk-weed pods. I was very happy for a time, since I was the fairest in the land. But then my stepdaughter turned sixteen and ruined it all by being even more beautiful."

"A thousand butterfly wings…" muttered the old man as he scribbled on the piece of parchment.

Another witch cackled. "You wasted your life trying to stay beautiful while I spent my days teaching lessons to those who deserved it. Every day I waited for some-one to come into my woods. If a maid shared her lunch with me, I cast a spell so that each time she spoke, pearls and precious gems fell from her lips. Maids who refused to share their food had frogs, snakes and lizards squirm-ing from their throats."

"What if it was a gentleman instead of a maid?" asked the old man.

"Generous gentlemen received swords of valor or enchanted cloaks. As for the stingy ones—"

A familiar voice broke in. "I transformed people as well, but not always for being selfish. I changed my daughter's betrothed into an otter because I didn't think he was good enough for her. When I told him how to break the spell, I made it so involved that he was bound to forget it."

"Is that your grandmother?" Eadric whispered into my ear.

I nodded, shushing him with a raised finger.

"So tell us what you said!" demanded one voice.

"I don't think I will. It was too delicious!"

Go ahead, I thought. *Tell them!*

"That isn't fair! I told you my recipe for beauty."

"We won't share anything else with you if you don't share with us."

"Oh, all right, if you're going to be that way. I remember it word for word, since it was so perfect."

A gossamer hair from mother-of-pearl,
The breath of a dragon green.
A feather from an aged horse,
The husk of a magic bean.

"I see what you mean. He couldn't possibly have gotten that right."

"It wasn't impossible, mind you, or it wouldn't have worked."

"But for an otter to remember that, or find half the things—"

"How long did he stay an otter?"

"As far as I know, he still is!" screeched my grandmother.

The hoots of laughter from the bottles made me so angry, I felt like shaking them.

"Now it's my turn!" screamed a voice over the din. "And have I got a story."

"Who said you could go next? You talked yesterday, so it's my turn."

I backed away from the window, tugging on Eadric's sleeve. "It's time for us to go," I whispered. "We've heard what we came for."

"But it's just getting good!" he whispered a little too loudly.

"What was that?" asked the bird. "I think I heard something."

"You're always hearing something," the wizard replied. "It's probably a loose seed rattling around in your skull."

The bird's outraged squawk hurt my ears. "Loose seeds! I'll give you loose seeds!" *Plip! Plip! Plip!* The last thing I saw through the window before I started to run was the bird flinging seeds at the old man.

We found Grassina seated on the blanket beside my grandmother, who had fallen asleep again. Haywood was chasing seagulls up and down the beach, and appeared to be having a wonderful time.

"We found the answer!" I said. "You have to come with us."

"There's a little old wizard named Olefat—" began Eadric, shifting his weight from one foot to the other.

Grassina stood and brushed the sand from her gown. "Olefat? I didn't know he was still alive. It's been years since I've heard anyone mention his name. I'm not surprised he's involved," she said, looking grim. "He has a shady reputation."

"He's the one behind all this," said Eadric. "You should see his hut. He put the memories in bottles and keeps them on a shelf."

Grassina began walking and we hurried to catch up. "He has the memories with him now?" she asked, a determined glint in her eyes. "Are you sure?"

"We heard them ourselves!" said Eadric. "He was arguing with a bird. It's the size of a crow, but it's green and red and has a much bigger beak."

"That sounds like a parrot."

"And then other voices started talking," I said. "They called themselves memories, but they weren't very nice."

Grassina shook her head. "No, they wouldn't be. A nasty group of witches lives in that retirement community. Maybe all the nice ones moved away—or never moved there in the first place, once they'd learned who already lived there. Not all old witches are nasty."

"That's good," said Eadric, smiling at me. He pointed at the hut down the beach. "We listened through the window and we heard your—"

Grassina held up her hand for silence. "You two did very well, but I think you'd better stay outside. It may get unpleasant in there."

Once again Eadric and I crouched beneath Olefat's window. Hearing my aunt knock on the door, I peeked over the sill, careful to stay out of sight. The old wizard looked startled.

"Who do you suppose that is?" Olefat asked his parrot.

The parrot squawked and threw another seed at him. "You're the wizard. You tell me!"

Olefat took off his hat, trickling seeds on the floor. His head was bald but for a fringe of hair that reached from ear to ear. Frowning, he rubbed his bald spot before jamming his cap back on his head. "Come in," he called, his eyelid twitching so much, it looked like a living thing trying to escape.

When Grassina opened the door, all the blood

drained from Olefat's face. Muttering under his breath, he began to reach into a fold in his robe, but Grassina threw up her hand and pointed her finger at him.

> No word, no gesture shall you make!
> Silence keep for your life's sake!

Olefat's mouth flew open, and it seemed as though he was about to speak. When nothing came out, his eyes took on a wild look. His jaw waggled, and his Adam's apple jerked up and down.

The parrot squawked, bobbing its head like a broken child's toy. "Would you look at that? That's the first time I've seen the old man speechless. You should have come by sooner. Why, we—"

Grassina pursed her lips and narrowed her eyes, a look that too often meant that someone was in trouble. "Silence, bird, or you'll never speak again," she said. The parrot's beak closed with a snap.

Grassina nodded, apparently satisfied. "Now let's get down to business." Pointing her finger at the old man once more, she recited a truthfulness spell.

> Let the truth be known to all.
> No more tales–short or tall.
> May the words we need to hear
> Pass from your lips to waiting ear.

From this day on, the truth you'll tell.
There's just one way to break the spell.
Three selfless acts you must perform
To aid a stranger who's forlorn.

It was a spell I'd heard before. Only a few months earlier a knight had boasted that he was responsible for the death of a dragon terrorizing a neighboring kingdom. When someone questioned the knight's story, Grassina was called in to verify the truth. It was an important point, for whoever had killed the dragon would win the hand of the princess and get half the kingdom. It turned out that a groom in the king's stable had really been responsible, which pleased the princess, for he was younger and much better-looking than the knight. The truth would probably never have come out if it hadn't been for Grassina.

As my aunt finished the spell, Olefat's eyes grew large and his hands began to shake. I wondered if he had heard of the spell and knew what it really meant. "You may talk now," said Grassina, "but I must say that you should be ashamed of yourself. It wasn't the first time you've done something like this, I warrant."

"No, I've done the same thing before." Even while he spoke, a look of horror altered Olefat's features. Stepping back, he clapped both hands over his mouth.

"Tell me, how did you get their memories?"

Olefat shook his head, but it didn't do him any good, for the words spilled out no matter what he did. "I bought a book from a merchant who didn't know what he was selling. Most of the spells were useless, but I tried the memory spell and it worked. I'm terrible at coming up with spells on my own, so I thought this was the perfect way to get some good ones."

The parrot squawked and flicked another seed at Olefat. "Stop talking, you idiot! You're going to tell her everything! Haven't you gotten us in enough trouble already?"

"I can't help it!" Olefat wailed.

Grassina's glance shifted from the parrot back to Olefat. "How did you get the ladies to come to the island?"

"I lied. I told them that I'd found some great swampland that was selling for next to nothing. When I gave them pictures, they wanted to leave right away."

"How did you get them all here?"

"That spell was in the book, too. The witches needed something as a focus, so I gave them bags of sand. I linked their brooms with a spell and took their memories the moment they landed."

Grassina nodded, as if something she'd suspected had just been confirmed. "Where is this book now?"

"Don't tell her, you idiot!" screeched the parrot.

Olefat struggled to keep his mouth closed, squeezing

his lips shut with his fingers. When he tried to speak anyway, his words were indistinguishable. Grassina sighed and reached out to pinch his nose so that he was forced to breathe through his mouth. The old man held out as long as he could, but when his face started to turn blue, he let go of his lips, gasped once and blurted out, "It's in the chest under the table!"

"Aagh!" shrieked the parrot. "Now you've done it, you old fool!"

Olefat began to weep enormous tears. When Grassina started toward the table, the parrot let out an earsplitting screech and flew at her in a flurry of beak and claws. I sensed movement beside me, and a furry body catapulted through the window. Although I hadn't known that Haywood had joined us, he seemed to know exactly what was going on. In a flash, he tackled the bird and had it pinned to the floor. The bird beat its wings in his face and tried to bite him, but I guess the otter was used to uncooperative food, for he knew how to hold it without getting hurt.

"Haywood, my darling, be careful!" Grassina said.

"I'm fine, my sweet," the otter assured her before turning back to the bird. Pressing down on the thrashing parrot, he said, "If you don't stop that right now, I'll rip off your beak and stuff it down your scruffy little throat."

The parrot's beak closed with a snap, and it jerked its

wings to its sides. "You wouldn't dare," said the parrot.

Haywood smiled grimly at the bird. "Try me."

"What's going on out there?" demanded a memory. "Who is that?"

"I heard my daughter Grassina," said my grandmother's voice. "I'd recognize the ungrateful wretch's voice anywhere."

My aunt's lip curled as if she'd tasted something foul. "Hello, Mother. If you don't mind, I'm a little busy now."

"What difference would it make if I did mind? My feelings never mattered to you before. But don't worry. I'll shut up and let you go about your important business, Lady High and Mighty!"

Ignoring the other memories who continued to mutter among themselves, my aunt raised the lid of the trunk and reached inside. When she sat back, she held a small brown volume in her hand. "Is this the book?" she asked, holding it up for Olefat to see.

The old man nodded, sniffling into his sleeve. His whole body seemed to slump.

"Good," she said, tucking the book into her pouch. "Then you won't be needing it anymore."

"In a way I'm glad someone showed up," said Olefat, wiping the tears from his cheeks. "Those old witches' memories were driving me crazy. You never met a nastier bunch of women. When I think about all the effort I put into this without getting much real information… They could gossip all right, and they loved to brag, but getting them to describe their actual spells—"

"Gossip?" shrilled a memory. "Did you hear that, ladies? The old geezer called us gossips! Just wait till we get our hands on you, you old—"

"You don't have hands!" Olefat said, smiling through his tears.

Grassina sighed and shook her head. "How do I return the memories to their owners?"

"Break the bottles," Olefat answered, gasping when he realized what he'd said. "But please, if you have any decency in you, let me go first. Those old bats would love to tear me apart!"

"After what you've done, that might be exactly what you deserve."

With an anguished groan, the old man fell to his knees and raised clasped hands to my aunt. "Please, I beg you, let me go!"

"Get up, old man, and get out of here. But you'd better hurry because I'm about to break every bottle in the room. These are all the bottles, aren't they?"

"Every one is on that shelf!"

Grassina reached toward a bottle. "Are you still here?" she asked Olefat.

"No! No, wait!" The old man moved faster than I thought possible. "Come along, Metoo," he said, snatching the parrot from Haywood. With the bird tucked under one arm, Olefat dragged the trunk out from under the table and climbed inside. The parrot hissed at the otter while the old man cast one last glance around the room before slamming the lid shut. I heard him mutter something, then the trunk began to move, rising off the floor and gliding out the door as smoothly as grease on water, passing Eadric and me on its way to the ocean.

Eight

As soon as Olefat was gone, Eadric and I hurried into the hut. We joined Grassina at the window to watch the trunk skim the tops of the waves. "That spell should put a crimp in his style, shouldn't it?" said Eadric.

"I hope so," said Grassina. She carried a black and green bottle to the window, where direct sunlight made it look diseased. "It almost seems a shame to let these go. The old witches are much nicer without their memories." Gesturing toward the shelf, she said, "Would you two like to help me with the bottles?"

Eadric grinned. "How can we resist?"

"I'll wait outside," said Haywood, and blew Grassina a kiss. "I'd just be in the way now."

"Thank you for all your help, my darling," called Grassina as the otter scurried out the door. "You were wonderful!"

We took turns smashing the bottles against the back wall, throwing them one at a time. As each bottle broke, the memories fled the hut in greasy, multicolored swirls. When all the bottles were broken, Eadric and I followed Grassina through the door, surprised to find that the sun was setting. We passed an angry group plotting their revenge on Olefat. Three witches had already set off in pursuit of the wizard.

We were crossing the beach when Haywood trotted over to join us. "Can we talk to your mother now?" he asked my aunt.

Grassina reached down to fondle his ears. "If we can find her. She may have left already."

We spotted my grandmother inspecting her broom near one of the huts. She had changed back into the black gown and pointy-toed shoes she normally wore.

"Mother, I need to speak with you," announced Grassina.

Grandmother swung around and glared at my aunt. "What is it? I'm in a hurry."

Slipping past Grassina, Haywood sat back on his haunches and stared up at my grandmother. "Hello, Olivene. Remember me?"

"By the breath of a cross-eyed bat, if it isn't that good-for-nothing Henley. So you finally found him, did you, Grassina? It took you longer than I thought it would, but then you always were a little slow. Tell me, daughter, what is he doing here?"

"Haywood and I still love each other, and we want to get married."

"So what's stopping you?"

Grassina sighed. "I've come to ask you to reverse the spell and turn Haywood back into a man. It's the least you can do since I saved your memory from Olefat."

Grandmother glanced at Haywood, who had chosen that moment to scrub his face with a paw. "You want a man, do you? There are enough men out there to pick from."

"But I want Haywood!"

This wasn't going at all the way I thought it would. Grandmother was supposed to be thankful and reasonable. Haywood was supposed to act less like an otter and more like a man. And Grassina wasn't supposed to lose her temper.

"Grandmother," I said, hoping to set things right, "I suggested they come. I know how much you've wanted more grandchildren, and I thought if they got married—"

"Why would I want another grandchild? The one I have is the greatest disappointment of my life! You refuse to follow the family trade, you let your mother bully you and you've never given a thought to what you want to do with yourself. When I was your age, I knew exactly what I wanted to do and I did it! You think everything should be handed to you on a platter, but life doesn't work that way. If you cared about your family, you'd live up to your responsibilities and learn to be a witch!"

"That isn't fair! I actually—"

"And as for you," she said, rounding on Grassina. "I may be old, but I haven't forgotten why I turned Horace into an otter in the first place. He doesn't have the talent the way you do. He comes from a family whose witches can't make a decent potion without reading it from a book. Forget about him. He's wasting your time and talents." With a wave of her hand and some foreign-sounding words, Grandmother gestured toward Haywood, who disappeared with an audible pop.

"Haywood!" screamed Grassina, her eyes wide with horror as she stared at the empty spot where the otter had just stood. "Mother, what have you done?"

"I've done you both a favor by sending him to a very nice place where he should be perfectly happy, if he survives. He's going to start forgetting you, Grassina. By the third day, he'll have forgotten that he was ever human. An hour after the sun rises on the fourth day, the change will be permanent. Now get out of my way. That half-baked wizard Olefat has a lot to answer for, and I'm going to make sure he has a miserable time doing it." Twirling her cloak around her shoulders, Grandmother swung her leg over her broom and leaned forward. Before my grandmother could take off, however,

Grassina darted in front of her and grabbed the broom handle.

"No, you don't, Mother!" Grassina said. "You're not leaving until you bring my Haywood back!" I had never seen my aunt so angry before. Her face was red and veins stood out on her forehead.

"Out of my way, you ninny!" screeched my grandmother. "It's not my fault that you're too dim-witted to know when someone's done you a good turn." She flicked her fingers at Grassina. Silver sparks shot from her fingertips, sizzling like fat on a hot pan. A spark landed on Grassina's wrist, burning her skin.

Grassina jumped back, gesturing with both hands while muttering something under her breath. A swirl of snowflakes whispered between the two women, extinguishing sparks with a hiss. When the snow cleared, my grandmother had already shot into the sky, cackling that nasty laugh of hers. "Horatio's not good enough for you, Grassina!" she screeched. "Forget about him!"

"That horrible witch!" exclaimed Grassina, scowling at my grandmother as she flew out of sight. "She can't do this to me again. I won't let her get away with it!"

I shook sparks from my skirt and resolved that I would never use my magic to hurt anyone. It hadn't occurred to me that my grandmother would try to hurt her own daughter.

"Now what am I going to do?" wailed my aunt.

"Even if I bring Haywood home before four days are up, Mother will refuse to change him back."

"You don't need her to do it! Eadric tried to tell you earlier—we overheard her explain to the other memories what you need to reverse it."

A gossamer hair from mother-of-pearl,
The breath of a dragon green.
A feather from an aged horse,
The husk of a magic bean.

Tears streamed down Grassina's face. I couldn't remember ever seeing my aunt cry before. "But I have to find Haywood!" she said. "I'm sure she sent him somewhere ghastly. I don't have time to find him *and* all those items."

"All you have to do is find Haywood," I said. "Eadric and I can start looking for the things you need. We'll meet you back at the castle. Today is Tuesday, so four days from now would be Saturday. If we work together, I'm sure we can do this."

"I don't know if I should let you," said Grassina. "It may be too dangerous. You'd need to look in the sea for the mother-of-pearl, and as to getting the dragon's breath—"

"That part should be easy. I already know where we can find a dragon. We came across one in the enchanted forest."

"I don't think—"

"Please, Grassina. It's my fault that you talked to Grandmother. If I hadn't been so sure that she would help us, we'd all be back at the castle right now and none of this would have happened. Please let me make it up to you. I can do this, I know I can."

"I can't—"

"You've helped me my whole life, and this is the first time I'll be able to do something for you. Please give me the chance."

Grassina wiped tears from her eyes with the back of her hand. "Are you sure about this? It won't be easy."

Eadric interrupted. "Of course we'll do it. Emma is your only niece, and I keep hoping that someday …" He put his arm around my shoulders.

"Then I suppose …" My aunt smiled feebly and reached for our hands. We took her hands in ours and held them tightly. "Thank you, Emma, Eadric," she said. "You don't know what this means to me. I need to go after Haywood before his trail gets cold. You may use the magic carpet, of course. I'll have it take you directly home. I already know where you can find the first item. Emma, open the silver chest in my bedchamber. Take the silver comb to the saltwater bowl. Run the comb through your hair three times, then do the same for Eadric. Put the comb in your pouch—keep it safe, for you'll need it to come back—and dip your hand in the salt water. This will take you into the sea, but don't worry, you'll be fine. When you get to the castle, ask for my friend Coral. She's a sea witch and she'll help you all she can. Be sure to take her a gift. When I come home, I'll get whatever you haven't located."

"How will you find Haywood without the carpet?"

"I have my ways." Sticking two fingers in her mouth, Grassina whistled, then turned back to me. "Tell your mother what your grandmother did. You can also tell her that she doesn't need to worry. I'll be home soon. Now climb on and be careful," she said as the carpet landed at our feet.

"How do you steer it?" I asked.

My aunt seemed edgy and impatient to go. She sighed and said, "I don't have time to show you now. It already knows the way home, so you won't have to worry about steering. Just say 'home' and it will do the rest."

Eadric and I looked at each other. He swallowed hard and said, "I'm ready when you are."

I nodded and tried not to think about falling off. Clenching my teeth, I stepped onto the carpet and sat down, taking deep breaths to calm my pounding heart. I was trying to get comfortable when my hand brushed the pouch hanging from my belt. "Maybe this could help," I said, taking out the string. "If I could turn this into some sort of strap to hold us on—"

"Emma, you clever girl! That's a marvelous idea."

Grassina's eyes lit up, and I realized that she was more worried about us than she let show. She gestured, and the string grew into a heavy cord that whipped around my waist, attaching itself to the carpet behind me.

I glanced at Eadric, who was secured as well. Although it wasn't much, it made me feel better. *Stay calm,* I told myself, closing my eyes as the carpet began to rise.

Nine

The flight back to the castle was nothing like our trip to the island. After I told the carpet, "home," it rotated until it faced the right direction and took off at a smooth and steady pace into the darkening sky. Eadric and I were tense at first, waiting for the ride to become bumpy or the carpet to suddenly go limp. When the flight remained uneventful, we both began to relax.

"You didn't ask me if I wanted to go," said Eadric, "but I really want to help you find those things for Grassina. She helped us break the spell and gave me back my life. I owe her, so I'm honor-bound to do whatever it takes to get her and Haywood together again. Anything less would be unworthy of a prince."

"I don't see how—"

"Anyway, I've been thinking about the things we have to find. Grassina said that her friend will help us locate the gossamer hair, and even I've heard of magic beans, so they can't be that hard to get. The feather of an aged horse might be tricky. I've never seen a horse with feathers, so I don't know how we'll handle that one. Your aunt will probably know what to do when she comes home. You were wrong about the dragons, though. It isn't going to be quick and easy, as you seem to think. 'The breath of a dragon green.'" Eadric shook his head. "It's too bad we don't have the vial I lugged around when I was a frog. That dragon's breath had lots of colors in it, and one of them must have been green. You don't suppose we could go find the swamp fairy and ask if we can have it back?"

"Even if we could find that fairy, and even if she agreed to give it back, there's no guarantee that the dragon who breathed into that vial was green. Breath of a dragon green isn't the same as green breath of a dragon. I think we're going to have to find a green dragon and get its breath somehow."

"I've had a few run-ins with dragons," said Eadric, "and they all have nasty tempers. Even when we find one, we can't just ask it to breathe into a vial. I'm going to need a new sword. I lost my old one in the swamp when that witch turned me into a frog. All I've got now is my dagger, and that's not nearly enough if I'm going to face a dragon. I've been thinking about that, too. Killing a dragon isn't so hard, but collecting its breath while it's still alive . . ." Eadric tapped his chin. "I suppose I could do it if the beast was asleep."

"Then that's our solution. I'll have a sleeping spell ready when—"

Eadric scowled. "I thought we'd get a sleeping potion."

"What would you do, toss the dragon meat laced with your potion and hope it eats the meat before it eats you?"

"I'd sooner do that than depend on your magic!" Eadric said. "For all I know, you'd put *us* to sleep instead of the dragon!"

"I'll have you know that my magic is getting better!"

"Oh, really? You already turned me into an old man with your magic, remember? I'll take my chances with a potion, if you don't mind. I'd rather you didn't come up with any more spells for a while. I think we'd both be better off without them."

"I didn't know you felt that way!"

"I didn't know you could be so stubborn!"

Eadric was right in a way. My magic wasn't very good yet, and it did complicate things. I didn't seem to be having any problems with the spells I read, only the ones I came up with myself. Grassina had told me to keep working on my magic, but maybe I should have just concentrated on learning the established spells. I seemed to have a good memory for spells, even though I'd never been very adept at remembering other things, like the social niceties my mother wanted me to learn.

The rest of the trip was spent in cold, miserable silence. I dozed for a time, coming fully awake as dawn was breaking behind the Purple Mountains. Although shrouded in mist, they were a lovely and welcome sight. Eadric woke when the carpet entered the tower window; the funny popping sound it made when the window widened was loud enough to wake the ghosts in the dungeon. The straps came undone as soon as we landed, slipping off us like an insult off an ogre. It felt good to have solid footing, and I bent and stretched, trying to work the kinks out of my legs and back.

Still refusing to talk to me, Eadric headed straight for the castle kitchen, but I wanted to say hello to Li'l first. I found her in the storage room, hanging from a rafter.

"So, there you are!" she said, sounding delighted to see me. "I heard you come in. Quick, tell me everything that happened."

I did, and I finished with the list of items we needed to transform Haywood. As it was Wednesday morning, we didn't have much time, so we'd have to go see Grassina's friend Coral as soon as we could. "And Grassina said that I should find a gift for the sea witch. Do you have any ideas?"

Li'l tilted her head and looked thoughtful. "I'd be happy to help, but I'm going to need time to think. Why don't you get something to eat before you scare everybody in the castle? Your stomach sounds like a dragon having a bad dream."

As I was leaving Grassina's apartment, I nearly ran into Eadric. He was juggling a tottering platter heaped high with cold roast duck, boiled partridge eggs, thick slices of dark bread and chunks of yellow cheese. "Hey!" he said. "What's the hurry?"

"I was heading to the kitchen."

He eyed the pile of food. "Good, then get me a couple more—"

Someone must have opened the door at the bottom of the steps, for suddenly the stairwell was flooded with noise. Because of the way the castle was constructed, anyone standing on the stairs could hear even the faintest sounds in the Great Hall when the connecting door was open. It sounded as if a large crowd had gathered and everyone was talking at once. Since one of the more distinctive voices was my mother's, I knew I probably couldn't avoid running into her if I went to the kitchen. I took my time going down the stairs while I thought about what I would say, scarcely noticing Eadric as he continued the list of food he wanted me to bring him.

Reaching the bottom of the steps, I saw that the Great Hall was bustling with servants, soldiers and courtiers. When I stepped into the room, I spotted my mother speaking with the castle steward. A short distance away, my father stood listening to the captain of the guard, who excused himself when he noticed me approaching.

"Father!" I said, pleased to see him. I would have liked it if he had opened his arms to me for a hug, but that was not his way. Skirting a trio of ladies-in-waiting, I bobbed my head to my mother, then hurried past her to my father's side. His smile was genuine, but the circles under his eyes and the weary stoop to his shoulders concerned me. My father was tall, with broad shoulders and blond hair turning to gray. A strong man, he feared little, so when I saw him looking worried, I worried as well.

"Your mother told me what happened to you," he said. "You must learn to be more careful."

"Of course, Father." I decided to postpone telling him about my latest adventures.

"Where is Grassina?" my mother asked, coming up from behind me. "I have to speak to her right away. Is she still upstairs?" Mother glanced toward the stairwell as if expecting my aunt to come down at any moment.

I shook my head. "She's not here. It was awful! When we asked Grandmother to help us, she refused, then banished Haywood to the wilderness. Grassina's gone to look for him. She said that you shouldn't worry."

Mother looked upset. "Of course I'll worry. Everything has gone wrong since she left. Limelyn, tell Emeralda about the spies."

The creases in my father's brow deepened. "All we

learned was that King Beltran had sent them to watch our family."

"Isn't King Beltran Prince Jorge's father?" I asked.

"Yes, unfortunately," said my mother. "I thought that if we made an alliance between our two countries, Beltran would leave us alone. He's coveted our western land for years. Your aunt Grassina's reputation for magic is the only reason he hasn't tried to take it by force."

My father nodded. "After we discovered Beltran's spies, I sent my own to his kingdom. I've just received their report. Jorge learned about your disappearance and thought that you had run away so you wouldn't have to marry him. When you returned with Prince Eadric, Jorge was convinced that he was right and swears that he no longer wants to marry you. Despite his son's wishes, Beltran plans to force the wedding. He's telling everyone that you and Jorge were officially betrothed and that you signed all the documents. I'm to give him half my western lands as your dowry."

"But that's ridiculous!" I exclaimed. "I never signed any documents, and there was no betrothal ceremony! And to demand that you give up land—"

"That's all he really wants. The rest is just an excuse," Mother said through clenched teeth. "I wouldn't let you marry that horrible man's son now for all the dust in East Aridia!"

"Beltran knows that the only way he'd get our land is

through force. He's called his men to arms," Father continued. "His spies have told him that Grassina is away, so he may well believe he has the opening he needs."

"This is the worst possible time for her to be running around in the wilderness," said my mother. "Greater Greensward has been at peace for centuries, although that could change if your aunt isn't here to use her magic. War can do horrible things to a kingdom."

I was puzzled. "How could Beltran's spies have told him about Grassina so quickly? She's been gone only a day."

"From the way they escaped, we think that at least one of the spies was a wizard," said my father. "They turned into birds and flew away."

My mother frowned. "That's why we need your aunt back here now. Your father is perfectly capable of dealing with any ordinary army. However, if Beltran has magic at his disposal, we need magic of our own."

"What can I do?"

"There really isn't anything—" Mother started.

"Please, Mother, there must be some way I can help. You've always said that I should take more interest in my duties as a princess."

"Very well, then. See if you can get Grassina home and focused on her work. She can't waste any more time on Haywood when she has a job to do here."

"I'll see what I can do. I already know what she needs

to turn Haywood back. Eadric and I are going to collect the items and—"

"Is he still here?" asked my mother. "Doesn't that boy have a home? It's bad enough that he ruined your reputation. Now we can't get rid of him. My steward has been complaining about him, too. It seems your Prince Eadric eats more than three knights."

"He's already been a big help—" I began.

My mother laughed. "I can't imagine how."

"And I'd be able to help Grassina better if Eadric was helping me."

Mother sighed. "I suppose he may stay, but only as long as he's being helpful."

"Has the young man given you any indication regarding his intentions toward you?" asked my father.

"He says he wants to marry me." I really hadn't wanted to tell my parents until I'd made up my mind, but I didn't want to lie about it, either.

"Perhaps it's his sense of chivalry that is making him say that," said my mother. "He must know that he's sullied your good name."

"I don't think that's it at all. I'm sure—"

My mother snorted, making a most unladylike sound. "You can't believe that he offered because he has feelings for you, Emeralda. You're too willful to make a good wife, and you're neither dainty nor delicate, as a princess should be. Heaven knows I've done what I could with you, but even I could only do so much. Since he's made an offer, however, my hard work must have had some effect."

If I didn't do something to stop her, my mother would be making wedding plans before I was even engaged. "I didn't accept his offer," I said.

Mother gasped. "What? I didn't realize that you were this foolish! His offer may be the only one you'll receive!"

"I didn't turn Eadric down; I just didn't say yes. I told him I'd have to think about it."

My mother's face was turning red. "This is preposterous. You should have jumped at the chance to …" She caught herself, and a slow smile softened her mouth. "No, wait, perhaps you're wiser than I realized. Sometimes playing hard to get—"

"I wasn't playing hard to get. I just don't know if I want to marry him."

"And that's exactly why you need your father and me, young lady," said my mother. "Without our guidance, you'd end up a pitiful old spinster like your aunt Grassina, and we would end up giving the country to relatives we don't even like."

I bit back the angry reply that burned in my throat. My aunt was far from pitiful and was only a few years older than my mother. Trying to look meeker than I felt, I thanked my parents for their advice and hurried to the kitchen, collected a hunk of bread and some cheese and left through the back door.

Eadric was still eating when I reached Grassina's rooms. He smiled at me, and I could tell that having food in his stomach had put him in a better mood, although he seemed a bit disappointed that I hadn't brought him more. While he nibbled a piece of duck, I told him about King Beltran and how he wanted to force me to marry Jorge.

Eadric's eyebrows shot up. "That's terrible!" he said. "He can't do that. You're going to marry me!"

"Jorge no longer wants to marry me, but my parents said that his father wants our western lands."

"I'll tell your father that I'll fight at his side. I know we aren't officially betrothed—"

"They said that the best thing we can do is help Grassina. They need her back here with her magic at full strength, and that means we have to help her take care of Haywood."

"Then that's what we'll do, but as soon as we've finished, I'm joining your father."

"I know he'd appreciate your help," I said. "You two will probably get along well together. You both enjoy a lot of the same things. My mother's a different story, though. Unless she decides that she likes you, she can be very unpleasant."

"Then I'll just have to get her to like me," Eadric

said, popping another egg in his mouth with greasy fingers.

"I hope you have better luck at that than I have. Even though she's my mother, I don't think she ever really liked me. But you have one factor in your favor that I never had—you're a boy."

While Eadric finished eating, I excused myself and went into the storage room to look for a gift for Coral. Li'l was inside, perched atop an old, dusty trunk that reminded me of Olefat's, except this one was in much sadder shape. Battered and dented, its surface was covered with grainy and badly pitted dark green leather. I couldn't understand why anyone would choose a hide of this type.

"What is that?" I asked, running my hand over the uneven surface.

"I asked your aunt that same question," said Li'l. "She said it's the skin off a troll's backside." Grimacing, I snatched my hand away and rubbed it on my skirt. "It's supposed to be tough and last a long time. That's the trunk your grandmother gave Grassina when the old woman retired. I thought we could look inside for a gift for that sea witch, although I have a few other things we could look at if there's nothing in there. Lift the lid and we'll take a peek. It's too heavy for me."

The little bat fluttered to the top of the magic mirror propped against the wall, leaving me standing by the trunk. Gritting my teeth, I grabbed hold of the lid and shoved.

It opened with the groan of ancient hinges, and I imagined that it was the voice of the long-dead troll. Kneeling on the floor, I reached into the shadowy recesses and began to take items out one at a time while Li'l named the things she recognized.

A ridged tooth as long as my thumb dangled from a golden chain. Li'l gasped, claiming it was from a manticore. The stiff gray hairs tied with silver thread were bundled werewolf whiskers. An ancient jar of yellow, crusty flakes was a collection of goblin earwax. Another jar held jagged black crescents that Li'l identified as nail clippings from an ogre. The little bat hissed when I held up a jar containing coarse, stringy hair caked with something brown and glossy. Shuddering, Li'l told me that it was the hair from a harpy and could empty even the largest castle with its stench.

I had just set the jar back in the trunk when Eadric stepped into the room. "Find anything yet?" he asked.

"Nothing we'd want to give anyone." I closed the lid of the trunk before he could dig around inside. "Li'l, didn't you say that you might have some other things?"

"There's the golden feather from the golden goose, but I don't think you'll want to take that. It has golden bird lice on it," Li'l said. "They're a pretty color, but they sure do tickle."

"And that's it?" I asked.

"There is something else in a little box behind the mirror, but I don't think you'll want it, either."

I found the box easily enough. When I opened the lid, there was only one thing inside: a silver hairpin with a ruby head shaped like a fish. "What's wrong with it, Li'l? Was it dipped in poison? Does it make the wearer sleep forever or turn her into a fish? What does it do?"

"That's just it. It doesn't do anything."

"So why wouldn't I want to take it?"

"Because it doesn't have any magic. I thought you wanted something special, and that pin is boring."

"A fish-shaped ruby is perfect for a mermaid! Since she's a magical being, she probably has all sorts of magical things already. We'll take the pin. I'm sure she'll like it." The box was too big to fit in my pouch, so I took the pin out and pushed it through the fabric of my sleeve until I was sure it was secure.

I had turned around to show Eadric when I heard Li'l exclaim, "What's that? Is it alive?"

"What are you talking about?" I asked.

"There, in the back," said Li'l, pointing at my gown with her wing.

I grabbed the back of my skirt and pulled it around to get a better look. I didn't see anything unusual until Eadric reached down and plucked something from my hem.

"Would you look at this!" he said, holding up a little

green crab identical to those we'd seen on the island.

I bent down for a closer look. "How did that get there?"

I'd thought the island crabs couldn't talk, so I was surprised when the little creature spoke. "I saw you change from a green hopping thing into a human," the crab said in a scratchy voice. "I wanted to see you do it again so I could learn how to do it, too. I've been holding on ever since you walked past. My claws are tired!"

"I can't show you how to turn into a human," I said. "I was a human before I was a frog, and I was just turning back. I've never heard of an animal turning into a human."

"I have," said Li'l, "but it hardly ever works out. Life as a human is too confusing, and the animal usually ends up feeling miserable."

Eadric waggled the crab, and its legs flapped. "What do you want to do with this thing, Emma? I think you should save it for Haywood. You know how much he likes to eat crabs."

The crab's claws stiffened, and it twisted its eyestalks to look at me. "Is Haywood that fuzzy monster that was eating my friends?"

I nodded. "He's an otter, and he likes to eat lots of things."

"Please," said the crab, pulling its little legs in toward its body. "Don't let that monster eat me! Surely I could come in handy someday!"

I hadn't liked watching Haywood eat the other crabs, and I already knew I didn't want him to eat this one, but I couldn't imagine what a crab could possibly do for me.

"I swear you won't regret letting me go!" said the crab, its eyestalks waving wildly above its head.

"Oh, really! And where am I supposed to put you?"

"I heard you talking about visiting a sea witch. You could take me with you."

I sighed. "I'll see what I can do. What's your name?"

"Shelton, which I think is a very good name for a crab. We pick our own names, you know, and I thought about it a long time before I chose it. My brother's name is Crabicus, but I don't like that one nearly as well. One of my sisters has an even funnier name. It's—"

"Here," I said, handing the crab to Eadric. "You hold him while I get the comb."

Eadric's jaw dropped. "Hold him? Why don't I just chuck him out the window and he can go live in the moat? The last thing we need is a crab tagging along."

"Be nice! You're a prince and you're supposed to set an example," I said.

"But he's just a—"

"And yesterday you were just a frog, remember? A frog who had friends who were also frogs. Think of him as a very small subject and you might find being nice a little easier."

Turning my back on Eadric and the crab, I hurried into Grassina's bedchamber and knelt beside her silver chest. Banded with silver straps, it was smaller and newer than the chest that held her clothes. I opened the lid and found the comb resting atop a creamy fabric embroidered with dragons. Shaped like a seashell, the silver comb was embedded with little pink pieces of coral. It was lovely, although it looked very fragile.

With the comb in my hand, I bade farewell to Li'l and joined Eadric by the saltwater bowl. Although I'd sometimes seen schools of miniature fish weaving back and forth through the bowl, the water now appeared empty except for the tiny castle. Perfect in every detail, the castle had two turrets and a few dozen windows, but as far as I could see, it had only one door, which appeared to be less than an inch high.

Ten

Eadric was staring at the bowl with a skeptical look on his face.

"Are you sure you want to go with me?" I asked. "You don't have to, you know. You can stay here until Grassina gets back."

"I'm going," he said. "Although that bowl is awfully small."

"We'll just have to use the comb and see what happens. I'm sure Grassina knows what she's doing."

"Maybe, maybe not," said Eadric. "Look at the way she handled your grandmother, not to mention the flying carpet. Here—if you want to take the crab, you'll have to carry him. I can't stand his chattering." Eadric handed Shelton to me and wiped his fingers on his tunic.

I glanced at the little creature. "I didn't know you were royalty when I met you," the crab said. "It's too bad, too, because I'm sure my family would have wanted to come with us if they'd known. My sisters—"

I shook my head. "No more talking, please. We have important work to do, so you'll have to be quiet."

"If that's what you really want, Your Highness, but I know all sorts of—"

"Starting now!" I said. Waving his eyestalks, Shelton scampered into my loose sleeve, pulling the lace down behind him.

I took a deep breath to calm my nerves, then undid my hair from its plait and separated the sections with my fingers. Before I could change my mind, I pulled the comb through my hair three times, then did the same for Eadric. I tucked the comb into my pouch, reached for Eadric's hand, and dipped my free hand into the salt water. There was a sound in my head like a thousand bubbles popping, and the next thing I knew we were swimming in the salt water, fully clothed.

I could see the outline of the bowl and the room beyond it, but they were enormous and far away. The castle lay below us, bigger than I'd thought it would be, although in every other regard it looked the same. To my amazement, I could breathe underwater and it seemed perfectly natural. Since Eadric looked the way he always did, I assumed that I did as well, so I knew we hadn't grown gills or turned into merpeople.

Enjoying our new ability, we smiled at each other and then turned toward the castle. It was obvious that Eadric had some experience swimming as a human, but I had not, and so I resorted to the strokes I'd used as a frog. It was awkward, as the fabric of my long gown hampered the movement of my legs.

The castle door had looked ordinary from a distance, but upon closer inspection, we found that it was made of a single slab of a smooth, white material, like a fragment of a giant seashell. We knocked, and after a few minutes a strange creature with a soft, sack-shaped body and eight ropelike arms answered the door. When it saw us, it blushed a fiery red and flung one of its arms across the doorway, blocking us from entering.

"What do you want?" said the creature, examining us with two bulging eyes that moved independently of each other.

Flustered by the way it was looking at us, I cleared my throat and said, "We've come to see Coral, the sea witch."

"Well, then, hurry and come inside before you let the cold water in."

The water seemed warm enough to me, but I followed the creature inside with Eadric bumping into me from behind. Once the door was closed, the creature looked us over again as if it wasn't sure it should have let us in.

"Wait here," it said, and floated through a nearby opening, leaving us standing in a narrow hallway.

I was tugging on my hair, gathering it into my hands,

when I realized that someone had entered the hall. Turning my head, I saw Eadric's face first, his expression so foolish that I had a good idea who it was before I even saw her.

"May I help you?" asked a voice melodious enough to make a nightingale sound like a half-strangled dog. When I saw her, I understood Eadric's reaction. She was gorgeous, with silver and dark blue hair even longer than mine, slanted dark blue eyes and pale skin with a faint tinge of green.

"I'm Emma, and this is my friend Eadric," I said, before Eadric could say anything. "My aunt Grassina suggested that we come visit you, if you're Coral, that is."

"I remember you!" said the sea witch. "I saw you in your aunt's room when you were just a little girl. You looked almost as surprised as I felt."

"That was me," I said.

"Come in, come in!" she said, ushering us down the hall. "You're just in time to join us for lunch. I have some friends over today and we were about to start, but there's plenty of room and more food than we could possibly eat."

"I don't know if we have time for—" I began.

Eadric grabbed my arm and pulled me toward him. "Be polite," he whispered in my ear, adding in a louder voice, "That would be wonderful."

We followed Coral through the door, down a short hallway and into a magnificent room. The walls and high ceiling were pink coral, the floor a bed of pure white sand. A table and eight chairs carved from some enormous creature's bones occupied the center of the room. Purple and yellow fanlike decorations had been arranged in a centerpiece around which tiny pink and yellow fish darted.

"These are my friends," Coral said, gesturing to five beautiful mermaids seated around the table. "This is Marina." A young mermaid with violet hair and amethyst eyes smiled in greeting. Another was named Kelpia and had dark green hair pulled back by two living starfish. Sandy had pale blond hair laced with darker strands of gold. She nodded hello to me, then turned and blew a kiss to Eadric. I was watching the color creep up his cheeks, so I almost didn't catch Pearl's name; she was a mermaid with striking silver eyes and pure white hair. At the far end of the table sat Starr, whose scarlet locks made my own hair look washed out. Each sat with her fishlike tail curled under her chair. Each had skin that bore at least a touch of green. Food and a room full of beautiful, green-skinned women. Eadric would certainly like it here!

"My friends and I have been rehearsing all morning," said Coral. "We get together to sing a few times a week. People call us the Sirens."

Eadric's eyes lit up. "I think I've heard of you. Aren't you the ones who sing to passing sailors?"

Starr shook her head and sighed. "Don't believe everything you hear. We never try to lure them onto the rocks. We're not responsible for the things our audience does."

Gliding to the head of the table, our hostess gestured toward two chairs. "Please be seated."

Eadric darted ahead, taking the chair beside Sandy, the blond mermaid, and leaving me the seat next to Coral. I was happy to sit beside my aunt's friend, but I was annoyed with Eadric, who was behaving as if I didn't exist. I bumped his arm to get his attention. When he didn't seem to notice, I decided to ignore him and let him make a fool of himself. I don't know what he said to Sandy, just that she found it terribly funny and burst into dainty peals of laughter that couldn't have been more unlike my laugh. I wondered how he would act toward her if I turned her into a patch of algae.

We hadn't been seated for long when the sacklike creature entered the room bearing four large bowls wrapped in four of its arms. A small parade of lobsters and snails followed. Using its free arms, the sack-creature picked up the first pair of lobsters and snails and dropped them on the table. After the monster had set a bowl on the snail's shell, the lobster climbed aboard. I couldn't imagine what was going on until the snail inched its way to Coral's plate. The mermaid nodded and the lobster dipped its claws into the bowl, serving her a portion of seaweed.

The snails continued their circuit around the table even after everyone had been served, perhaps on the chance that someone might want more. Each of the four serving bowls held some kind of seaweed. I suppose they were different, but they all looked alike to me, and I found myself wishing I'd eaten more bread and cheese when I'd had the chance.

Served raw, the seaweed was chewy, hard to swallow and too salty for me. After the first few bites, I just pushed it around my plate, wishing that a few large dogs sat under the table waiting for scraps the way they did at home.

I'd almost convinced myself to take another bite when Coral leaned toward me and said, "Now tell me, Emma, what is the reason for this delightful visit?"

I set down my fork, grateful for the excuse. "Actually, we're looking for something and hoped that you might be able to help us. We need to find some mother-of-pearl."

Coral smiled. "Is that all? Then you need look no further. I have some very fine specimens here in the castle. Octavius, please bring us one of the shells."

The sack-creature had been waiting in the corner so quietly that I'd forgotten that it was there. When it left the room, its eight arms appeared to ooze bonelessly across the floor, while the one eye that I could see jerked back and forth, looking first in one direction, then another.

"I don't mean to be nosy," I said, turning to Coral, "but how did you get a sea monster to work for you?"

Coral giggled and covered her mouth with her hand. "Octavius isn't a sea monster, he's an octopus! They make the best butlers. I don't know what I'd do without him. He can do more than one job at a time, and he's all the defense I need."

Octavius returned only a few minutes later with a large seashell. Extending his arm, he set it on the table in front of me. I heard a tiny pop as a disc on one of his arms let go of the shell, which looked like a flattened wheat bun sprinkled with sugar. Rubbing my fingers along a row of small holes, I wondered why anyone would think it special.

"Turn it over," urged Kelpia. The shell was rough and coarse, so I was surprised when I flipped it over and found a smooth, lustrous lining of creamy white with pink and blue shimmering highlights.

"Now, that's mother-of-pearl!" said Starr, the mermaid with the scarlet hair.

It was beautiful, but it wasn't at all what I'd expected. I must have let my disappointment show, for Coral asked, "What's wrong?"

"Nothing's wrong," I said. "It's just that I don't see any hair."

A wave of laughter swept through the room. "Why in Neptune's name would you expect to find hair?" giggled Starr.

"It has to have hair. We've come here to get a gossamer hair of mother-of-pearl."

Someone gasped. I looked around and saw the white-haired mermaid cover her mouth with her hand and flee the room, knocking over her chair. The other mermaids looked away, avoiding my eyes as if I'd done something shameful. "What is it?" I asked. "Did I say something wrong?"

Coral shook her head, making her hair swirl around her like a blue halo. "Not really. Pearl's just a little sensitive about her mother. Whoever told you to get a gossamer hair of mother-of-pearl was trying to trick you. There is no hair on mother-of-pearl. However, the mother of Pearl is Nastia Nautica, who has hair so fine it's almost transparent. I suppose you can call it gossamer. Why do you need this hair?"

"It's one of the things we need to turn Grassina's betrothed back into his human self. My grandmother changed him into an otter and—"

Coral clasped her hands in front of her chin and beamed. "You mean Grassina finally found Haywood? But that's wonderful! Of course we'll help you get the hair. I'll talk to Pearl about it. Under the circumstances, I'm sure she'll be glad to take you."

Kelpia cleared her throat and gave Coral a look.

"Maybe *glad* isn't the right word," said Coral, "but Pearl has heard Grassina's story and I'm sure she'll do it. We mermaids have soft spots in our hearts when it comes to true love. You stay here and finish your meal. I'll go talk to her."

I felt awful about upsetting Pearl, but I had no idea how to apologize. "I didn't mean to—"

"You couldn't have known," said Kelpia. "Pearl's mother is a sea witch, and she's a great embarrassment to our sweet Pearl. If you really want that hair, you're going to have to see her yourself." Leaning toward me, she lowered her voice. "Just be careful when you go. Nastia's nickname is Nasty for a reason. Not all sea witches are as nice as Coral."

Eleven

"I'll take you to see my mother," said Pearl, "but I can't guarantee that she'll help you."

"I understand," I said. "I can't make promises for my mother, either."

"My sisters have already moved to another ocean to get away from her. I'm sorry I overreacted at Coral's, but I couldn't bear hearing my friends talk about Mother. It's just that she's always doing things.... You'll see what I mean when you meet her."

As we swam, I began to envy Pearl's lack of confining clothes. Blue and green scales covered her from the waist down, while shells and some kind of sea foam dressed her upper body. A string of seed pearls woven into her hair kept it under control. Unhampered by trailing fabric or constricting laces, Pearl's movements were so fluid, they appeared effortless. I was fascinated by the way her tail moved up and down and by how quickly it could propel her through the water. My clumsy attempts at swimming were as exhausting as they were slow.

After crossing the bare ocean floor, we entered a kind of forest composed of a great stand of seaweed swaying in the current. Alleyways opened and closed with the movement of the plants, confusing the way.

"We're getting close," Pearl told us after some time. "I'll help you however I can, but you're going to have to do whatever my mother says if you want that hair. Tell her that you've come to ask a favor of her. She'll give you a task to perform. Once you've completed it, you should ask for the hair."

"I'm sure we can handle it," said Eadric, resting his hand on my shoulder. I was still annoyed with him for the way he'd acted in Coral's castle, so I shook off his hand and swam after Pearl, leaving him to follow as best he could.

The seaweed parted, revealing the hulk of a round-bellied ship lying on its side. A gaping hole exposed the heavy planking and allowed us easy access. Pearl led us through the dimly lit interior, stopping here and there to point out handholds that we should avoid or rotten sections of flooring that would crumble if touched. Brightly colored fish darted out of our way, while a long, snakelike creature with a flattened tail wiggled past. What light there was slanted through holes in the hull at strange angles. I tried to picture where we were in the ship.

Entering a short passageway, we reached a large cabin that appeared to be someone's living quarters. My eyes were drawn to an opening in the opposite wall where a wide window must have provided the captain with a wonderful view of the ship's wake. A high-backed chair sat facing the window, angled so that anyone sitting there could watch the creatures swimming by.

"What do you want, Pearl?" asked a voice from the chair, and I realized that someone was in the room with us.

"Some friends of mine have come to see you, Mother," said the mermaid, motioning for us to stay back. "They have a favor to ask."

An old sea witch rose from the chair and floated toward us. Her hair was indeed so fine as to be almost transparent. Her scales, which reached her collarbone, were a dark shade of green. Her nose was thin and pointed; her pale green skin was taut, as if she defied wrinkles to appear. Yet it was her eyes that made me stop and stare. They were terrifying, so dark and lifeless that they seemed to be two black holes.

"A favor?" said the sea witch. "You mean they didn't come here just to gawk?"

"A favor, yes, that's right," I said, embarrassed that I'd been caught staring.

Something inside a sea chest growled. Snatching a long pole from where it leaned against the wall, Nastia

Nautica rapped the chest until the growling stopped. When the sea witch turned to me, I shrank back from those terrible eyes. "Before you can ask a favor, you must earn the right. Bring me the giant pearl that the ancient sea monster guards before the sun sets this day and I will grant your favor. However, if you don't succeed, I will cut off your heads and feed them to the sharks." Raising her arm, the sea witch pointed at a wall where a long-bladed knife rested on two curving hooks. I gulped and backed away.

Pearl's mouth dropped open when she heard her mother's threat, but her amazement quickly turned into anger. "A beheading, Mother? Isn't that a little severe?"

"Not if they want a favor."

"But they're friends of mine. You can't threaten to cut off my friends' heads!"

"I can do whatever I want to, my dear. This is my home, and they came here to ask something of me."

"You're always saying, 'Pearl, why don't you ever introduce me to your friends?' This is why, Mother! This is exactly why I never bring my friends around! I like my friends the way they are—with their heads still attached!"

Eadric took my arm and pulled me to the side. "Maybe we'd better go," he whispered. "We don't want to get in the middle of a family argument."

I nodded. "We can come back later."

"Believe what you want, daughter. Your friends will

have to get that pearl from the sea monster or I'm using my carving knife!"

We fled the cabin without waiting to hear the end of their argument. The moment we were outside the wreck, Eadric turned to me and said, "Emma, we're going home. That sea witch is crazy. No hair is worth losing your head! I'm sure your aunt wouldn't want you to take any unreasonable risks, and I'd call this unreasonable."

Getting the hair was going to be far more dangerous than I'd expected. If Grassina knew what the old sea witch had threatened to do, she would have whisked us away in an instant, but she wasn't there and I couldn't forget the look of fear in my mother's eyes and the worry on my father's face.

"I can't give up now, Eadric. You can go home, but if I don't get that hair, Grassina won't be able to turn Haywood back and she won't be in any condition to help my father. If Greater Greensward goes to war without any magic on its side, East Aridia will win, my father will lose his western land and I'll have to marry Jorge. I am going to get that hair with or without your help!"

"Huh," grunted Eadric. "If you put it that way… We should hurry if we're going to find that pearl before sunset."

Suddenly, someone raced through the gap in the wall. I thought it was Nastia Nautica coming to cut off our heads without giving us a chance, but I was wrong. It was Pearl.

"I wanted to tell you where to find the sea monster. It never occurs to my mother to give directions. The seaweed thins out on this side of the ship. Swim straight ahead until you're in the clear. Follow the first reef you come to. It will look like a ridge made of coral. When you reach a gap in the reef, turn right. Look for the biggest cave and you'll find the sea monster. It's one of the old species that you don't see very often anymore. The Old Wizard of the Sea cast a spell on it so it would guard the pearl until he came back. It's been there for as long as anyone can remember. Do you have all that?"

"Sure," said Eadric, tapping his forehead. "I've got a mind like a wolf trap."

I rolled my eyes. "Thanks for your help, Pearl."

Pearl shrugged. "Any friend of Coral's is a friend of mine. I should keep an eye on Mother and make sure she doesn't pull any of her tricks. See you when you get back."

Twelve

The seaweed thinned after only a few yards. We spotted the reef right away, a great colony of coral that must have been growing for many years. The pinks, greens, yellows and oranges were as beautiful as any flower garden, the branching towers more intricate than any castle ever built. We passed sea fans like those that had decorated Coral's table and fish so brilliantly colored they could rival the most exotic birds. More than once I noticed eyes watching us from niches and tails disappearing into crannies.

The reef curved like the arc of a giant circle, seeming to go on forever, but we finally reached the gap Coral had mentioned. A sunken island lay ahead, its base riddled with caves, its top worn away by the scouring waves. Even from a distance, we could tell which cave was the largest because the others were small nooks in comparison. Jagged rocks guarded both the ceiling and the floor of the wide entrance.

Swimming toward the cave, we searched for some sign of the sea monster. There was nothing that might indicate that a monster lived there, no pile of bones, no scarring of the ocean floor, no ominous growl or glint of hungry eyes. Instead, yellow and turquoise fish darted through the entrance, flashing here and there as they changed direction. I followed Eadric into the cave; the rocks were sharp, snagging my skirt and tearing it. Smaller rocks, equally jagged and dangerous, protruded from the ground beside the larger ones. I tried not to touch the floor, for it looked odd—red, soft and squishy like a strange kind of coral that grew sideways rather than up. The cave was fairly large, nearly twelve feet across, but there was no sign of the pearl. There was a narrow opening at the back of the cave, however, and I had the awful feeling that there was where we'd have to go.

Eadric agreed. "Let me go first," he said. "I've dealt with more monsters than you have."

"What are you talking about? You don't know any more about sea monsters than I do."

"Monsters are monsters, no matter where you find them." Eadric peered into the opening and waved me back. "There's a passage here. You'd better stay behind. It's so dark I can't see a thing."

"Wait a minute. It's too cramped for a witches' light, but I have a candle I can use." Fumbling in my pouch, I took out the candle stub that Grassina had given me. "Let me think about this for a minute. I've never tried to light a candle underwater before."

Since it was such an unusual situation, I was sure I had never read a spell that would fit. I concentrated, picturing what I wanted and trying to think of the words that would get it for me. Eadric had started to fidget by the time I finally said,

> Little candle burning bright,
> Make the day out of the night.
> On the land or in the sea
> Keep your wick aflame for me.

With a muffled hiss, the candle lit itself, although its light wasn't nearly as bright as it would have been on land. "Will this do?" I asked, handing it to Eadric.

"As long as it doesn't go out," he said. "Who knows what we'll find in there?"

I followed Eadric as closely as I could, trying not to bump into him. Being near him made me feel a little safer, although I was still so nervous that I jumped at the slightest thing. When a fish swam past and its tail brushed my cheek, I shrieked and grabbed Eadric's arm, certain that the monster had found us.

"What is it?" Eadric asked, whirling around with his dagger in his hand.

I felt my face grow warm. "Nothing. Never mind. It was just a fish."

"Huh," he grunted, shaking his head. Feeling like a fool who jumps on a chair when she sees a mouse, I resolved to be braver next time, no matter what I saw.

As the passage narrowed even more, Eadric's body blocked most of the light, but I could see that the walls were ridged and kind of squishy. Something wasn't right.

When the passage widened into a small chamber, Eadric paused to look around. "Do you see anything?" I asked as he held the candle high.

"No monster, but I think I see the pearl. That thing is huge!"

"Let me look," I said, trying to see past him.

Caught in a swirl of seaweed on the floor of the chamber, the pearl was enormous. It was almost the same size as my head, yet perfectly round and pure white. Handing me the candle, Eadric bent down and reached for the pearl. When he tried to pick it up, he couldn't budge it. "Something is holding it," he said.

Eadric braced himself to try again and was able to lift the pearl a few inches. "Maybe if I help," I said, wrapping my arms around his waist and adding my strength to his.

The pearl came away from the floor, inch by inch, until whatever had been holding it suddenly let go and we flew backward, hitting the opposite wall with a splat. Slimy globs dripped from the pearl, coating Eadric's hands. When we stood, we saw a depression where the pearl had been attached. Glistening with an oily sheen, a liquid heavier than water bubbled from the depression until it overflowed onto the floor.

I felt a tremor beneath my feet. "Eadric," I said, but he was too engrossed in the pearl to notice. Another tremor, stronger than the first, made Eadric look up in surprise.

"What was that?" demanded a familiar voice. I glanced down and saw the little green crab climbing up from the folds of my hem. "You forgot about me already, didn't you? I know it's because I'm so little. If I were as big as one of my brothers, you'd never forget that I was around. My brother Clawson—"

The next tremor was enough to make me stagger.

"What are you waiting for?" asked the little crab. "Get out of here while you still can! I'm a little dizzy, but it looks to me like those walls are moving in."

"Eadric," I said, "we've got to go!"

He put his hand on the small of my back and propelled me toward the passage. "You go first."

With the little crab tickling my arm as he crawled into my sleeve, I dove toward the opening. We had gone only a few feet when the walls pressed close enough to brush my shoulders, and Eadric had to turn sideways to move at all. My heart was pounding, but I kept going, determined not to panic in front of Eadric.

The walls continued to close in until they were squeezing me. Many years ago, one of the ghosts in the dungeon had died by being buried alive under a collapsed wall, and he had described it to me in horrible detail. I had had nightmares about it for weeks. I felt like I was living one of those nightmares now.

I squirmed, forcing my way between the walls. The pressure would have been tremendous if the walls hadn't been so soft. I dug my fingers into their surface, dragging myself forward while they squeezed the breath out of me. Suddenly I reached the end, popping out of the passage like a seed from a grape. When I turned to help Eadric, his arm and shoulder were already emerging, but the pearl held in the crook of his arm seemed to be in the way. I wrapped my fingers around the pearl and braced my feet against the wall. Tugging as hard as I could, I pulled the pearl free. A moment later, Eadric slipped out.

We were back in the larger cave and all I wanted to do was leave, so I was horrified when I saw that the opening had disappeared. The ceiling was lower, and the jagged rocks now met, blocking our way. I set my feet down but regretted it immediately, since the floor started to writhe and take shape beneath me. It wasn't a floor at all, but a giant pink sluglike creature that rose up and slapped me against the back wall. Stunned, I drifted helplessly.

When I opened my eyes, I saw Eadric wrestling the monster in a dim half-light. I shuddered when something moved across my arm. It was Shelton, brandishing the fish-headed pin that he had pulled from my sleeve. "What is he thinking?" grumbled the crab, waving his eyestalks at Eadric. "You can't fight a sea monster that way!" Pushing away from me, the little crab swam toward the monster while holding the pin with his big front claw. Shouting, "Leave him alone, you ruffian!" he jabbed the pin into the fleshy slug.

The slug retreated momentarily, then reared up once again and slapped Eadric, spinning him around until he slammed into the wall. I flailed my arms, trying to stay out of the monster's way.

"Take this!" yelled Shelton, plunging the pin into the slug again. A moment later, Eadric had his dagger in his hand and was slashing at the flapping, squirming monster.

The candle was lost somewhere in the cave, but the rocks blocking the entrance allowed a small amount of light to enter. I was watching Eadric and Shelton, wishing that I had a weapon as well, when I noticed that the monster always stayed in the front of the cave, making it more vulnerable to attack. It was almost as if it was anchored in place. I studied the monster, following its silhouette to the floor of the cave and gasped. The monster *was* attached to the ground, but that wasn't all. Its soft pink body *became* the ground and led all the way back to … I couldn't believe how blind I'd been. If I hadn't expected to find a sea monster hiding in a cave, I might have realized the truth sooner, but to have gone so long without knowing …

"Eadric," I shouted. "That's not the sea monster. We're *inside* the sea monster. The thing you're fighting is just its tongue!"

"Its tongue?" he shouted, backing away while droplets of the monster's blood formed a haze around his dagger.

"We have to get out of here! The monster is trying to push us back down its throat. It's trying to swallow us! Those rocks must be its teeth."

Shelton paddled furiously toward me, grabbing hold of my shoulder. His wiggling eyestalks tickled my ear. "We're in for it now!" wailed Shelton. "This reminds me of the time—"

"Emma," said Eadric, "please do something about that crab before I forget how nice I'm supposed to be."

"I think we have something else to worry about now," I said.

Although the tongue had retreated under Eadric's assault, its tip was probing the sides of the cavelike mouth. We tried to swim away, but it wouldn't be long before the tongue found us and drove us back.

The monster growled, a deafening sound that hurt my ears and shook me until my bones rattled, but I wasn't going to let it stop me. It was up to me to come up with a spell, whether Eadric liked it or not. I evaded the tongue while I tried to think of the right words. Somehow, knowing what kind of creature we were dealing with made it a little less scary. "All right, monster," I said at last. "Your people-eating days are over."

Teach this monster, let him know,
That he cannot treat us so!
Where his gums are strong and firm,
Make his teeth loose, make them squirm.

Make them loose until they jiggle,
Make them looser till they wiggle.
So we're not killed while in our youth,
Make him lose each great big tooth.

There was a crackling sound, and one by one, the monster's oversized teeth came loose, although the smaller row beside it was untouched. It wasn't dramatic, but it was effective just the same.

"Now you've got it!" shouted the crab. Two more teeth wiggled in the monster's gums, tumbling to the floor of its mouth. As one tooth after another sagged and fell out of his jaw, the sea monster opened his mouth and howled. Propelled by the blast rushing from the monster's throat, we tumbled head over heels out of its mouth and past the coral reef before hitting the ocean floor.

I rolled to a stop yards away from Eadric. Dizzy and shaken, I staggered to my feet and asked him, "Are you all right?"

Eadric rubbed his shoulder and winced. "Uh-huh. How about you? I thought you were too frightened to be of much use in there, but you were actually pretty brave."

"Not brave, just desperate."

Eadric shrugged. "Sometimes there isn't much difference between the two. So how about a kiss? I think we should celebrate."

"Celebrate what?"

"After what we just went through? Being alive, for one; getting the pearl, for another. And what about your second successful spur-of-the-moment spell?"

"I'll feel more like celebrating after we give this to Nastia Nautica and get a hair from her," I said, tapping the pearl. Something tugged at my sleeve, and I looked down to see the little crab swinging from the fabric, his eyestalks crossed and his legs shaking. I dumped the pearl in Eadric's lap. "How are you?" I asked the crab. When I realized that he was still holding the pin like a tiny sword, I took it away and tucked it in my pouch.

"Nothing wrong with me!" Shelton said as I set him more firmly on my shoulder. "I have felt better, though. Why, just the other day I was saying to my brother—"

"Tell us later," Eadric interrupted. "We'd better get moving. That monster could be anywhere. Look!" he said, pointing back the way we had come.

The monster was gone, and I wondered what had happened to it until I noticed a mottled gray shape curled between the sunken island and the coral reef. It had a blunt head, short grasping arms, a tall, curved back fin and a long, pronged tail. Knowing the size of the head gave us a better idea how big the sea monster really was; it was enormous and could easily have wrapped itself around Aunt Grassina's tower.

The creature moaned, a strange wavering sound that left my bones vibrating. Keeping near the ground in the hope that we wouldn't be observed, Eadric and I swam to the coral reef, staying as close to it as we dared. With the water growing dark around us, I knew that dusk was approaching and we would have to hurry if we were to get the pearl to the witch in time.

Skirting the coral reef, we saw menacing shapes with curved fins and pointed faces circling overhead. Eadric swam near me, his dagger in his hand, his eyes moving constantly as he tried to keep watch in every direction.

When we reached the wreck, it was surprisingly quiet, with only the creaking of the timbers and the mysterious thuds and whistles that we always seemed to hear in the ocean. Pearl greeted us at the door while her mother, Nastia Nautica, remained in the high-backed chair facing the wide window in the stern.

"We got it!" Eadric held the pearl so that the last of the light shone on its creamy surface.

"Mother will be pleased," whispered Pearl.

When Nastia Nautica neither turned around nor acknowledged us in any way, I began to wonder what was wrong. Gesturing to Eadric to stay where he was, I swam around the side of the sea witch's chair and peeked at her. She sat slumped in her seat with her head tilted back. Bubbles drifted from her open mouth, and I could see her eyes moving beneath their closed lids. "Is she all right?" I whispered to Pearl.

"She's fine," said Pearl. "I sang her a lullaby and put her to sleep. She'll be furious when she wakes up, but by then you'll be long gone and she won't have any power over you since you've accomplished the task."

Eadric looked appalled. "Why would you want to put your mother to sleep?"

"You should be glad I did. She told me that if you brought the pearl, she was going to have you steal the crown of the Sea Worm King, a ridiculous request since the crown is useless to anyone who isn't a worm. It's so typical of my mother. She's never been able to live up to her end of a bargain without adding other conditions."

Mother used to tell my sisters and me that she'd give us a treat if we picked up our toys. When we did, she'd make us polish her barnacles or brush the sharks' teeth before we saw any treat. It's why my sisters, Clamela and Anemone, left home as soon as they were old enough. I'll probably join them one of these days."

Pearl held out her hand, opening it to reveal a single strand of gossamer hair. "Here, I got the hair for you. I knew that if you asked her for it, she'd never give it to you, even if you met all her demands. You can't trust her at all. It's gotten so bad that everyone considers her the white cod of the family. I'm the only one who will even talk to her anymore."

I tucked the hair in my pouch and was pulling the drawstring closed when I pricked my finger, drawing a bead of blood. It was the pin decorated with the ruby fish. Pearl deserved a gift for all she'd done, so I took it out and handed it to her. "This is for you. Thank you for the hair and for your help. I'm glad we don't have to go on another errand—the last one was bad enough."

"What a lovely pin!" she said, her eyes sparkling.

"I'm afraid it doesn't have any magic."

"Pah! I have enough magic as it is. It will be a relief not to have to worry about what might happen when I'm wearing it."

Eadric was already backing toward the door. "I'm looking forward to going home. Ready, Emma?"

"Aren't you forgetting something?" I asked.

He had both arms wrapped around the pearl, and I think he was hoping that no one would notice. "Oh, yeah," he said, looking sheepish. "Here, Pearl. Please give it to your mother."

Pearl smiled and reached out her hands. "I'll make sure she gets it."

Thirteen

We had worked our way through the seaweed and were swimming side by side when I glanced at Eadric and was surprised to see that he looked worried. "Is something bothering you?" I asked. "We got the pearl there in time and we have the hair now, so everything is fine, isn't it?"

Eadric frowned. "Why did you give away the pin we'd brought for Coral? Now we don't have a gift for her."

"I guess I wasn't thinking," I said. "I know how fairies act when you don't give them a gift they'd been expecting. I hope Coral isn't like that."

"Why does everyone forget about me?" asked the crab, tugging on my sleeve. "If it's because of my size, I'll be molting soon and then I'll be much bigger."

"What about you?" growled Eadric. "We're not giving you a gift, if that's what you're thinking."

"No, no, no! I don't want a gift, although that would be nice. Maybe if you—"

"Shelton!" I could see Coral's castle up ahead, and I didn't want to arrive at her door arguing with a crab.

"I was just going to say that I could *be* a gift for Coral. I like it here, and there wasn't much for me back at your castle, Princess. If you want to say that I'm the gift, I wouldn't mind at all. As soon as I realized that they were weeditarians—"

"Weeditarians?" Eadric asked.

"You know, people who eat only seaweed. As I was saying, since they're weeditarians, they're not about to eat me, so I'm sure I'd be safe here. Much safer than at your castle once that awful otter comes home. So, what do you say? May I be the gift, because it would be the answer to both our problems, don't you think?"

We had almost reached Coral's castle, and I didn't have much time to consider my decision. "If that's what you really want," I said. If the little crab annoyed Coral as much as he did Eadric, she might come to resent my gift … and me. On the other hand, we didn't have anything else to give her, and Shelton did want to stay.

"Shelton, let me get this straight," said Eadric. "According to your theory, people who eat weeds are weeditarians. What about animals who eat humans? Say, dragons, for instance. Would you call them humanitarians?"

"Maybe," said Shelton, "depending on who it is they eat!"

Seeing movement out of the corner of my eye, I turned my head to look. One of the sharp-faced creatures had come to examine us more closely. "Gentlemen," I said. "I think we have company." I darted to the castle door and tried the latch, but it was locked. Eadric turned to face the creature, bracing himself in the sand. While he guarded my back, I banged on the door as loudly as I could, which isn't easy underwater. "Hurry up, Octavius," I yelled. "Please open this door!"

"That's a shark," said Shelton. "Some are nice enough, but others are nasty. See the way he's looking at us? It's all right as long as he looks, but be careful when he comes closer. I've heard some really scary stories about those guys. Remind me to tell you about the one who—"

"Will you please get that crab to be quiet!" Eadric said. He had his dagger back in his fist and was trying to stay between the shark and me.

"Shelton!" I said, shaking my arm to get his attention.

"I got the point!" said the little crab, scrambling into my sleeve.

The shark was closer now, so close that we could see its cold, round eye staring at us. "Shelton," whispered Eadric without turning his head. "Do sharks have any weak spots?"

The little crab poked his eyestalks out of my sleeve. "You're asking me? I thought you wanted me to be quiet!"

"Shelton!" I cried.

"Oh, all right! I've heard that they'll go away if you hit them on the nose with something heavy. Keep in mind I don't know anyone who's actually done it, so it may not even be true. I'm kind of small to try it myself, but you can if you want to."

Eadric grunted. "Thanks for nothing, Shelton. Watch out. It looks like it's coming this way." Eadric pushed me against the door, then stood with his back to me, his feet firmly planted, the dagger clenched in his fist. I held my breath as it came straight at him, veering off at the last second.

"Got any spells in mind?" Eadric said so softly that I could hardly hear him.

"You'll have to give me a minute."

"I don't know if I have a minute to give you."

"Then I'll do the best I can. Here goes."

You don't want us in your belly.
We'll taste bad, like stinging jelly.
Turn around and head straight back.
We would make a lousy snack.

"Is that supposed to make a shark decide that he doesn't want to eat you?" said Shelton from the depths of my sleeve. "Because I think I've heard that some sharks eat jellyfish, although I may be wrong."

"Emma," said Eadric, "he isn't going away."

"Sorry about that. I told you I needed more time."

"Get ready," said Eadric. "Here he comes!"

I was furiously trying to think of a better spell when the door jerked open and a voice snarled, "What, may I ask, are you doing?"

"It's a shark, Octavius, and it's—"

"Oh," he said, and suddenly his arms seemed to be everywhere. He wrapped one around my waist, and another around Eadric, then dragged us both through the opening. A third arm was yanking the door shut as a gaping mouthful of teeth hurtled toward us. Octavius slammed the door an instant before the shark hit it with a resounding bang.

"That was close!" I said, rubbing my head where I had bumped it on the wall.

Eadric helped me to my feet. "Time to go," he said.

Octavius had barred the castle door. Loud thuds told us that the shark was trying to bash its way in.

"Thank you for your help!" I told the octopus as we followed him down the hall.

"It was nothing. I was merely keeping out some of the riffraff. It's a shame I can't keep it all out," he said.

I swam closer to Eadric and whispered in his ear, "Were we just insulted?"

"Lady Coral," said Octavius, leading us into a little sitting room. "They're back."

"Wonderful!" declared the sea witch. "I was beginning to worry."

"*You* were worried?" said Shelton. "You should have been there. If you had seen what I saw, you would have been worried from the start."

Tilting her head to one side, Coral raised an eyebrow. "Who are you?" she asked.

"This is Shelton," I said, not sure how to introduce him. "He's—"

"I'm your present!" said the little crab. "They want to thank you for everything you've done. And I must say that you have a lovely place here. It's certainly prettier than that other sea witch's home, although not nearly as well located."

"Thanks, Shelton," I said, certain that Coral wouldn't want such a chatterbox. "As for your present—"

"He's delightful! Thank you for such a thoughtful gift. Everyone gives me combs and jewels for my hair, but you can only use so many. A nice little crab who can keep me company is a wonderful idea. Octavius isn't much of a conversationalist. We'll get along very well, won't we, Shelton?"

"You bet, Miss Coral. Why, I can tell you some great stories. And I know—"

"We'd better be going," said Eadric. "If you could show us the way?"

"Of course. Octavius will guide you to the door."

Coral took a tiny glass bell from a nearby table and rang it. "Give my love to Grassina, and please come back again to visit. I enjoyed meeting you both. Now, Shelton," she said, setting the little crab on the chair beside her, "tell me all about yourself."

Eadric grinned. "That should take a while."

"Hmph," said Octavius, who was waiting in the doorway. "Please follow me."

"What about the shark?" I asked the octopus.

"It won't bother you. The world beyond the shell door follows its own rules. Whatever happens in the waters around the castle will not affect the waters beyond that door."

Good! I thought. I'd already seen enough big, sharp teeth to last me a lifetime.

The shell door wasn't far from the sitting room, and I could hear the murmur of Coral's and Shelton's voices all the way down the hall. They must have been enjoying each other's company, for the last things I heard before the door shut behind us were the high-pitched giggles of a beautiful sea witch and a funny little crab.

Fourteen

We were standing beside the tank with water pouring from our clothes when we heard Li'l's cheerful voice. "Hi!" she said. "How'd it go?"

"Li'l, where are you?" I asked, trying to find her in the darkened room.

"Can't you see me over here?" The little bat gasped. "Don't tell me that salt water makes you go blind! Because if it does—"

"No, Li'l, it's just dark in here, that's all. Do you mind if we have some light?"

"Well, of course! I keep forgetting that just because it's light enough for me, that doesn't mean—"

"Lights!" I said, flicking my fingers toward the ceiling where the witches' lights bumped together. A rosy glow filled the room, making everything look soft and dreamy.

"So you're back!" said a voice, and I turned to see Grassina emerge from her bedchamber. Her face was pale and she had large, dark circles under eyes red and swollen from crying. "Here, let me help you with those wet clothes." Pointing her finger at us, she muttered a few words. There was a blast of warm air, and our clothes were dry, although my dress suddenly felt a size smaller and Eadric's tunic looked shorter. Maybe Mother had been right when she said that Grassina might find it difficult to concentrate on magic that didn't concern Haywood.

"Thank goodness you're home!" I said. "Are you all right? Have you spoken with my mother?"

Grassina scowled. "She pounced on me the minute I got back. Your mother always has been a worrier. I've already checked out Beltran's wizard, and he won't be a problem. He's Olefat's brother, Olebald, and he's even less competent than his sibling. I can't do anything about him until he crosses our border, so it will have to wait until after I've seen to Haywood."

"Where did you find Haywood?" I asked my aunt.

"I haven't yet," she said as fresh tears trickled down her cheeks. "My mother is wicked! I'll never forgive her as long as I live. She laid false trails, and I'm still trying to find the real one. I came to pick up a few things. I'll be leaving again soon."

"But what about Beltran? Mother says that—"

"I told you, there's nothing to worry about." Grassina sounded impatient. "Your mother jumps at shadows. Right now the only thing that concerns me is taking care of my darling Haywood."

"Is there anything I can do to help?"

"Just tell me what you've gotten so far and what you still need to find."

"It wasn't exactly what we expected, but we got the gossamer hair of mother of Pearl." I opened my pouch and handed the hair to Grassina. "And here's your comb," I said, handing her that as well. "Your friends were very helpful."

"Can they have the fruit tarts now?" said Li'l.

Grassina shrugged. "They can if they're hungry."

"I love those things!" Eadric said, hurrying toward the table where Li'l had just uncovered a platter of tarts. After stuffing a tart in his mouth, he carried the platter to the soft, moss-colored carpet in front of the hearth. I sat down beside him and held my hands toward the warmth of the fire.

Li'l landed on the floor and cocked her head to the side. Peering up at me, she asked, "What else do you need to get?"

"Since we have the hair, we need the breath of a dragon green, a feather from an aged horse, and the husk of a magic bean."

"You don't have to get them in any special order." Grassina wiped her eyes with the back of her hand and settled into one of the chairs. "And I know where you can go next, although you'll have to wait until tomorrow morning. You need your rest, and the magic market is closed now, anyway." She pointed at the tapestry behind me, and I turned around to look.

It was an old tapestry that had hung on the wall since before I was born. The picture showed a town centered around a marketplace; it was fairly dark now, with only a few lights glowing in the windows. When I was younger, I'd spent hours studying it, delighted with the way it changed from one second to the next.

"Not only is that the map of a real place," said Grassina, "it's also the best way to reach the magic market. Just touch the wall surrounding the fountain and you'll go straight there. Touch it again when you want to come home. You should be able to get the magic beans at one of the stalls, and someone might have the feather or the dragon's breath as well."

"Do you think they sell swords at that market?" asked Eadric. "I need to get a new one."

"They probably do," said Grassina. "They sell just about everything there."

I gave my aunt a sketchy account of our trip into the saltwater bowl, leaving out a few details like the sea monster, the shark, and Nastia Nautica's threat to chop off our heads. I'd tell her later, when she didn't have so much else to worry her.

"I want to thank you," Grassina said when I'd

finished my tale. "You don't know how much it means to me that you two are helping." She smiled at us through drying tears. "I couldn't possibly look for Haywood as well as find those things. I don't know what I'd do without you."

"We're glad we can help," I said.

After saying good night, I went downstairs to sleep in my own bed. Tired as I was, I still couldn't fall asleep because I couldn't stop worrying. Without Grassina's help, my father's men would be unprepared to face an opponent armed with magic, yet my aunt wasn't doing a thing about it. If only I hadn't led her to Haywood. If only I hadn't persuaded her to go see Grandmother! I didn't agree with my mother very often, but this time I couldn't help feeling that she was right to worry. Even if Grassina couldn't do anything until Beltran crossed the border, she should be trying to find out what he had planned. When I finally drifted off, my dreams were filled with weaponless soldiers marching into battle against some faceless horror. I didn't stop tossing and turning until I'd heard a rooster crow at one of the neighboring farms.

When I woke later that morning, my stomach was already growling, so I headed to the kitchen for something more substantial than fruit tarts. I saw more soldiers than usual on the way there, including some I'd never seen before. The cooks were busy, but they took the time to tell me that Eadric had come and gone already, having eaten enough for two grown men. He was considered a phenomenon in the kitchen, and the cooks and scullery maids were keeping a running bet on how much he could eat.

I was on my way out, my stomach pleasantly full, when I ran into my mother. "Did you talk to Grassina last night?" she asked. "What did she tell you?"

"She said that she can't do anything until Beltran has crossed the border."

Mother bit her lip and nodded. "That's what she told me, too, but she's wrong, you know. There are so many things she could be doing to get ready. I'd feel much better if only she would make some sort of effort."

"I'm sure she knows what she's doing," I said, although I really didn't believe it.

"I hope you're right. I can't talk to her anymore. She's too distracted to concentrate on anything important and only wants to talk about Haywood. I couldn't dissuade her from leaving again, although I told her that she should stay here and plan her strategy. The woman has lost all sense of responsibility to this kingdom. She was so distraught. If she isn't able to find Haywood or turn him back into a man, I'm afraid she might become melancholy, and then she'll be no use to anyone. That's what happened the first time he disappeared, you know."

I left my mother talking to her ladies-in-waiting and hurried through the crowded halls. Armed soldiers stood guard outside the throne room door, further evidence that my father was preparing for war. Reaching my aunt's rooms, I found Eadric waiting in a chair by the fireplace and Li'l seated on Grassina's worktable beside a small cloth bag.

"Grassina left last night after you went to bed," the little bat said. "She asked me to give you this."

"What is it?" I asked. Peeking inside, I saw a handful of coins.

"It should be enough for the magic beans," said Li'l. "Now you'd better go. You're already getting a late start."

Although the tapestry took up a large part of one wall, the picture of the fountain wasn't very big. Our fingers covered most of it when Eadric and I touched it at the same time. I knew it was woven cloth, but the picture felt as cold and smooth as real stone. A rush of air made me blink; there was a brief sensation of flying, and suddenly we were standing beside a marble fountain.

The fountain was on a small raised platform, giving us a good view of the market. Pausing at the top of the steps, I tried to make sense of the market's layout, but the arrangement of stalls and carts didn't seem to be in any order. "Let's look around," said Eadric, taking the steps two at a time.

A yellow canopy the color of daisies shaded the stall at the bottom of the steps. Pictures of tankards had been worked into the canopy's fabric, and on the shelf running the length of the stall a dozen pewter tankards rested, polished and ready for sale. Eadric stopped a few yards away, his mouth gaping in disbelief. A gray tabby cat with white paws stood behind the counter, polishing a tankard it had taken from a crate.

"Will you look at that!" said Eadric, staring at the cat.

"Close your mouth, Eadric," I said, nudging him with my elbow. "It's not polite to stare."

"But he's a cat—"

"And this is a *magic* marketplace. You can't expect it to be like a normal one."

"Tankards for sale!" sang the cat. "Bottomless tankards for sale here! Never run out of ale again. Fill it once and it stays filled, no matter how much you drink."

"My uncle would like one of those," said Eadric. "Except he'd find it a challenge and try to drink it dry."

"We're not here to buy gifts for people. We're here for the bean, remember?"

"The bean—right. Hey, cat," said Eadric, "do you

know where we can buy a magic bean?"

"No, sorry, mate. I'm new here and don't know the other stalls yet. You might ask the dog two stalls over. He makes deliveries and seems to know his way around. Can I interest you in a tankard?"

"Maybe another time. Thanks, cat."

The pale blue canopy of the next stall showed a picture of a cloud, its cheeks puffed out with lines curling away from its mouth as if it was blowing something.

"What do you have there?" Eadric asked, pointing to a carved wooden box resting on the counter.

A young man with straw-colored hair flipped open the lid and removed four slim pieces of glass dangling from a round silver plate. A silver cylinder hung in the midst of the glass pieces, and as we watched, the man tapped the cylinder. It bumped against the glass strips, setting off a tinkling chime. A breeze sprang up in the stall, ruffling Eadric's hair and the few curls that had sprung loose from my braid.

"You see," said the young man, tapping the cylinder again and setting off a brisker wind. "It's a wind chime, and its operation is simple. Each touch amplifies the effect. Amaze your friends, confound your enemies, command the wind whenever you wish!"

"We have other shopping to do first," I said, seeing from the expression on Eadric's face that he was wavering.

The cat had mentioned a dog at the second stall over,

but the only occupant was an old woman dressed all in blue. "May I help you, young miss?" she asked. "I have some lovely stones for sale." Setting a small chest on the counter, she lifted the lid, displaying an assortment of colored stones. "Stones for every occasion—stones that can make you successful or brave, stones that will cure a stomach ailment or make a toothache go away. These purple stones will banish bad dreams if that's what's troubling you." She held a violet-colored stone in the sunlight.

"It's very nice, I'm sure, but it's not what I'm looking for. Actually, I was told that a dog worked at this stall who might be able to help us. He makes deliveries."

The old woman pursed her lips and shut the lid with a snap. "Oh, you want Archie. He's off on a delivery now, and I don't expect him back anytime soon."

"We're looking for a magic bean. Do *you* know where I could purchase one?"

"A magic bean, you say?" The woman shook her head. "Sorry, I can't help you with that."

A knot formed in the pit of my stomach. Finding the bean might not be as easy as I'd thought.

"Emma, come over here!" called Eadric from a stall on the other side of the narrow alley. A beefy man stood behind the counter holding a stout stick in his hand. Stuffing dribbled from a cloth dummy hanging from a post in the corner. "This stick is amazing! Watch what it can do." Eadric nodded to the man.

"Beat it, stick," said the man, tossing the stick at the dummy. Whirling through the air, the stick beat the cloth body with loud thwacks and puffs of dust. The dummy swung from the pole, twisting and turning with every whack of the merciless stick until I thought its seams couldn't possibly hold together any longer.

"You use it if someone tries to steal from you," explained Eadric. "You never know when you might meet a thief."

I shook my head and started to walk away. "I don't think so. It would be just as easy for the stick to be used against the owner as against a thief. I'll take my chances without the stick, thank you."

Eadric ran after me. "But Emma, you take too many chances. At least with the stick I'd know you were safe."

"I *am* safe," I said, giving Eadric my most dazzling smile. "I have you with me, don't I?"

Eadric appeared to be speechless. He stared at me for a moment, perhaps to see if I was joking, but I didn't let him see how I really felt. I didn't want a stick to protect me; I could protect myself.

"You're right," he said, shrugging. "Let's go find that bean."

We continued between the stalls, pausing to examine the items that interested us, like the acorns that could hold an entire wardrobe and the shoes that could carry a person enormous distances, but we still didn't see the dog or hear anyone hawking fresh vegetables. I was beginning to wonder if we'd ever find the stall when I saw a little dog with white, fluffy fur carrying a leather bag in his mouth.

"Pardon me," I called to the dog. "Are you Archie?"

The little dog stopped abruptly and turned to look at me, the bag gripped tightly between his teeth. He nodded without opening his mouth.

"We were told that you might know where we can find someone who sells magic beans," I said.

Archie tilted his head to one side and looked me up and down. I must have passed his inspection, because he set the bag on the ground, although he was careful to place both front feet on top of it. "Look for the stall with the dark green canopy. Old man Bosely is the only one I know who sells magic beans. If he's not there, ask Milky White. She's learning the trade."

"Who is Milky White?" I asked, but the little dog had already grabbed his bag and trotted off through the crowd, his plumed tail swishing.

I found Eadric nibbling the leg of a roast partridge. He offered me a wing and didn't seem offended when I refused.

"We need to look for a green canopy, a man named Bosely and someone called Milky White," I said.

"It must be another cat. I can't believe what they

have these cats doing. I'll tell you, though, that cat back there really knows how to cook a partridge," he said, smacking his lips.

It took us a while to work our way across the marketplace, as Eadric wanted to stop at every food stall. It wasn't until we'd reached the last row of vendors that we found the right one. A large stall shaded by a canopy of darkest green, it reminded me of the velvet-lined chest where my mother kept her jewels. The colors were more brilliant than those of ordinary vegetables—ruby apples, amethyst plums, topaz squash, and sapphire berries. I saw fruits and vegetables that I had never seen before, like the long yellow fruit that grew in bunches like fingers, and enormous striped melons as big as a horse's head. They seemed to have everything—everything but beans.

A man with a scraggly beard and a shock of white hair watched us approach. He was so short that his chin could have rested on the countertop, yet his hands were enormous and I could see the swell of his muscles under his brown jerkin. The cow standing behind him was entirely white but for the tip of her nose and her enormous dark eyes. I decided that she had to be Milky White.

I was opening my mouth to ask about the bean when Eadric reached for a plum, squeezing it between his thumb and forefinger. The man's eyes were crossed, so it was hard to tell exactly where he was looking, but it was clear that he'd noticed Eadric. "Can I help you?" he said. "We have a policy here—you touch it, you buy it." He pointed to a sign on the table written in glowing script.

You touch it, you buy it.
No free samples. No refunds.
Shoplifters will be persecuted by harpies.

"How many plums would you like?" the man asked. "They're magic plums, so they're guaranteed to be delicious."

"Four," said Eadric.

"What we're really looking for are magic beans," I said.

The man shifted his gaze in my direction. "We don't have any now. They're not in season. Come back in six months. We should have some by then."

"We need them to counteract a spell," said Eadric. "We can't wait six months!"

"Sorry, I can't help you. I traded my last beans for Milky White. That'll be one penny for four plums."

"Is there anyone else who might have some?" I asked. "Maybe Milky White's former owner could spare one."

The cow blinked her long, dark lashes. "Those are

gone, too. Jack told me that his mother threw them out the window when he brought them home."

Bosely grunted and scratched his nose. "As I said, come back in six months. You can buy as many beans as you want then."

Fifteen

Unwilling to give up yet, we wandered through the marketplace, asking merchants about magic beans. Most of them looked at us as if we were crazy and said, "Not at this time of year." Others were sneakier, acting as though they might know, then trying to sell us their own merchandise instead.

Although we weren't having any luck finding a bean, we did come across a lot of other tempting magical goods for sale. I was examining a quill pen that never needed dipping when someone screeched, "Emeralda!" from across the marketplace. I cringed, recognizing my grandmother's voice.

"What are you doing here?" she called, elbowing people aside.

"Looking for a gift for Mother," I said. It was as likely an excuse as any, although I doubted my mother would really want anything from a magic marketplace. I had no intention of telling Grandmother about our real errand, however.

Grandmother rubbed the tip of her long nose and squinted. "My cat tells me that you've begun practicing magic. It's about time. Are you any good at it?"

"I can do a few spells," I said. Eadric coughed and I felt my face grow hot, but my grandmother didn't seem to notice.

"Excellent. Keep studying. We need more witches in our family. Come see me when you're ready to learn from an expert!" It was the first time in my life that I'd earned my grandmother's approval, and I wasn't sure what to say. "You haven't seen Olefat, have you?" she asked. "I tracked the old scoundrel here, but he's good at hiding."

I shook my head. "I haven't seen him."

Her gaze darted around the marketplace, settling on a pudgy witch carrying a large woven basket only a few stalls away. "I almost had him in Arabia, but he disguised himself as a dancing girl and hid in the sultan's palace."

"Olefat?" said Eadric, his eyebrow quirked in surprise. "He's an old man!"

"You'd be amazed what a few veils can hide." Squinting, Grandmother stared at the witch and said, "There, on her shoulders. Does that look like birdseed to you?"

The specks on her cloak could have been seeds, although I couldn't really tell from a distance. "Maybe," I began, but Grandmother was already scurrying toward the other stall.

A green feathered head popped above the rim of the pudgy witch's basket. "They're here!" shrilled a distinctive voice as Metoo flapped his wings, making the basket lurch and bounce.

"Not now, you stupid bird!" shouted the witch, struggling to hold on to the basket. Olefat was wearing a disguise so good, I wouldn't have recognized him if I hadn't heard his voice. The hood of his cape covered his head, and he wore a long black dress much like my grandmother's. He'd shaved off his beard and mustache and darkened his skin. When he saw my grandmother jostling her way through the crowd, his eyes went wide and he stepped back a pace, then turned and darted toward the fountain.

"Stop him!" screamed Grandmother. At the sound of her voice, a half dozen furious old witches began to run after Olefat. I recognized them as some of the witches from the retirement community.

Olefat pounded up the steps to the fountain, his heels kicking up his hem, while Metoo squawked and floundered about in the basket. I was surprised to see how fast my grandmother could run once she was free of the crowd. Even so, she was only at the bottom of the steps when Olefat reached out his hand and touched the low wall surrounding the fountain. Grandmother cursed and flung herself at the old wizard as the air shimmered around him. She was too late: he disappeared seconds before her hand slapped the wall. The air shimmered again, then suddenly she was gone as well.

"Why didn't she use magic to catch him?" Eadric asked.

I shrugged, looking up when a merchant standing nearby answered. "Only licensed magic works inside the town limits. The merchants' guild handles the licenses, and they've placed a damper over the town to prevent the use of random magic. Without a damper, unscrupulous customers could steal whatever they wanted and no one could trace them."

Eadric nodded. "Maybe that's why Olefat thought it was safe to come here."

"But won't they end up in the same place?" I asked. "She touched the wall, too."

"They'll go back to wherever they came from," said the merchant. "Can't say where that might be."

We continued on for a few more minutes and had reached the section of the marketplace where potions were sold when we heard shouting. A crowd was running toward us, growing louder and more frantic. Something roared in a voice so loud that the shutters behind me shook. I covered my ringing ears with my hands, while Eadric clapped his hand to his dagger. "I have *got* to get a sword!" he said, his eyes scanning the crowd as he looked for the source of danger.

The crowd opened up, revealing a black-maned lion

and a silver-horned unicorn facing each other. The unicorn screamed, rearing up on his hind legs to crush the lion's skull with his flailing hooves. As the unicorn was about to strike, the lion leaped aside, then turned to slash at his opponent with raking claws. The same people who had been so eager to get away moments before now seemed more interested in gawking.

"We'd better go," I said. "We don't have time to stay and watch."

"I want to see how it ends."

"Fine," I said, starting to walk. "You stay here while I keep looking."

"Can't you wait another minute?"

"Not if we want to look for the bean *and* a sword."

"Oh, right," said Eadric, hurrying after me.

I was almost ready to abandon our search for the bean, when we reached a stall with a faded gray canopy and an assortment of merchandise for sale. A white-haired old woman looked up as we drew near. She smiled toothlessly and said, "What can I do for you?" Even if she'd had teeth, her appearance would have been unusual, since she had only one eye and it never seemed to look directly at us, rolling around in its socket as if it had a life of its own.

"We're looking for magic beans," Eadric said bluntly. "Do you have any?"

"You're out of luck. No beans this time of year.

They're out of season."

"Maybe you can still help us," I said to the old woman. "Do you know anyone who has dragon's breath for sale? Or a horse feather or two?"

"Dragon's breath is rare. It's too hard to collect without getting fried. I've never heard of horse feathers. Are you sure someone isn't playing a trick on you?"

"It's possible, but it isn't likely. We'll just have to keep looking," I said and began to turn away.

"Perhaps I have something else you might like. Let me see." The old woman bent over, reaching under the counter for something, but as she leaned down, her eye popped out, rolled across the counter and fell to the ground with a soft plop.

Eadric bent down to search the ground for the eye. *He's a kind person,* I thought, watching him pick up the filthy eye and hand it to the old witch. A lot of people wouldn't have wanted to touch it.

"Thanks," said the woman. "I used to have a jar of them, but my husband took it when he ran off with a younger witch. When I finally caught up with him, he and his little tart had already broken up and he'd left the eyes with her. I never did find out the name of the witch or what had become of my jar of eyeballs."

"Really?" I said. "I might know where they are."

The old woman gasped as her mouth dropped open, giving off an odor that made my eyes water. "Where are they? Tell me where they are and I'll give you your beans!"

"I thought you said you didn't have any," said Eadric.

"That was before I knew you had something I wanted. I always like to keep a couple on hand. You never know when they might be useful. Tell me, where is my jar of eyeballs?"

"Well, I don't actually know that they're *your* eyeballs," I began.

The old woman waved her hand, dismissing any question of ownership. "That doesn't matter. I'll know them when I see them. Where are they?"

"The beans first," said Eadric.

The witch reached for a box tucked beneath the counter. Hefting it onto the wooden board, she rummaged through it while muttering under her breath. "Magic buckles, magic baubles, magic bones … ah, here they are—magic beans!" Taking two shriveled yellow things from the dirt in the bottom of the box, she held them up between her thumb and forefinger, showing them to Eadric and me. "Now, tell me about my eyeballs."

"Wait a minute," said Eadric. "What are those?"

"Magic beans, of course. They may be old, but they're still potent! If you don't want them, you can wait six months for fresh ones."

"Never mind," he grumbled. "I guess they'll do."

The old woman turned to me. "My eyeballs?" she prompted.

"I saw a jar filled with eyeballs in a witch's cottage about a week ago," I said. Eadric and I had been stuck in the cottage when we were frogs, but I wasn't about to tell her that.

"Were they alive?" the old woman asked, holding her breath.

"Yes, very much so. They kept looking at me."

She clapped her hands, unable to control her glee. "And where is this cottage?"

"In the enchanted woods at the edge of Greater Greensward."

"That's all I need to know! Thanks! Enjoy your beans!" she said dropping them into Eadric's outstretched hand. Grabbing a box from under the counter, the old woman dashed from her stall.

"Now we can go see about your sword," I said, pleased with our newest acquisition. "If we hurry, we can be back at the castle before dinner."

Laughing, Eadric set his hands on my waist and picked me up, spinning me around until I was dizzy. "This day has turned out better than I thought it would! We got your beans, I'm going to get my sword and we'll still be at your castle in time for a hot meal. How about a kiss to celebrate?"

"You and your celebrating! Are you sure we have

time for a kiss? Shouldn't we hurry before all the swords are sold?"

"I hadn't thought of that!" he said, setting me down so fast that my teeth clacked together. "You can give me that kiss later."

"Wait! I just thought that—" But Eadric was already gone, disappearing between the stalls as he rushed to find the armorers' section of the market. I hurried after him, not sure where we should be looking, so I was surprised when I heard someone singing and realized from its words that it was a sword.

Alas, my master, you do me wrong,
To cut me off from sight and song.
For I can serve you oh so well,
Fighting better and faster than any!

It was still singing when I reached the stall where Eadric stood in line, a look of great longing on his face. There were only two other young men in front of the stall, both dressed in dark green. The man wearing a pointed cap was paying for his sword while the other waited to test one.

After collecting the customer's money, the tradesman gestured to the young man in front of Eadric and handed him a sword. "Here, try this one, young master," he said.

The sword seemed to come alive the moment it left its scabbard, glowing with a soft light that almost vibrated. When the young man stepped to the well-used practice dummy and raised his sword arm, the gleaming metal began to sing.

I am the sharpest sword around.
My blade can cut through butter.
I slice through trees with equal ease,
Carve stone without a mutter.

"No two are exactly alike," the tradesman explained. "They're named swords, the best in the known world. They bond to their owners very quickly."

"I'll take it," said the young man, tossing him a leather sack filled with clinking coins.

The merchant smiled and ducked his head, but he counted the coins before the young man was out of sight. A bell chimed, and I saw other merchants begin to close their stalls, helped by cats, dogs and a few human assistants.

The sword merchant frowned when he saw that Eadric was still waiting. "I'll be closing now, young master," he said as he lowered the first of the shutters that protected his stall.

Eadric placed his hand on the next shutter, preventing the merchant from moving it. "Surely you can take the time to show me one of your fine swords. I need to buy one today if possible."

The merchant glanced at Eadric out of the corner of his eyes. "We're not supposed to transact business after the bell has rung. I'll be back in a fortnight."

"I can't believe that you don't want to sell one more sword. If they're as good as you claim they are, it won't take me long to decide."

"Ah, well, I suppose it couldn't hurt." The merchant reached into a box, pulling out an ornately carved scabbard from which a filigreed grip protruded. "Here's one of my finest." He held up his hand in protest when Eadric began to pull the sword from its scabbard. "No, no! We don't have time for that. The watch will be coming soon, and I must have everything put away. Do you want the sword or not?"

"Without trying it?" asked Eadric. "I'd like to feel the weight of it in my hand."

It was getting dark, and men with tapers were lighting raised lanterns by the fountain. The merchant's eyes flicked toward the light, then back to Eadric. "There isn't time. Never mind, young master," he said, laying his hand on the scabbard as if he were about to reclaim his property. "It was a mistake to think that—"

"I'll take it!" Eadric declared. "Emma, if I could borrow a few coins—"

"Here," I said, handing him the bag Li'l had given

me. "Do you really want to buy a sword without even looking at it?"

Eadric stepped closer and whispered in my ear. "I don't have any choice. When else will I get a magic singing sword? Here you go, my good man," he said, counting out the coins into the merchant's hand.

"I don't know about this," I said as Eadric tucked the scabbard under his arm.

"Let me do the worrying. You've never purchased a sword before."

I laughed and shook my head. "I've never purchased anything without seeing it first, but then I'm not the one who is going to use it!"

Sixteen

When we reached the castle, the first thing I did was ask Li'l about Grassina. She hadn't come back yet, but there wasn't a thing I could do about it except keep looking for the rest of the items. With only one more day left, I was beginning to feel desperate: the two items we still had to acquire seemed the hardest to find. I tried not to think about what would happen if we couldn't find them.

Exhausted, I took my time going downstairs and was surprised by how quiet the castle seemed. Eadric hurried ahead and was already on his way back up with his food before I'd even crossed the kitchen threshold. My mother entered the room while I was looking for a plate. Eyeing my dusty hem, she asked, "Where did you go this time?"

"The magic marketplace," I said without thinking.

"Oh, really?" Her eyes narrowed to glittering slits. "You're practicing magic, aren't you? I knew it was only a matter of time."

I realized my mistake, but it was too late. I'd already said too much. "I've learned a few things," I said, watching her warily.

"I've been telling you for years that you weren't to get involved in magic!" Mother said, her voice getting shrill. "You never can listen, can you? It was for your own good, you know. I was trying to keep you from getting your heart broken. I suppose you're already hoping to be the next Green Witch. Well, it will never happen. You're not smart enough, and you're so clumsy that you'll probably drop the wrong ingredients in your potions. You simply don't have what it takes."

"I've only just started."

"This is a terrible time for you to do this. Our kingdom is at war—because of you, I might add—and Grassina is off to who knows where." Mother sighed. "Your father and I had hoped that the talent would pass you by. The ability to use magic can ruin a woman's life. Is Prince Eadric aware that you're involved in the practice of magic?"

"He knows all about it."

"And is he still serious in his intentions toward you?"

"Yes, Mother, he is. He knew about my interest in magic before he ever mentioned marriage."

"Extraordinary! Few men want to marry a witch, princess or not. I take it that you haven't accepted his offer yet."

"Not yet, no."

"Accept before you do something stupid and scare him off. Men don't wait forever! Now tell me, did you get what Grassina needs?"

"We have two of the things, but we have to find two more."

"Then you'd better get busy. We need her back here concentrating on her work now! Your father has taken his army and started for the border. Our informants tell us that Beltran's army has passed through the Crimson Hills and will reach the border tomorrow night. His wizard rides with him, which is how they made it past the trolls and through the hills so quickly."

"Grassina knows who the wizard is. She doesn't think he'll be a problem."

"To the old Grassina, perhaps, but I'm not sure what she can handle the way she's acting now. Even in the best of times, love and magic don't always mix well, which is something you should remember." Turning abruptly, Mother stalked from the room, leaving me even more worried than before.

I crept up the stairs to join Eadric in Grassina's room, where we sat in front of the fireplace while Li'l peppered us with questions about our excursion. By the time she ran out of questions, I could barely keep my eyes open.

"We'd better get some sleep," Eadric suggested when

I yawned. "We're going to have another busy day tomorrow."

"Before we go, I have to tell you that I spoke with my mother. She said that Father is leading his army to the border. Beltran is only a day's march from there, and Mother is worried that Grassina won't get back in time to help. I just wish there was something that I could do."

"You are doing something—you're helping your aunt so *she* can help your father when she does get back. You can't do everything."

"I can't even seem to do this one job right. We still haven't found the dragon's breath or the feather, and time has almost run out."

"I'm sure we'll find them," he said. Suddenly, I heard the swish of straw brushing against stone, and a figure shrouded in black shot through the window on a broom. Halfway into the room, my grandmother hauled in her broom handle, stopping it in midair. She hopped off with a grunt and turned to look around. Frightened by Grandmother's sudden arrival, Li'l scurried across the table and crouched behind the bouquet of crystalline flowers.

Grandmother scowled at us when she didn't see what she wanted right away. "Where's my old trunk?" she demanded.

"Which old trunk?" I asked, thinking there might be more than one.

"Don't be a ninny!" said Olivene. "The trunk I gave that whelp Grassina."

"It's in the storage room." I pointed at the door and would have opened it for her, but she stomped across the carpet, flung the door open and disappeared inside.

"What's that all about?" Eadric asked.

"I don't know," I said, "but I think I'd better find out." Motioning for Eadric to stay where he was, I followed my grandmother through the door and found her crouched on the floor beside the trunk, clinking the jars together. "What are you looking for?" I asked, trying to see around her hunched shoulders.

"Here it is," she crowed, holding up the bundle of werewolf whiskers. "Best thing for tracking over distances less than fifty miles. Werewolves have an excellent sense of smell. That old charlatan Olefat doesn't stand a chance now!" Climbing to her feet, she slapped the lid shut with a bang. I cringed, not sure what would happen if the jars were to break.

"Now, what about you?" asked my grandmother, leaning close to stare into my eyes. "Have you been practicing your magic?"

I took a step back. "Yes, I have. I think it's improving, too."

"Good!" she barked. "Keep it up. It's the most important thing a girl your age can do." Shoving past me, Grandmother stomped back into the main room. "So where's Grassina, that worthless daughter of mine? I have to set that feeble-brained nitwit straight about a few things."

I shrugged. "I don't know."

"'*I don't know*,'" she said, mocking me in a shrill falsetto. "Well, somebody has to know, and if I don't hear in one minute … Wait, let me guess. She's out looking for that brainless bumpkin Halpert, isn't she? But it won't do her a bit of good. Even if she finds him, I'm not going to turn him back. In fact, I think I'll wait right here, and when she gets home, I'll—"

"You'll do no such thing," said a deep male voice. I shivered as the temperature of the room dropped.

Eadric's face turned pale as he stared at the blue glow taking shape by the door. "Is that a ghost?" he asked, his voice a faint whisper.

"That's my grandfather, King Aldrid," I said. I was surprised to see him outside the dungeon.

"Haven't you plagued these poor children enough, Olivene?" Grandfather asked, looking a little more solid. "I could hear you down in the dungeon. You have no right to be here, pestering Emma and her friends."

"And who's going to make me leave?" Grandmother asked.

"I will, if I must." Although we could still see through him, Grandfather seemed to grow larger and more threatening.

"You can't do anything to me, you weak old fool! I have more power in my little toe than you'll ever have, ghost or not!"

"Perhaps," said Grandfather, "but I know more about you than you know about yourself. For as long as you lived in this castle, I kept track of everything you did, even after I died. If you don't leave immediately, I'll tell everyone your secret recipe for witches' brew, the potent kind you use for your most powerful spells."

"You wouldn't dare!" shrieked my grandmother, flinging up her arm as if to ward him off. "Do you know how many years it took me to come up with that formula?"

"Seven, I believe, so you'd better get out of here before I give it all away. Lizard lips and nose of—"

"All right, I'm going! But Grassina will regret the day she turns Harlin back into a human. That girl should have learned to listen to her mother!"

"His name is Haywood," said my grandfather as Grandmother stuck out her hand and snatched her broom from the air when it flew to her.

"It could be Huckleberry for all I care," Grandmother screamed, hopping onto her broom. With a shriek of rage, she shot through the window and was gone.

"Thank you for coming by, Grandfather," I said.

"My pleasure, Emma. If there is any way I can help,

be sure to ask. I'm not stuck in that old dungeon like some of the ghosts. Now go get some rest, my dear. You look like you could fall asleep standing up."

Indeed, my head had scarcely touched my pillow before I was asleep. Even so, I woke earlier than usual and dressed in a hurry, anxious to get on our way. It was Friday, and we had only one day left to find the dragon's breath and the feather.

When I reached Grassina's rooms, Eadric was taking his new sword out of its scabbard for the first time. This sword didn't sound at all like the others.

Why was I made into a sword?
Why not a pen for writing?
I much prefer the written word.
I do not like the fighting.

Fighting hurts both friends and foes,
Brings us naught but heartfelt woes.
If I could, I'd stop it now.
Never fight again, somehow.

Eadric grimaced. I could only imagine how disappointed he felt on hearing the sword's song. "Whatever you do," he said to me from between gritted teeth, "don't say I told you so."

"I don't really need to, do I?" I said. "It's supposed to

be a named sword. Why don't you ask it for its name?"

Eadric snorted. "Talk to it? It's a sword, not a person!"

"It's an enchanted sword. You could try, at least," I said.

"I will!" said Li'l, hopping up and down. "Sword, tell us your name!"

Light shimmered on the sword's blade, but it remained silent.

"Don't bother, Li'l," I said. "I think Eadric has to do it. The sword has been his since the moment he drew it from its scabbard."

"If it means you'll leave me alone … Sword, what's your name?"

Light flashed on the blade as it began to sing.

My name is Ferdinand,
But you can call me Ferdy.
I've been told I sing too much,
I am a little wordy.

"My sword's name is *Ferdy*? What kind of name is that for a sword?"

"I think it's a nice name," said Li'l. "It's kind of friendly."

"A sword's name shouldn't be friendly! It should be elegant and powerful, a strong name for a strong weapon!"

Li'l ruffled her wings. "But that's just it. I don't think he wants to be a weapon."

"That's great! I'm about to face dragons with a sword that doesn't want to be a sword."

"Face dragons?" asked Li'l.

"We have to get the dragon's breath, remember?" I said. "Since we can't ask Grassina for suggestions, we have to look in the one place where we know we'll find dragons. We saw one in the enchanted forest when we were frogs, and from the signs they left it looked like there were probably more. Does Grassina have a vial that we could use to collect the dragon's breath? It would help if we could do it while the dragon is asleep, so we're going to need some sleeping potion, too."

"I might have something you can use. Oh, dear. Grassina isn't going to like this at all." Li'l was still muttering to herself as she fluttered into my aunt's storage room.

"Before we go, we should put the magic beans in the silver chest," I said, holding out my hand to Eadric. "Do you have them with you?"

"Of course," he said, dipping into his belt pouch. "They tasted strange, though."

I couldn't believe my ears. "You ate them?"

"Just the insides. We only need the husk, remember?"

"But they're magic beans. You have no idea what they can do!"

Eadric's face flushed and he looked away. "Actually, I do. They gave me a stomachache right after I ate them, but that went away when the gas started. It's kind of embarrassing to talk about."

"When will you learn that there are some things you can't eat?"

"I'll be fine once I get over this little problem. You worry too much."

"One of us has to, because you don't worry enough!"

Seventeen

Eadric's horse, Bright Country, was happy to carry us to the enchanted forest. A handsome steed, he had grace and speed worthy of a prince. His mane and tail flew like silver banners as we galloped along the dirt road that led from the castle to the village, turning toward the ancient trees as soon as we could.

Although it was midmorning when we entered the forest, it looked like dusk under the leafy canopy. The trees grew so close together that little sunlight reached the ground. We had passed through the forest only days before, but we had been frogs then and largely ignored by the magic creatures. It was different now, and we could both feel it. This time, the forest was just as aware of us as we were of it.

While Bright Country picked his way over tangled roots, I looked around, half expecting to see the beckoning hand of a nymph, the watchful eye of a satyr or the twinkle of fairy lights. Instead I saw the roots of two trees hunching above the ground, dragging the trees closer together as their branches bent and made way for each other. The only sound was a prolonged rustle and the creak of shifting limbs.

"Did you see that?" Eadric whispered, his lips so close that his breath tickled my ear.

"The trees really did move, didn't they? Look," I said, pointing to my left. "Those trees are doing it, too."

Two enormous trees lurched across the ground, leaving a space too narrow for a horse to pass. The moving trunks had thick, green-tinged bark, whiplike branches and leaves shaped like the palm of a hand. I couldn't recall ever seeing such trees before. While we watched, other trees began to shift, blocking our way into the forest. I turned to look behind me. The only way still open was a path leading back to the road.

Pulling on the reins, Eadric reached down to pat his horse's neck. "We'd better stop here. I don't think Brighty can take us any farther."

"Yes, I can," said Bright Country. "I'll find a way around—"

"And the trees will move again," interrupted Eadric. "Sorry, Brighty, but you need to go home. It's probably for the best anyway. I have to travel through the forest without attracting attention, and you're too big for that. We're looking for dragons, but they aren't the only beasts that live in this forest. It's even more dangerous here than we thought, so Emma should go, too. Brighty, I want you to take her—"

"What do you mean, take me? I'm going with you, and you can't stop me!" Wiggling out of Eadric's arms, I slid off Bright Country's back and stumbled, landing on my knees. Eadric followed, slipping to the ground with the nimbleness of long practice, while I scrambled to my feet and glared at him. "You need me and my magic to help you get that dragon's breath."

"Emma, I'm not taking you with me. I don't want to see you get hurt. I've been thinking about the dragons, and when I do find one, I don't want you anywhere around. I've fought dragons before, and you haven't. I know how dangerous it is."

"But we're not here to fight dragons!"

"That doesn't mean it won't happen."

"I understand that, but look," I said, reaching into my pouch. "Li'l found this sleeping potion." I shook the small vial of blue liquid that Li'l had given me. "And she gave me a bottle to collect the dragon's breath. You don't have to worry. I'll stay out of the way if there's any fighting involved, but I'm going to do my best to see that you don't have to fight anyone. Killing a dragon isn't going to get us its breath, although magic might. I know my magic isn't perfect, but it's all we've got. I don't want to lose you any more than you want to lose me."

Eadric grinned. "Then how about that kiss you owe me?"

"What kiss? I don't owe you any kiss!"

"Sure you do. We're engaged to be engaged, aren't we? As far as I'm concerned, you always owe me a kiss."

Eadric's lips had barely brushed mine when hot horse breath wuffled my hair. "Should I take her back or not, Your Highness?"

"I guess she's staying with me, Brighty. You'll have to go back to the castle by yourself."

We watched until Bright Country had turned onto the path and passed the more threatening trees. With his head hanging lower than his hocks, the horse was a picture of dejection. "He'll be fine," I said, squeezing Eadric's hand.

Once his horse was out of sight, Eadric and I wriggled between trunks and climbed over roots, running when the trees began to move again. When we finally came to a more natural section of the forest that seemed to be firmly rooted, I relaxed. A flickering shadow made me hurry to catch up with Eadric.

Eadric kept his hand on Ferdy's hilt. I knew that he didn't dare take the sword out of its scabbard until he needed it, as the enchanted weapon would sing and draw more unwanted attention. "Look for a dragon sign," said Eadric. "Scorched bark, leaves brown and curled from intense heat, claw marks ... things like that."

As I looked, I tried to think of possible spells I could say, quick and easy ones that would work against any attacker, but it was hard to concentrate on spells while searching for dragon signs in the near dark. I was studying a suspicious patch on a tree when I heard Eadric say, "What do we have here?" Suddenly, he took two steps forward and jumped into a trench I hadn't even noticed. Nearly ten feet across, the trench appeared to be about three feet deep. "Stay there!" he said, holding up his hand when I gathered my skirts to follow.

I peered into the trench, trying to see what might have created it. Fairly uniform in width, it extended as far as I could see in both directions, but I could find no sign of its origins. "What is it?" I asked.

"I'm not sure, but I think it might be—"

We heard the sound of approaching footsteps at the same time. Even from a distance they made the ground shake. "Giants!" we said in unison, understanding now what had made the trench.

The shaking made the trees shiver and dislodged clods of dirt from the trench's sides, showering Eadric as I reached down to help him out. He grasped my hand and I leaned the other way, falling onto my back when he jumped. Scooping me up, Eadric began to run. I struggled to get down, but he refused to let go.

"You can't run as fast as I can, not dressed in a long skirt," he said, puffing in my ear as he carried me deeper into the forest. I was wearing my old green gown and kirtle, lighter in weight than some I owned, but the fabric was still enough to hamper my legs.

We crouched behind a broad tree trunk and covered our ears. The ground throbbed beneath us, and we had to fight to keep our balance. Peering between the trunks, we saw enormous shadowy figures passing single file through the trench. Although we couldn't see much more than their legs and feet, it was enough to tell us that any one of the giants could have flattened us both without noticing.

We stayed where we were, our muscles cramping, until the last giant finally moved on and the ground stopped shaking. Although my parents' castle was only a few miles away, I'd never known of the presence of so many giants in the enchanted forest. I dreaded to think of what else we might encounter.

A few yards past the giants' trench, I saw a scorched tree. The bark was blackened, as was the ground around it. Eadric found another a short distance away. The burned trunk was still warm; the dragon was probably nearby. We were trying to determine which direction the dragon had gone when we heard a voice screaming for help.

"The dragon's caught someone!" I said.

With his hand on Ferdy's hilt, Eadric dashed between the trees, leaping over downed trunks, while I followed as quickly as I could. The sound of Eadric's footsteps led me on until they stopped suddenly and I heard a muffled oath.

"What is it?" I said, hurrying to catch up.

"Don't come any closer!" shouted Eadric.

I didn't stop entirely, just slowed my pace while I studied the trees ahead. I was surprised to find Eadric suspended in midstride, one arm raised in front of his face.

"What's wrong?" I asked, and then I saw it. An enormous web glistened between two trees, ensnaring anything that tried to pass. Taller than my grandmother's cottage and broader than three of my father's most imposing knights standing with arms outspread, the web was hard to see unless a breeze moved it and the light hit it just right.

A bedraggled raven flapped feebly at the top of the web, its beady eyes fixed on me. "Fly while you still can!" it said in its raspy voice.

Eadric had been caught in the end closest to me, his left arm held in place as if to ward off a blow. Only a few feet away, a flying squirrel hung suspended, its limbs spread wide for flight. Shivering uncontrollably, it made pitiful mewling sounds. The biggest surprise, however, was the creature trapped at the other end of the web. It was a young dragon no bigger than a large dog. A pretty shade of blue, it was covered in overlapping scales and had a raised ridge running from the back of its head to the tip of its long tail. The two wings sprouting between the dragon's shoulder blades beat the air behind it but were too entangled to free the dragon from the web.

"Stay where you are," Eadric told me. With the whisper of metal against metal, he pulled Ferdy from his scabbard. The sword immediately began to sing.

Why was I made into a sword?
Why not a—

"Be quiet!" Eadric said, shaking his sword. "We don't need to tell the whole forest where we are."

As if we haven't already, I thought.

Ferdy took the hint. He stopped singing abruptly and began to hum. It was slightly off-key, but at least it wasn't as loud. "Mmm hmm hmm hmmm hmm hmm …"

Reaching back with his humming sword, Eadric swung at the web, easily slicing through the strands. Another stroke and his left arm was free, although tattered bits of spider silk still clung to his sleeve. Eadric stepped back and hacked at the web, freeing the squirrel and the raven before moving on to the little dragon.

The dragon shrieked when it saw him coming with his sword upraised. Puffing up its chest, it opened its mouth and tried to blast Eadric with its flame, but the creature was young and didn't have the strength it would have as an adult. Its feeble trickle of heated smoke dispersed in the air, carried away by a light breeze.

While watching Eadric cut the rest of the web from

around the struggling dragon, I saw movement out of the corner of my eye. I turned my head and gasped. It was a huge black spider, its back as high as my shoulders, its legs longer than a big man's reach.

"Look out!" I screamed as the spider darted forward, its mouthparts clashing.

Eadric whirled around. With an angry shout, he hurled himself at the creature, hacking and stabbing as the spider danced back, avoiding his blade.

"Thief! Scoundrel!" screamed the spider. "Just wait till I catch you! I'll wrap you in silk, bite off your head, then suck the juices from your body!" The spider darted forward, swinging a hairy leg and knocking Eadric to the ground. Grunting, Eadric rolled to his feet with Ferdy aimed and ready.

Humming louder and louder, Ferdy broke into song as Eadric chopped at the living nightmare.

Take that, you nasty monster.
Take that, you beastly beast.
You shall not hurt my master,
Nor add him to your feast.

The spider had a long reach and greater strength. Keeping its multiple eyes fixed on Eadric, it quivered in anticipation. As if the sword were an extension of his arm, Eadric slashed at the spider, vaulting over one reaching leg, cleaving another in two.

The spider shrieked, staring at the stump of its severed limb. "Forget what I said!" it shrilled. "I'll suck out the juices before I cut off your head! I want you to feel my mandibles piercing your flesh and your life slipping away."

Freed from the web by Eadric's efforts, the little dragon took advantage of the commotion to scurry into the forest, running with the awkward gait of a puppy. I watched it go, which was a mistake, since I should have been watching the battle. Suddenly, the spider was forcing Eadric in my direction.

Eadric had already cut off two of the spider's legs. When he hacked off a third, the spider slowed but kept coming at him with an uneven step. Swept aside by Ferdy, the third leg flew at me like a spear, shuddering into the ground beside me. I shrieked and tried to run, tripping when my feet became tangled in my skirts. Flailing with my arms, I fell headfirst into a patch of puffball mushrooms, crushing them so that dustlike spores rose in a cloud around me.

Taken by surprise, the tickling was more than I could handle. "Ah … ah … ah-choo!" I sneezed, and in an instant, I was a frog again. Too horrified to move, I was still sprawled on the forest floor when Eadric barreled into me. He was a frog, too, of course, but even worse, he no longer had Ferdy.

"What have you done? I've lost Ferdy! I needed that sword to defend us!"

"I couldn't help it!" I wailed. "I didn't sneeze on purpose!"

While the spider looked around in confusion, we hopped under a large fern, hoping that the monster would pass us by. A dry twig snapped. Suddenly, the fern quivered and was gone, yanked out of the ground. "Ah-ha!" said the spider, looming above us, its multiple eyes gleaming with malice. "I thought I saw you go in there!"

"Hop!" shouted Eadric.

We leaped straight ahead, directly under the spider's belly, while its hairy legs skittered around us. A dark blue, foul-smelling fluid dripped from a wound in the spider's underside, and we took an extra second or two to hop around the splashing puddle. The spider staggered as it turned to follow, shrieking high-pitched notes that hurt my eardrums.

"You come back here!" screamed the spider. "You can't get away with this! No one does this to me and lives!"

With all its legs, the spider could easily have overtaken us, but its lopsided gait sent it careening off tree trunks and stumbling over the uneven ground. We hopped around fallen branches, and when our path lay straight before us, we leapted in ground-eating bounds. Eadric was a better hopper and could have left me behind if he'd wanted to, but he stayed by my side, encouraging me when I began to tire.

"I wish I had Ferdy," said Eadric, who wasn't the least bit out of breath. "I was getting used to him. He's a good sword."

"We'll come back … for him … when we change … again."

The spider was persistent, staying on our trail no matter how we dodged and circled. Every few minutes I looked back over my shoulder, hoping I wouldn't see it, but the spider was always there. *If I could make up a spell,* I thought, but all I could come up with were some silly rhymes using *spider* and *beside her,* which I didn't like at all.

When the ground began to shake again and I stumbled and fell, I thought it was just my usual clumsiness, but the ground was still shaking as I got back on my feet. Suddenly, I had an idea. "Head for the giants' trench!" I shouted to Eadric.

"Are you crazy? That's the last place we should go. We don't have any way to defend ourselves."

"That's exactly why we're going there," I said.

The shaking ground had tripped the spider as well. When I glanced back, it was staggering to its feet, keening so loudly it made me cringe. I hurried on, bounding across the forest floor, ignoring the pain in my side and the burning in my lungs. When we finally reached the trench, another group of giants was already in sight, striding along their path. I looked back to make sure that the spider was still following us, but I needn't have bothered. Even the sight of the approaching giants wasn't enough to scare it away.

"Emma, come back," shouted Eadric as I put on a burst of speed and jumped past him, sailing down into the trench.

When Eadric jumped in after me, I didn't know if he wanted to drag me out or if he understood what I was planning to do and wanted to help, but either way it was enough to entice the spider to follow us into the trench. I headed straight toward the approaching giants whose slow, steady pace covered more ground in just a few minutes than it would have taken me hours to hop.

"Emma," shouted Eadric, but I didn't have time to talk. The spider had learned to compensate for its lost limbs and had started to pick up speed.

I was hopping as fast as I could when I realized that with his next step, the first giant would be upon us. "Now!" I shouted to Eadric. Spinning around, I tensed my muscles, then put all my strength into jumping out the other side of the trench. When I soared through the air with my legs extended, it felt almost like flying. I'd misjudged the distance and landed on the edge, my breath whooshing out of me. Using the last of my strength, I pulled myself onto level ground while Eadric sailed past me in a graceful arc.

Looking back at the trench, I saw that the spider was trying to follow us, its remaining legs scrabbling at the soil. With the ground shuddering wildly beneath our feet, Eadric and I fell. The spider, who had climbed halfway up the side of the trench, fared even worse, tumbling down the crumbling dirt to land on its back. In an instant, the giant's foot came down with a loud splat.

Trying to be inconspicuous, Eadric and I stayed where we were until the giants had passed. Once they were gone, we crept to the edge and looked down. The spider was a blotch on the floor of the trench, its legs dark lines embedded in the dirt.

"Whatever made you think of coming here?" Eadric asked.

"I couldn't think of a spell, so I tried to think of how I would kill a spider at home. Stepping on it seemed like the best idea."

"Good thinking, except for one thing—you could have been killed!"

"I guess," I said, shivering at the thought.

"Good going!" said a strange voice. "That spider got just what it deserved."

I looked around, but there wasn't anyone in sight. "Who was that?" I asked.

"I'm Ralf," said the voice, and the little dragon popped his head out from behind a tree trunk, a crumpled violet dangling from his mouth. "I wanted to thank you for helping me. If you hadn't come along, I'd probably be spider food by now."

Eadric smiled. "Glad we could help."

Ralf swallowed the flower, flapped his wings and rose into the air, creating a small gale that whipped the leaves on the trees nearby. Eadric and I had to grab each other's arms and lean into the wind to keep from being blown to the ground.

"I saw you turn into frogs," said Ralf, landing beside us. "That was really something! What else can you change into?"

I coughed and wiped my eyes with the back of my hand. "Nothing. That was it."

"Oh," said Ralf, looking disappointed. Then his eyes brightened as if he'd thought of something else. "You're not werefrogs, are you? I've heard of werewolves, but I've never heard of werefrogs."

"No, we're just having a problem with a spell. I'm Emma, and I'm a witch in training. This is my friend Eadric."

"Pleased to meet you," Ralf said, nodding to us one at a time. "You were both awfully brave. I was really scared when I got caught in that web, but you two weren't frightened at all, even when the spider was chasing you."

"Maybe we didn't look scared, but I was terrified!" I said. "I was hopping as fast as I could and it still didn't feel fast enough."

"Tell me something," said the little dragon. "If you're not were-anything, why are you here? This is a very dangerous place, especially for humans."

"We're looking for a few things," said Eadric. "A green dragon and the feather from an old horse. You haven't seen any green dragons around, have you?"

Ralf frowned. "I don't know any green dragons. How about yellow?"

"It has to be green," I said, shaking my head. "We're trying to reverse a spell. It's very important."

"You should ask my grandfather. He's the king, so he knows all the dragons. I can take you to see him if you'd like."

"He won't want to eat us, will he?" I asked.

"Maybe if you were humans, but dragons don't eat frogs. Anyway, you saved my life and you're my friends now, so he'll want to meet you. Hop on."

"Hop on where?" Eadric said, looking at the dragon as if he was a horse.

Ralf squatted and let his wings droop. "My back. Grandfather lives in a cave at the base of the Purple Mountains. It's a long way from here."

I cringed, mindful of my tender frog skin. "We can't. Your scales are too rough."

"Not at the base of my neck. There's a little gap in my ridge where you'll fit if one of you sits behind the other. It's smooth there and you won't get hurt."

I had never heard of riding a dragon, and after our experience with the magic carpet, I wasn't sure either of us wanted to fly anywhere, but we had only one day left and needed the dragon's breath. "I'll climb on his back if you will," I said to Eadric, pointing at Ralf's wing.

Eadric grasped two knobs where the wing bones met and began to pull himself up. "What about Ferdy? I should go see if he's all right."

I followed, watching to see where he placed his feet. "You're a frog now. You couldn't lift him anyway."

Grunting, Eadric heaved himself onto Ralf's back. "Then we have to look for him after we've seen Ralf's grandfather. You wouldn't mind taking me, would you, Ralf? I left my sword near the spider's web."

"I'd be happy to, Eadric," said Ralf. I grabbed hold of his ridge when the little dragon stiffened his wings and began to flap. Eadric wrapped his arms around me as he whispered into my eardrum, his voice so soft that I could barely hear it over the swish of the dragon's wings. "What do you think of Ralf?"

"I like him."

"So do I," said Eadric, "and I *never* thought I'd meet a dragon that I liked. I just wish we weren't going to meet Ralf's grandfather. We're frogs, and I don't have any way to protect us."

"You heard what Ralf said. Dragons don't eat frogs.

We should be fine. Tell me something. What would you have said if someone had told you a few weeks ago that you soon would be riding on a dragon's back with a princess in your arms?"

I felt Eadric shrug. "I'd have asked her name. A few weeks ago, I was looking for a princess to kiss. I never imagined I'd be lucky enough to find you."

I sighed and settled back against his chest. For a frog who could be all too thickheaded, Eadric could be awfully sweet sometimes.

Eighteen

Even young dragons like Ralf have powerful wings that can carry them at great speeds. Although the Purple Mountains were many miles from the enchanted forest, it wasn't long before Ralf was following the contours of the foothills and skimming the mountainsides.

Angling into a valley pocked with caves, he suddenly darted into a larger opening. The cave narrowed at the back, forming a long, smooth-sided tunnel. It was dark and gloomy inside, and I couldn't imagine how Ralf could see well enough to fly. However, the deeper we went, the better I understood why his grandfather lived there. Great patches of lichen grew on the walls, glowing like witches' lights. Delicate crystalline flowers bloomed on the walls and floors. We passed through larger caves where columns of multicolored rock rose from the floor to the ceilings high above. I saw solid rock that looked like flowing water and clear pools of water that seemed to be bottomless.

It was cooler than it had been aboveground, but not uncomfortable. We began to smell a pungent odor soon after we entered the first tunnel. The deeper we went, the stronger the smell became, until the air seemed thick with it. The tunnels branched occasionally, and a few of the passages belched hot air. I was happy when Ralf passed those by.

"When we get there," whispered Eadric, "I'll look around in case we have to get out fast. You can't trust dragons, and we may have to escape if the situation turns bad. Whatever you do, don't sneeze."

My fingers were growing numb from clutching Ralf's ridge when we finally entered a chamber larger than any others. "This is Grandpa's treasure room," said the little dragon as he landed on the floor. "He spends most of his time here."

Eadric immediately hopped down while I took my time and looked about from my elevated vantage point. Pink and white striped columns seemed to hold up the ceiling, while squat cones rising from the floor glistened with dripping moisture. All kinds of objects were stacked one on the other in tottering piles. Some, like the enormous mounds of precious stones, were glittering and obviously valuable. I wasn't so sure about others, like the old shoes and stacks of yellowing parchment.

A low-voiced murmur ran through the cave. "You should go over here, although maybe you're more pink than red. Where did I put that other one? I thought I had six of these."

"Grandpa likes to sort his treasures in different ways. Sometimes he does it by size, sometimes by shape or—"

"*Who dares enter my cave?*" boomed a voice so loud that the piles shook and small objects clattered to the floor. What I had thought was a mound of golden treasure wasn't treasure at all. It was an enormous dragon.

"It's me, Grandpa. It's Ralf! I've come to visit you, and I've brought two of my friends."

"Ralfie, my boy! Come over here where I can see you!" said his grandfather.

Wishing I had gotten off sooner, I clung to the ridge on the back of Ralf's neck as he flapped his wings and skimmed over the treasure. My heart thudded wildly; the nearer we got to Ralf's grandfather, the bigger he seemed. The Dragon King was the largest creature I had ever seen. Each of his scales was bigger than a human head and ranged in color from yellow-gold on his throat to red-gold on his tail. The ridge along his back was tall and spiky, although some of the points had broken off and others were missing altogether. His age was evident from the scarring on his scales, the hair sprouting from his long, pointed ears and the way his claws were blunted by wear.

"There you are, my boy!" said the old dragon, crouching down to peer nearsightedly at his grandson.

"But what's that on your back? It's not some kind of parasite, is it? Or have you caught some new disease? Maybe I should find my special ointment."

"No, Grandpa, that's my friend Emma. Eadric is around here, too. They're frogs, Grandpa, and they saved my life!"

I scrunched down as low as I could behind Ralf's ridge while he told his grandfather about the spider and our rescue. The little dragon made us sound wonderful, but I held my breath, hoping he wouldn't mention that we were actually humans.

The king was so close, his breath nearly blew me off Ralf, and the smell was enough to make my eyes water. Blinking, he bowed down until his snout nearly touched my head. He sniffed me, and I could feel his hot breath dry out my skin. When he sat back, he said, "You're right. They *are* frogs. Maybe you and your friends would like to help me. I'm sorting everything by color now. Come see my red treasures. Just don't eat my rose, Ralfie. I know how much you like flowers, but that rose is very special."

The pile of red treasures wasn't large, but it was interesting. A red riding cape lined with a wolf skin had been neatly folded and lay atop a mound of sparkling rubies. A half dozen pairs of dancing shoes shuffled around the pile, while a blooming rose trembled beside a restless magic carpet woven in every imaginable shade of red.

"Very nice, Grandpa," said Ralf. "But Emma and Eadric were wondering if you know of any green dragons."

"Green dragons? Why didn't you say so? Of course I have some green dragons! Would you like to see them?"

"Yes, please," I said, my voice coming out in a little whisper. The old dragon was frightening even when he wasn't trying to be, but if he actually knew a green dragon and could take me to him, our search might already be over.

Turning his enormous bulk, the king of the dragons reached into a mound of emeralds. "Now, where did I put them?" he muttered to himself, scattering the emeralds beneath his groping claws. Squinting, he lowered his head so that his nose was only inches from the pile. "Ah, here they are!" he said, holding up two small dragons carved from jade. "Is this what you wanted?"

"No," I said, my disappointment making the word come out more sharply than I'd intended. "Thank you, but we need to find a *real* green dragon."

The old dragon huffed and dropped the jade figures back onto the pile. "Why didn't you say so? There's no such thing as a real green dragon."

"But they have to be real! You must be mistaken."

"I don't make mistakes, young frog! Kings never do!" I shrank back as the old dragon's nostrils flared and smoke puffed out of his gaping mouth.

"I'm sorry, but we have to find a green dragon to break a spell. Spells don't work if they're impossible to break, and this spell has lasted for years."

"Nevertheless, green dragons don't exist. Dragons are red or blue, yellow or purple, black or silver or gold, but in all my years, I have never heard of a green dragon. Now if you'll excuse me, I was looking for something." The old dragon turned away, his tail knocking over a small mountain of sapphires. "I wonder where I put that scarlet pumpernickel," he muttered.

Ralf sat back on his haunches and watched the old dragon go. "I'm sorry we couldn't help you, Emma."

"It's not your fault. Thanks for trying. It's just that I don't know what we're going to do now. We'll never break the spell if we can't find a green dragon, and if we can't break the spell, the kingdom of Greater Greensward is going to be invaded and I might have to marry that awful Jorge!"

"Don't give up yet," he said. "Why don't you look around while I help my grandpa? We don't have to stay long, but we'll hurt his feelings if we leave too quickly." The little dragon crouched so I could climb off. "Come find me if you need anything."

"I was going to ask if your grandfather had a feather from an old horse, but I don't think we need it anymore. How about some water instead?" I said, rubbing the skin on my back. "Your grandfather's breath dried me out."

“I have something even better,” Ralf said. Leaping into the air, he disappeared behind the stacks, returning a minute later. “Try this. It’s the salve my mother put on me when I was a baby. Little dragons don’t have tough skin until they’re a year old. This gunk keeps them from getting fried when they’re around other dragons.”

Ralf’s salve was thick and white and smelled kind of minty, like spearmint leaves. Tilting the vial into my hands, Ralf poured out enough to cover me in a thin, sticky layer. It felt cool to the touch, and when I’d smeared it on my skin, I felt cool all over. “Thanks,” I said, wishing that all my problems could be solved so easily.

Once I was alone, I started thinking about Grandmother’s spell. If there were no green dragons, they couldn’t really be part of the cure. My grandmother must have tricked us back on the island, and I’d been foolish enough to believe her. But she’d been so convincing!

I was wandering around, not really looking at anything in particular, when I saw something move. A group of mirrors, both ordinary and magic, had been stacked against one another. The mirror closest to me showed an overweight peasant kneeling by a fireplace in a cottage with a sagging roof. I was already turning away when I realized that it was Olefat with his hair cut short and his beard just starting to grow back.

"I wonder how close Grandmother is to finding him," I murmured to myself. The image blurred, and when it became clearer I saw Olefat again. He was standing now and appeared to be talking to someone. Although I couldn't hear what he was saying, I could tell from his expression that he was in the midst of an argument.

I was watching Olefat gesture with his arms when I noticed that shadows were filling the room behind him. I gasped when they took shape, recognizing my grandmother and the other witches from the retirement community. The old man turned suddenly, but the witches were too fast for him. My grandmother's hand flashed, and Olefat disappeared. In his place cowered a small, brown dog with sad eyes, floppy ears and a white-rimmed muzzle.

I jumped when Metoo streaked into view, his hooked beak and claws reaching for my grandmother. She gestured again and the bird was gone. A moment later, the little dog began to scratch behind his ear with a frenzied kicking of his hind leg. It seemed she'd turned Metoo into a flea.

Something clattered on the other side of the mirrors, and the image disappeared. Following the sound of clinking metal, I found Ralf stacking gem-studded cups in the gold pile while Eadric ogled a golden helmet. From the way his skin was shining, I could tell Ralf had given him the salve, too.

"Are you ready to go yet?" I asked.

"Sure," said the little dragon. "We can go now if you want. I just have to say goodbye to my grandpa." Setting down the last of the cups, the little dragon left to find the Dragon King.

"Come here," said Eadric. "I want to show you something. Just look at the hinged visor on this helmet. I've never seen anything like it before. I could really use this when we hunt for the green dragon."

"There aren't any green dragons, Eadric. Didn't you hear the Dragon King? And if there aren't any green dragons, then Olivene must not have told the other witches the real cure. Maybe she was holding back her secrets from Olefat. It's all been a waste of time." I kicked a spindle of gold wool lying on the floor and watched it spin in a circle. "We might as well go home and tell Grassina. You don't suppose there's any chance that she'll give up and help my parents now, do you?"

"I don't think so," said Eadric. "From the way she acted before, I think she'd fall to pieces if she thought she couldn't get Haywood back. But I don't think you should give up just yet. The old witches' memories seemed to think it was possible. Wouldn't they know if green dragons were real or not? And just because the king says that there aren't any green dragons doesn't mean that it's true. He's half blind and spends most of his time in a cave. I think we should keep looking. There has to be at least one green dragon somewhere."

Ralf was still talking to his grandfather when we found him. "Thanks, Grandpa. We'll be going now."

"You're welcome, Ralfie. Come back any time." The Dragon King smiled a toothy grin that showed off his fangs. I flinched, and Eadric put his arm around my shoulder in a protective sort of way. The old dragon lowered his head to look at us. Pointing with one gnarled claw, he said, "Those two belong in my green pile. What are they doing over there?"

"They're my friends, Grandpa. They're with me!"

"Then you'd better take them out of here. I'm working on my green pile next."

"You heard the king. Climb aboard, you two." Ralf squatted down and extended his wing. "There's someone I want you to meet."

"Is it another dragon?" Eadric asked, helping me onto the little dragon's back.

"Nope, but he's a friend of my grandpa's. His name is Shirley, and I think he can help you with something. Hold on tight!" said Ralf, spreading his wings. "Here we go!"

A current of hot air buffeted us as we headed up the tunnel. I held onto Ralf's ridge so tightly that my hands hurt. "Where does Shirley live?" I asked the little dragon.

"On the highest peak of the Purple Mountains. He's

a nice old guy, just a little deaf."

I closed my eyes and sighed. If only we could go home now and didn't have to worry about war or magic spells. If only I *knew* that I'd never have to marry Jorge.

Nineteen

When we finally left the tunnel and flew into the open air, Ralf circled above the ground once before starting an upward spiral. "Hold on tight!" he shouted.

The air had been pleasant at ground level, but the higher we flew, the colder it became. Although Ralf generated a lot of heat, keeping us warm, the heat didn't reach his wings and snow began to accumulate, weighing him down and slowing our flight. What had started out as a few drifting flakes became a blizzard, obscuring everything around us.

"We're almost there!" Ralf shouted just as I was beginning to think we might be flying into a white void forever. "Shirley's cave is at the top of the mountain." I was grateful that dragons were famous for their sense of direction.

"Why would anyone want to live on the top of a mountain?" I shouted.

"My grandpa says that Shirley moved here to get away from the flies when he retired. It's too cold up here for them. Here we go!" I nearly fell off when Ralf landed with a thump. "Hold on just a little longer. I'll get us inside where it's warm."

The little dragon caught hold of a string blowing wildly in the wind and pulled with all his might. Peering through the falling snow, I saw that the string led into a tiny hole in the rock face of the mountain. Ralf let go of the string, and a door opened, revealing a hole twice as tall as I was when I was human.

Something moved out of Ralf's way when he shuffled through the opening, but I couldn't see what it was until my eyes adjusted. After the glare of the snow, the cave interior seemed dark, making it difficult to see. Dim light came through holes in the cave walls, and the room finally became visible. We were in a cave about the same size as my bedchamber at home. Its rock floor was level, its ceiling too high to see clearly.

I was startled when an old, sway-backed horse wearing a thick wool blanket whinnied and trotted toward us. White with gray stockings, the horse's splayed hooves clacked against the stone when it stepped into the wind to push the door closed. Once the door was shut, the old horse turned and looked at Ralf. "I know you!" said the horse, nudging Ralf with his nose. "You're old Gargle Snort's grandson. What brought you all the way up here?

Your grandpa's all right, isn't he?"

I bit my lip and tried not to laugh. *Gargle Snort?*

"Grandpa is doing fine," said Ralf, flapping his wings to shake off the snow. "These are my friends Emma and Eadric. They want to ask you a question."

"Your grandpa is dying fast? I'm sorry to hear that. I always liked the old lizard, even if he did have a temper like a … never mind. You're a young one and shouldn't hear such language. So what brought you all the way up here?"

Ralf glanced at me and rolled his eyes. Then, rising up on his hind legs, he shouted into the horse's ear. "My friends Emma and Eadric want to ask you a question."

"There's no need to shout! So, you brought your friend Amandedric. Another one of those newfangled names? Who's your other friend?"

"You don't understand. One of my friends is Emma, the other is Eadric."

"They each took half the name, huh? Well, that's fine, too."

The little dragon cleared his throat, which was sounding scratchy from yelling. "We're looking for the feather of a horse. Do you have one you could give us?"

"Brother of a Norse? Why would you look here? I was an only child."

"Not Norse, horse! Do you have an old feather that you could give us?"

"Leather? Why would you want my old leather? All

I've got are my old saddle and tack, but they wouldn't fit any of you pipsqueaks."

"I didn't mean—" began Ralf.

"I don't understand what's wrong with you young people. First you want one thing, then another. You can't make up your minds, can you? Why, in my day, we knew exactly what we wanted." The old horse yawned, showing us what was left of his yellowed teeth. "I was about to take a nap when I heard you at the door. You wouldn't mind showing yourselves out, would you? My old bones need a lot of rest these days."

"Actually, we were hoping—"

"Don't forget to shut the door behind you," Shirley said, trotting out of the room.

"I'm sorry," Ralf said, turning back to Eadric and me. "I can't seem to make him understand."

"But we don't really need the feather if there aren't any green dragons. We can't reverse the spell if we're missing even one ingredient. Besides, why would we come to Shirley for a feather?" I asked. "I really think we should be getting back." I couldn't figure out what we were doing wasting our time there.

"I thought you knew," said Ralf. "Shirley's great-great-great-great-great-great-great-great-grandfather was Pegasus."

"You mean he has feathered wings under that blanket?" I asked.

"Pretty gray ones."

"Then all we need is one of his feathers!" Eadric said.

Ralf nodded. "If you can get him to give it to you."

"Couldn't we just take one?" asked Eadric. "I doubt he'd miss it."

"Take it without asking?" Ralf sounded shocked at the idea.

"You tried asking, and you saw where that got us."

"That's true," Ralf said, tilting his head to the side as if it helped him think. "Well, maybe we can find a loose one on the floor."

"But what's the point?" I asked.

"We said we weren't going to give up yet, remember? I say we get the feather and then see about the green dragon," said Eadric.

"Fine." I said. "We're here, we may as well."

Ralf carried us to the next room, where he let us off at the door. It was little more than a large stall, with a trough for water, a bucket for grain and a rack for hay. Clean straw covered the stone floor, and the air smelled sweet and fresh.

"How does a horse keep his own stall so clean?" Eadric whispered.

"Magic," answered Ralf. "I've been here with my grandfather a couple of times, and this cave is always like this."

"I could use some magic for Bright Country," said Eadric. "He makes a real mess of his stall."

I peeked through the doorway again. Shirley lay in the middle of the room, stretched out on his side. His eyes were closed, and his deep, even breathing told us that he was asleep. Eadric and I kept our eyes on the old horse as we hopped into the room.

The prickly straw stabbed the bottoms of my feet. Eadric, however, didn't seem to notice the straw and hopped all the way to Shirley's side. The blanket was slack around the horse's belly, so it was easy for Eadric to slip his hand underneath and feel for a loose feather.

I watched him for a moment, then decided that I'd better go help. I was studying the ground, preparing for my next carefully placed step, when I saw something gray partly buried by the gold-colored straw. Stretching out my arm, I pulled out a long, sleek feather. Excited by my find, I whispered, "Eadric!" but he didn't hear me.

I took another step, waving the feather like a flag. Without turning around, Eadric said, "I can't reach his feathers from here," then lifted up the corner of the blanket and slipped underneath. I could see him moving about under the blanket, a frog-sized lump crawling across the horse's side like a mole burrowing in the kitchen garden.

"Eadric," I said, hopping one step closer.

"I can't find any loose ones," he said in a muffled

voice. "I'll just pull out one of these."

"No, Eadric, I found—"

The lump under the blanket jerked, and Shirley snorted, opening his eyes partway. He flicked his tail, whipping his hindquarters and narrowly missing the lump that was Eadric. Lifting his head, Shirley looked blearily about. When he didn't see anything, he muttered, "Darn flies," then dropped his head and went back to sleep. The lump moved again, and I held my breath until Eadric tumbled out from under the blanket.

Wearing an enormous grin, he hopped toward me, holding the feather high. He stopped when he saw my feather. His grin disappeared.

"Great," I said, wishing I could put the grin back on his face. "We'll keep my feather in case we ever need another one."

When we finally set out, sitting on the feathers so we wouldn't lose them, the wind was blowing just as fiercely as before. The snowfall was so heavy that I couldn't see the back of Ralf's head. Comfortable from the dragon's body heat, I closed my eyes and let myself relax against Eadric. I was almost asleep when he shouted to Ralf, "How did the grandson of Pegasus get a name like *Shirley?*"

"It's a nickname, really," said Ralf. "Even when he was too young to fly, he was so surefooted that he could go just about anywhere. The name stuck, and—"

I sat up a little straighter. "You mean he's called *Surely,* S-U-R-E-L-Y?"

"Of course. What did you think I said?"

"You don't want to know." I chuckled and closed my eyes again.

"What about your name, Ralf?" said Eadric. "How did you get a name like that if your grandfather is called Gargle Snort?"

"I still have my baby name, even though I haven't been a baby for a couple of years now. I'll get to choose my real name when I grow up. I want a strong name like my hero Flash Red-Snout. My mother's name is Flame Snorter, but everybody calls her Snorty. She's known for how far she can belch flames. My father is Grumble Belly because his belly grumbles before he breathes fire. I haven't decided on my name yet."

"If I had to choose my own name, I think I'd want it to have something to do with bravery," said Eadric. "Yours could be about your magic, Emma."

"Are you kidding? I'd probably be called Fumble Fingers or Clumsy Toes. Even if it were about my magic, it probably wouldn't be very complimentary. My magic still needs a lot of work."

"I'm sorry I couldn't find a green dragon for you," said Ralf. "I owe you for saving my life."

I patted the dragon's shoulder. "Don't worry. You did your best, and that's all anyone can ask."

Ralf turned his head and peered at me with one eye. "What did you need from the green dragon, anyway?"

"Nothing much," I said. "Just some breath."

"I have an idea. How would you like to come with me to the Dragon Olympics?" asked Ralf. "My mother is entered in the distance flame-belching contest tonight."

I scratched my head with my toe. "Distance flame-belching? We appreciate the offer, but it doesn't sound like the kind of place that would be safe for frogs. Frog skin is kind of tender, and those flames—"

"Don't worry. The salve I gave you in my grandpa's cave will protect you."

"That's a great offer, but—" said Eadric.

Ralf looked so eager. "All the dragons will be at the Olympics. If any green dragons exist, they'll be there."

"But your grandfather said—" I began.

"It's worth a try, isn't it?" asked Ralf.

He was right. If there was even the smallest chance that we might be able to get the last ingredient, then we'd have to go. It was already Friday afternoon, and we had to have everything before dawn the next day. "Of course we'll go with you," I said. "Won't we, Eadric?"

Eadric nodded, although his mouth was set in a thin line and his eyes looked uneasy. "Thanks for inviting us, Ralf," he said.

Twenty

Grassina had told me about the ancient Greeks and their fondness for athletic contests, but I couldn't imagine how the dragons would compete. I wondered if all their contests involved fire.

After flying back down the side of the mountain, Ralf carried us into the same main tunnel where we'd met his grandfather, then turned into the first branching tunnel we encountered. Hot air met us like an invisible wall, but the ointment kept us from feeling much more than a slight change in temperature. It was dark inside, perhaps too hot for the fungus that illuminated the other caves.

Flying through a network of connecting tunnels, we entered a cave filled with bats and another that reeked so badly it gave me a headache. Eadric said that it smelled like trolls, so I was glad we weren't on foot. When we finally emerged from the last tunnel, we found ourselves in an enormous, bowl-shaped arena open to the sky.

With a level floor and high rock walls, it was the perfect spot for a gathering of dragons. It was hotter than inside the tunnel, and I could see why when Ralf flew up onto a small ledge so we could look around. A bubbling pool of red liquid seethed in the center of the arena, the air above it wavering in the rising heat.

"What is that?" I asked Ralf.

The little dragon glanced at the scarlet pool. "That's lava—liquid rock. My dad likes to swim in it."

"Eadric, did you hear that?" I asked, but he wasn't paying attention. His face had turned a paler green, and his eyes looked like they were about to jump out of his head. I followed his gaze back to the floor and understood why. There must have been at least ten times the number of dragons than there are people in my father's castle, with more dragons arriving all the time.

I studied the dragons, hoping to see a green one, but none of their colors was even close. This seemed to reinforce what the Dragon King had told us, yet I couldn't stop hoping that Eadric was right, that the old dragon really didn't know everything, and that a rare green dragon might still show up.

At first, I thought the dragons were just milling about, but as I watched, I noticed a purpose to their movements. While a few dragons darted across the floor on errands of their own, most were heading toward the low stone walls that defined the fields of competition.

Only a short distance from where we sat, athletes raced around an oval with other dragons standing by, watching. A roar went up when a yellow dragon passed a blue one, a sound that would have been terrifying if I'd heard it anywhere else.

A little farther away, dragons wearing armbands ran back and forth between brightly colored tents. Each tent was big enough to fit at least twenty grown dragons, although I never saw more than a few enter at once. I couldn't read the symbols on their banners, so I had no idea what they stood for, but when I saw an injured dragon carried into one tent, I assumed that it housed a healer.

I grabbed hold of Ralf's ridge when a gust of heated air almost knocked me off his back. Looking up, I saw six dragons chasing one another around the giant bowl, flying faster than any bird ever could. A pink cloud floated above the flying dragons, distorting my view of the mountains surrounding the arena, making them seem closer, then farther away. I turned to watch the dragons in the oval ring again. When one of the racers flamed, a small pink cloud formed in the air above him. The smell of boiled cabbage drifted by, reminding me of the magic miasma.

"Ralf," I said, "does anyone use this arena when the Olympics aren't going on?"

"Sure. Lots of dragons come here to practice. My

mother comes here almost every day. It's one of the reasons we live where we do."

I heard shouting and glanced down at the crowd directly below us. A group of giants had arrived, carrying baskets filled with skinny brown pods and long purple peppers. The dragons seemed eager to get at the baskets, following the giants to a low ledge carved into the far wall. When the giants emptied the contents onto the ledge, the dragons lined up behind them and helped themselves to the food.

"Those are flamers," said Ralf, pointing to the eating dragons. "They're stoking themselves with gunga beans and hot flami-peppers. Those peppers are one of the reasons the Olympics are held here. Gunga beans will grow just about anywhere, but flami-peppers grow only in volcanic ash."

"Why do the flamers like them so much?"

"If you combine big batches of them and mix them with a dragon's digestive juices, you get the best flames in the world. My mother eats them all the time. The beans are okay, but the peppers are too bitter for me. Look, there's my mother. Let's go down so I can introduce you."

Taking a step forward, Ralf dropped off the ledge and glided across the arena above the heads of the walking dragons. There were more giants here now, and Ralf had to swerve around them while trying to keep his mother in sight. The giants were sweating profusely, the huge drops that beaded their faces dripping onto the ground and anyone unfortunate enough to be standing nearby. Neither the dragons nor the giants seemed to mind, although some of the drops were as big across as my father's shield.

"What color are your mother's scales?" I asked Ralf as we approached the group of flamers.

"Red. My father's scales are blue like mine, although his are a lot darker. I hope mine get dark like his when I'm older."

"Hey, Ralfie!" called a voice from behind us. An enormous blue-black dragon only a little smaller than the Dragon King was trotting toward us from the direction of the lava pool. His head was huge, his eyes deep-set and shadowed by jutting ridges. When he opened his mouth to talk, I saw a long forked tongue and teeth so brilliantly white, they didn't seem real.

"Hi, Papa!" said the little dragon. With a bounce in his step, Ralf bounded across the rock floor to the larger dragon's side. "Where's Mama? I thought I saw her."

"She had to get ready. The competition is starting soon and she was afraid you weren't going to make it in time, so she asked me to find you. Are these friends of yours?" When the dragon leaned down to get a better look at us, Eadric dug his fingers into my arms.

"They sure are," Ralf said, a hint of pride in his

voice. "The little one in the front is Emma. The bigger one in the back is Eadric. Don't worry. They don't bite."

Ralf's father snorted. "That's good! I don't think I want to know a biting frog."

When Grumble Belly picked up his son and set him on his shoulders, Eadric and I clung to Ralf's ridge, wobbling back and forth until we were dizzy. Pushing his way through the crowd, the big dragon headed to the area set up for the distance flame-belching contest. The next contestant, a large yellow dragon, was lumbering up to the line when we arrived. Nodding to a black dragon wearing an armband, he took a few deep breaths and belched a flame half as long as the field.

"Huh," said Ralf's father. "Not bad."

A murmur went up from the crowd when the next athlete came forward. A slender dragon with red scales verging on magenta, she looked very feminine, with a refined head and delicate features.

"That's my mother!" Ralf said.

Eadric ducked, knocking his head against mine when Ralf's father reached up and patted his son on the back. "Hold still, Ralf. You don't want to distract her."

When his mother began her series of deep breaths, Ralf's wings stiffened, and I could feel his muscles tense beneath us. "Here we go," his father whispered. "Come on, Snorty, you can do it!"

Taking one last breath, Ralf's mother opened her

mouth and raised her wings, sweeping them back as a flame nearly as long as the field shot from between her gaping jaws. The flame was hot, glowing white where it left her mouth, fading through yellow and orange to red where its tip licked the rocky ground.

The crowd cheered wildly as the black dragon raced to the end of the field before Snorty's flame died down. The noise drowned out the announcement of her distance, but it was obvious that she had won. "Next year they're going to have to lengthen the field just for her, aren't they?" an older dragon with rust-red scales bellowed to Ralf's father.

"Sure looks that way," the huge blue dragon agreed.

"No knight would stand a chance against her," Eadric whispered into my eardrum.

It was impossible to get through the crowd, so we waited for his mother at the side of the field. She disappeared behind some of the bigger dragons, then suddenly she was beside us, reaching for Ralf.

"I knew you could do it!" Ralf shouted, flinging himself at her.

"Ralfie!" she said, sitting back on her haunches as she caught him. "How did you like it?"

"You were super, Mama! You're the best!"

His mother laughed and fondled the ridge atop his head. Turning toward the larger dragon, she smiled. "And what about you, Grumblekins?"

"You were great, Hot Lips," the big dragon said.

Eadric snorted, and I poked him in the stomach with my elbow. Laughing at your hosts is not a good idea, especially when they're dragons.

"Guys," Ralf said, covering his eyes with his wing. "Do you have to do that now? You're embarrassing me."

His mother laughed again and looked down at Ralf, noticing us for the first time. "You must be the frogs who are searching for a green dragon. My father told me about you. Any luck yet?"

Eadric shook his head. "Not so far."

"Why don't you three go look around?" she suggested, gesturing with her wingtip to encompass the entire arena. "It will be a while before they announce who won. Perhaps you'll get lucky and find your green dragon."

"That sounds like fun!" Ralf said, squirming out of his mother's grasp. "Roar for me when the ceremony's going to start."

Leaving his parents behind, Ralf flew across the arena, looking for a place to land. While the little dragon studied the crowded fields, Eadric whispered into my eardrum, "What did you think of his parents?"

"They're nice," I whispered back, "but I don't think they take us very seriously."

Eadric glanced at a passing deep purple dragon. Long and lean, the dragon had a surly expression on his face and wary eyes that probably didn't miss much. "I don't mind," said Eadric. "In fact, I think it's better this way. I'd rather be ignored as a frog than eaten as a human."

Twenty-one

There was so much to watch, we didn't know where to look first. Teams of seven dragons each were performing synchronized flying routines in the air above us. The group directly overhead did barrel rolls and flips, then climbed through the air in a giant spiral. On the way down, they went into flat spins and linked claws to form a star.

I never would have thought that watching dragons compete would be so much fun. The giants seemed to be enjoying themselves, too, laughing and talking across the heads of the dragons. I saw a red-bearded giant taking bets, jotting down figures on a piece of bark that had probably covered an entire tree.

Neither Eadric nor I had stopped looking for a green dragon. I saw a gold dragon, whose scales took on a greenish tinge when the light hit him right, but Eadric and I agreed that the color wasn't green enough and that he probably just needed a good polishing. We continued to look, but it had already come to seem like a hopeless quest. In a way, I thought it was just as well. I was a frog now and no longer had the bottle Li'l had given me. Even if I did find a green dragon, I doubted that any dragon would wait for me to find a container.

A squat blue dragon was strolling along a low stone wall that separated the fans from the athletes, urging everyone to stay well back. "Overheated dragons snort fire to cool off," he warned.

"What do they do in this event?" I asked Ralf.

"They run around the arena twice. Then they swim the length of the pool and fly around twice. Most of them end up at the flame-belching field afterward, letting off the heat they built up, but some of them can't wait that long and do it during the race." The little dragon had started to wiggle again, more violently than before. "I've got to go take care of something. You wait here and I'll be back in a few minutes."

"But Ralf," I said as he plucked us off with his claws and set us on the ground. Ralf ignored me. Turning tail, he flapped his wings and took off, heading toward the flame-belching field.

Eadric and I waited by the track, watching the dragons run past. When the first dragons left the pool and took to the air, we decided that we'd given Ralf more than enough time.

"So much for a few minutes," Eadric grumbled,

peering into the forest of scaly legs.

"Maybe he got lost."

"Maybe he found something better to do than spend time with two frogs."

"Ralf wouldn't desert us, Eadric. He's our friend. Something must have happened. I think we'd better go look for him."

"Where do you propose we start?" he asked.

"That way." I pointed in the direction Ralf had gone.

"Fine," said Eadric. "Then follow me and stay close while I try to keep us from getting squashed."

Eadric wasn't always right, but I was learning to trust his judgment in certain matters. He'd lived as a frog longer than I and had learned all the tricks he'd needed to survive. If anyone could get us through a stomping herd of dragons, it was Eadric.

We hopped alongside the stone wall until it turned one way and we had to go the other. Venturing out into the open for the first time, I took my cue from Eadric, hopping when he did, waiting when he waited. We were approaching the first tent when a giant came along, weighed down with an armload of tent stakes. Stopping to adjust the load, he dropped one and it landed with a crash only a few yards away, sending up a swirling cloud of ash. It made a few dragons cough, but its effect on me was much worse. It made me sneeze.

Suddenly we were humans again in a place where

humans were definitely not welcome. I froze, certain that we were more likely to be seen if we moved, but Eadric had other ideas. "I was afraid this would happen!" he said, grabbing my arm and yanking me toward the cluster of tents. "Come on! We've got to get out of here before—"

"Humans!" roared a short, fat dragon with dingy yellow scales and droopy ears.

"—a dragon sees us," Eadric finished, tightening his grip on my arm.

Although the yellow dragon had spotted us, he seemed to be the only one who had. The rest were looking around in confusion, which gave Eadric and me the chance to dart behind the giant's stake. It didn't help that we were no longer covered with Ralf's salve and that sweat was pouring off us. The heat demanded our attention and sapped our strength. Each step was an effort at a time when speed was our only ally, but even speed would not have been enough. No human can outrun a dragon. If we didn't want to be flame-broiled, our only chance was to hide.

The giant who had dropped the tent stake was still standing in the same spot, reaching for the piece of wood. He didn't notice Eadric drag me behind his hand as it closed around the stake. We were much bigger than we'd been as frogs, but we were still small when compared to most dragons and tiny compared to the giant, who could have held us easily in his hand.

I was so frightened, I couldn't get my feet to move, so Eadric had to pull me behind the stack of giants' baskets to hide us from dragon eyes. We used an old folded tent for cover when we heard the voices of the dragons grow louder. Rounding the mound of fabric, we found ourselves only a short distance from the standing tents.

We heard voices inside the first tent and had to pass it by. The next tent was also occupied, but the third tent appeared abandoned. Eadric and I slipped under the flap that covered the doorway and looked around. A low stone bench had been set up at one end. Crudely made, it looked strong enough to hold anyone, even the Dragon King. Someone had dumped a pile of robes in a corner of the tent, although I couldn't imagine why dragons would need them. Aside from a scattering of flower petals on the floor and lanterns hanging from the tent posts, the rest of the tent was empty.

Satisfied that we were alone, Eadric wiped the sweat from his eyes. "I know it wasn't your fault that you sneezed, but can't you sneeze again and turn us back? We're cooked meat if those dragons find us, and they're not going to stop looking until they do."

"I can't sneeze on command any more than you can. Something has to *make* me sneeze." Afraid that I'd lose my nose or do something else just as awful, I wouldn't even consider making up a sneeze-inducing spell.

A muffled moan came from the pile of robes. Eadric

and I jerked our heads around, but we didn't see anyone there. I started across the floor of the tent, moving as quietly as I could. When I heard the sound again, it was more of a whimper than a moan. Grasping his dagger with one hand, Eadric reached the pile first, tossing the top robe aside. Ralf lay curled up in a ball with his eyes shut, his scales a sickly blue.

"Ralf!" I said. "Are you all right?"

"I don't feel so good."

"You don't look so good, either," said Eadric. "You're turning a funny color."

"When did you start feeling sick?" I asked the little dragon.

"After I ate the bouquet Mama got when she won."

I didn't like the way his scales were taking on a yellowish tinge and his lips were starting to swell. "Then here's what we're going to do—"

"Get away from our son!" a voice growled behind me. I glanced back and saw Ralf's parents pushing through the entrance to the tent.

"Dad, is that you?" Ralf asked. "I don't feel so good."

"What have you done to him?" Snorty demanded, her eyes flaring red as she hurried to Ralf's side.

I tried to swallow, but my mouth was dry and my throat felt tight. Even if I could get the words out, I wasn't sure how to explain what had happened before the dragons roasted me.

Eadric brushed past, shielding me from the dragons with his body. "Don't worry, I'll protect you," he whispered.

Grumble Belly snarled and lowered his head, his eyes narrowed. Smoke trickled from his nostrils, and the smell of boiled cabbage grew stronger. I gulped when I saw his muscles bunch beneath his scales. The huge dragon was preparing to charge. "You filthy humans won't get away with this," he growled. "I've always known that humans weren't to be trusted. You kill innocent dragons sleeping in their caves, steal their treasures and attack them when they're providing for their families, but I didn't know you were so low that you'd deliberately hurt children. When I get through with you, there won't be enough ashes to—"

"Dad, it wasn't them. I ate Mama's bouquet and now I feel sick."

The blue-black dragon's head whipped around to look down at where his little son rested. "You mean the humans didn't hurt you?"

"Of course not. That's Emma and Eadric. They're having problems with a spell."

"Grumblekins, look at him," whispered Snorty. "He's turning yellow."

I peered around Eadric and caught a glimpse of Ralf. The little dragon's scales were pale yellow, and the tip of his nose had turned gray.

"Find those humans!" shouted a gruff dragon voice

from somewhere outside. "Wipe them out before they multiply! The things are worse than rats!"

"What's going on in here?" said the Dragon King as he thrust his head past the flap and trotted into the tent. "Good, you caught the humans. Have you found out how they got here?"

Snorty raised one brow ridge. "Through the entrance, I imagine. Ralfie says they're his frie—"

"Would you look at that!" interrupted her father. "A green dragon. So they do exist. Those two frogs weren't crazy after all."

"Dad," said Snorty, "that's Ralf, your grandson. He's sick."

I peeked around Eadric again. Ralf's scales had turned pale green, his swollen lips a deep emerald.

A voice shouted so loudly that it must have come from right outside the tent. "You go that way, Thunder Gut, and I'll go this way. They've got to be around here somewhere."

"Wait till I get my claws on them," growled another voice. "They killed my parents when I was just an egg. Humans don't deserve to live!"

I shrank away from the side of the tent as if they might see me somehow. The ground shook as they ran past, and ash puffed through a small tear in the bottom.

"Ooh," moaned Ralf. "I feel awful." His scales were deepening into emerald.

"Nice shade of green," said the Dragon King.

Ralf opened one eye and peeked up at his father. "Am I really green?"

Grumble Belly nodded. "But I'm sure it's only a temporary condition," he said in an overly hearty voice. "You'll be back to blue in no time."

"I need to breathe into something," said Ralf, trying to raise his head.

"What's wrong, sweetie? Are you having trouble breathing?" asked his mother. Ralf moaned again, and his mother turned to her mate. "Grumblekins, we have to find the healer. This is serious."

"No, Mama," Ralf whispered. "I need to do it for Emma."

Suddenly, I understood. Despite his illness, Ralf was thinking of Eadric and me and our quest for dragon's breath. If he did what he proposed, we'd have everything we were looking for, but even so …

"That's all right, Ralf. You don't have to do that. You just have to get well, and I think I know how to help you."

Ralf shook his head. "Not until I help you first. Do you have something?"

I shoved my hand into my pouch and grabbed the bottle. Yanking out the stopper, I knelt beside Ralf and held the bottle to his nose. He puffed a few gasping breaths, filling the small container, then lay back, his eyes half closed.

"What did you mean when you said you could help him?" Ralf's mother asked as I shoved the stopper back into the bottle and tucked it in my pouch.

"I know a spell for tummy troubles. I read it in a book of magic."

Ralf's father snorted. "A spell! What are you, some kind of witch?"

"A witch in training, actually. I won't try the spell unless you want me to, so it's up to you."

The old king scratched his head with a claw and looked confused. "There's something I should tell you, something about dragon smoke. It's on the tip of my brain. If only I could remember."

Ralf groaned again. Clutching his tummy, he curled up into a tight little ball.

"Not now, Father!" said Flame Snorter. "If she can help Ralfie …"

"Do you want me to try?" I asked. Ralf's mother nodded and the little dragon's father frowned, but no one objected. I pointed my finger at Ralf, hoping the spell would work on dragons as well as humans. "Here goes," I said.

> Soothe the aching tummy,
> Quench the belly fire,
> Calm the quaking stomach,
> Douse the pain so dire.

As I lowered my finger, the room seemed to throb with a light so bright that I had to squeeze my eyes shut and cover them with my hands. There was a hissing sound like steam escaping from a cook pot, and Ralf sighed.

"Was that it?" said his father. "I expected a lot more."

"How do you feel?" I asked Ralf, but his color was already returning to its normal shade of blue.

Ralf blinked up at me and smiled. "I feel better. Thanks."

"Sorry about the fire dousing. It was part of the spell and I was afraid it might not work if I left that out."

"It doesn't matter," said the little dragon's mother. "As long as my baby feels better. He's too young to have a real fire yet anyway. When he's a little older, I'll start feeding him gunga beans and hot flami-peppers. That'll get his fire going."

"Mama! I'm not a baby anymore. And you know I don't like flami-peppers! You're not really going to make me eat them, are you?"

"Every day. And no more flowers for you, young dragon. You'll eat normal dragon food and nothing else. Have I made myself clear?"

"Yes, Mama," said Ralf.

"He's not the only one who eats things he shouldn't," I said, glancing at Eadric.

I'd grown used to the constant din outside the tent as the dragons scoured the area for us, only now it seemed to be getting louder. When I listened, I could make out one word above all the rest. *Humans* sounded like a name for evil when shouted by an angry mob of dragons. We were in serious trouble.

The Dragon King peered nearsightedly at Eadric and me and shook his head. "I can't believe I'm going to say this, but I think you two had better hide for a while. I'll try to head everyone off, but I can't help you if they find you. Even though you've done my family a mighty big favor, there's only so much I can do. Too bad you're humans, that's all I can say."

"What if they weren't humans?" asked Ralf. "What if they turned back into frogs? Then they could leave the tent and no one would notice them. You can do it, can't you, Emma?"

"That's a great idea, Ralf, but there's only one problem. I have to sneeze if we're going to turn back, and I don't know how to make myself do it."

"Isn't there some other way you can change? You fixed me with magic. Why don't you fix yourself?"

"When I fixed you, I used a spell I'd read in a book. I don't know any spells that would change me back."

"Then make one up," said Ralf. "Witches do that kind of thing, don't they?"

"I'm not very good at making up spells yet. They

never turn out quite right."

Grumble Belly pointed a sharp claw at my chest. "You mean you'd try your magic on our son but not on yourself?"

I glanced from dragon to dragon, hoping that at least one of them would understand. "It's not that I don't want to. I just can't." I swallowed hard when the adult dragons' eyes began to glow red and pink smoke trickled out of their nostrils. The temperature in the room seemed to be rising as swirling smoke filled the air and the smell of boiling cabbage became overpowering.

"I think you'd better try, Emma," said Eadric. "You don't have much of a choice."

"What about you, Eadric? I know how you feel about my spells. Whatever happens to me is going to happen to you, too. Are you sure you want me to do this?"

"I'm willing to risk it if you are. We've made it through so far, haven't we?"

I took a deep breath and nodded. "All right," I said with a halfhearted smile. "Just don't expect any great poetry."

"About that smoke," said the old dragon.

Flame Snorter glared at him. "Not now, Father. Give the girl a chance."

"This is important. I remember what I wanted to tell her, and it's something she'd better know. Young human," he said, turning to me, "do you see the dragon smoke in this tent? There's a lot more now than there was a minute ago."

"Yes, but—"

"Dragon smoke is pretty powerful stuff. We have our own special magic, and so does our smoke. After you've been breathing the smoke the way you have, if you try to cast a spell on yourself, it will change your magic, one way or another. Just thought I'd better warn you."

"What do you mean?" asked Eadric.

"If you're a friend to dragons, it'll make your magic stronger, but there aren't too many dragon friends around. If you're like most humans and wouldn't mind using your magic against us, you might lose your magic altogether. If that happens, I don't think you'll be leaving here alive. My family will try to help you, but those fellows outside aren't feeling too friendly. It's your choice, so make it a good one. Once you cast your spell, what happens next will be out of your hands."

I was frightened. Trying to sneak past the other dragons wasn't much of an option. I didn't want to die, and I didn't want to risk losing Eadric, who would do his best to protect me and end up getting himself killed. I didn't want to lose my magic, but the more I thought about it, the more I felt that I wasn't about to lose anything. I never had used my magic against dragons, and I had no intention of starting. Wouldn't that count for something?

When I tried to talk, the words seemed to stick in my

throat. I tried again, and they came out sounding funny to me, as if someone else was saying them. "I have to try the spell."

"All right," said the old dragon. "It's your decision."

I closed my eyes so that the dragons wouldn't distract me. It took me a minute to come up with something that I thought would work. When I was ready, I took a deep breath and said,

I wish I might,
I wish I may,
Have the form
I want today.

Please let me choose
Which it will be.
No longer human
Make it froggy.

The pink smoke seemed to be drawn to me, swirling around me in an ever-thickening cloud. Eadric and the dragons faded from sight and everything grew silent, leaving me alone in a world of shadows. Despite the heat, a chill walked up my spine and I shivered. With Eadric at my side, I had felt braver and more able to face whatever came, but now … I tried to tell myself that everything would be fine. I had sworn that I'd never use my magic to hurt anyone, and as far as I knew, I'd never done anything worse than make a sea monster lose his teeth. Even then, he'd had another set coming in.

Something whispered at the edge of my hearing. I dug my nails into my palms and held my breath, straining to understand it. The sound came again, louder and more distinct. It was a voice, but it didn't belong to a human and it spoke no words that I could understand. Another voice joined in and then a third, and before I knew it, a chorus of voices surrounded me. They grew louder until suddenly they stopped, leaving me in silence once again.

Flashes of light broke through the smoke, red and yellow in a bed of dusky pink. *This is it,* I thought. *The dragons are going to turn me into charcoal.* I think I even forgot to breathe. Arrows of light with no beginning and no end shot through me as if I was no more substantial than a shadow. I heard soothing music and screams of terror, I tasted blood and sugar, smelled the stench of decay and the perfume of wildflowers. The arrows were cold and hot, they itched and burned and soothed … and then they were gone.

I felt light-headed and as fresh and full of energy as if I'd just stepped from an invigorating swim in a cool mountain stream. My senses seemed sharper, my thoughts clearer. I knew that I'd turned into a frog, but I also knew that something bigger and far more important had happened to me. Whatever it was, I was no longer the same person I'd been just minutes before.

The smoke was almost gone when the noise of the Olympics returned. It was loud and harsh, yet I welcomed it as proof that everything was all right.

"Would you look at that!" exclaimed the Dragon King. "I should have known it would turn out like this after the way you helped our Ralfie!"

"You have a funny sort of glow now, Emma. I can see it when I squint my eyes real hard, like this," said Ralf, squeezing his eyes into little slits.

"When you said that her magic would be more powerful, how much of an increase did you mean?" asked Eadric.

"That depends on the person," said the Dragon King, "but it's usually quite substantial."

Although I didn't know what to say, Eadric didn't have the same problem. "That's just great!" he said, shaking his head. "You made some mistakes with your magic before, but I can imagine what you'll come up with now!"

A dark red dragon with jagged brow ridges lifted the tent flap and stuck his head inside. "Has anyone seen a pair of humans?" When his eyes fell on the Dragon King, he ducked his head, murmuring, "Sorry, Your Majesty. Didn't mean to intrude."

"Hmph," said Gargle Snout. "See that it doesn't

happen again. And take your search for humans elsewhere. There aren't any here."

The red dragon bowed and backed away, muttering apologies. When the flap had fallen closed, Eadric said, "I think we should leave before anything else happens."

Ralf rubbed his eyes and stifled a yawn. "I'll take you to find your sword—"

"You certainly will not!" said his mother. "You're not going anywhere with your friends now. You can hardly keep your eyes open, and I don't—"

"Mama!" wailed Ralf, his face crinkling.

"Don't worry, son," said his father. "I'll take your friends wherever they need to go. You listen to your mother, and I'll come see you when I get back."

"You don't mind?" the little dragon asked. "Because it's kind of far."

While Ralf gave directions to his father, I tried to think of a good reason for not going with the big dragon. I knew and trusted Ralf, but his father was intimidating even when he was trying to be friendly. I was opening my mouth to make some excuse when Grumble Belly picked us up, plopped us behind his neck ridge and trotted out of the tent.

"Goodbye!" yelled Ralf as the tent flap closed behind us.

"Goodbye!" I called back, but we were already airborne.

Twenty-two

Night had fallen while we were inside the tent, but the glow from the lava pit cast an otherworldly light over the arena. Instead of taking the tunnel through the mountain, Grumble Belly avoided the crowd by flying straight up. I was convinced that we were going to fall off his back at any moment, but he carried us safely through the mountain passes and over the forest, his great wings beating with a strong and steady rhythm.

It was a beautiful night with the stars twinkling overhead, the pale face of the moon nearly full and the crisp, clear air washing away the smell of Ralf's salve. If it hadn't been for the whump of the dragon's wings, it would have been silent as well.

Ralf must have given his father excellent directions, since the big dragon carried us directly to the trees where the spider's web had hung. It was dark in the woods, making it hard to see much of anything. The moment the dragon landed, Eadric sprang to the ground. I hopped off the dragon's back, too, not wanting to stay there by myself. "If you'll wait, I'll make a light," I said, hearing Eadric stumble in the dark.

"Don't bother," said Grumble Belly. He closed his eyes and concentrated until his stomach made a grumbling sort of sound, like an old man makes when his bones are aching. Taking a deep breath, the dragon exhaled with his mouth partly closed, letting out a thin tongue of flame and the now-familiar cabbagey smell. The flame created enough light to illuminate the nearby ground all the way to the lowest branches of the closest trees. It went out when he inhaled, lighting again with his next breath, illuminating the area in a pulse of light, dark, light, dark. It was helpful, but not perfect since I could see Eadric for a moment, and then he disappeared as the flame went out.

"Ow!" said Eadric. I could see him now, standing by a tree and rubbing his forehead, apparently having run into a branch. Staring at the ground by his feet, he said, "I know Ferdy is around here somewhere."

"Grumble Belly," I said, taking a step back when the dragon's huge head swung around to face me, "would you be able to carry us if we were humans?"

"Easily," the dragon answered.

"Then I think it's time we stopped being frogs." Since it had worked so well the first time, I used the same spell again—with a small adjustment.

I wish I might,
I wish I may,
Have the form
I want today.

Let me choose
Which it will be.
A human form
Is right for me.

My magic felt different now. While it had taken a lot of effort and concentration before and I had to hope I was saying the right thing each time, now I knew when it was right, and it wasn't just because the spell was similar to the one I'd said in the tent. Now I could see what effect my words would have before I said them. This time when I said the spell, the change took place in an instant and I didn't feel queasy afterward. Powerful magic definitely had its advantages.

While Eadric shuffled through the dead leaves, searching for Ferdy, I tried to remember where he'd been standing when we turned into frogs. I knew where I'd been and he'd been right. "What's this?" I asked when my foot hit something hard. I knelt down to brush the leaves aside and uncovered his sword, only a few feet from where he'd been looking. Eadric reached for Ferdy, then stood up, holding the sword at arm's length.

"I'm sorry I left you, Ferdy," said Eadric. "I didn't mean to. Please forgive me."

Ferdy didn't stay silent for long.

> I'm never one to hold a grudge.
> I never can stay mad.
> I'll never be the kind to judge.
> To see you makes me glad.

"Ferdy's better than a faithful hound," I said. "A sword that forgiving won't chew up your shoes when it's starving for attention."

"He is a good sword, isn't he? I'd say he wasn't such a bad purchase after all."

The trip home took only a few minutes. We were within sight of the castle when Grumble Belly said, "I'd drop you at your front door, but that would bring out all the guards. Is there somewhere out of the way where I can let you off?"

"Over there," I said, pointing to the tower on the left. "That's where my aunt lives. She won't mind if we use her window. In fact, she'd probably like to meet you."

"Another time, perhaps." Grumble Belly dipped one wing and swerved toward the tower, gliding up to the window silently.

"Thanks for the ride," I said, jumping onto the ledge.

Eadric checked to make sure that he had his

possessions with him before following me through the window. "Thanks," he said.

Grumble Belly smiled. "You saved my son's life and became his friends. Here," he said, snapping off the tip of an already cracked claw and depositing it on the window ledge. "If you ever need me, hold this in your left hand and call my name. Dragons don't forget their friends."

Eadric and I stood by the window, watching the dragon's silhouette winging through the night sky. A shout went up from the guard on the next tower, but Grumble Belly was already too far away for an arrow to reach.

I picked up the dragon's claw and tucked it in my pouch, intending to examine it in the daylight.

The door to the storage room creaked open and a small head peeked out. "Is it gone?" Li'l whispered, peering around the room.

"Yes, Li'l," I said. "The dragon's gone."

"Thank goodness!" said the little bat. Li'l leaned forward and peered at me. "So, did you get the dragon's breath and the feather?"

"We got it all! I have the dragon's breath right here," I said, patting my pouch.

"And here are the feathers," Eadric said, handing them to me. I was carrying them to Grassina's workbench when he pointed toward the back of the room and whispered, "Who's that?"

A pale figure seemed to be floating toward us, and I

thought it must be one of the castle ghosts until she stepped in the puddle of moonlight shining through the window. It was my mother, her hair streaming loose around her shoulders and down her back, her long, white gown brushing her ankles and reaching past her fingertips.

I pointed at the witches' lights, lighting a half dozen or so.

"You're back," she said, sounding relieved. "Is Grassina with you?"

"You mean she isn't here? But she knows we have to turn Haywood back within the next few hours!"

"Haywood! I wish I'd never heard that name. He's made her forget everything, and now she isn't even here when we need her so desperately."

"What happened? Is something wrong?"

"Of course something's wrong! King Beltran's army has almost reached the border. Your father is waiting for him there. If Grassina doesn't help your father, Beltran's wizard can destroy our entire army before a single arrow is shot. Emeralda, you told me that you'd learned a little magic. Do you know how to locate Grassina? We need her back here right away!"

"I'll see what I can do." It occurred to me that my mother had to be truly desperate to accept my magic so suddenly, which made me want to help even more. I searched Grassina's workbench for her dragon scale, but she must have taken it with her again. "I can use this," I said, finding her old far-seeing ball. Although she had a newer and more powerful one, that seemed to be missing as well.

"Eadric, help me find something personal of Grassina's that I can use to locate her. Try checking her comb or her pillow. If we're lucky, her cleaning spell missed a hair or two."

Unfortunately, Grassina's spell was too thorough. We didn't find any of her hair, but we did find a clump of Haywood's fur on the window seat.

"This will have to do," I said. "We'll see if we can find Haywood and hope that Grassina is nearby."

"I don't understand," said Eadric. "If you can find Haywood this way, why didn't Grassina try it? It has to be easier than whatever she's been doing."

"It depends on the distance involved," I said. "This won't be easy if he's too far away. My aunt is a powerful witch, but this may be too hard even for her. And remember, she had to eliminate all those false trails."

I already knew what I was going to say when I set the fur on Grassina's workbench and placed the far-seeing ball on top of it.

> In the day or in the night,
> In the dark or in the light,
> Show me where the otter's gone,
> Show me now before the dawn.

An image formed inside the ball, fuzzy at first, but it grew more distinct as we watched. The sun was high over a riverbank where an otter, his fur wet and shiny, slipped and slid across the mud. A shadowy figure was chasing him, but the otter was too wild to catch. Twisting around as the figure reached out, he snapped and bit, then scampered toward the water as the figure fell back, nursing an injured hand.

"Is that Grassina?" Eadric asked, squinting at the image. "Why is she so hard to see?"

"Because she isn't the one I asked to see," I said.

"Can you contact her?" asked my mother.

"I can do better than that." I was feeling stronger and more confident in my magic than I ever had before, and making up spells no longer seemed such a challenge.

"Step back," I said, "and stay out of the way. This might be messy." Taking the ball in my hands, I turned to face the center of the chamber.

Bring the otter to this room
So that he can be a groom.
Bring my aunt who's chasing him,
Keep them safe in life and limb.

The splat of something wet and heavy hitting the floor made me jump. Haywood had landed first, tumbling across my aunt's beautiful carpet and smearing it with mud. Grassina appeared next, sprawling on the floor with a whoosh as the air was knocked out of her. Stunned, she lay still for a moment, and I began to worry that she'd been hurt. She was shaky when she stood up, but I thought she looked fine until I noticed the blood dripping from her hand.

"Oh, my!" exclaimed my aunt, staring at us in surprise. "How did that happen?"

"Emma used a spell," Eadric began.

Grassina looked at him as if he was crazy. "Who?"

"Emma," Eadric said again. "She found you in that ball thing, and then she said a spell to bring you here. Queen Chartreuse said she needed you, so Emma—"

"Emma couldn't possibly do that. I don't know anyone who could bring two people over such a distance. There must be—"

Haywood was acting like any wild thing suddenly let loose indoors. He panicked, his claws digging into the carpet as he scurried from one end of the room to the other, trying to find a way out. I stopped listening to Grassina when he ran into the table holding the crystalline bouquet. The table fell over with a crash, and the bouquet would have been smashed on the floor if Eadric hadn't launched himself across the room, catching it with both hands.

"Good catch!" I said, and darted after the frantic otter. I chased him into the corner of the room, which I decided wasn't a good idea when he bared his teeth and growled. Backing away one step at a time, I pointed my finger at him and said,

> Send this otter to the pond
> Where I first met Eadric.
> Do not let the otter leave,
> By free will or by magic.

The instant I finished the spell, Haywood disappeared, leaving behind mud and the musky scent of wet otter. I heard Grassina gasp, and when I turned around, she was staring at me as if I'd grown another head.

"I'm sorry, but he couldn't stay here," I said. "He's too wild to keep inside."

"I know. I would have done the same thing. I just can't believe how much you've changed. The Emma I used to know couldn't have done that. And if you were really the one to bring us here—"

"She was," my mother said, surprising me by looking proud. "Now hold still and let me look at that hand." Muttering to herself, my mother made Grassina sit down and began to dab at her wound using water from the pitcher and a clean cloth. "You two can talk later," Mother added. "Grassina has to go help Limelyn. She said that when she came back—"

My aunt frowned at her. "I said that I'd help him

after I took care of Haywood. I still have to turn my darling back, and I don't have much time."

"But Beltran's troops have almost reached the border," said Mother. "His wizard—"

"Isn't going to do anything until morning. Olebald isn't very powerful, so he needs to see what he's doing. He'll wait for daylight. As I said before, I'll go directly there once Haywood is changed back. Now if you don't mind, I have a lot to do."

"Do you swear you will on your honor as the Green Witch?" my mother asked, tightening the bandage that she was wrapping around her sister's hand.

"*Ow!*" yelped Grassina. "Yes, I swear! Now, get some sleep. You'll need to be rested for Greater Greensward's victory celebration." Taking my mother by the arm, Grassina led her to the door.

"All right, as long as you swear." Mother said, letting her sister push her across the threshold.

Twenty-three

Grassina gestured, and more witches' lights began to glow, the light soft and diffuse. Eadric's stomach rumbled, and a crimson fog floated around the room. He blushed, his face turning nearly the same color as the fog.

"Eadric ate the seeds inside the magic beans," I said, certain that that was all the explanation my aunt needed.

Grassina shook her head sadly, although a smile tugged at the corners of her mouth. "You shouldn't have eaten those seeds, Eadric. Those were old magic beans whose magic gets stronger with age. Every month for the rest of your life your problem will return when the moon is full."

My grandfather was known as Aldrid the Wise, my father was Limelyn the Courageous, yet the man I might marry one day could be called Eadric the Flatulent. Eadric groaned when his stomach grumbled, and I couldn't keep from smiling. What a time to realize that I really *wanted* to marry him!

"I think I'll go down to the kitchen," Eadric said, heading for the door. "It's been a while since we ate last. Emma, are you coming?"

"No, I need to stay and help Aunt Grassina." I settled into my usual chair in front of the fireplace. Grassina joined me in the other chair, and we waited until Eadric had closed the door behind him. When my aunt sighed, I knew that something was wrong.

"Father will be all right, won't he?" I asked.

"Oh, yes. This has nothing to do with your father. It's just that I'm not sure I'm doing the right thing about Haywood."

"What are you saying? Don't you want to get him back the way he was?"

"Yes, of course I do, or at least I think I do. But what if we've changed so much that we don't like each other anymore? Or what if we discover that we've fallen out of love? I'm no longer the young girl who fell in love with the romantic young wizard in training. I've had a lot of time to think about this. It took me much longer than I thought it would to find Haywood. Then when I did, Mother had made him forget that he was ever human, just as she said she would. He was happy as an otter, happier than most men ever are. What right did I have to bring him back here to life as a human?"

"He was happy as an otter because of Grandmother's spell, you know that. But he'll be happier with you. I saw the way he looked at you when you found him the other day. He'd even carved your name in the bark of an old oak, although it must have been terribly difficult for an otter. He loves you, Aunt Grassina, and if he was in his right mind, he'd tell you so."

Grassina held up her hand, showing me the wrapping stained with blood. "He bit me, Emma! When I finally found him, he bit me like a wild animal!"

"It was Grandmother's spell. I know the real Haywood loves you!"

Grassina sighed again. "Perhaps you're right, Emma. I know so little about affairs of the heart. It's been so long." She closed her eyes and rubbed her temples as if in pain, but when she looked at me again, she seemed a little more cheery. "If we're going through with this, we'd better get busy. Dawn will be here before we know it."

While Grassina started toward her room to fetch the items from the silver chest, I reached into my pouch for the bottle of dragon's breath. I was about to take it out when I heard a rustling by the window. I gasped when Grandmother shot through the opening. Hopping off her broom, she pointed a finger at Grassina. "There you are! Did you find him?"

Grassina turned her head and glared. "What are you doing here?"

"I've come to keep you from making a terrible mistake!"

"The only mistake I've made was letting you near Haywood again," said Grassina. "I should have known better than to ask you for help."

"Is that any way to talk to your mother?"

"In your case, yes. Now please leave."

Grandmother muttered something as she squinted, her tiny eyes nearly disappearing in a mass of wrinkles. Grassina must have guessed what her mother was up to, because she put her hand in front of her face and recited something very fast. With a high-pitched whistle, Grandmother's spell bounced off Grassina and attached itself to its creator. Furious, Grandmother clawed at her lips, tearing away strands of something thick and white that seemed to writhe in her hands.

"Why, you little pipsqueak!" shrilled my grandmother once she'd uncovered her mouth. "You restore Henry and your life will change forever!"

"I hope so, Mother, and his name is *Haywood!*"

"This is for your own good, daughter!" screamed Grandmother as she hurled a ball of the tangled white strands at Grassina.

My aunt ducked, and the ball splattered against the wall behind her. "Mother, I'm warning you, you aren't going to change my mind."

"Let's bring Howard here and we'll see what he thinks." Grandmother muttered something and made clockwise circles with her hand. A puff of orange smoke clouded the corner of the room, and when it cleared, Haywood stood blinking at the light. Grandmother spoke again, and a dozen wasps buzzed through the window, heading straight for the otter. If I hadn't known the strength of my spell, I might have been convinced.

"Haywood!" screamed Grassina as he snapped and batted at the wasps. Without thought for her own safety, my aunt rushed to help him. The moment Grassina turned her back, Grandmother pointed at her and muttered. It must have been a binding spell, for my aunt froze in midstep. Her body trembled as she fought to break the spell.

"Harvey isn't worth the breath it takes to say his name," my grandmother shrilled. "I don't know why you're being so thickheaded!"

"Because she loves him!" I said, surprising even myself. I couldn't bear it any longer. My grandmother had done everything she could to stand in the way of true love, and even that hadn't been enough for her. "You may have fooled Grassina, but I know that's not Haywood. He's still right where I put him, and that's where he'll stay until we're ready. Your tricks aren't going to work with me, so you might as well stop now."

Grandmother grumbled and waved her arm. The false images of the otter and the wasps began to fade.

"What you're doing is wrong, Grandmother!" I continued. "Can't you see that they should be together?"

My grandmother's eyes flashed. "I see. You've learned a little magic, so you think you can interfere. Well, this is none of your business. This is between my daughter and me." With a flick of her fingers, silver sparks shot from their tips, sizzling as if they burned the air.

Keep it simple, I thought, and a spell formed in my mind almost effortlessly.

The wind must blow,
It can't be slow.
Put out each spark
And leave no mark.

A sudden gust of wind shook the tapestries on the walls, whipped my hair about my head, blew the loose parchments off Grassina's desk and turned the sparks into fizzling dust that fell harmlessly to the floor when the wind died down.

"Very nice!" exclaimed Grandmother, and suddenly I had the impression that she was pleased. "Now how about this?" I was surprised to see her vanish, but even more surprised that I could still sense her presence in the room.

"I know you're here, Grandmother. Hasn't this gone on long enough?" When she didn't answer. I said, "Fine. If that's the way you're going to act, let's try this."

Let each life here
Give off a glow,
To help me learn
What I must know.

My skin tingled, and the air around me began to shimmer while a golden aura formed around my aunt and Li'l. I blinked, and when I looked again I saw a glowing light roughly my grandmother's size and shape. The light moved, and I heard my grandmother laugh. "Very good! Maybe we'll make a witch of you yet."

Somehow, what had started as a fight between my aunt and my grandmother had ended up feeling like a test for me. From the tone of my grandmother's voice, it seemed that I had passed.

A blue mist floated through the door, and my grandfather materialized in the middle of the room. "Back so soon, Olivene? You stay away for years, and now you visit twice in one week?"

Grandmother reappeared with a small pop. "Mind your own business, you old fool," she said, her bristling eyebrows drawn together in a V. "This is between me and my granddaughter."

"She's my granddaughter, too. Leave her alone, Olivene. She doesn't need you interfering in her life."

"And I don't need your advice, Aldrid. I was leaving anyway. I've already said what I wanted to say and learned what I wanted to learn." Grandmother smiled at me, then turned to waggle her fingers at Grassina. My aunt's foot hit the floor with a thump, and she staggered a step or two.

"Then why are you still here?" asked Grandfather.

"I'm not," Grandmother said. Hopping onto her waiting broom, she flew around the room, cackling like an old hen and making us duck to avoid her. When she flew out the window, a full moon framed her silhouette.

Grandfather shook his head. "That woman gets crazier every time I see her."

"I heard that!" Grandmother shouted over her shoulder, her voice fading with distance.

"Thanks for stopping by, Father, although I could have handled it myself," said Grassina. "I was running through the standard releases for binding spells. I would have broken it soon, and then I would have taken care of Mother."

"I know, but I wanted to see her, even if it was just for a minute. She has the personality of a crazed she-bear, but I miss her just the same. Nice or nasty, your grandmother has always been the most exciting woman I've ever known. It wasn't her fault that she turned mean. Good night, ladies. Come visit me when you can."

Grassina waited until Grandfather had dematerialized, then raised her eyebrows and turned to me. "So what have you been doing? Your magic has improved more than I would have thought possible in such a short time."

"It was the magic miasma at the Dragon Olympics," I said. "It seems that when you do magic—"

"Never mind," she said, shaking her head and smiling. "It sounds like a long story, and I want you to tell me all about it when we have time. Right now, we'd better see to Haywood. The sun will be up before we know it."

I followed my aunt to her workbench. Taking out a small clay bowl, Grassina dropped in one of Surely's feathers, Nastia Nautica's gossamer hair and the husk of a magic bean. Li'l watched every move, her head swiveling back and forth. I handed Grassina the bottle of dragon's breath. She shook it, then said,

Solids become liquids,
Liquids turn to gas.
Reverse the process
With my next pass.

Make this gas a liquid
For an hour or two.
Return it to its present form
When its work is through.

When she waved the bottle over the bowl once more, the contents sparkled, becoming so bright that I had to look away.

"I find that liquids are much easier to use in some

circumstances, gases in others. In this case," she said, holding up the bottle so I could see the blue-green fluid inside, "a liquid is handier. Now watch."

Slowly tilting the bottle, Grassina poured in three drops, waited a moment, then poured in another three. My heart beat one, two, three times, then the liquid dragon's breath grew hot, bubbling like the lava in the dragon's pool, and the feather, the hair and the bean husk curled into tight little balls before dissolving. The liquid, now a creamy blue, was light and frothy with bubbles rising and falling.

"Good," said Grassina, setting a lid on the bowl. "Now we're all set." Recapping the bottle, she handed it to me before picking up the potion. "Keep that bottle safe. There's no telling when you might need it next, and it was probably very difficult to get."

You have no idea, I thought, but when I saw her secret little smile, I decided that maybe she did after all.

Twenty-four

Dressed in heavy cloaks against the early morning chill, Grassina, Eadric and I hurried along the path to the swamp, lighting our way with torches. The sky was already growing brighter when we reached the pond. It wasn't a terribly large pond, but it had always been my favorite. I loved the stand of cattails at the far end, the willows trailing their lance-shaped leaves in the water, and the wash of gravel where I had often stood to survey my own, small kingdom. Haywood was floating on his back in the morning mist, seeming as if he didn't have a care in the world.

Grassina wasn't about to wait any longer. Holding out her hands, she called,

> Come to me, my darling.
> Come to me, my friend.
> When you have sipped
> The drink I hold,

Your feral life will end.

As if in a trance, Haywood rolled over onto his belly and swam toward Grassina, his liquid brown eyes never leaving her face. Uncovering the bowl, Grassina crouched by the water's edge. When Haywood's paws touched the mud of the bank, she tilted the bowl, pouring its contents into his open mouth.

Haywood blinked up at Grassina. Gradually, more mist rose from the water around him, and his edges began to blur. The dark, furry form that was Haywood grew longer, his head and body larger, his tail disappearing altogether.

I glanced at Grassina. Although her eyes had been troubled just moments before, they were now lit with the purest joy I had ever seen. She gazed into Haywood's eyes; her face softened. As the mist dissolved, I could see that Haywood was human again. A middle-aged man, he was dressed in clothes twenty years out of style. His sandy brown hair was tinged with gray, his brown eyes warm and friendly. From the way he looked at Grassina, it was plain that his memory had returned and that he still adored my aunt.

They reached toward each other with trembling hands. Their faces seemed to glow with happiness, and I felt my throat tighten when they leaned toward each other and kissed. I was still watching them when a breeze sprang up, chasing away the last of the mist and bringing with it a shower of rose petals, pink, red, purple and every shade in between. They drifted around us in a gentle blanket, filling the air with their sweet scent.

I was brushing a few clinging petals from my face when I felt something hard rub against my cheek. I glanced at my hand and was startled to find Grassina's green leaf ring on my finger. "Why is this—" I began, and then I heard someone gasp. I turned back to Grassina and Haywood. The breeze had died, leaving them covered with petals. Jerking his hands away from Grassina, Haywood struggled to back up, but his feet slid out from under him and he landed in deeper water with a splash.

I wondered what could have caused the look of horror on his face, and then Grassina turned around, the petals fell away, and I knew. No longer the beautiful woman I had known my entire life, she had become just like my grandmother. The curse we'd all feared, the curse the fairy had put on my ancestor, Hazel, had taken its toll, turning Grassina's glorious auburn hair stringy and black, her well-shaped nose so long that it almost reached her jutting chin. She had more hairy warts on her face than I had toes on my feet, and her fingers were bent and gnarled.

It was the rose petals, I thought. *Grandmother must have added that to the spell she cast on Haywood. She's had her way after all.*

"What are you pea brains gawking at?" Grassina asked, her voice as scratchy as a rusty knife.

"You've changed," I squeaked.

"Of course I've changed, fly breath. I've gotten a whole lot smarter. The wedding's off. I wouldn't marry fur-boy if he was the last wizard in the swamp. Now go away and stop bothering me. I've got to get out of these disgusting clothes and into something more suitable."

Grassina stormed off in the direction of the castle. Dumbstruck, we watched her stomp away, then turned and looked at each other.

"What just happened?" asked Haywood, water dribbling from his clothes as he slogged his way out of the pond. "Where's my Grassina? I thought that was Grassina, but then that hag ... Did that woman do something to her? Is she in danger?"

"No, I don't think so," I said, and gave him a brief description of the curse. His expression changed from horrified to woeful as I explained what must have happened. "That woman was your Grassina, at least until the curse took hold. I don't think she's anyone's Grassina now."

"There must be something we can do about it! You're training to be a witch, and I was studying wizardry before Olivene changed me. Between the two of us, we should be able to think of something. What did the curse say, exactly?"

"That's just it. The only one who would know is the fairy who said it, but we don't even know who that was. It's hopeless." The enormity of what had happened finally began to sink in. The woman who had been the kindest, most caring person in my life was gone, replaced by a horrible crone. Fighting back tears, I could feel my throat close up, making it hard to speak. "I'm sorry that this happened. If I hadn't insisted that we see my grandmother—"

"I'd still be an otter and Grassina and I would have spent the rest of our lives trying to find a solution. And as soon as we did, Grassina would have turned nasty anyway." Haywood grimaced and rubbed the back of his neck, turning his head from side to side.

"You'll be stiff for a while," I said, "but it won't be long before you're back to normal."

"Normal, eh? For twenty-three years normal was being an otter. It wasn't a bad life, either. The only thing I really missed was Grassina."

"I know. We never thought that my grandmother would go to such lengths."

"Olivene must have hated me even more than I realized, although I don't know why. If I could get my hands on her now, though, I'd give her plenty of reason."

"That would only make things worse. Why don't you go to the castle? Cook will give you something to eat, and I'll talk to my parents. I'm sure we can find a place for you to stay until you decide what you want to do."

Haywood took a step, his legs shaking beneath him. "Thanks," he said. "This is going to take some getting used to."

While I probably should have helped Haywood get to the castle, I couldn't make myself go back just yet. I was angry at my grandmother for her spell and at Grassina for succumbing to it, but mostly I was angry at myself. Turning back to the pond, I glared at Eadric, although I knew that none of it was his fault. "I can't believe this!" I said. "Why did I have to be such an interfering busybody who couldn't stay out of other people's business? If only I hadn't been so convincing when Grassina wanted to give up. If only I hadn't encouraged her to ask my grandmother for help. If only I hadn't brought them back together in the first place. I should have known my grandmother would do something like this!"

"What about your father?" asked Eadric, a puzzled expression on his face. "Isn't Grassina going to help him?"

"Oh, no!" I said. "She was supposed to go now, wasn't she? What are we going to do?"

"What do you mean? Just because she looks different, it doesn't mean that she's lost her ability to—"

"That's true!" I said, and began to run. "I'm sure she's just forgotten." When I saw my aunt up ahead, using a stick to whack the heads off daisies while she walked, I shouted, "Grassina! Wait for me!" Instead of waiting, my aunt began to walk faster.

I jerked my hem from the grasp of clutching brambles and hurried after Grassina, finally catching up with her on the path that led into one of the kitchen gardens. "What do you want?" she asked, glaring down the length of her long nose at me.

"My father!" I gasped, out of breath from running. "You have to go help him!"

Grassina sniffed loudly. "No, I don't. It's no longer my responsibility. I don't have to do anything I don't want to."

"But the Green Witch—"

"That's right. It's up to the Green Witch, and that's you now. See this ring?" she asked, grabbing my wrist and twisting it to get a better look at my hand. "It means that you have to protect the kingdom." Her eyes glittered when she shoved my hand away and started up the path.

"But I don't know what to do!" I wailed.

Without stopping or turning around, she shouted, "You'll figure it out!"

Eadric caught up with me while I stood open-mouthed, watching Grassina stomp off. "Is she going to help your father?" he asked.

I shook my head. "No. She says that I'm the Green Witch now, so it's up to me." I held out my hand and showed him the ring.

Eadric's jaw dropped. "You're the Green Witch? You've got to be kidding!"

The dumbfounded look on his face was almost insulting. "It's not that hard to believe! I'm sure I can do it. I just have to figure out how."

"You mean she didn't tell you?"

"No," I said, "and I don't think the job comes with a list of instructions. Just give me a moment to think!"

"Sure." Eadric stepped back a pace and raised both hands in the air as if surrendering. "Go right ahead."

I didn't know what I should do. Because of me, my father had been left without any magical defense. I was sure that Grassina would have known exactly what steps to take before she'd changed, but even if she still knew, she wasn't about to tell me. And what about my grandmother? She had seemed awfully pleased with my improved magical abilities. Maybe she really had been testing me. Maybe she was trying to see if I was good enough to be the next Green Witch. She had to have known what would happen when Grassina kissed Haywood, so maybe Grandmother wanted to see what I was capable of doing before letting her daughter have her way. I don't know what would have happened if I hadn't been good enough, yet the fact that the ring had ended up on my finger meant a great deal to me. Even so, just because I was the new Green Witch didn't mean that I knew how to help my father. *If only I had some help,* I thought, and suddenly I knew what to do. I smiled, glad that I hadn't had time to clean out my pouch.

"He said to call on him if I ever needed to," I said, reaching into the cloth bag.

Eadric frowned. "Who said that?"

Taking the broken fragment of dragon claw in my left hand, I yelled, "Grumble Belly!"

"You didn't have to shout," said Eadric. "It was just a simple question."

"I wasn't shouting at you; I was calling him. I hope it doesn't take him long to get here."

I tried to wait patiently, but Eadric kept muttering things like "stupid idea" and "waste of time." "Listen," he said finally, "why don't I get Bright Country? The sooner we start—"

There was a clap like thunder, and Grumble Belly dropped out of the sky, his shadow gliding across the pond. His leathery wings made a rustling sound as he landed beside us. "When I said you could call on me, I didn't mean right away. Dragons need to sleep sometime, you know."

"I didn't think I'd have to call you this soon, but everything has changed." I explained that I'd become the Green Witch and that my father was counting on me. "And you were the only one I could think of to ask for help."

"What am I, the invisible prince?" muttered Eadric. "You could have asked me."

The dragon sighed. "I'll do what I can. Is he coming, too?" Using a blunted claw, Grumble Belly rapped Eadric on the chest, nearly knocking him to the ground.

"Of course," I said, climbing up onto the dragon's scaly shoulder. "I always need Eadric."

Twenty-five

Greater Greensward is a fairly large kingdom, but it didn't take long to cross it on the back of a full-grown dragon. I was familiar with the border, having visited it many times, so when we didn't hit the correct spot immediately, I told Grumble Belly to head north.

Long before we saw the armies, we spotted dragons circling in the sky. There were three of the scaly beasts, all a vivid orange shading to crimson and all larger than Grumble Belly.

"Do you recognize them?" I asked our dragon friend.

"I've never seen them before. They must not be from around here. Siblings, probably, since they're all the same color and their shading matches."

I studied the dragons as we flew closer. They didn't look at all like the dragons I'd seen at the Olympics. Even the way they moved seemed odd; the sweep of their wings was jerky and the way they turned their heads too abrupt.

"Hello!" Grumble Belly called, but the trio of dragons ignored him.

We finally passed the last of the trees in what had seemed to be an endless forest. Below us lay farmland already taken over by the two armies. They faced each other in straight rows with only a few hundred yards and a trickling stream between them. Both sides appeared to be waiting for a signal.

"I'd better see my father first," I said, and leaned forward to tap Grumble Belly's shoulder. "Can you take us down now, please? I want to talk to the king in the green armor."

My father had to calm his plunging horse when Grumble Belly landed beside him. When he finally stood still enough that we could talk, Father turned to me. "So, Emma, I expected to see Grassina. What are *you* doing here, and *what* are you riding?"

"Grassina finally fell victim to the family curse, so I'm the new Green Witch. This is our friend, Grumble Belly. He's helping us."

"Grumble Belly, huh?" Father said, eyeing the enormous dragon. "You say he's a friend? Then he isn't under a spell?" I noticed that my father's hand had moved toward his sword, but when I nodded, he took his hand away. "Someday you'll have to tell me how you two met. And you mean to say that Grassina acts like Olivene now?"

I nodded. "And Haywood is a man again."

"I'll have a lot to get used to, won't I?" he said. "What do you plan to do, Emma?"

"Whatever you need." I glanced at the knights trying to calm their frightened horses. "But I think we'd better get back in the air before we scare away your army."

"Then see what you can do about those orange dragons. We can handle Beltran's troops, but not while dragons are attacking."

When Grumble Belly leaped into the air, he headed straight for the other army. The men in the front lines looked like peasants fresh from the fields. Wearing stiffened leather for armor, and carrying pitchforks and axes for weapons, I didn't think they stood much of a chance against my father's trained soldiers. Beltran had kept his own trained men toward the back and it looked like he was there as well, seated on a black horse behind the foot soldiers and the mounted knights. I decided that another, trimmer figure seated on a white horse to his right must be Prince Jorge since they were dressed almost alike. Helmeted and wearing suits of chain mail, the triple griffins of their family crest decorated their horse's trappings as well as their shields, but while the king wore black, Jorge was dressed in shining silver.

Another man sat astride a gray horse to the left of the king. Taller than Beltran or Jorge, he had flowing white hair and wore a long black cape. His face was uncovered, and from where I sat, he looked like he might be handsome, although not as handsome as the prince. When the man gestured at the dragons, I realized that he must be the wizard. *That can't be Olebald,* I thought. *He doesn't look anything like Olefat.* Realizing that Grassina must have been mistaken, I swallowed hard and tried to ignore the tight feeling in my chest. This was no incompetent wizard who would be easy to defeat.

My father sat at the head of his mounted knights, his visor raised as he watched the dragons descend. The beasts flamed and my father's men cried out. Horses reared and pranced, creating havoc in my father's ranks.

"Beltran's wizard must be controlling those dragons," said Eadric. "It would take a strong wizard to control three dragons at once, wouldn't it, Grumble Belly?"

The dragon snorted, and a sour puff of air wafted past us. "I've never met a wizard who could control one dragon so completely, let alone three. Dragons don't normally involve themselves in the affairs of men. He must be a powerful wizard indeed."

I watched as the dragons swooped and veered, flying low over my father's men and scattering the more skittish horses. Some of the foot soldiers broke ranks and ran, leaving the lines in even greater disorder. The dragons were fearsome enough, yet they seemed so odd.

"Let's challenge them," I said to Grumble Belly, "and let them know we're here."

"But there are three of them, and they're the biggest dragons I've ever seen," said Eadric.

I sniffed the air. "That doesn't matter. Do you smell boiled cabbage?"

Eadric grunted. "What are you talking about? Even I can't think of food at a time like this."

The orange dragons swerved and came back toward my father's troops. Beating their wings in unison, they swooped low over the cowering men. Horses screamed and fought their reins, and a full third of my father's army disappeared into the forest.

"You're right!" exclaimed Grumble Belly. "I don't smell anything even though they've been flaming."

"Exactly! Now, how about that challenge?"

"Cover your ears!" Grumble Belly's sides expanded as he inhaled. The roar was deafening, even with my fingers stuck in my ears. My father's remaining troops looked up, but they stood their ground and watched us with their swords raised and their bowstrings taut. Beltran's men looked surprised, and I saw fear in the way his foot soldiers drew closer together. The three dragons' movements became jerkier for a moment, then they turned and headed toward us.

When Grumble Belly flew higher, the three orange dragons rose to meet him, flaming long before they were within reach. After seeing how far a dragon could flame at the Olympics, I thought their flames looked meager.

"Watch out!" shouted Eadric. "Those flames may not hurt you, Grumble Belly, but we'll be burned to cinders."

I shook my head. "I don't think so, but you can close your eyes if you want."

"Close my eyes? What good will that do?"

"Sometimes your eyes can trick you even though your brain knows the truth," I said.

A moment later, the flames from the orange dragons reached us. I felt nothing, however, except the rush of the wind against my face as Grumble Belly beat his wings and soared.

"What's going on?" asked Eadric.

"Watch and learn," I said, and recited a quick and easy spell.

Let all that's false
Now disappear.
We do not want
To see it here.

The orange dragons flickered, then one by one they faded away, leaving nothing behind to mark that they had ever been there. "They weren't real," I said.

An excited shout went up from my father's troops, echoed by a groan of despair from Beltran's men. Suddenly a lone horseman broke away from the enemies' lines, galloping toward the closest trees. Beltran's wizard was kicking his heels into his horse's sides to make it go faster. "Follow that man," I told Grumble Belly, and an instant later we were passing over the heads of my father's foes. Drawing closer, I was surprised to see that the wizard was bald-headed and pleasant-faced; he looked a lot like Olefat. Just like the three dragons, the wizard's appearance had been a lie.

Grumble Belly was almost directly over him when Olebald turned and looked up. I was too far away to hear what he said, but I saw his hands wave and suddenly a small dark cloud appeared above us. Thunder rumbled in its depths and a bolt of lightning zigzagged through the sky.

"Hold on tight!" bellowed Grumble Belly as he tucked his wings and dove. Eadric reached around me and we both clutched the dragon's ridge, our knuckles white from pressure. The first bolt missed us, but the second hit the dragon's tail, jolting him with a surge. He plummeted, tumbling head over heels. The lightning had stunned us as well, and we fell from his back, unable to control our muscles enough to hold on. I couldn't hear anything but the ringing in my ears, although I must have screamed, since I made my throat sore. I was too numb to think, let alone say a spell, and Eadric and I would have been killed if Grumble Belly hadn't come to his senses and beaten the air with his wings, bringing him level beneath us. He caught us with his skull, a lumpy and uncomfortable place to land. As the air woofed out of me, I knew I'd bear the bruises for days.

Although I couldn't hear, my head cleared as Eadric helped me back to my seat on Grumble Belly's neck. I realized that even though the cloud was shrinking as it leaked rain, it probably still held enough energy to shoot more lightning. Bending toward the dragon's neck, I shouted, "Would you mind heating up that cloud?"

"I'd be delighted!" said Grumble Belly, and with a blast of flame, he turned the cloud into steam, which quickly dissipated in the clear blue sky.

Before Olebald could aim his magic at us again, I pointed at him and said,

> Go to the isle of sun-warmed sand,
> Where memories were taken.
> Stay there till your king's gone home,
> His urge to fight forsaken.

A tiny whirlwind sprang up under the horse's hooves, growing until it engulfed both horse and rider. I watched as the swirling wind rose from the ground and carried them away.

When Eadric spoke, his voice was faint in my still ringing ears. "It looks as though the fighting has started without us."

While fleeing the storm cloud, we had flown over the forest, leaving the battlefield behind. I turned and saw that the archers had sent their first volleys into the opposing armies' ranks. Men had already fallen, and more fell as we watched, cut down by the iron arrowheads. I had to do something fast. People's lives were at stake, and one of those lives was my own father's.

"I have to stop this!" I said.

Although Grumble Belly circled above the battlefield, no one on the ground seemed to notice us. "I could fry them if you'd like," the dragon suggested, and his belly began to grumble.

"No," I said. "I don't want you to hurt them, either."

Eadric tapped my shoulder. "What kind of magic did the Green Witch use in the tapestry?" he asked. "Maybe you could do something like that."

"I don't know what she did. I'm going to have to come up with something on my own. Wait a minute." A bizarre picture had popped into my head. I couldn't keep from laughing, a deep-down belly laugh that made Grumble Belly snort blue flame and turn his head to look at me in surprise. It was loud, and I know I sounded strange, but it wasn't anything I could control. I had just had the most wonderful, impossible, amazing idea.

"What's so funny?" demanded Eadric when I'd started to calm down.

"You'll see," I said, wiping tears from my eyes. "Just

sit back and give me some room. First of all, I need a way to deliver a spell. Pointing my finger from up here wouldn't work very well. How about this?" I used my hands to shape a ball bigger than a witches' light. Although I hadn't asked it to be, the ball turned out to be green. "Now to add the right spell, and I think this one is perfect!"

Strangers came to steal our land,
To take what they could carry.
They're free to go, if they leave now,
As long as they don't tarry.

If they stay to fight a war,
They'll have to pay a price.
While they remain upon our land
They'll live as frogs or mice.

"You're turning an entire army into frogs or mice?" asked Eadric.

"Not the *whole* army," I said. "Just enough so they'll get the point. Grumble Belly, would you mind flying lower? Right over Beltran's army would be fine."

While the dragon swooped and turned, I tossed the ball as hard as I could, aiming for the center of the front line. The ball glittered as it fell, and some soldiers in the back shot arrows at it but missed. Grumble Belly flamed and turned the arrows to ash before they could hurt anyone.

When the ball hit the ground, it exploded in a shower of green droplets. The men closest to it disappeared immediately, then the men next in line disappeared as well. My father's men cheered as an ever-widening green circle devastated the front lines. It looked as though Beltran's men had simply vanished. It wasn't until the soldiers behind them pointed at the ground and began hopping around like they'd suddenly lost their minds that I knew that my spell had worked. Grumble Belly flew lower, and I saw that the ground was swarming with brown mice. Although the frogs blended in with the spreading green magic, I thought I saw a few of them as well.

"Good!" I said. "Now let's go see King Beltran."

"The king might listen to you better if you go armed," warned Eadric.

I nodded and hurried through the spell, making another green ball.

Grumble Belly flapped his wings, creating a wind that knocked over a half dozen foot soldiers. The archers raised their bows, but he ignored them and soared past the army before they could let any arrows fly.

The clanking of armor was loud when the knights turned to face us, but Grumble Belly began puffing smoke the moment he landed, and the knights seemed reluctant to engage an angry dragon. I could see only a little of the king's face beneath his helmet, since the metal came low over his brow and the nosepiece covered his nose. He was an old man with a short beard and thin lips, and his eyes were two dark smudges against a face turned pale. Jorge sat beside him, his long blond curls peeking out from under his helmet, his deep blue eyes watching me with disdain.

"King Beltran," I announced, "I am the Green Witch and protector of Greater Greensward. I demand that you leave our land at once."

The mounted knights muttered, their horses shifting restlessly, but the king raised his hand and the voices stilled.

"If you leave now," I said, "you may go home, but each man who stays to fight will turn into a frog or a mouse."

"What about the men you've already changed?" asked the king.

"Take them with you. They'll turn back into men once they cross the border into your kingdom."

"Don't believe her, Father," said Prince Jorge. "That's Emeralda, the princess you insisted I marry. I've seen the Green Witch, and she's older than that girl."

"Hello, Jorge," I said.

" 'Your Highness' to you," he said, his nostrils flaring. "You were lucky that I was willing to marry you, but you were too stupid to know it. Is that the commoner who carried you off?"

"I'm not a commoner, and I didn't carry her off." Eadric sounded indignant. "I'm as much a prince as you are, Jorge, and I'll have you know that I'm going to marry Emma!"

Jorge took off his helmet. "Prince Eadric, is that you? I thought you looked familiar. Where did you get a dragon? I don't suppose you'd sell it? I'd look marvelous on a beast like that."

Grumble Belly's stomach rumbled, and smoke trickled out his nostrils. "Dragons aren't for sale!" I said as his muscles tensed under me.

"Then we have nothing more to talk about," Jorge said, setting his helmet back on his head.

"You can still marry him, girl," said King Beltran. "If your father gives me enough land, I'd be willing to ignore your foolishness."

"I didn't want to marry your son before, and I certainly don't want to marry him now. You'd better leave and never come back. I'm watching over this kingdom, and you aren't welcome here!"

"I see," said the king. "Then you leave me no choice but to use force to change your mind." Turning to the knights behind him, Beltran raised his hand and nodded. Without bothering to look at us again, the king and his son trotted toward the forest. Once the king was out of the way, his knights lifted their swords and urged their horses forward.

"I wish I'd brought Ferdy, but I didn't think I needed him when we went to the swamp," said Eadric.

"That's all right. I'm the one who's armed this time. These people don't seem to believe in magic unless it happens to them. I guess I'll have to give them a taste. Grumble Belly, I think it would have a greater impact from the air."

Snorting again, the dragon pumped his wings, and we rose above their heads, making the horses rear. A few of the knights slid off their horses' backs to the ground, where they lay struggling under their armor's weight. We hadn't gone far when archers began to shoot at us, so I didn't hesitate before throwing the next ball. It landed in the midst of the knights, and I was pleased to see that it didn't affect the horses, although their riders disappeared into the depths of their armor.

King Beltran and Prince Jorge had already moved out of my weapon's range and were fleeing the field when Grumble Belly flew after them. "And what about you?" I called while shaping another green ball with my hands.

"We'll go!" shouted the king. "Just leave us alone and let us gather our men!"

"Very well," I said. "You have one hour to collect your soldiers." Resting the ball between Grumble Belly's spikes, I leaned back against Eadric while the dragon's enormous wings carried us higher.

"Should I take you home now?" asked Grumble Belly, swerving over the remaining soldiers.

"Not yet, if you don't mind. I think we'd better stay and make sure they really do leave. I need to talk to my father, too. I'm sure he'd like to know what's happened."

We were higher than the treetops when Eadric and I leaned over to watch the soldiers scurrying about, collecting frogs and mice in their helmets and on their shields.

"I wonder how many will actually make it home," said Eadric.

I shrugged. "I don't know, but life as a frog isn't too bad." Squirming in my seat, I turned to face him. "I'm sorry if I seem to take you for granted sometimes. I dragged you into some awful predicaments, but you've helped me more than I could have dreamed possible. I appreciate everything you've done."

"Enough to give me a kiss?"

"Mmm," I said. The kiss was long and loving and I enjoyed every second of it.

After a time, Eadric pulled away to murmur, "You're wrong about one thing. Those were adventures, not predicaments. I like adventures, and maybe that's one of the reasons I'm crazy about you. When you're around, I never know what's going to happen next!"

Once Upon a Curse

One

When I was a little girl, I never gave much thought to doing magic. I'd watch my aunt Grassina perform it every day and she never seemed to have any problems. When I started practicing magic, I expected it to be as easy for me as it had been for her. I couldn't have been more wrong. My first attempts at magic were a series of small disasters. I made crab-apple tarts that grew claws and pinched us. My cleaning spells were so strong that my bed made itself even when I was in it, and a whirlwind swept up everything I dropped, including my shoes and hair ribbons, dumping them in the dung heap behind the stables. I became a frog because of one kind of magic, while another kind turned me back into a frog at the worst possible times. Sometimes my magic didn't do what I'd intended, sending me to the dungeon or making me prematurely old. When dragon steam enhanced my magic and I became a powerful witch, I thought that my problems with magic were over, but once again, I was wrong. Suddenly I had bigger problems to face—problems caused by magic that I soon learned only magic could fix.

I'd been visiting my aunt Grassina's workshop in the dungeon every day for the last few weeks and I had almost finished studying her parchments and the books she'd brought down from the tower rooms. With only a few more left to check, I was getting increasingly frustrated since I hadn't found a single spell that would help me.

When I'd arrived in the dungeon that morning, Grassina had dashed out of her room without saying where she was headed. Knowing her, she probably had some sort of mischief planned. I would have followed her to see what she was up to if I hadn't had something more important to do.

Massaging my forehead with one hand, I pushed the parchment aside with the other. I was tired of sitting in the dungeon. It wasn't as bad as it could have been, since there were plenty of candles and I'd dressed warmly, but the candles kept sputtering and going out, and the stink of decay was so strong it made my head hurt.

Something ran over my shoe, and I jerked my foot under my chair. *It's probably Blister,* I thought, shuddering. Once, before she changed from being the kind and gentle Green Witch to being the nasty, bewitched self she'd been for the last year or so, Grassina had kept a small, inoffensive, apple-green snake that had never bothered anyone. Now she shared her room with an old gray rat she'd found in the dungeon—Blister. He smelled awful, his fur was patchy and his naked tail was covered with sores, but his worst feature was his disposition, which was as nasty as my aunt's. I didn't mind the chill of the dungeon, the magic fogs that drifted from room to room or even the ghosts who popped in unexpectedly. Blister was a different story, however, since he loved tripping me and jumping out of shadows to startle me.

For the hundredth time, I thought about creating my own witches' lights so I wouldn't have to strain to see the words on the pages and the creatures that lurked in the darkened corners of the room. I knew better, however, because this was my aunt's workshop and she didn't like anyone doing magic in it except her. She was always nasty, but she was even worse if you did something she didn't like, which is why I'd gone to the dungeon in the first place. The feeble light from her flickering candles would have to do.

I'd been looking for a cure for the family curse for over a year. My aunt had been its most recent victim, and if I didn't do something about it before my sixteenth birthday, I might fall prey to it as well. Like our magical abilities, the curse had been passed down from generation to generation. It had started when my long-ago ancestor Hazel, the first Green Witch, had given out everlasting bouquets at her sixteenth birthday party and hadn't brought enough for everyone. A disappointed fairy had cursed her, saying that if Hazel ever touched another flower, she'd lose her beauty as well as her sweet disposition. Unfortunately the spell hadn't ended with Hazel, who had died centuries before I was born. Women in my family learned to stay away from flowers, with life-altering consequences if they didn't. They not only became ugly to look at, they turned so nasty that hardly anyone could stand them.

I finished reading another parchment and sighed. One more collection of useless spells for turning sows' ears into silk purses and lead into gold. The last spell, so long and involved that it had almost put me to sleep, had explained how to make mountains out of molehills.

"Almost finished, Emma?" said a high-pitched voice. My friend, a bat named Li'l, peered at me from the ceiling where she hung upside down.

"It shouldn't be long now," I told her. Rolling the parchment into a tube, I set it beside the others that I'd already studied. I was reaching for the last two, when I heard scratching at the door. "Grassina's back," I said, pulling my hand away.

My magic had improved remarkably since the day I had learned that I had the talent. Not only had I become a Dragon Friend, but I'd also become the Green Witch after Grassina lost the title. I could do a lot of things that I would once have considered impossible. Now I knew who was standing on the other side of a door without opening it. This was particularly handy when I was trying to avoid talking to my mother.

The scratching came again.

"Why would Grassina scratch the door?" Li'l asked.

"Good question." I reached for the latch and had opened the heavy wooden door only a few inches when it smacked into me, and an enormous lizard bounded across the threshold. At least seven feet long, the stocky creature's body seemed to fill the room. It raised its head to hiss at Li'l, but didn't pay any attention to me.

Li'l shrieked and flew to the ceiling, trying to hide in the cracks between the stones. The lizard cackled and its edges grew fuzzy, then suddenly my aunt was standing in its place. "Why are you still here?" she asked me. "I thought you were almost finished."

"I would have finished days ago if you had more light."

"There's enough light in here to do *my* spells, but if it stops your whining, I'll give you your rotten witches' lights. Anything to get rid of you sooner." With a wave of her hand and a few muffled words, Grassina sent a flurry of small globes bouncing against the ceiling. Instead of the rosy glow her witches' lights had made before she changed, these cast a sickly shade of green, making us look mortally ill.

A fuzzy little animal with a stubby tail and tiny ears scurried across the table. The creature squeaked as it ran off the edge and fell to the floor, where it lay on its back, twitching. Although it was about the size of a mouse, it didn't look like any I'd ever seen. "What is that?" I asked my aunt.

"A hamster," she said. "I saw them on my travels once. It used to be a spider, but hamsters have more meat on them. Being a lizard makes you hungry."

"That's disgusting!" I exclaimed.

"Do you really think so?" Grassina asked, her eyes brightening.

I looked up when one of the witches' lights went out. An ugly brown fog smelling of rotting vegetables was smothering the lights one by one. Grassina darted across the room to a barrel and rolled it to the center of the floor. The fog had almost reached the last witches' light when she muttered a few words and the barrel began to shake. Hissing like an angry snake, the barrel swelled as it sucked the fog through a small opening in its side. When the last wisp had disappeared, Grassina rammed a plug into the hole and rubbed her hands together. "Good!" she said. "I could use more of that."

"What do you need it for?"

"This," she said, stomping to her workbench and

uncovering a bowl filled with lavender dust. "I distill the fog and collect the residue."

"What does it do?" I asked.

"None of your business," she said, slamming the cover back on the bowl. "You're too nosy for your own good. I think you'd better leave. I'm sick of seeing your face around here."

"I'm not finished yet. I have two more parchments—"

"Here, take them," she said, snatching the parchments off the table and tossing them to the floor. "And don't come back!"

Li'l fluttered from her hiding place in the ceiling while I picked up the parchments. We'd hardly crossed the threshold before the door slammed shut behind us.

"At least you got the parchments," said Li'l, landing on my shoulder. "I thought she didn't want them to leave her workshop."

"That's what she said when I first asked to see them. It's the only reason I didn't take them upstairs before this. Unfortunately these probably won't be any more helpful than the others. I guess I'm going to have to look somewhere else."

"Where else can you look?"

"That's a good question," I said. "My sixteenth birthday is next week and I have to find a counter-curse before then. Father has scheduled his tournament to start the day before. He says it's to celebrate my birthday, but I think that's just an excuse. He's invited Eadric's parents and half of their kingdom, so I think he's hoping to impress my potential in-laws before any marriage contract is signed."

Li'l looked puzzled. "Why do you have to find the counter-curse before your birthday?"

"Because the curse could change me anytime after I turn sixteen. If that happens, there won't be a Green Witch to protect the safety of Greater Greensward. At least Grassina had me to take her place, but I don't know anyone who could take mine!"

"There you are!" my mother called as I closed the dungeon door behind me. "I can't imagine why you spend so much time in that horrid place, but then you always were peculiar."

Hearing my mother's voice, Li'l slipped off my shoulder and fluttered toward the darker recesses of the corridor. I couldn't blame her for being afraid of my mother.

"I was visiting Grassina's workroom," I said, hoping to distract my mother from the fleeing bat.

Mother looked as if she'd swallowed something bitter. Since the curse had taken effect, she'd avoided my aunt as much as she did my grandmother.

I nodded to my mother's lady-in-waiting who was hovering close enough to hear her name called, but far enough away to appear discreet.

"Your Highness," she replied, curtsying lower than she used to before I was the Green Witch. Being a princess hadn't meant nearly as much as being the most powerful witch in the kingdom, and I now received a lot more respect than I ever had before.

Cradling the parchments in my arms, I joined my mother as she entered the Great Hall. "I told you," I said, "I'm looking for a cure for the family curse. Grassina has been letting me look through her books and parchments."

"Have you found anything?"

"Not yet."

"I'm not surprised. If all the witches before you weren't able to come up with a cure, what makes you think you can? Don't get an inflated opinion of yourself, miss, just because you're the Green Witch."

"I won't, Mother." I certainly wouldn't with her around. "I just think that they might not have looked hard enough or in the right places."

"More likely there's nothing to find. You're wasting your time when you should be seeing to your new gowns. You'll be meeting Prince Eadric's parents next week when they come for the tournament and I want you looking your best, although there isn't much we can do with someone as tall and gangly as you. The seamstress will need all the time she can get to make you presentable, so I want you to go see her now."

"What I'm doing is very important—"

"Getting married is very important, and if you don't make a good impression on your future husband's parents, there may not be a wedding. We're going to have to use every trick we can to make them like you, and it's not going to be easy."

"I still haven't told Eadric I'd marry him."

"But you will soon, if you know what's good for you," Mother said, narrowing her eyes.

I left my mother with the promise that I would see the seamstress as soon as I could, but I had no intention of going straight there. Fittings were torture as far as I was concerned because my mother always showed up to point out my physical shortcomings as if I were the work of an inept sculptor.

I hadn't told anyone why I'd put off answering Eadric. Even he didn't know the real reason, although he'd made me promise to give him my answer at the tournament. I was afraid it wasn't going to be the answer he wanted to hear. Although I knew I loved him, I wasn't sure that I should get married. It was one thing to marry the man you love with the idea of living happily ever after, but it was something entirely different knowing that you could turn nasty any day and abandon your husband and children. I didn't want the same thing to happen to Eadric that had happened to my grandfather—left on his own when my grandmother Olivene had changed from normal to mean. My mother, who had so far avoided the curse by completely banning flowers from the castle, may not have thought it possible to find a way to end the family curse, but I had to believe that such a cure existed. If I was unable to end the curse, I had no intention of marrying anyone.

The tower rooms I now used had once been my aunt's, but I'd claimed them when Grassina moved to the dungeon. It was difficult to run up the uneven steps, and I had only reached the first arrow slit when Li'l dropped from the ceiling and landed on my shoulder. "What took you so long?" she asked. "I've been waiting here for ages."

"I was talking to my mother," I said.

"Your mother doesn't like me. She makes people hit me with brooms."

"She's afraid of bats. You'll just have to stay away from her."

"I'd be happy to, but she's hard to avoid. So are her eeks."

"What are *eeks*?"

"The people who try to bash me. They come running every time she covers her head and shrieks, 'Eek!'"

I smiled. "*Eek* isn't a title or a name. It's sort of like saying, 'Ick, a bug!'"

Li'l snorted. "That's insulting, isn't it? As if trying to bash me wasn't enough."

The moment we entered my chamber Li'l headed for the storage room where she usually slept, leaving me on my own. I hadn't made many changes to the tower after I had moved in, so it looked much the same as it had when my aunt lived there. A new workbench occupied the main room, replacing the one Grassina had taken with her to the dungeon. The two chairs and the table still sat before the fireplace; the dappled green rugs still covered the floor. Grassina had left her tapestries, the saltwater bowl and the living-crystalline bouquet behind, and I had seen no reason to move them.

I was comfortable in the tower and had all the space I needed to do my work as the Green Witch. Along with the title had come the ring on my finger and the responsibility of watching over Greater Greensward. Protecting our beautiful kingdom was a job I enjoyed. I used a farseeing ball to keep watch over the kingdom and toured the countryside by magic carpet every few weeks. Since becoming the Green Witch, I'd fended off an invasion from a neighboring kingdom, chased away a pack of werewolves, routed a trio of nasty trolls and taught a flock of harpies not to harass our villagers. I'd also taken on the responsibility of keeping the castle moat clean, which wasn't easy because Grassina insisted on dumping her trash into it. A witch's trash is different from that of an ordinary person, and sometimes noxious fumes and bizarre creatures emerged from the moat.

My aunt had been the kindest living adult I'd ever known, and I missed her real nature more than I could say, which was the other reason I had to find a cure for the family curse. Grassina was now as horrible as she had once been wonderful, and her nasty tricks were getting worse every day. She'd been terrible to Haywood, the man who had been her betrothed. He had lived with us for nearly five months after Grassina had changed, finally moving out when the tricks she played on him began to torment other people as well. He hadn't moved far, however, and still visited the castle now and then.

Grassina had driven away my mother's favorite ladies-in-waiting and more servants than we could afford to lose. Lately my aunt had even turned herself into strange beasts like the lizard I'd just run into, terrorizing the people and animals in and around the castle. Turning Grassina back into her old self would make everyone's life more pleasant.

I unrolled a parchment and settled down to read, but it proved to be as useless as the others. After glancing at the last parchment, I set them both aside and went to see Li'l. She blinked when I opened the door to the storage room. "Find anything?" she asked.

"Nothing useful, unless I want to remove rust or turn myself into a bird. I don't want to give up, but I don't know where to look next. I've talked to every bookseller at the magic marketplace, I've gone through my grandmother's books and parchments, and now I've looked at all of Grassina's—and I haven't found anything I can use."

"What about Vannabe's cottage? Mudine left a lot of good books there."

When I was fourteen, Li'l, Eadric and I had been imprisoned in a witch's cottage deep in the enchanted forest. A previous occupant had left her books of magic spells behind. The spells had been reliable, and I'd used a number of them before I learned how to create my own. Remembering that book, I felt a surge of hope. If the other books were just as helpful, perhaps one of them might contain the information I needed. "That's a good idea," I said. "If I go now, I can be back before dark."

"You sent the magic carpet to be mended, remember?" Li'l said. "How are you going to get there?"

I was about to answer when I glanced out the window. A dove was flying past the tower, the bronze-edged pattern on its wings distinctive in the bright summer sun. I leaned against the windowsill to watch the bird. *I wish I could do that,* I thought as the dove swooped and turned.

I loved trying new spells. Because Eadric had been involved in the original spell that had turned me into a frog, every time I had turned into one he had as well. However, once my power had become strong enough and I was better able to control it, I could turn into other creatures without changing Eadric. "I think I'll fly." I climbed onto the window ledge and recited the spell from the parchment.

Fleet of wing and sharp of beak,
Turn me to the shape I seek.
When I say the final word,
I will be a feathered bird.

My magic was stronger now, so the change was swift and painless. I no longer felt queasy when I changed from my human form to that of a creature, although the difference in perspective was still disorienting. I spread my wings and saw that I was covered with pale brown feathers. I had turned into a dove, the last kind of bird I'd seen. Cocking my head, I bent down to examine my orange feet tipped with small, sharp talons.

I'd watched birds before, of course, so I didn't think that flying could be too hard. After all, it didn't take baby birds long to learn, and I was certainly smarter than a sparrow. Raising my wings, I brought them down in a short, sharp movement. I was thrilled when my feet rose from the ledge, but raising my wings again forced me back down. *There must be some trick to this,* I thought.

Beating my wings once more, I moved out the window and found myself high above the moat. Surprised, I forgot to flap and dropped like a stone, remembering to flap again when I was only a few feet above the water. A long, gray tentacle shot through scum floating on the surface, its leaf-shaped tip brushing my tail. I beat my wings again, zigzagging up and down, trying to stay out of the monster's reach. Grassina must have dumped more trash into the moat, but I couldn't do anything about it until I got back.

I was over dry land again when I discovered that if I twisted my wings and folded them partway, I wouldn't force myself down each time I raised them and could finally fly like a real bird. I experimented, soaring higher than the castle tower and swooping low to skim the meadow grass. A sunny day with only a gentle breeze nodding the buttercups that edged the farmers' fields, it was the perfect day to practice flying.

Two

Dark clouds were scudding across the sky by the time I saw the enchanted forest. Hoping to find shelter before the rain began, I fought an ever-strengthening breeze. The leaves on the trees were dancing, exposing their paler undersides, when I reached the forest's edge. Even on sunny days, the interwoven branches of the ancient trees prevented most of the sunlight from reaching the forest floor. The forest was even gloomier when the day was overcast.

I hadn't been in the forest long before I passed a green-skinned nymph slipping into a pond. A pair of unicorns huddled under a sheltering tree. I was still watching the unicorns when a griffin flew past, buffeting me with its eaglelike wings so that I had to fight to regain my balance.

Winging my way through the forest, I studied the trees, trying to find a familiar landmark that would lead me to the witch's cottage. I finally spotted a singed tree that I recognized and was able to get my bearings. It wasn't long before I reached the clearing and saw the cottage, looking much the way I remembered it, although the roof seemed to be in better repair.

Noticing the smoke escaping from the crooked chimney, I realized that someone was inside, and I had to force myself not to flee. I reminded myself why I was there. Although I knew I had to visit the cottage to examine the old books, the closer I got to it, the more nervous I became. While we were frogs, Eadric and I had mistakenly asked a witch named Vannabe for help, but instead of offering her assistance, she had kidnapped us, carrying us to this very cottage. Threatening to cut off our tongues and toes, she had locked us in a cage until I had found a spell in a book that opened every lock, latch and knot in the house. The thought that Vannabe might still live there almost made me turn around and go home, but I was no longer a helpless frog. As the Green Witch, I was more than a match for an aspiring witch like Vannabe.

When I heard voices coming from the cottage, I decided to investigate. I hurried closer to the house, skimming over the tops of the wildflowers that filled the clearing. The first drop of rain splatted on my wing as I landed on the windowsill.

Two women were seated inside, but neither one was the young, black-haired Vannabe. I couldn't see the face of the white-haired woman who sat at the table with her back to the window. The other one, however, was facing me, a tiny, thin woman with gray hair and a sour expression that matched the tone of her voice. "You promised me fresh air and sunshine," she said. "Ha! Fresh dust, fresh pollen, fresh manure—I bet you even have fresh mold in this dung heap, but no fresh air! Why would you live in such a hovel? My dog has a better home than this."

"It suits me. I invited you to visit because I thought you'd like the change. You're always complaining about the town."

"Who's complaining? I love the town. At least a witch can make a difference with her magic there. What can you do out here in the middle of nowhere?"

The white-haired woman sighed and turned around. I was surprised when I recognized her, although I shouldn't have been. After all, I had been the one to tell her about the cottage. Eadric and I had met her in the magic marketplace the year before while searching for magic beans. She had given us the beans in exchange for information about a jar of eyeballs that she claimed belonged to her. I'd seen the jar in the cottage when I was a prisoner, and I saw it again now, sitting on the table in front of her.

Unlike the day we'd met when she had one eye rattling loosely, she now had two eyes in her head, although they didn't match each other. The vivid blue eye seemed to fit better; the brown eye with flecks of gold bulged from the socket. She had a large black mole on her cheek, and her toothless mouth seemed to collapse in on itself. Surprisingly her words were clear when she spoke. "I can *rest,* Dyspepsia. It was peaceful here until you came."

I needed to talk to these women and ask if they could help me. Jumping to the ground, I thought for a moment and recited my usual spell to become human. As I shot up to my normal height, everything seemed smaller and less intimidating. My skin felt stretched and pulled, prickling all over when my feathers disappeared. I sighed with relief.

Smoothing my hair with one hand, I knocked on the door with the other. A moment later it opened with a bang. It was darker inside, lit only by the fire in the fireplace and the pale light coming through the window. After a drizzling start, it was raining in earnest now.

"Would you look at that, Oculura," said the gray-haired witch from where she still sat by the window. "We finally have company."

"You were the bird on the windowsill, weren't you?" Oculura asked, motioning me into the room.

I nodded. "I didn't mean to eavesdrop …," I began, stepping into the cottage.

"Why not?" said Dyspepsia. "Listening in on conversations is often the only way to learn anything. I used to turn myself into a fly for that very reason."

"Until that man swatted you," said Oculura.

"He missed, which was a good thing for him. I would have been furious if his aim had been better."

"You would have been squashed if his aim had been better and in no shape to do anything about it."

"Hmph!" said Dyspepsia.

While the two women argued, I glanced around the room. It was neater than it had been before; the cobwebs and the old bird skeletons were gone, and the bat droppings had been scrubbed from the table and floor, which might have been why the room smelled so much better.

I looked toward the shelf where the books had rested. The dust was gone, and I was dismayed to see that the books were also missing. I was going to ask about them when Oculura turned to me, looking me up and down the way one might inspect a horse that was for sale. I half expected her to demand to see my teeth, but instead she said, "I know you from somewhere, don't I?"

I nodded. "We met at the magic marketplace. You gave us some magic beans."

"Hmm." Turning to her jar, the old woman selected two more eyes, popped out the ones in her head and stuck in the new ones. She blinked, then looked at me again. "That's better," she said. "I remember you now. You were with that nice young man. You told me about my jar of eyeballs."

I nodded again, unable to look away from her face. I

could swear that the black mole that had been on her cheek was crawling onto her chin.

"So," she said. "How were the beans? Did they do what you needed them to?"

"Yes," I said, dragging my eyes from her chin. "They worked quite well, thank you."

"And the young man? Is he still as handsome?" Oculura asked, looking through her eyelashes coyly.

I couldn't help it—my eyes flicked back to her chin. "He's the same as ever."

Oculura frowned. "Hasn't anyone ever told you that it's rude to stare?"

I could feel my face turning red. "I'm sorry, but your mole—"

"It's not a mole; it's a facial tick. I got it the first night I slept on that lousy bed," she said, pointing at the sagging mattress in the back of the room. The old witch tapped the tick with her finger, but made no move to dislodge the little black insect. "I like it now. It's grown on me—kind of like a beauty mark, don't you think?"

"Very nice," I said, trying not to grimace.

"Why are you here?" demanded Dyspepsia. "I know you didn't come just to get beauty tips from my sister."

"I'm trying to find a way to end a curse put on my family. I was hoping I could look at the books that used to be on that shelf."

"You can. I put them in the trunk with my own

books. You can look at those, too. Mind you, I wouldn't let just anyone look at them, but you told me about this place and I've been very happy here, despite my sister's complaints." Oculura looked pointedly at the gray-haired woman, then stomped to the trunk and flung open the lid.

"Take your time," said Dyspepsia. "It'll be nice having someone else around. All my sister does is play with those eyeballs of hers."

"Here you go," said Oculura, dumping a stack of books on the table. "You can look through these."

While the rain drummed on the roof of the cottage, I skimmed through the books, taking note of the more interesting spells. Dyspepsia sat in her chair by the window, complaining about her aching feet, the rain, the size of the cottage, her sister's lack of attention, the time of year and everything else she could think of. Ignoring us both, Oculura examined her collection of eyeballs, trying each eye one at a time, then in different combinations with the others.

"Each one sees things a bit differently," she explained when I glanced at her for a moment. Holding up a startlingly blue eye, she said, "This one belonged to a poet. Everything I see through it is very clear." She pointed at another floating in the jar. "A camp follower owned that one. It's always looking for a certain kind of man. And this," she said, reaching into the jar and plucking out an eye with a dark brown iris, "belonged to an old wizard who could see the magic in everything."

Oculura fished around in the jar and took out two milky-white eyes. I wondered how anyone could see with them. "These are my real seer's eyes," she said with obvious pride. Bending over the table, she popped out the eyes she was wearing and tucked the seer's eyes into the sockets. "Now give me your hand." Taking one of my hands in both of hers, she closed her eyes and hummed tunelessly, then said, "You're having a tournament at your castle, and you're going to invite me! I accept. And I'll bring my sister. We're going to have a marvelous time. There will be jousting and food and some ill-used magic and—"

"What's that about magic?"

"But before the tournament you're going on a long trip."

"I am?"

"Yes," she said. "Just don't ask me where. These eyes are old, and they tire easily."

"What was that you said about ill-used magic?" I asked as she changed her eyes again.

"You should have asked while I had those eyes in. It's too late now. I can wear them for only a short time before they need to rest. Would you like to see any others?" Oculura picked up the jar and swirled the liquid inside. The eyes swirled, too, and I thought they looked a little queasy. "I can show you my first eyes if you'd like. They were a beautiful, deep blue and matched my favorite gown. My ex-husband thought they were my best features. I have them here somewhere. My mother named me Oculura because of my beautiful eyes."

"You always were her favorite child," muttered Dyspepsia.

"She was a colicky baby," Oculura said, gesturing toward her sister. "So Mother named her Dyspepsia. She's had problems with her stomach her whole life."

"Problems with my stomach, problems with my feet, problems with men.... I never did get married," said Dyspepsia. "Never met the right man. What about you, girl? Anyone special in your life?"

"Yes, as a matter of fact." My chest tightened as I thought about Eadric. He'd gone back to Upper Montevista nearly six months before to help his father, and I missed him so much. He was due to come back the following week, but sometimes even a week can be an awfully long time.

"Was it that handsome young man?" asked Oculura.

I nodded. "That was my Eadric," I said, trying to look cheerful.

It didn't take me long to finish going through the books, simply because there wasn't much in them that interested me. I kept hoping up to the very last spell in the very last book that there might be something...

"Find anything that you can use?" Oculura asked, dropping an eyeball back into the jar.

I sighed. "Not a thing," I said as I set the last book aside. "Now I don't know what to do. I've looked every place I can think of, but there hasn't been anything."

"Hmm," said Oculura. "You did say it was a curse, didn't you?"

"That's right. It affects the girls in my family after they turn sixteen."

"And you're not sixteen yet?"

"I will be next week."

"Then if I were you, I'd talk to my sister."

"But I don't have a sister."

Dyspepsia snorted. "She doesn't mean your sister; she means me! I used to specialize in curses. I had to give them up, though. Curses take a lot out of you. You have to be really worked up to cast a good, strong one. All that anger made my stomach hurt more."

"So you know a lot about curses, including how to end them?"

"Of course I do, and I'd tell you, too, if only…."

"If only what?" I asked.

"My feet really hurt. What I could use right now is a good foot rub."

"Foot rub? But I…."

"My own sister won't touch my feet, but I'd feel so much better if someone rubbed the ache out of them.

I'm sure I'd feel like talking then."

"Fine," I said. "I've never rubbed anyone's feet before. I suppose you'll have to take off your shoes."

"Of course, but my back hurts, so if you don't mind. . . ."

I sighed and reached for her foot. *The things I do for my family,* I thought as I slipped off the old woman's shoe.

Fortunately for me, Dyspepsia knew what she was talking about. I was soon so caught up in what she had to say that I forgot about the stickiness of her stubby toes and the way her feet smelled like rotten cucumbers. According to her, there were only two ways to end a curse. You could either persuade the person who had cast it to remove the curse, or you could do whatever the curse dictated. Unfortunately I couldn't do either since I didn't know who had cast it or exactly what it said. True, I knew a fairy had cast it; but that made it worse, according to Dyspepsia, since bargaining with fairies rarely worked. However, if I could find out which fairy was responsible for the curse, I *might* be able to get her to end it. Failing that, I'd have to try the solution imbedded in the curse, although fairies never made anything easy. I'd need the exact wording, and even that might not be enough.

"First things first, however," Dyspepsia said. "If you can't find any record of what really happened, you're going to have to go back to when the curse was cast."

"But it happened hundreds of years ago."

"You'll travel over time instead of distance. If you're strong enough, you'll be able to control the forces involved. If you're not, well, the curse won't matter to you anymore. The spell itself is simple. Just modify a basic search spell using an object from your destination as a focus. Since you want to go to a different time, your focus object must be from that time. When you want to come back, include when you want to return to in your spell. You won't need a focusing object since you're from this time."

I set her foot on the floor and picked up the other. "Oh, before I forget," she continued, "you'll need something to give your spell a little oomph. Everyone has a personal preference. I knew a wizard who could harness lightning to make his spells stronger."

"How did that work?"

"I can't say. No one ever saw him again, so it either worked or blasted him into dust."

"I don't think I'll try lightning," I said.

"Good idea. But whatever you choose needs to be portable so you can use it to come back."

"Anything else I should remember?"

"Of course. You're heading for a different location in time, but your location on the ground will remain the same. If the curse was cast long ago, most buildings and places will have changed since then. You're going to have to work your spell somewhere that has changed very little, or you might appear in the middle of a wall or at the bottom of a pond. Keep in mind that it should be out of the way. It wouldn't do to pop into the Great Hall or the queen's chamber. If you want to get the information you desire, you won't want anyone to know who you are or why you're there."

"It sounds complicated."

"It isn't really. I'm sure you'll do just fine. Oh, one other thing—make sure you don't change anything when you go back in time. Any change then could have a big effect later. Everyone always gives the same example: if you kill your ancestor, you'll never have been born."

"That doesn't make sense. If I killed someone, and then I didn't exist, how could I have killed him in the first place?"

"Don't ask me. I don't understand the details, I just use the spell and try to be careful. Now about my feet. . . ."

Three

The rain had stopped by the time I was ready to go. After taking my leave of the two sisters, I turned into a bird again. Flitting beneath the dripping branches, I tried to remember everything Dyspepsia had said and wondered how I'd ever make it all happen. Perhaps talking to someone who knew our family history and was familiar with the castle might help me locate an object that I could use as a focus. My grandmother could probably help if she wanted to, although the chances of that were slim even if I did catch her on one of her friendlier days. She was the oldest living direct descendant of the first Green Witch and probably knew more about her than anyone, so I would just have to risk her bad temper. My next stop would be the Old Witches' Retirement Community.

With the entire width of the enchanted forest ahead of me, I had plenty of flying time to think. Even so, when I finally smelled the perfume of the rose-covered cottages, I still didn't have any idea what I was going to say. By the time I spotted the gingerbread walls of Grandmother's home, I'd decided to come right out and ask her.

My stomach grumbled as I landed on the edge of Grandmother's garden, my beak almost watering at the thought of all that delicious gingerbread. I hadn't eaten anything other than a bowl of porridge that morning and I was beginning to feel a little light-headed. Drawn by the sugary scent of the cottage, I was hopping toward it, opening my beak to recite the spell that would turn me back, when something struck me from behind. I sprawled beak-first on the rain-soaked ground, pinned down by a warm, heavy object. "I like a meal that delivers itself!" a voice murmured into my ear.

I recognized the voice. It was Herald, my grandmother's old orange tabby and one of the most disagreeable cats I'd ever met. Yanking my beak out of the dirt, I spluttered and shouted, "It's me, Emma, you lousy cat. You'd better let me up right now!"

Herald snarled. "Lousy cat, am I? Considering your position, princess, I don't think you should have said that."

I gasped and tried to think of a banishing spell, anything to get the cat off me. Herald picked me up with his teeth, pinning my wings to my sides. I struggled to get free but he clamped his jaws harder. The cat had taken only a few steps when suddenly something barreled into him, knocking him to the ground. Herald growled deep in his throat, a curious sound that made me vibrate in his mouth.

"Let her go!" said a gruff voice. Herald bit down instead, sending sharp pains through my wings. "Fine," said the voice. "If you're going to be that way—get him, Metoo!"

The cat twitched. When he opened his mouth to yowl, I fell onto the wet grass and staggered to my feet, reciting the spell that would change me back. The moment I opened my eyes as a human again, I turned to thank my rescuer. A small brown-and-white dog had the cat by the back of the neck. It was Olefat, the wizard my grandmother had turned into a dog to punish him for tricking her.

"Thanks," I said.

Olefat blinked up at me, then deliberately opened his jaws and let the cat go. Still yowling, Herald ran up a tree and onto a branch, where he stopped to scratch himself with a frenzied kicking of his hind leg. Obviously Metoo, Olefat's parrot that Grandmother had turned into a flea, had reached his target. "That's one!" the little dog shouted as he turned and trotted toward the back of the cottage.

My grandmother had told me that she'd tied the curse she had cast on Olefat to one Grassina had used to make him tell the truth. As long as one spell lasted, they both would be in force. According to Grassina's spell, "Three selfless acts you must perform, to aid a stranger who's forlorn." Apparently Olefat was trying to break the truth spell. I was giggling when I started toward my grandmother's front door.

"Who's there?" screeched Grandmother as she shoved her cotton-candy curtains aside and popped her head out the window.

"It's me. I've come to visit."

"No, you haven't. You've come to pick my brain. Grassina told me about your search. Still looking for a way to end the curse, are you?"

"I have some questions to ask you that might help. Do you mind if I come in?"

Grandmother cackled. "Of course I mind. If I'd wanted to see you, I would have gone to the castle. I don't like visitors. They always expect me to talk to them and give them something to eat. They either stay too long or leave before they should; they snoop around and ask nosy questions. There ought to be a law against unexpected visitors. But you're here now, so I guess I'm stuck with you. Come in if you have to."

My stomach was grumbling again when my grandmother met me at the door. She scowled and said, "See, I told you so! You'll be wanting food now!" Without waiting for an answer, she turned and stalked off to the kitchen. Jabbing a finger at the bench by the table, she ordered, "Sit down," then slammed a mug of cider in front of me. While I wiped the cider from my face, she broke off part of the windowsill and tossed it onto the table. It was magic gingerbread, which stays fresh for years. Its gingery, sweet taste made my whole mouth tingle.

"Now, what did you want to ask me?" Grandmother said as soon as I had a mouthful of gingerbread.

I hurried to swallow and nearly choked. Coughing, I took a sip of cider, then cleared my throat and said, "What can you tell me about Hazel, the first Green Witch?"

"Nothing!" Grandmother snapped. "There, I answered your question. Now go home and leave me alone."

"Surely you know something about her. Of course I could just go ask Grassina. She always says that she's forgotten more than you ever knew." The curse had made my aunt and my grandmother so much alike that they were always trying to outdo each other, a fact I'd learned to turn to my advantage.

"She did, did she? What a liar. Say, she hasn't gotten a lizard for a pet, has she? I found one hunting moles in my garden the other day. It took off before I could get a good spell going, but something about it made me think of your aunt. I had to come up with a new spell to replant my rosebushes. The ugly brute tore them all out of the ground."

I sighed. My grandmother did have beautiful roses, something that was of course forbidden at our castle. "Grassina doesn't have any new pets aside from a smelly rat," I said, "but she likes turning into a big lizard so she can terrorize everyone in the castle."

"She would, wouldn't she?" said my grandmother. "I thought it looked like Grassina. It smiled at me before it ran off."

"You were going to tell me about Hazel, the first Green Witch," I prompted.

"I was, was I?" Grandmother shrugged. "Might as well. Can't have you thinking that nasty daughter of mine is the only one who knows our family's history. Hazel's father was King Grunwald the third or maybe the fourth. He built the castle you live in now. They say the magic came down through her mother's side, but then it would have to, wouldn't it? The only ones in our family who have the talent are the girls."

"What part of the castle did King Grunwald build?" I said, remembering Dyspepsia's comment about finding the right location.

"The oldest part, of course. Use your head, girl! The whole back half was added on later by your great grandfather and so were many of the towers."

"Would any of his possessions still be in the castle? A suit of armor, perhaps, or a piece of furniture?"

"There might have been before your mother became

queen, but she had the castle cleaned from top to bottom the year after she married your father. The nitwit even had servants scrubbing out the dungeon. I doubt there's anything in there older than two hundred years. She always has preferred new things over old."

"I meant to ask you, are you coming to the tournament?"

"Of course I'm coming. You know I love tournaments. What tournament are we talking about?"

"My parents are putting one on next week. Eadric's parents are coming."

"Eadric who? Do you mean your pudgy friend with the big ears?"

"Eadric doesn't have big ears!"

"Ah-ha! So, it *is* him. I'll be there. Or at least I think I will. Let me get my scrying bowl so I can see and make sure."

I took another bite of gingerbread while Grandmother snatched an old, chipped bowl off the shelf. After pouring a dipperful of water into the bowl, she set it on the table. "Now don't yammer at me while I do this. I have to concentrate. Let's see," she said, leaning over the bowl so her long nose nearly touched the water. I couldn't see whatever she was looking at because her head blocked my view, but apparently she saw something. "Tournament … next week … will I be there? There's Eadric, big ears and all. There's your mother, looking prissy as usual. I see a couple of dotty, old witches. Wait, one of them's me. Yeah, I'll be there. And so will … say, look at this. There'll be some magical trouble at your tournament, girl. Something's going to go very wrong."

I nearly choked on the gingerbread again. When I could talk, I said, "Oculura mentioned something about that. What is it? Can you see?"

Grandmother sat back and glared at me. "I told you not to talk! How am I supposed to concentrate with you blathering away? Now let me look. I think it's—"

With a thump and a swish of his tail, Herald the cat landed on the table beside the bowl, then stuck his face in it and started lapping the water. Whatever picture Grandmother was studying disappeared in ripples.

"Darn cat!" Grandmother grabbed Herald and tossed him out the window. "Want a drink of water?" she asked me. When I shook my head no, she carried the bowl to the window and dumped it over the ledge. The water must have hit Herald, because he howled. My grandmother cackled. "Serves you right, you old sour-puss!" she said and slammed the bowl back on the table. "Say, I have some liver I've been meaning to cook for weeks. It has a nice, blue sheen to it now, so I'm going to boil it with a few turnips before it goes bad. I'm making beetle-wing biscuits, too. Care to stay for dinner?"

My stomach flip-flopped at the thought. "It's getting

late. I should go home before it gets dark," I said, scooting off the bench. "Thanks so much for your help."

Grandmother glared at me. "See, it's like I said. You're leaving just when I'm getting used to you being here. Well, good riddance, and don't come back soon!"

I probably would have forgotten all about Grassina's newest moat monster if it hadn't tried to catch me again as I flew toward my tower window. Although its body was still hidden in the murky depths, its thick tentacles with their leaf-shaped tips were clearly visible, flailing in the air.

No normal creatures lived in the moat anymore because Grassina's previous monsters had eaten them all, so it wasn't surprising that this one was always hungry. Keeping an eye out for the tentacles, I recited the spell I'd used on the other monsters.

> Find the monster in this moat
> And send him far away
> To a place where monsters dwell,
> A place where he can stay.

I swerved out of the way when one of the tentacles whipped past me. Some spells take longer to work than others, and this one seemed to take an extra-long time. I was relieved when I heard a sucking, slurping sound and the thrashing tentacles disappeared.

My rooms were dark when I landed on the windowsill although torches burned in the streets of my favorite tapestry, which depicted a town and its marketplace. My golden canary trilled a greeting as I fluttered into the room, twittering in excitement when I turned back into a human.

"Lights," I said, flicking my fingers at the ceiling where witches' lights bobbed. Like most spells I used often, I no longer had to recite the complete spell out loud.

With the lights glowing gently overhead, I hurried to my bedchamber, intent on locating a special box. Although I had no idea where I could find a focus object from the past, I already knew just what I would use to strengthen my power. Hidden in a box in the bottom of my trunk was a small bottle containing dragon's breath, the most powerful substance I'd ever encountered. While dragon's breath was a key ingredient in a potion that had changed an otter back into a man, it had been dragon's steam—a heated form of their breath—that had enhanced my own magic, making me the most powerful witch in the kingdom.

Taking the box from the trunk, I lifted the silver lid. Pinks, blues, yellows and greens swirled in the gas that nearly filled the bottle. I slipped the little bottle into the pouch that I carried at my hip and reached for my warmest cloak. With the tournament less than a week away, I didn't dare waste time.

I locked the door behind me, keeping an eye out for any of Grassina's magic tricks, but I didn't notice the noise in the Great Hall until I'd reached the bottom of the stairs. It was a bit late for dinner, which meant that my parents probably had guests and were dawdling at the table. Unless I wanted to be drawn into their conversation and spend the rest of the evening with them, I'd have to slip past unnoticed.

I peeked into the Great Hall. The smell of roast pheasant would have tempted me once, but I could no longer eat meat, having been an animal myself. It was the reason I usually avoided eating with my parents now, since they didn't understand my reluctance and still tried to make me eat it.

Drawing my cloak around me, I hoped that keeping to the shadows would be enough, but the moment I stepped into the hall, my mother spotted me. "Emeralda," she called, using my full name. "It's so good of you to join us. Come see who's here."

I sighed and turned to face the raised table where my parents sat side by side, surveying the Hall. Seated on my father's other side was a middle-aged man with a pleasant face and sand-colored hair tinged with gray.

"Haywood!" I hurried to the table, hoping to avoid sitting beside my mother. Haywood had been a wizard-in-training before my grandmother had turned him into an otter, long before I was born. He'd been working on his magic ever since he had turned back into a man and was getting fairly good at it. "It's nice to see you," I told him. "Are you staying long?"

"Just a few days," Haywood replied. "I'm building a house by the river, and I still have a lot to do. I'll be back next week, though. Your father has invited me to his tournament."

"Wonderful!" I'd gotten to know Haywood during the months that he lived with us and had found him to be very likable. Even my mother's opinion of him had changed. He would have been welcome in our home anytime if it hadn't been for my aunt. "Have you seen Grassina?" I asked.

"Briefly," said Haywood. "She threatened to turn me into a hamster, which I thought was rather odd."

"She was probably hungry," I said. "You might want to fly home and avoid any lizards you see."

"Emeralda, come sit by me," my mother ordered, leaving me no choice unless I wanted to create a scene. I took my seat beside her reluctantly. It looked as though everyone was nearly finished, but my mother had the pages bring the platters around again. Fortunately having a guest meant that she might not notice when I chose only vegetables and a hunk of bread.

Mother's eyes narrowed when she turned to me.

"Where were you today? You know the seamstresses were going to fit you for your gowns."

"I was seeing to something important," I said.

"I hope this important matter doesn't prevent you from having your fittings tomorrow! You've wasted too much time already. Luckily for you, you missed your aunt's mischief making. Your father went hunting today. The hounds flushed a hare from the underbrush right away. Your father said that it led him a merry chase until the hounds finally ran it to ground. Then what do you suppose the hare did?"

"Got eaten by some half-wild dogs?"

Mother's eyes snapped. "It turned into a monstrous lizard that chased *them*. The horses were terrified and the dogs.... Well, see for yourself," she said, pointing to the corner of the room.

During meals, Father's hounds normally waited under the tables watching for dropped food or the occasional handout, so I was surprised to see them cowering in the corner with fearful eyes.

"Grassina did that?" I asked.

"And thought it was very funny when I confronted her. Your father is furious."

A squire who had come into the hall slipped behind the tables until he reached my father. They spoke for a moment, before Father turned to me. "It seems your prince Eadric has returned earlier than expected,

Emeralda. He's in the stable with his horse."

I hopped to my feet, nearly knocking a platter from a page's hands. "May I be excused?" I asked.

"Of course my dear," said Father.

Mother started tapping her fingers on the tabletop, a sure sign that she wasn't pleased. "He wasn't supposed to be back for another week. I hope his parents' plans haven't changed."

"I'll find out," I said and dashed from the room before she could think of a reason that I should stay. Once I was out of my parents' sight, I hiked up my long skirts higher than was probably modest and ran as fast as I could.

The animals had been fed, and the comfortable sound of horses munching their grain filled the stable. I peeked over the door of Bright Country's usual stall and saw Eadric brushing his horse until the stallion's white coat shone. Ferdy, Eadric's singing sword, hung from a nail on the wall, close to Eadric. Since the day when Eadric had been unprepared for the battle between Greater Greensward's army and the army of East Aridia, he'd always kept his sword nearby.

Eadric looked wonderful standing in the stall, his sleeves rolled up and his clothes muddy from a hard day of riding.

"Eadric," I said, and then the door was open and I was in his arms, which was exactly where I wanted to be.

Four

It was nearly an hour before I returned to my original errand. Eadric and I had spent a few wonderful minutes while Bright Country eyed us with disgust. When he finally snorted and said, "Get a stall," we stopped kissing and grinned at each other. Eadric looked different from when I'd seen him last, and I was surprised by how much he'd changed in a few months. He'd grown another inch or so and was now nearly as tall as me. His chin and upper lip were rough from stubble, and his curly, brown hair was longer than he used to wear it. What really surprised me, however, was that his paunch was almost gone and the muscles in his arms and across his chest had gotten bigger.

"How have you been?" Eadric asked, his voice a bit deeper than I remembered it.

"Miserable while you were gone. Wonderful now that you're back. And you?"

"So lonely that I couldn't stay away any longer. My

parents are coming next week. They wanted me to travel with them, but I told them I had to help a lady in distress."

"Oh, really? And who was the lady?"

"You. You did say you were miserable."

"Devastated."

"Good. I'd hate to think I lied to my parents."

"What else did you tell them?"

"That you're beautiful and exciting and the only woman with whom I could live happily ever after. That they'll like your parents, but your aunt Grassina is a little unusual."

"Aunt Grassina! I was on my way to see her when my mother stopped me. I have so much to tell you! I met Oculura's sister, Dyspepsia, who told me how we can learn about the curse, and now Grandmother is coming to the tournament where some magic is going to go wrong."

Eadric held up his hand and laughed. "Slow down! One thing at a time, please."

I started over again and told him about seeing Oculura, the witch we'd met at the magic marketplace, and her sister who used to be an expert on curses. He nodded and said, "How nice," but I could tell he wasn't very interested until I told him that I'd have to travel back in time to learn the actual words of the family curse.

"Really?" he said. "You can do that?"

"According to Dyspepsia I can. All I need is something that came from that time and something to make my power stronger. I already have the vial of dragon's breath, which has the strongest magic you can get."

Eadric rubbed his chin. "What time are we talking about?"

"The Dark Ages. That's why I need to see Grassina. Maybe she knows of something old."

"If you really think she'll help us, she must have changed since I was here last."

"She's gotten worse, if anything, but it's worth a try," I said.

"Wow," said Eadric, his eyes lit with excitement. "Going back in time! I never thought I'd do that."

"Eadric, you aren't going. It isn't safe. I have no idea what I'll find or even if it will work."

"Of course I'm going. You don't think I came back early to visit with your parents, do you? And I've heard what knights used to be like in the Dark Ages. One of them could kidnap you, drag you back to his castle and force you to marry him. You're not going without me."

"Are you threatening to drag me off to your castle?"

"If I have to," he said, trying out a wicked leer.

I knew there was no arguing with Eadric. I started to tell him about everything else that had happened to me since he left. I was still talking when we headed for the dungeon, and I had to cut short my description of Oculura's eyes as we reached my aunt's room. Grassina didn't answer when I knocked, although we could hear someone banging around. Curious, I opened the door a crack and peeked inside. A lizard once again, my aunt was chasing a hamster, her nails scraping the floor, her scaly tail slamming into the bench and knocking over the chair. The hamster squeaked and tried to run up the wall, falling flat on its back with a tiny thump. Grassina pounced on the helpless creature and snapped it up in an instant.

"Aunt Grassina!" I said, shoving the door open all the way. "Stop that right now! How can you eat those hamsters?"

"Oh, bother!" rasped Grassina in her lizardy voice. "Don't you have anything better to do than to spy on me? Hold on, I'm going to—*Brap!*" She burped, gave me a toothy grin and turned back into a human. "What are you doing here? How can I get any work done if you keep popping in?" She peered at Eadric in the dim light. "Who's that with you? It's not that dunderhead Eadric is it?"

"Hello, Grassina," said Eadric. "How have you been?"

"When?" she barked. "Be specific, boy."

"I wanted to ask you some questions," I began, "but if you're too busy—"

"Don't be silly. Of course I'm too busy. Go away and bother someone else."

"You sound like Grandmother. She didn't want to talk, either."

Sticking a grimy finger in her mouth, my aunt probed her teeth with her fingernail. "You went to see my mother? What about?"

"I had some questions about our family's history," I said. "Grandmother seemed to think she knew more about it than you did, but I thought I'd ask you, anyway."

"Huh," grunted my aunt. After examining her fingernail, she flicked something off it onto the floor. "Don't believe a word she says. That old bat can't remember her middle name, let alone family history. Besides, I know more than she ever did."

"Then you must know all about Hazel, the first Green Witch. Was her father King Grunwald the third or the fourth?"

"The third," she said, running her fingers through her hair until it stood out around her head like a squirrel's nest. "But his wife was a commoner. Don't stand there like an old stump—fetch me that bowl of powdered nightshade. You might as well make yourself useful while you're here." Going to her workbench, Grassina lifted the lid off a cold, iron cauldron and reached for a wooden spoon. "Now where was I? Oh, yes, Hazel. She liked plants. Had a real green thumb. What else did you want to know?"

"Would there be anything of Hazel's here in the castle? Or something that belonged to one of her parents?" I went to the shelf where my aunt stored most of her dried plants and took the containers down one at a time.

"Never seen anything like that. Why do you want to know?" Grassina glanced in my direction and pointed. "The nightshade is in the cracked bowl on the end."

"Just wondered." I took the bowl down and shook it. "You're almost out."

"Don't tell me that! I need five spoonfuls for the next step!"

"I don't think you have more than two here," I said, handing her the bowl. "What are you making?" Grassina caught me peeking into the cauldron and slammed the lid back on, but not before I'd seen that it was half filled with sparkly, lavender dust.

"None of your business! Now get out! I need more nightshade if I'm going to do this right, and I don't want you in here while I'm gone. You don't have any nightshade upstairs, do you?" she asked, squinting at me.

"No, sorry, I don't keep—"

Grassina snorted. "Well, you should. Never know when you're going to need it." Grabbing an empty sack, she hustled Eadric and me out of the room and waved her hand over her door to lock it. "And keep out!" she said, glaring at me before turning on her heel and steaming off down the corridor.

Grassina hadn't told me anything very useful, but I still wasn't ready to give up. Pointing my finger to light the torches on the wall, I gathered my skirts around me and sat down on the dungeon steps, leaving room so Eadric could sit beside me. "Maybe I could use a chip from one of the original stone walls as my focus," I said. "I could take it from one of the older sections and. . . ."

A blue mist seeped through a door at the end of the hall, thickening until it took the form of an elderly man with long white hair and a regal posture. He drifted down the hall toward us, his refined features becoming more apparent as he approached. When he finally reached my side, he seemed to loom over me.

"Is something wrong, my dearest Emma?" asked the ghost.

I drew my cloak more tightly around my shoulders since the air was chilled by his presence. "Hello, Grandfather. I have a puzzle to solve, that's all. By the way, this is Eadric. I believe I told you about him. Eadric, this is my grandfather King Aldrid."

"I remember. I've seen him around the castle," said Grandfather, "although we've never officially met."

"Hello, sir," said Eadric. For someone who was talking to a ghost for the first time, he did very well. His voice was only slightly shaky and his cheeks only a little pale. My grandfather was charming even as a ghost—

he'd chosen to live in the dungeon when my grandmother had fallen victim to the curse, and he had stayed on as a ghost even after he'd died.

"It's a pleasure to meet you, young man. Emma, you said you have a puzzle? How delightful. Perhaps I can help you."

"I hope so," I said. He already knew about my desire to find an end for the curse, so I told him what I'd learned from Dyspepsia. "I have something to make my power stronger, but I still need an object from Hazel's time. Grandmother said that my mother had all the old things thrown away. Hazel's father was King Grunwald the third. I don't suppose you know of an object from his reign that I could use?"

Grandfather rubbed his chin and frowned. "Grunwald the third, hmm. I don't know of anything from that time—"

I sighed. "Then I suppose I'll have to use a chip from a wall he had built."

"Oh my, no!" said Grandfather. "That might take you back years before the day you need to arrive. It should be from something that happened closer to that party, I suppose. I know someone who should be able to help you. Come back in the morning, and I'll try to have him here."

We left Grandfather with the promise that we'd meet him first thing in the morning. Eadric was yawning broadly when we left the dungeon, so we said good night, and he stumbled off to the bedroom he'd used before.

When I passed through the Great Hall, the room was empty except for the hounds still cowering in the corner, startling at every sound. Upstairs in my chamber, I crawled into my bed grateful for its comforting warmth, but I couldn't stop worrying about what I planned to do. Who was Grandfather bringing, and how could this person help me? What if the spell didn't work, and I didn't go anywhere or ended up in the wrong time? And even if the spell was successful and I reached Hazel's time, who knew what I would face?

Sleep was impossible as I thought about why I should go. If I couldn't find a way to end the curse and it changed me before I found someone to replace me as Green Witch, Greater Greensward would be without magical protection. Even if the curse never changed me, I'd have to spend the rest of my days trying to protect everyone I cared about from my crazy aunt and worrying that I still might be the curse's next victim. When I finally fell asleep, I dreamed of sharp-clawed monsters with teeth like daggers chewing up the trestle tables in the Great Hall where my entire family sat, waiting to be devoured.

I was up early the next morning collecting everything I thought might be useful on my trip: a piece of string, a candle stub, a vial of protective salve my dragon friend Ralf had given me and, the most important, the bottle of dragon's breath that I'd put in my hip pouch the day before. The string could always become rope; the candle, an ever-useful light; the salve, a great protector; and the dragon's breath, a way to get me there and back. I hung my smallest farseeing ball on a chain around my neck, dressed in a comfortable gown and warm cloak, fed my canary, then went to check on Li'l. My mother wouldn't need to know, as I figured on returning the same day.

"Where are you going?" asked the little bat from her favorite rafter.

"Into the dungeon for now. If everything works out, I'll be going to find the cure for the curse."

"Can I come with you?" she asked, fluttering to my shoulder.

"You can come as far as the dungeon, if you'd like, but after that I'll need to be on my own. I'm going to try to travel back in time, and I'm not sure what I'll find. I don't dare take anyone with me."

This time when I went to the dungeon, I took a witches' light tethered to me by magic. Lighting my way with a warm glow, it kept pace like a well-trained hawk, staying a few feet above my head. Eadric was waiting for me in the Great Hall, taking bites from a hefty chunk of cheese. He offered me some, but my nervous stomach gurgled and I decided not to take it.

Grandfather was already waiting for us in the dungeon with two ghosts I'd never seen before. Wary of strangers, Li'l hunched down on my shoulder, gripping my cloak with her claws. The room was so cold from the presence of three ghosts that I could see each puff of our breath. Even with the cloak wrapped around me, my teeth chattered and I had to listen hard to hear my grandfather.

After nodding to Eadric, Grandfather drew me to his side so that we faced the other ghosts together. "Emma, I'd like you to meet Sir Jarvis," Grandfather told me. The ghost wore a peaked cap, over-tunic and leggings that had long been out of fashion. His noble bearing would have been the same in any time period. "And this is his friend, Hubert. Hubert tells me that he worked in the stables of Grunwald the third." The ghost was stooped with age, his long hair straggled almost to his knees, his tunic was little more than a rag and his legs and feet were bare. The finely wrought chain that he wore around his neck seemed very much out of place.

"*King* Grunwald to you, youngster. You need to learn respect for your betters," said Hubert.

Sir Jarvis looked appalled. "Sorry, Your Majesty! Hubert hasn't been the same since guards came down a few months back and opened the trapdoor to the oubliette." The oubliette was little more than a hole in the cellar of the castle covered by a rusty, metal grate. It was where the old kings put prisoners who they wanted to forget. "Hubert was sure that they'd finally remembered him and had come to let him out. A bit late, if you ask me, but he has trouble with his memory even on the best of days. He forgets that only his bones are left in that pit, and the guards weren't interested in those. Hubert," he said, turning to his friend, "this is King Aldrid. You've met him before!"

"He's not the king!" grumbled the stooped ghost. "King Grunwald the third is the king and has been for as long as I can remember. I've worked in his stables since I was just a lad."

Sir Jarvis shook his head. "That was many years ago, Hubert! Limelyn is king now. This is his father-in-law, King Aldrid. He wants to ask you some questions."

"What kind of questions?"

"Actually," I said, "I'm the one who wants to talk to you, Hubert. I'm Princess Emeralda and I'm interested in King Grunwald the third. Can you tell me anything about him or his daughter Princess Hazel?"

"That I can. Princess Hazel is lovely, much prettier than you. She has the most beautiful golden hair, with eyes the color of robins' eggs and skin as smooth as cream. She has a green thumb and can grow anything she has a mind to. Why, I've seen her grow a potato vine up the stable wall that sprouted potatoes in less than a day.

Lots of talent our princess has; you can be sure of that! It was the little princess who gave me this medallion just before the big party," Hubert said, pulling the chain out from under his tunic. A silver disk spun on the end of the chain. "Said it was for bravery. I never took it off. Had to hide it or many's the time they would have taken it from me." Eyeing me as if I might try to grab his ghostly medallion, Hubert tucked it back under his filthy tunic.

"It was a lovely medallion," I said. "And it was very kind of the princess to give it to you. What about King Grunwald? What was he like?"

The aged ghost's shape wavered, his form growing faint, then more distinct. "Why are you asking all these questions? You aren't a spy, are you? The king doesn't take kindly to spies! I'll call the castle guards; that's what I'll do. They'll throw you in the oubliette, and you'll never get out!"

"That's all right, Hubert," said Sir Jarvis, patting the older ghost's arm. "Calm down now, old fellow. There are no spies here!" Hubert muttered to himself while his friend turned to Grandfather and me. "Hubert spent his last days in the oubliette. Grunwald the fourth had him tossed down there when something went missing. I think Hubert was caught someplace he shouldn't have been, but he certainly paid the price. The oubliette was a terrible place to die."

"I'm not going back there!" shouted Hubert. "You can't make me!"

I couldn't blame him.

"There, there, Hubert. No one is going to make you do anything. I think it's time for us to go. Good day, Your Majesties," said Sir Jarvis, bowing to Grandfather and me.

"What did they say?" Li'l piped up as the two ghosts faded into blue mist and floated down the hall. "I could understand him all right," she said, waving her wing at my grandfather, "just not those other two."

"Really? And can you understand Li'l?" I asked Grandfather.

He nodded. "Quite well, actually."

"How is that possible?" I said. "I thought that only witches and people who had been turned into animals for a time could understand them when they talk."

"That's true," he said. "And when the family curse changed your grandmother, and she sent me to the dungeon, she turned me into a rat for a few days. I've been able to talk to animals ever since. I know every creature in this dungeon, living and dead. It was a centipede who first told me about Hubert. I'm sorry Hubert wasn't very helpful."

"But he was, Grandfather. He gave me just what I needed. Now I know where to go. Can you show us the way to the oubliette?"

"Nasty place," said Grandfather. "Why would you want to go there?"

"Because that's where Hubert died. I think it's time we found his bones."

Five

The oubliette wasn't at all where I thought it might be, so I was glad I'd asked Grandfather to lead us there. Over time, magic had moved doors and holes in the floor so often that even a map wouldn't have helped. When we found it, the metal grate didn't look very sturdy. A lattice of holes as wide as the palm of my hand, it was about three feet square and quite heavy. The grate felt brittle and was hard to move, but Eadric and I were able to lift it free of the opening and set it aside on the floor.

"Now what?" asked Grandfather, floating over the hole as he peered into the darkness below.

"Now I go down there." Taking the piece of string from my purse, I laid it on the floor and made it grow. With a soft hiss, the string stretched until it was longer and thicker. One end of the string fastened to a hook in the wall as the other dropped down into the hole. I listened until I heard the end of the rope slap the floor of the oubliette.

"Let me go first!" said Li'l. She fluttered her wings, circled me once, then swooped into the absolute dark of the hole. "Not much down here," she called. "Just a lot of bones."

"I'll go look," said Grandfather. "Maybe I'll find someone I know." Drifting through the opening, he disappeared from sight.

"I'll go next," said Eadric. "I want to make sure it's safe." Sitting on the edge of the opening, Eadric grasped the rope, hooked one foot around it and slipped down its length. "It seems all right," he called, his voice sounding strangely hollow.

"I'll be right there," I called down and was reaching for the rope when a scrabbling of nails on the stone floor made me stop to listen. At first I thought it was Grassina turned back into a lizard, but when a scrap of shadow detached itself from the gloom, I knew exactly what it was.

"Emma, are you coming?" Eadric called.

"In a minute," I said, stepping back from the edge of the hole.

The glow of my witches' light wasn't very bright, but it was enough to make the shadow moving toward me obvious. The size of a newborn calf, it had no discernable features except for its red eyes. Aunt Grassina had taught me how to deal with the shadow beast years before, so it no longer frightened me as it once had, but

I didn't want it to follow us down into the oubliette where I might not have space to maneuver. Bracing my legs, I waited for it to attack. It came at me in a rush, the scrape of claws on stone its only sound. I waited until the last second, then hit it between the eyes with my fist while I jumped out of the way. Unfortunately my foot caught on the grate that I'd left lying on the floor, and I tripped and fell headfirst into the hole.

"Emma, what are you doing?" Eadric shouted as I plunged toward the floor. Something grazed my hand and I snatched at it, catching the rope and nearly dislocating my arm. The rope swung wildly as I flipped over so I was right side up again. My witches' light bobbed around like a crazy thing, casting shadows that shrank and stretched on the walls and floor like some strange kind of monsters.

I felt Eadric grab my legs. "Let go. I've got you," he said.

Li'l circled me, so close that her wings nearly brushed my face. "Why did you do that?" she asked. "I thought you were going to climb down the rope."

"Are you all right?" Grandfather said, floating up to where I still hung. "Do you need help?" he asked.

"I'm fine," I said, although my voice sounded forced even to me. I took a deep breath. My heart was pounding so hard I was sure everyone could hear it. *Just let go,* I told myself. Unfortunately my fingers weren't listening, and I couldn't make them do anything. "I think I'll stay here awhile," I announced, although my hand hurt and my shoulder shrieked with pain.

"Why?" asked Li'l. "You've almost reached the floor, anyway."

Eadric tightened his grip on my legs. "It's all right, Emma. You aren't going to fall."

"Tell that to my fingers."

"I'll help," said Li'l. Fluttering closer, she nipped my little finger.

"Ow!" I said, more surprised than hurt, and my hand jerked away from the rope. I was relieved when I fell into Eadric's arms.

"Got you!" he said, planting a kiss on my lips. "Now are you glad I came?"

"Yuck!" said Li'l. "Do you have to do that in front of me?"

Eadric laughed. "We're practically engaged, Li'l."

"That doesn't matter. You humans do the strangest things."

"And bats don't?" Eadric asked.

"Not like that!"

"Eadric, put me down," I said. "I have work to do."

"Fine," he said, setting me on my feet. "But you have to admit that I'm handy to have around."

The room was roughly eight feet wide and ten feet long. While one end was dry, I saw gaps in the wall at the other end where stones had shifted, letting water from the moat trickle in. A single skeleton lay sprawled against the driest wall, its legs extending into the middle of the room. However, it was the two corners filled with piles of bones that interested me most. Someone had sorted them neatly, stacking all the skulls in one corner, the rest of the bones in the other. Glancing at the whole skeleton, I decided that he'd probably been the last occupant of the room and the one who'd piled the bones.

"Poor fellow," said Grandfather, hovering above the skeleton. "Even his ghost has abandoned him."

"I don't like this place," said Li'l. "It has a bad feeling. Can we go now?"

"Not until we find what we came for," I said. "Let's start over here." I was picking up an arm bone when a skeletal hand wrapped its fingers around my wrist.

"Not so fast," said a skull in the other pile.

"What do you think you're doing?" asked a second skull.

"Thief! Grave robber!" shrieked a third.

Setting his hand on Ferdy's hilt, Eadric said, "Emma, step back and let me handle this," and drew his sword from his scabbard. Ferdy began to sing.

I can fight an ogre
I can fight a troll
Plain old bones don't....

"That's enough, Eadric," I said. "I can take care of it."

Since skeletons don't have muscles to give them strength, it was easy to pry the bony fingers off my wrist. The hand twitched when I set it on the pile and some finger bones reached up, trying to pinch me while another hand plucked at my sleeve. I sighed and tried not to lose my temper.

The sound of gnashing teeth made me glance up. "All for one and one for all!" hollered a skull with a bad overbite. "Don't let her take a single bone!"

"I don't want any bones," I said. "I just want to borrow a medallion."

"What kind of medallion?" asked a skull with a cracked jaw.

"It's for bravery, and I think it's made of silver. It belonged to Hubert, who worked in Grunwald the third's stables."

"Oh, that medallion!" said a skull.

Another skull grunted. "What do you mean, *that* medallion? There's only one here!"

Something clattered behind me. "Look out!" shouted Li'l, and I turned to see the skeleton clambering to its feet. Tottering on wobbly legs, it raised its arms, its shaking hands reaching for my throat.

"Oh, stop it!" I said and gave the skeleton a shove. It fell against the wall with a thump. Its skull must have been loose, because it fell off and rolled across the floor until it bumped into the opposite wall.

"Serves you right, you big bully!" shouted a skull halfway up the pile.

"You always thought you were special just because you had all your parts!" shouted another on the bottom.

"I never knew you felt that way!" said the skull on the ground. The skeleton patted the stone floor until it located its head, then set it in place on its neck before turning its back to the other skulls.

Putting my hands on my hips, I glared at the skulls and said, "I'm here to do a job, and I'd appreciate it if you'd let me get on with it."

"Maybe we should just leave," said Li'l.

"They won't bother you anymore," said Eadric, scowling at the skulls as if daring them to defy him.

Grandfather floated across the room, his blue outline growing larger and darker until it looked quite menacing. "Perhaps they can help," he said with an edge. "I'm sure they know where we can find the medallion."

"Why should we help you?" asked a wavering voice.

"Because," said my grandfather, "if you don't help, I'll scatter your bones across the kingdom for the wolves and wild dogs to find." The pile of skulls shifted uneasily. "However, if you do help, I'll sort you and see that you get proper burials."

The skulls muttered among themselves until one of

them spoke up. "Do you promise? Cross your rib cage and hope to rest in peace?"

"I promise," Grandfather said solemnly, "on my honor as a king and as a member of the Council of Ghosts."

"Then we'll give the girl the medallion," said the spokes-skull, "but she'll have to return it to its proper owner when she's through with it."

"I'm down here," said a muffled voice that I assumed came from Hubert's skull.

The pile of bones shuddered and heaved. Bones slipped off the top while others were pushed up from the bottom. Finally a bony hand gripping the medallion rose to the surface. Tarnished with age, it was the same medallion that Hubert's ghost had worn on a chain around his neck.

"Thank you," I said, taking the silver disk. "You've been a big help."

"Can we go now?" asked Li'l, flitting around my head.

"You can," I said, "but I won't be going with you." Reaching into my pouch, I took out the bottle of dragon's breath. I had everything I needed now, including a secluded spot from the right century. It wasn't ideal, but I didn't think I'd find anything better.

"What do you mean?" asked Li'l. "You said we could leave as soon as you had what we came for."

"I know I did, and I'm sorry, but I'm going to go learn what I can about the curse. I shouldn't be gone long—not if I do this right."

"Be careful, my dear," said Grandfather. "The past was a harsh and cruel time."

"I will, Grandfather. I'll be back before you know it."

Eadric came to stand beside me and rested his hand on my shoulder. "Don't worry, Your Majesty, I'll keep her safe."

I frowned and shook my head. "I told you, Eadric; you can't go with me."

"And I told you that I am," he replied, looking as serious as I'd ever seen him. "You need me as much as I need you."

"I need you to stay here where it's safe. Who knows what I'll find in the past."

"Exactly," said Eadric.

I didn't want to waste my time arguing, so I shook his hand from my shoulder and edged away, confident that I could move beyond his reach when the spell started to take effect.

Dyspepsia had said that I needed something to enhance my power, but she hadn't said how much I should use. Dragon's breath is very powerful as well as hard to get, so I decided to let out a tiny bit and hope that it was enough. Holding the medallion in one hand, I took the stopper out of the bottle for a moment to let some of the breath escape, then said the spell I'd already decided to use.

> Take me to the day before
> The fairy cast the curse
> That changed my dear aunt's
> temperament
> From kindly to much worse.

I was saying the last line when I heard something scrape against the stones above my head. When I looked up, the glowing eyes of the shadow beast were peering down through the opening.

"Emma!" Grandfather shouted, drifting between the creature and me.

I could hear the shadow beast's nails on the stone floor as it launched itself down into the oubliette. I tried to move out of the way, but the only path open to me was the corner where the pile of bones rested.

"Look out!" screeched Li'l, fluttering around my head.

"Emma, over here!" shouted Eadric. He threw himself at me, pulling me out of the way as the shadow beast lunged, but we were both off balance and we started to fall.

"Careful!" screamed a skull as the whole pile trembled.

Eadric and I were about to land on the pile of bones

when the oubliette disappeared, and we found ourselves rushing down a dark tunnel, propelled by a buffeting wind. A thunderous roar filled my ears, and at first I thought we'd brought the shadow beast with us. When the wind spun me around, I tried to see something, anything in the dark, but my witches' light was gone and I couldn't see a thing. *I hope this is supposed to happen,* I thought as the darkness swept us away.

Six

The air was thickening around me and it was getting harder to breathe. I no longer felt like a wind was whisking me along, but more like something was forcing me through a thick and lumpy, sour-smelling pudding. I could still feel Eadric's arms around me, just as they'd been when he'd pulled me away from the shadow beast. I was frightened, but not nearly as much as I would have been if I'd been alone. Although I hadn't wanted him to come, in a way I was glad he had.

The air grew hotter, and a high-pitched whine filled my ears. I was gasping for breath when something shoved us through a warm, moist layer. Suddenly the air was normal again. We fell—how far I couldn't tell—until we slammed into cold, hard stone, landing on our sides. With the air knocked out of us, we lay sprawled on the ground, too numb to get up.

"What was that?" croaked a voice from somewhere

nearby. "Either I'm dreaming or the rats have gotten a lot bigger."

Wherever we were, we weren't alone. I drew in a ragged breath and was nearly overcome by the stench of dung and an unwashed human body. I tested my limbs, afraid that I might have broken something, but I was fine—aside from scrapes and a few tender spots.

Eadric let go of me and sat up, Ferdy's scabbard scraping the floor. "Are you all right?" he whispered.

"I will be," I said as quietly as I could, "as soon as I find out where and *when* we are."

I was stuffing the medallion and the bottle of dragon's breath into my pouch, when something small and bony landed on me with a Whump! It moaned softly, then started to move around, poking me with knobby edges. "Stupid spell," grumbled a familiar voice.

"Li'l, is that you?" I whispered.

"Emma?" she said. "What happened? One minute I was in that oubliette, and the next thing I knew a wind grabbed me, beat me up and spit me out. Where are we? Did we go back in time?"

"I'm not sure," I whispered. "Shh! Someone's in here, and he thinks he's dreaming."

I set Li'l on my shoulder while I peered into the darkness, hoping for some glimmer of light. I couldn't see a thing until I looked up and saw a swirl of color rising above me—either the dragon's breath or some ghostly apparition that had decided to leave. When it disappeared through a checkered shape that could only be a grate, I knew that we were in the oubliette, although I still had no idea *when*.

I thought about creating a witches' light or using the candle stub so we could see, but if I did, I might have to use more magic to convince the man that he really was dreaming. The longer I thought about it, the more complicated it seemed. No, I'd have to manage without any light at all.

Something shifted in the dark. "Speak up!" said the voice, sounding more like a man and less like a nightmare. "You're awfully quiet for a dream. Why don't you sing me a song? Last dream I had, a minstrel sang about a great knight. Made me feel like I was there, fighting dragons and all. How about a song like that?"

Eadric spoke up, saying, "I'd like to sing, but I don't know any good songs."

"Then I'll sing one," said the voice. "I made it up myself. It's the story of why I'm down here. Want to hear it?" The voice chuckled. "Listen to me—asking a dream what it wants!" He started to sing, scratchy and so far off tune it made me cringe.

They sent Old Derwin to the pit
Because he dropped a platter.
It landed on the good king's crown,

And made an awful clatter.
The king told him to clean it up
As if it didn't matter.
But Princess Hazel threw a fit.
And made the servants scatter.
She said he'd ruined her new gown
Because of what did splatter.
That he was worthless and no good
For anything but chatter.
She sent him down here with no food,
And said he'd get no fatter.
That he was such a clumsy oaf....

"She sent you to the oubliette because you were clumsy? That's horrible!" I said. I'd grown up being ridiculed for my clumsiness, and I thought that had been bad!

"Aye, but the goose gravy made an awful mess. I can't blame the princess for being upset."

"But throwing you into the oubliette—"

"Is that what you call it? I call it the pit."

"And Princess Hazel sent you here?" I asked. If that was true, then the curse must have taken effect already. No one with a shred of kindness in her heart would send anyone to the oubliette. I didn't expect Derwin to have heard the curse firsthand, but nothing stays secret in a castle for long. If people had been discussing it, he might have heard them and. . . .

Derwin sighed. "I should have been more careful," he said. "The princess has been in an awful state what with all those suitors come for her party. Her relatives have come, too, rich and poor alike, and she's trying hard to please them. She's very particular, our princess Hazel, and she deserves the best. Although sending me to the pit does seem a bit harsh, to my way of thinking. I hope they'll let me out when the celebration's over and not just forget about me altogether. It isn't for two more days, though, so I don't expect them anytime soon. Want to hear the rest of my song? Or maybe the one about the milkmaid's dream, since you're part of a dream yourself? It's my longest, so we'll just have to hope that I don't wake up soon."

> A milkmaid dreamed that she could be
> A princess for a day.
> She made a crown of buttercups,
> A throne of fresh-cut hay.

The party hadn't been held yet, although I was earlier than I'd hoped. Now I'd have to stick around for two more days to find out exactly what the fairy had said. Maybe the little bit of dragon's breath I'd used hadn't been enough. I pursed my lips and tried to think, but it wasn't easy with Derwin's singing grating my ears.

"Can't we go now?" Li'l asked, nudging me with her wing. "I don't like it here."

The little bat was right. It was time to go. I'd have to think of some way to get out of the oubliette and go where I could blend in while waiting for the party.

"Just say a spell," said Li'l, "and take us somewhere else."

Engrossed in his song, Derwin didn't seem to hear us, although it wouldn't have made much difference even if he had. We were talking in Li'l's language, and the chances weren't very good that he could understand Bat. "It isn't that simple," I said. "We can't just appear out of nowhere. There's no telling who might be around."

"Isn't that what we just did?" asked Eadric.

"That was different," I said. "Derwin thinks he's dreaming. We don't want anyone else to see us until we're ready. I have to think of a way to get us out of here, but I can't see a thing, so…."

"I can," said Li'l. "I'll show you the way. Although if you were a bat…."

"That's it!" I whispered. "I'll turn us into bats."

"Bats!" said Eadric. "I don't know about that."

"What's wrong?" asked Li'l. "Do you have something against bats?"

"Not at all," Eadric hurried to say. "Bats are very nice."

I don't know why I'd never turned into a bat before.

I'd always admired my little friend's ability to navigate in the dark and hang upside down without getting dizzy. It wouldn't be hard to do, either. After all, it couldn't be much different than turning into a bird, and I'd already done that. Setting Li'l on the floor, I took Eadric's hand and murmured the spell that would get us out of the oubliette, although Derwin was singing so loudly that I doubt he would have noticed even if I'd shouted.

Silky fur
And wings of skin
Change the shape
That we'll be in.

Neither birds,
Nor frogs, nor cats,
We'll now be
A pair of bats.

Although I couldn't see a thing, I knew when the change was finished because I felt so different. I was smaller, and my body and head were covered with soft fur. Bare skin stretched between my fingers, which had grown long and thin, though my thumb was shorter and could still move freely. The skin between my fingers stretched all the way to my feet, forming wings. More skin connected my tiny feet, and my toes were tipped with long, curved claws.

"Good job!" exclaimed Li'l. "You make a pretty bat, Emma."

"What about me?" Eadric asked.

"You're not bad, either," said Li'l with a lot less enthusiasm.

I glanced up, hoping to see in the dark, but it still looked black as pitch. "Why can't I see? I thought bats could see in the dark."

"We can, but not with our eyes. We make a sound, and it makes a picture in our heads. Try it. You'll see what I mean."

I tried making all kinds of sounds, but nothing unusual happened. Frustrated, I finally made a little sound in my throat, surprising myself when the sound came back, smaller yet quite distinct. A picture of the wall in front of me formed in my mind. *That's funny*, I thought. Turning my head, I made the sound again. When it came back this time, I could tell that the next wall was farther away. *So that's how Li'l does it.* Keeping my mouth open, I made the sound over and over again, until I had a good idea what the oubliette looked like. In this time, there weren't any bones, and the back wall was sturdy and dry.

I'd located Derwin sitting against the wall on the other side of the room, where he was singing with great gusto. When he gestured with his arms, I could see it with my mind, although I still couldn't see anything with my eyes.

I could see Li'l and Eadric, too. "I know what you mean, Li'l," I said. "This is great! Come on, let's get out of here."

"Finally!" exclaimed the little bat.

I tried to move my wings the way I had when I was a bird. My bat wings were very different, however, and it took me a while to get it right. Even then I didn't fly very well. I had to learn new movements while keeping my mouth open so I could make the sounds to see where I was going. It was a lot to master all at once, and I bumbled around the oubliette for a while before it began to feel right. Eadric seemed to have problems, too, although he caught on sooner than I did.

When we finally reached the grate in the ceiling, I was relieved that we fit through the spaces easily. I crawled through one of the holes, still making my sounds, and found that the oubliette was at the end of a short corridor. As we flew away from the grate, I could hear Derwin singing his song, his scratchy voice growing faint with distance.

We reached another corridor, longer than the first and lined on both sides with cells. From the sounds coming through the doors, I could tell that many of them held prisoners. Eadric and I tried to follow Li'l's example, fluttering down the corridor while staying out of the flickering light cast by the occasional torch. This was just as well, for we passed two guards outside the guardroom door and had to make a wide detour around one who'd stopped to relight a torch.

The door at the top of the stairs was closed. We looked carefully, but we couldn't find even the smallest opening through which we could escape. Since there weren't any other ways out of the dungeon, we had to wait until someone opened the door. Li'l chose a point midway between two torches where the shadows were deepest and showed Eadric and me how to cling to the ceiling with the claws on our toes.

My claws held me firmly in place, and I was surprised at how comfortable hanging upside down by my feet could be. It was so comfortable, in fact, that I began to grow drowsy, and I might have fallen asleep if a guard hadn't opened the door at the top of the stairs, letting in a draft that made the torches gutter and rocked us back and forth. The guard was already shutting the door when we zipped past and found ourselves in a dimly lit corridor.

We needed to find someplace private where I could turn us back into humans. The corridor led into a large room smelling strongly of old herbs mixed with bits of rotting refuse strewn over the floor. It was the Great Hall, and it looked much the way it would in my day, just messier. A small group of women talked in a corner while two young men playing chess lounged on a bench nearby. Seeing so many people, Li'l darted toward one of the narrow windows set high in the wall. Eadric and I were following her when a woman shrieked, "Eek, it's a bat!"

"There's a flock of them!" shouted someone else.

Hearing other people behind me, I tried to fly faster and had almost reached the window when a pear sailed past, splatting against the wall and showering me with sticky bits of fruit. They were throwing things at me! I veered away, struggling to keep my balance and saw Eadric dodge someone's thrown shoe.

"It's trying to get in my hair!" shrieked a girl, pulling the end of her surcoat over her head. Other female voices cried out in alarm as they tried to cover their hair as well.

A shoe grazed my back, ruffling my fur. Li'l had already reached the window, but I had to veer off, heading back into the Hall. The women shrieked. I wove back and forth, hoping to dodge anything else they might throw at me as I aimed for the other window. Suddenly the dry straw of an old broom came swishing through the air, knocking me across the room. I tried to right myself, but before I could get my wings sorted out, I landed in a tangle of something limp and greasy.

"It's in my hair!" screamed a voice so close it hurt my ears.

I struggled to free myself until someone started slapping me. Covering my head with my wings, I shut my eyes, curled up into a tight little ball and tried to think of a way out of the mess I was in without using something as conspicuous as magic. If only the woman would stop screaming!

"Got it!" said a triumphant male voice as a hand closed around me, pulling me out of the woman's hair.

My eyes popped open. The florid face of a young man with light brown hair was staring down at me. "Watch this," he said to someone behind him. "I can kill it with one hand!"

My response was automatic, but even if I'd thought about it, I probably would have done the same thing. I bit him squarely on the thumb.

"Aargh!" he shouted, and I was free.

I didn't think I'd bitten him hard enough to do any real damage, although I checked my teeth with my tongue just to make sure. The aftertaste was awful.

Eadric had been trying to reach me, but another young man was chasing him, struggling to trap him in a woven basket. When Eadric saw me, he changed direction and followed me to the window where Li'l was waiting for us on the ledge. Before I followed her into the sunshine, I stopped to look back and was surprised to see that everyone had fled the room. *So much for being inconspicuous,* I thought.

Seven

"Did you have to fool around like that?" asked Li'l. "I thought you were right behind me."

"We were, but those people had other ideas. We need to go outside and…. Oh!" Eadric's jaw dropped as he stared past us out the window.

Even during my short excursion through the castle, I had noticed differences from the way it was in my time. The furniture was sparse, the people's clothing simpler. However, the biggest difference was outside. Unlike our time when flowers were forbidden on the castle grounds, I saw them blooming everywhere. I recognized the roses climbing the walls and growing in massive hedges, having seen the rose-covered cottages at the Old Witches' Retirement Community, but I didn't know the names of most of the rest.

Vines dripping with purple blooms covered the castle. Dark blue flowers nodded at the edge of the moat while small yellow flowers and broad, green pads floated on the water. Trees heavy with pink-and-white blossoms stood like rows of soldiers waiting to be inspected on either side of the road leading away from the drawbridge. Although I didn't know much about such things, it seemed odd that so many plants should bloom at the same time.

"Why would anyone plant flowers around the castle?" asked Eadric. "They make it harder to defend."

I tapped him on the wing and pointed to the other side of the road where hedges of deep pink roses grew in an intricate maze. "That will be perfect," I said, hopping off the ledge.

Li'l and Eadric followed me as I flew to the maze, dodging droning bees and butterflies intoxicated with nectar. "Perfect for what?" Eadric asked.

"For turning back, of course."

"Already?" asked Li'l. "But we were just starting to have fun!"

When we passed the drawbridge, I was shocked to see that vines twined around the chains and threaded through the portcullis. Eadric must have seen it, too, because his wings faltered, and I heard him mutter to himself.

Reaching the maze, we skimmed the rosebushes until I found a secluded niche invisible even to someone looking down from the higher tower. I settled to the ground and used my usual spell to turn us back into humans. No sooner had I smoothed my gown over my hips and adjusted my hem, than I heard voices coming through the maze of shrubs. Eadric heard them, too, and set his hand on Ferdy's hilt, but I shook my head and he took his hand away.

"Why does Millie need a new gown, Mother? It isn't her birthday," someone whined.

Startled, Li'l slipped into a dense section of the hedge where even I couldn't see her.

"I'm sorry, my darling Hazel," a sweet voice replied, "but you want her to look her best for your party, don't you? We wouldn't want her to embarrass you in front of your guests."

"Really, Mother," said a softer voice. "I don't need another gown."

"Nonsense," said Hazel. "Mother is right. You'll get a new gown, but it won't be nearly as nice as mine. Will it, Mother?"

"Of course not, dear. You are the birthday girl, after all."

"And don't forget, Millie," said Hazel as they rounded the hedge, "stay out of my way when … goodness, who are you?" she asked, spotting us for the first time.

Hazel was lovely, but not what I'd expected. She looked like a flower herself, with her porcelain skin, pink cheeks and delicate features. Her thick blond hair reminded me of my mother's. Her lips were the same deep pink as the roses and her eyes a deeper blue than the sky. She didn't look anything like the Green Witch in the tapestry decorating my chamber at home.

The older woman who walked beside Hazel wore a simple gold circlet to secure the veil covering her hair. Shorter than Hazel, she was plump and had worry lines etching her forehead. Her eyes were green, although not as dark as mine, and I could see our family resemblance. However, the face that really surprised me was that of the young girl peeking from behind her shoulder. Except for her dainty, freckled nose and the carrot-red shade of her hair, which was much brighter than my auburn, I might have been looking in a mirror.

"I said, 'Who are you?'" Hazel repeated.

I curtsied and said, "Emma." I wasn't really sure how I should explain my presence since I'd never intended to meet the royal family. I had hoped to talk to one or two people about the curse and leave.

"You must be one of Aunt Frederika's daughters," said Hazel. "There are so many of you; it's hard to keep track."

"Are you settled in, dear?" asked the queen, smiling at me kindly.

"Not really," I said. "I just—"

The queen frowned and shook her head. "Don't tell me that my steward didn't assign you to a room. I'm so sorry. With all our guests, we simply don't.... I know. Millie," she said, turning to the girl behind her, "you have ample space in your chamber. Your cousin can sleep there. I'll have the steward see that a pallet is brought up before supper."

The redheaded girl behind her smiled shyly at me and nodded.

The queen turned to Eadric, who'd been staring at Hazel with obvious admiration. "And you are ...?"

Eadric blinked and cleared his throat. "I'm Prince Eadric, a friend of Emma's."

Hazel smiled at him coyly. "Another prince? How nice. Do you come from very far away?"

"Farther than you can imagine," he said. I could have sworn I heard Li'l giggling in the bushes behind us, but no one else seemed to notice.

"Ah," said Hazel. "That explains your unusual clothes. Perhaps one of the other princes could lend you something more becoming. You can share a room with them. We'll have to find a way to fit in one more pallet." She looked me up and down, her eyes lingering on my gown. "Send a tunic and surcoat for her, Mother. That *thing* she's wearing is most peculiar. One of your ladies-in-waiting should have something that would fit her."

"I'm sure we can find her something—" the queen began.

"She is tall, though, isn't she?" Hazel said, brushing

past me on the path. "And I can't imagine where she got that nose."

"We mustn't be unkind to those less fortunate, dear," I heard the queen say as she hurried after her daughter. I could feel the heat rushing to my cheeks, and I knew that I was blushing—something I hadn't done in a very long time. When I glanced at Eadric, he was staring after Hazel with a dazed look in his eyes.

"Don't pay any attention to her," said Millie, patting my shoulder. "My sister is like that with everyone."

"Your sister?" No one had told me that Hazel had a sister, older or younger. It was a shame that so much of our family's history had been lost.

Millie sighed. "I just turned thirteen, so she's only three years older than me, but she acts twenty years older. Come with me. I'll show you where you're going to sleep. I'll have one of the pages take Eadric to meet the princes."

"How many princes are there?" Eadric asked.

"Five," said Millie. "That room is going to be crowded."

I glanced around, hoping to see Li'l, but she must have still been hiding in the bushes. I resolved to come back and find her as soon as I could. "It's awfully kind of you to let me stay in your room," I said, following Millie through the confusing maze.

"Oh, I don't mind," she said. "I'm surprised they

didn't put someone in with me sooner. Mother tends to forget about me, and as for Hazel—well, sometimes I wish she would as well. I shouldn't complain, though. You come from a big family. I suppose it's even worse for you."

"Big family? I don't. . . ." I stopped, remembering that I was supposed to have a whole gaggle of sisters. If my long-ago relatives wanted to believe that I was one of Aunt Frederika's daughters, I wasn't about to try to change their minds.

"The drawbridge is this way," said Millie, leading us between two banks of heavy-headed roses that looked exactly like all the others we'd passed. We had left the maze and were passing the first of the flowering trees when Millie exclaimed, "Oh, look, there are your sisters now!"

Any hope of passing myself off as one of the cousins died the moment I saw them. A cluster of six or seven girls—ranging from a few years older than me to a toddler clinging to her mother's hand—turned to look at us. Like their mother, each one was petite and finely boned; even the oldest girl was fairly short. Although their mother's hair was dark brown, all of the girls' hair was red, but none of them had my high cheekbones or distinctive nose. I wasn't sure what to do, so I waggled my fingers at them in greeting and hurried past, spurred on by their puzzled expressions.

True to her word, Millie called to the first page she saw and had him escort Eadric to the princes' chamber. After that, Millie didn't say another word until we reached her room. Closing her door behind us, she plunked herself down on her narrow bed and turned to me with a determined look in her eyes. "We need to talk," she said, patting the blanket beside her.

I climbed onto the bed. "If it's about Frederika—"

"Don't worry," Millie said. "I understand perfectly. You aren't really one of her daughters, are you? I didn't think you were."

I searched her eyes, hoping she would understand. "When Hazel said—"

"Hazel is wrong more often than she's right, but you'd never get anyone else to admit it." Millie drew her knees up to her chest and hugged them. "You can tell me the truth. I'm very good at keeping secrets."

I shook my head. "You wouldn't believe me if I told you."

"It doesn't matter. I think I already know. Aunt Frederika isn't your mother, but I bet Uncle Markus is your father, and he made his wife take you in and raise you as one of her own. She resents it, doesn't she? The look on her face said it all. Don't worry; it happens in the best of families. I'm right, aren't I?" Millie said, looking very pleased with herself.

"You're too clever for me," I said, delighted that

she'd found her own explanation.

Millie sighed. "Not really. It's just that every family has secrets. Some are easier to figure out than others."

"Don't tell me that you have a secret, too."

Millie turned her head away. Something was troubling her, but I couldn't blame her if she didn't want to tell me about it. After all, we'd only just met. I was about to apologize for being nosy when there was a knock on the door and a pair of chambermaids came in carrying a pallet and an armful of clothes. It didn't take them long to arrange everything to their satisfaction. They were leaving when one of them glanced at my shoes and frowned. As the door was closing, I heard her say to her companion, "Did you see that girl's shoes? They looked like a dog chewed them."

I tucked my feet under me, hoping Millie hadn't heard her. My shoes were scuffed and dirty from tripping in the dungeon, but I didn't think they looked chewed. Certainly none of my father's hounds could have done it, and as for King Grunwald's.... When I thought about it, I hadn't seen a single hound since I'd arrived, although they always seemed to be underfoot in my own time.

"Don't your parents allow dogs in the castle?" I asked.

Millie shook her head. "Not anymore. It's not my parents' idea, though; it's Hazel's. She doesn't like dogs. I suppose she's afraid they'll dig up her precious plants."

"She does have a lot of influence, doesn't she?" I said. I didn't know anyone who could make my father get rid of his favorite hounds.

"Hazel usually gets what she wants. It wasn't always that way, just since she discovered that she could do magic. My parents are afraid of her now, and they do everything they can to make her happy."

I was shocked. The only people in my family who had tried to use magic against a relative had been under the influence of the family curse. The thought that someone might *want* to do it…. "Has she ever used her magic to hurt anyone?"

"Not so far, but she's always dropping hints that she could if she wanted to. Even the threat of withholding her magic is enough to get people to do what she wants. Before she came into her abilities, the kingdom's crops were failing. Hazel turned all that around. I just wish she'd left it at that."

"Then she hasn't actually done anything to anyone?"

"I wouldn't say that. After she figured out that she could do magic, she experimented all the time, and she wasn't always nice about it. She used to have vines tie me up just for fun. Sometimes she'd grow prickly plants on my chamber floor during the night so I'd step on them when I woke up in the morning. She doesn't bother me so much since I learned to stay out of her way and let her think she's getting what she wants."

"But she doesn't always get what she wants, does she?" I asked, seeing a hint of defiance and something I couldn't quite name in Millie's eyes.

"No," she said, a secret smile curving her lips. "Not anymore."

"Doesn't she use her magic for anything productive besides growing crops? What about protecting the kingdom or helping your parents?"

"If only she would! Everyone likes to pretend otherwise, but Greater Greensward is in trouble. Werewolves have been raiding the outlying villages, and I overheard my father talking to his men about vampires. What's even worse is that a dragon has moved into a cave near here. Father sent knights after it, but we never saw them again. He finally stopped sending people, although I know he's been hoping one of Hazel's suitors will kill the dragon for us. It's not going to happen, though. All they want to do is eat our food, drink our wine and flirt with Hazel. Although there is one suitor…."

"What about him?"

"His name is Prince Garrid. He's very handsome if you like men who have wavy, blond hair; deep gray eyes; and cleft chins. He's a good hunter. Every day when the weather is fair he goes off by himself, yet he never fails to come back with some sort of game. Garrid may be the only one who would stand a chance against the dragon. Prince Fenton is said to be good on the jousting field, but that isn't the same as fighting a dragon. What about your friend Prince Eadric? Is he a good hunter?"

"Yes, he is. He's gone hunting with my father many times, and their hunts are always successful. But you shouldn't need to send a hunter after your dragon. Isn't there anyone who could take care of it with magic?"

Millie shook her head. "No one's ever tried, although it wouldn't be a bad idea," she said, getting a faraway look in her eyes.

"So there are werewolves, at least one dragon and who knows what else in the kingdom. Why are your parents still having the party with all this going on?"

Millie shrugged. "It's what Hazel wants and what Hazel wants—"

"Hazel gets!" we said in unison and grinned at each other.

Millie assumed that I was ashamed of my meager possessions and didn't want to fetch them from among Frederika's belongings, so she lent me what I needed, borrowing what she didn't have from others. Once I'd changed my clothes I didn't stand out so much, and I began to relax and enjoy myself. That afternoon Millie showed me around the castle, pointing out her favorite places to hide from her parents and sister. The castle was smaller than in my time, without the entire back section that my great grandfather had added. I acted as if I'd never been there before, oohing and aahing over each of the innovations she pointed out that seemed so old-fashioned to me.

I was amazed when I saw how many flowers had been introduced into the castle, often in inappropriate ways. The larger windows were overgrown with blossoming plants so big they blocked most of the sun, making the castle dark and dismal inside. Climbing the tower stairs, I found the arrow slits filled with blossoms as well, many of which I recognized from their leaves. I'd grown up picking medicinal plants with my aunt Grassina, but had been forbidden to touch them when they bloomed. Finding sweet woodruff, wild thyme, lovage and cowslip growing in the niches that archers used to defend the castle seemed wrong to me. I found sunflowers on the battlements, turning their yellow faces as the sun crossed the sky, while melon vines crisscrossed the stone, forcing me to step carefully. Because of Hazel, the castle was more green than gray, pretty rather than practical.

When we went to supper that night, Millie was careful to keep me away from my supposed parents, telling me how uncomfortable she was sure I must feel around Frederika. Instead of sitting at the high table with her parents and her aunt and uncle, she led me to a table where other young nobles were taking their places. Hazel saw where we were going and abandoned her seat with her parents, scampering off the dais. Smiling gaily at every guest she passed, Princess Hazel shoved her sister aside, taking her seat on the bench beside one of the princes. The trestle tables were arranged in a U with royalty seated at the closed end, so I could see Millie's parents' faces easily. Although King Grunwald didn't seem to notice, the queen—whose name I'd learned was Angelica—watched her daughters flouting protocol with a resigned look on her face, as if she'd seen it all before.

Eadric came in a few minutes later, talking to a young nobleman. He spotted me sitting beside Millie and took a seat on my other side after persuading a sandy-haired prince to move over.

"How are you getting on?" I asked him as pages served the eel-and-prawn stew.

"All right. The room is clean, and the princes seem friendly. That's Prince Fenton over there," he said, indicating the young man beside Hazel. "He follows the tournament circuit and can't resist bragging." He nodded toward the youth with dark hair. "And that's Jasper. He seems nice enough."

When Eadric pointed out Prince Fenton, I recognized him as the leering monster who'd captured me when I was a bat, threatening to kill me with one hand. He seemed affable sitting with Hazel and the visiting princes, but I couldn't keep from shuddering every time I looked his way.

The only other prince who seemed noteworthy was the one Eadric had identified as Jasper. He wore his straight, dark brown hair chin-length like most men of his time. His eyes crinkled when he smiled, and he had an easy, infectious laugh. Even so, I probably wouldn't have noticed him if Millie hadn't spent most of the meal peeking at him, turning away with a guilty start whenever he glanced in our direction. At thirteen, Hazel's little sister was a bit too young for marriage, but not too young to think about it.

"Where is that prince Garrid you mentioned?" I asked Millie, looking down the line of well-dressed nobles for someone fitting his description.

Millie selected a leg of roasted capon from a passing platter and set it on her plate. "He isn't here. On the days he goes hunting, he doesn't come back until after dark. Prince Garrid is the only one of Hazel's suitors who contributes to the table. I think my parents already favor him because of it."

Maybe Eadric should do that, I thought. My mother resented him because he ate so much, but she might not mind his long visits if he provided food on a regular basis.

I was serving myself some beets when two pages bumped into each other, nearly dumping their heaped platters on the floor. It reminded me of Derwin's song about what had happened when he had dropped the platter.

"Millie," I said, "do you know a servant named Derwin?"

"How do you know Derwin?" she asked. "He's one of our oldest servants."

"Have you seen him lately?"

"Hmm," she said, twirling a lock of hair around her finger. "I guess I haven't seen him since the night he dropped the goose on Father. It was kind of funny. Even Father laughed. The only one who didn't was Hazel. She doesn't have much of a sense of humor."

"I heard that she sent Derwin to the oubliette." Maybe I was interfering, but something had to be done.

"I didn't know that! I hope the poor old man is all right. I'll talk to Father about it. There was no call for Derwin to be treated so!"

We were nibbling the final course of cheese and fruit when I overheard some women seated nearby discussing the vicious creature that had attacked them. According to one, a slobbering horror with blazing, red eyes had swooped on them, baring its daggerlike fangs. It took me a while to realize that she was talking about me.

"If it hadn't been for Prince Fenton, we might all have been killed," said one young noblewoman, smiling past her friends to where the prince was helping himself to another slab of venison.

The prince looked down at his thumb wrapped in a strip of clean linen. "Vicious beasts, bats," he said.

I covered my mouth so no one would see my smile, but Jasper must have noticed because he met my eyes and winked. Some of the other princes turned to Fenton and demanded to hear the story.

I was worried about Li'l since we hadn't had a chance to make our plans before Eadric and I had left her. I just hoped she wasn't too frightened alone in the unfamiliar maze. "I need some fresh air," I told Millie. "I'm going for a walk in the garden."

A juggler was strolling past the table, and Millie seemed entranced by the balls he kept circling through the air. "Hmm?" she murmured. "Then I'd better go with you. We're not allowed to walk alone at night."

"But it isn't dark yet," I said, glancing out the window.

Millie gathered her skirts and slipped off the bench. "My father's rules. There are too many dangerous beasts in the area. I told you about the werewolves."

"I can go with Emma," said Eadric, swinging his legs across the bench so he could stand.

"Then you won't need to go, Millie," I said. "Eadric will keep me safe."

Hazel frowned at me. "Perhaps we should all go," she said. Gracing him with her sweetest smile, Hazel took Eadric's arm and led the way. It was almost as if she thought I'd brought her another suitor. I couldn't help feeling a pang of resentment when Eadric bent down to hear what she had to say.

I bit my lip and followed them, trying not to glare at

Eadric and Hazel. I didn't want company. If a group of people went with me, I wouldn't be able to talk to Li'l. I would have said something, except everyone was already heading out the door. Only Jasper dawdled behind as if waiting for me. Hazel glanced back. She made Eadric wait while she held out her hand to Jasper and said, "You may also escort me." Jasper looked my way and shrugged, then linked Hazel's free arm with his.

Millie bumped my elbow. "Look at her," she whispered. "Hazel would have all of them on a tether if she could, and even that probably wouldn't be enough."

The shadows were getting long as we approached the rose-hedge maze, and the scent of the flowers hung heavy in the air. Hazel stepped lightly down the path, surrounded by the princes and a few of the giggling, young noblewomen. Since Millie trailed after Jasper like a lost puppy, it was easier to get away on my own than I'd expected. All I had to do was dawdle until I was left behind, then take an opposite turning once they were out of sight.

The roses were lovely, but after a while they all looked the same to me. I hadn't gone far before I stopped to look around. "Li'l!" I called softly. "Where are you, Li'l?"

It was a little soon for bats to be out hunting, but mosquitoes came out earlier in the shade of the hedge. I could appreciate a good insect, having lived as a frog for a time, but that didn't mean I wanted to feed them. I was slapping my cheek when Li'l fluttered over the top of the hedge and landed on my shoulder.

"Where have you been?" she asked, straightening her wings. "I've been waiting here all day. I can't say that I mind, though. They raise some good, juicy bugs in these shrubs."

When I slapped my neck again and studied the smear of blood and the squashed mosquito on my palm, I noticed that my ring was gone from my hand. I must not be the Green Witch in this time. "So you don't mind staying here for a few days?" I said. "Hazel's younger sister is sharing her room with me, but I don't think she'd understand if a bat joined us."

"I'm fine here. Once you get past the leaves and thorns on the outside, some of these shrubs have nice, cool spaces in their middles. Sit still for a minute and the bugs come right to you. Good place for a nap, too."

"If you're sure you're all right—"

"Sure, I'm sure. It's not as nice as a good cave, but a bat can't have everything."

"I'll try to come see you at least once a day. We have to stay until after the party."

"Fine with me," said Li'l. "I might take a look around, come dark. What's the use of visiting a new time if you can't see the sights?"

"Don't go too far."

Li'l beat her wings and rose into the air. "Don't worry about me. I can take care of myself."

After Li'l left, I retraced my steps, but I guess I'd made more turns than I'd thought. It all looked the same to me, and I might have gotten lost if Millie hadn't shown up. "I took a wrong turn," I said, gesturing back the way I'd come.

Millie gave me a sympathetic smile. "That's easy to do. We have to go now. They'll be raising the drawbridge soon."

I could hear the voices of the others coming through the maze, but there was something else nagging to get my attention. I concentrated and then I had it—the faintest hint of a scent, one that I'd hoped I'd never smell again.

"Hurry," I told Millie, reaching for her hand. "We have to get inside."

A woman screamed, or at least it sounded something like a woman. People in the maze shouted, and I heard the sound of running feet.

Millie tried to pull away from me. "Someone is hurt! We have to go help her."

"No one is hurt," I said, pulling her along behind me as I started for the castle. "That was a harpy. If there's one, there's a whole flock. They rarely travel alone."

"Really?" she said, stopping to look over her shoulder. "I've never seen a harpy."

I tugged on her hand and got her moving again. "Believe me," I said, "you'd be better off if you never did."

I'd seen harpies before. In fact I still had nightmares about them. Foul-smelling creatures with the bodies of vultures and the heads of women, in my time they had taken over a small village in Greater Greensward by chasing away the people who lived there. Once a harpy occupied a house, it took a massive effort to make it clean enough for anyone to live in it again. Harpies smell worse than skunks and leave their odor behind long after they've gone. It had taken me three days and a lot of magic to chase them away, and then the villagers had still refused to come back. If possible, it was better to keep them out in the first place than to have to clean up their mess afterward.

I was pulling Millie onto the drawbridge when the first harpy appeared. Shrieking wordlessly, it swooped down on us. I would have used my magic to turn the creature away, except I didn't want anyone to know that I was a witch. When I threw up my hands to ward it off, a boy dressed like a stable hand shouted and came running with a stout staff. Waving the staff in the air, he forced the screeching harpy higher. We were almost beneath the portcullis when the creature began pelting us with dung. It missed Millie and me, but hit the boy squarely on the back. It would have hit him again if he hadn't kept running.

Once we were inside, Millie and I thanked him profusely. After he ran off to the stable, Millie said, "That boy saved us from a stinky fate. I think he deserves a reward."

Although he looked very different from his ghost, the shape of his nose and the jut of his chin were similar enough that I'd recognized him. It was Hubert. "I think so, too," I said. "In fact I think he deserves a medal."

Eadric had been with Hazel and her friends when the harpies attacked. According to Hazel, nearly a dozen harpies had pelted them with sticks and clods of dirt. Eadric was the only one carrying a sword, and he'd made a real impression with his skill and bravery. I heard all about it after they reached the castle. Hazel's voice was almost as loud as the harpies' by the time she joined us.

The entire castle was in turmoil as soldiers ran to defend the gates and the battlements, servants rushed to fetch water from the castle well to heat for baths and everyone else ran around, shouting questions that no one seemed able to answer. We found the queen in the Great Hall, wringing her hands. "What a time for this to happen!" she wailed. "We have a castle full of guests and more on the way!"

"Where is Father?" Millie asked, trying to get her mother's attention. "I have to see him."

The queen grabbed her daughter by the arm and held on tightly. "Oh, no you don't, young lady. You'll just get in the way! You're staying here with me until this is over."

Although I understood how frustrated Millie must feel, her mother's interference helped me. I needed to go somewhere without anyone following me or suspecting that I had gone. Afraid that the queen might try to make me stay as well, I slipped into the milling crowd and headed for the stairs that led to the unfinished tower.

The stones were thick with dust and the door leading to the tower was jammed, but when I finally forced it open I had the ideal vantage point. Soldiers stationed on the battlements across from where I watched thrust their swords at the harpies, who flew just out of reach, pelting them with dung. Although archers shot one volley after another at the bird women, only a few found their mark. A group of harpies was concentrating on the battlements just above the gate, but there were so many of them that I found it hard to see why, until a harpy fell and I spotted the king surrounded by his knights. A sword flashed and another harpy fell, making the rest of the creatures draw back. The knights moved as a group, trying to escort the king to the only completed tower and safety.

Although I remembered Dyspepsia's warning about

not changing the past, I had to interfere. It may not have been my time but it was my home, and I couldn't stand to see it taken over by harpies. While everyone watched the monstrous creatures, I hid in the tower doorway to recite the spell I had in mind. I knew how persistent harpies could be, so I had the spell cover their return just in case.

Oh, ye wind of far-flung places,
Keep these harpies from this home.
Should they force themselves upon us,
Blow them all from here to Rome.

At first it was a light breeze caressing my cheek and lifting the hair that had come loose from my braid. Within seconds it was a wind strong enough to blow a man's cap from his head. In less than a minute, I had to fight to get back into the tower room. The harpies flying over the battlements were carried off while I strained to shut the door. From the sound of their screaming, the rest of the harpies soon followed them.

When I rejoined the crowd in the Great Hall, the king and queen were standing near the high table, talking in muted voices. They looked up at the approach of one of their knights.

"Your Majesties," said the knight, "the harpies have gone."

"But how? Why?" asked the king.

"It was the wind, sire. It carried them away."

"Wind? You're making no sense, man. There is no wind today."

"It started suddenly, sire, and it's already stopped."

"You don't suppose it was magic, do you?" asked Queen Angelica.

The king nodded. "It must have been."

"Then it had to have been Hazel's doing."

"Where is the girl?" asked the king. "I wish to talk to her."

"She's locked herself in her chamber," said one of the young ladies who had followed the princess into the maze, "and she refuses to come out."

"Then she performed the magic from there," said the king. "I must thank her."

"I don't know what we would have done without that darling girl!" the queen gushed.

"Let's go," Millie whispered, coming up behind me. "If I have to listen to any more of this, I'm going to be sick."

I followed Millie up the stairs to her chamber. We got ready for bed and Millie went to say good night to her parents. When she came back, she told me that Hazel had kept her door locked, refusing to come out until her parents had assured her that the harpies were gone. "She'd blocked her windows with climbing roses," said

Millie. "Their perfume was so strong it gave everyone else a headache. My father no longer thinks that she was the one who got rid of the harpies."

"Really?" I said, trying to sound surprised. "Then who does he think it was?"

"That's just it," said Millie. "No one knows. Maybe it was one of the princes. We don't know much about them. That's what I wanted to discuss with you. I hate to ask you for a favor since you're a guest, but I need your help."

"What do you need me to do?" I asked.

"Hazel is supposed to announce the name of the suitor she's chosen at the party. When we went for our walk, she was discussing Fenton's tournament wins with him, so she didn't hear the other princes, but I did. They didn't say anything wrong exactly, and I know they were joking, but they said some things that made me wonder why they're asking for her hand. Is there even one among them who loves her? I'd feel better if we could find out what they really want."

"I'll talk to Eadric. Since he's sharing a room with the princes, maybe he can learn more about them."

Millie sighed. "Thanks. At least that's a start." Her bed creaked as she turned over.

I lay awake thinking, long after Millie's breathing became soft and even. She was a sweet girl, and we'd taken to each other right away. She was also a relative, although a distant one. If she needed my help, I would try my best.

As I lay in bed, wishing I could fall asleep, it occurred to me that there might be something more I could do than just find out what the curse had been after it happened. Maybe I could do something about the curse itself. Maybe I could keep it from being cast. I already knew that Hazel had offended the fairy by failing to give her an everlasting bouquet. It shouldn't be hard to make sure that didn't happen. She'd just have to make more bouquets—enough to give one to everyone, including every fairy. If I ended the curse before it began, Grandmother and Grassina would never have turned nasty, Grandfather wouldn't have died in the dungeon, Grassina could have married Haywood and I could marry Eadric. It sounded like the perfect solution to everyone's problems. I remembered Dyspepsia's warning about the dangers of altering history, but it wasn't hard to convince myself that the kind of change I had in mind couldn't hurt anyone. Believing that I'd just had the best idea yet, I drifted off to sleep, worry free for the first time in months.

Eight

When we went downstairs the next morning, the Great Hall was empty except for some pages polishing swords. I had hoped to catch a glimpse of the elusive prince Garrid, but when I asked one of the pages where I might find him, I was told that the prince had already gone hunting.

Breakfast in the castle was haphazard, since most people preferred to wait for dinner at noon. Millie and I were hungry, however, so we collected bowls of porridge from the kitchen. We had just finished eating when Queen Angelica took Millie off to see to her new gown. Left on my own, I went in search of Hazel, prepared to do whatever it took to make sure she was ready for all the guests at her party. I finally ran into her when she was leaving her mother's chamber. She barely glanced at me as she swept past.

"Hazel," I said, hurrying after her. "I've been meaning to ask you how the preparations are coming for your party."

She turned to look at me, curling her lip in a way that reminded me of my mother. "Ask the castle steward. I have better things to do with my time."

"I just meant that I'd be happy to help," I said as she started to turn away.

She looked me up and down, and said, "What could you possibly do?"

"Help with the decorations, I suppose. Or perhaps the gifts for the guests."

"Gifts for the guests?" she said, frowning ever so slightly. "I have thought about giving them something. I'll decorate with flowers, of course, and I daresay I'll give out flowers as well. I'm known for my green thumb, you see," she said, holding up her left hand. Her thumb was actually green, the same shade of green as the skin of some wood nymphs I'd seen. I wondered if the blood of a wood nymph flowed in her veins. "People come to me from all the kingdoms around when they need help with their crops. Giving them flowers, an everlasting bouquet perhaps, would remind them of how much they need me."

"I'm sure everyone will love them. How many do you plan to make?"

"Why does that concern you?"

"I just want to help, that's all. It would probably be a good idea to make extras. You never know how many guests will show up at the last minute."

"You don't have to worry. I'm sure there will be enough for you to have one, too."

"That isn't what I meant—"

"Greedy thing, isn't she?" Hazel said to one of her mother's ladies-in-waiting. "But then the poorer relatives often are." She sneered at me, then tossed her head and walked away.

I tried not to let her attitude bother me. It wasn't so much the way she treated me as the knowledge that this girl was my ancestor. I'd always wanted to believe that my ancestors were better people than they probably really were.

After talking to Hazel, I needed to see a friendly face. Millie was still busy with her mother and I couldn't find Eadric anywhere, so I decided to go outside to visit Li'l. Except for the droning of the bees, the maze was quiet when I reached it. Li'l didn't come right away when I called her, and I was beginning to wonder if something had happened to her when she finally showed up.

Landing on a full-blown rose that bent double under her weight, Li'l opened her mouth to yawn, then said, "What's up?"

"I'm sorry I woke you. I wanted to know about your night. You said you might go exploring."

The little bat shifted her feet like she does when she's excited. "It was great! I went to the forest. It's bigger now than in our time. There are fewer farms between here and there and a lot more places for a bat to live. Lots of bugs, too. I was chasing a firefly when I met him."

"You met a bug?"

"Course not! Just the handsomest bat I've ever seen. He was chasing the same firefly, but he let me have it. A real gentlebat, that's what he was. I wish you could meet him. You'd like him; I'm sure of it."

I had to smile. "A gentlebat, you say. How nice."

"He showed me around. We saw the waterfall where the wood nymphs wash their hair and the ring where the fairies dance. We missed the early show, and the musicians were taking a break when we got there, so we waited for them to come back. The dancers were so graceful and light on their feet."

"They have wings, don't they?"

"That's true. Anyway I didn't get back until it was almost dawn. Bugsy brought me home."

"Bugsy?"

Li'l ducked her head as if she was embarrassed. "That's what I called him, and he didn't seem to mind. He's so good at catching bugs."

"Hmm," I said, watching my little friend preen her wings, something I'd never seen her do before. "Do you think you'll see him again?"

Li'l bobbed her head. "He's coming back tonight. We're watching the unicorn races in the Silver Glade and going out for beetles afterward."

"Then you'd better get your rest," I said. "It sounds like you're going to need it."

It was still early, so I went for a walk around the castle, admiring the variety of flowers that grew at the edge of the moat. After a while I heard the distant clang of metal on metal. The sound grew louder as I approached the practice field where the princes were showing their sword-fighting techniques to a group of squires not much younger than themselves. Jasper was correcting a squire's stance when he looked up and saw me. He smiled and waved before turning back to his pupil.

I noticed Eadric at the same time that he noticed me. Excusing himself from his companions, he joined me in my walk. "Millie wants to know more about the princes," I said. "It would help if you could keep your eyes and ears open and find out what you can."

Eadric laughed. "That won't be a problem. You learn a lot about people when there are six of you crowded into one little room. I already know who snores and who doesn't like to wash. And Garrid must be having some sort of intestinal trouble."

"You mean you've met him?"

Eadric nodded. "He came in late last night and left the room a short time later. We were all asleep, but my pallet is so close to the door it wakes me every time someone leaves the room. Poor guy didn't come back until it was almost dawn."

"Maybe it was something he ate," I said.

"Maybe," said Eadric. "Say, you should see some of the birthday gifts the princes have brought for Hazel. Jasper has this cup...."

"I forgot about the gift! We have to get her one!"

"At the magic marketplace?" asked Eadric.

"We don't have time for that. We'll have to make it."

Eadric rubbed his jaw. "I suppose I could find some wood and carve a buckle...."

"Never mind," I said, rolling my eyes. "I'll think of something."

"Tell me," he said. "Why have you been making faces at me ever since we got here? You look as if you're angry half the time."

"I haven't been making faces! I'm just not happy about the way you've been acting."

"What do you mean?" Eadric said, scowling. "I've been doing my best to fit in. I helped fight off the harpies and have spent most of my free time giving lessons to the squires. What more do you want from me?"

"That's wonderful, but it's not what I'm talking about. It's the way you hang on everything Hazel says and let her whisper in your ear. You really like her, don't you?"

"Hazel? You've got to be joking!" said Eadric. "Sure, she's pretty, but she has as much substance as one of your cook's pastries and isn't nearly as sweet. The girl doesn't think of anything except herself. Do you know she wanted me to sit at her feet singing songs about her beauty when I'd already promised the squires I'd show them how to track werewolves? I had to lie and say I couldn't carry a tune before she'd leave me alone."

"You mean you can sing?"

"Sure, when I have to. So, that's what this is all about? You think I've been paying too much attention to Hazel?"

"You don't seem to mind the way she flatters you and touches your arm or your hand."

"I'm trying to fit in, remember? Watch Fenton, or any of the other princes, and see how they act around her. I don't spend nearly as much time with Hazel as they do."

"But they're her suitors. You're supposed to be mine!"

"And I am," he said, pulling me into his arms.

The royal family was sitting down to dinner when we returned to the castle. I took a seat between Eadric and Millie again, with Hazel on Eadric's other side. Hazel made a big show of praising Eadric for fending off the harpies, and I noticed that she felt the muscles in his arms more than once. I ground my teeth and didn't say anything, even when Hazel took morsels off her plate and put them on his. But when she offered to show him the gardens, I couldn't keep from telling her, "He's already seen them with me."

Hazel sneered. "It wouldn't be the same, Emma dear. I know all the gardens' secrets. I could show him things he's never seen before."

"I just bet you could," I muttered into my mug of cider.

An elderly servant carried a platter the length of the table, offering everyone a slice of boiled mutton. "Derwin looks well now, doesn't he?" Millie said to me, using her knife to point out the elderly man. "I had them give him a bath when they pulled him out of the oubliette. I think it was the only bath he's ever had."

"Thank you," I said. "I'm sure everyone here appreciates your thoughtfulness."

I was listening to Millie describe her new gown when there was a commotion at the far end of the Hall. One of the king's foresters was trying to get past a guard who seemed determined to keep him from entering.

"You can't see him now," said the soldier.

"It's an emergency, I tell you," said the forester. "King Grunwald needs to hear about this."

"About what?" asked the king from the raised dais.

"The dragon is back, Your Highness. He's been spotted carrying off a prize bull. We think he ate the farmer."

King Grunwald set down the drumstick he'd been gnawing and rose to his feet. "I need volunteers," he said, looking directly at the row of princes. "Some brave young men skilled in fighting who aren't afraid to take on a dragon. Who among you is man enough to kill the foul beast?"

One prince looked away as if meeting the king's eyes would commit him to going. Another pretended to be busy with his food, acting as if he hadn't heard a word the king had said. Only a few young men stood, Eadric, Fenton and Jasper among them.

"I'll go, sire," said Eadric. "I need the practice."

Fenton made a rude sound, then said, "I'll go, sire, to prove I'm worthy of Princess Hazel's hand."

"I'll go, sire," said Jasper, "to rid the countryside of a terrible scourge."

"I'll go, sire," said two knights.

"For honor," said one.

"For glory," said another.

"For goodness' sake," I whispered to Millie. "Do they all have to be so dramatic?"

"Perhaps they are braver than I thought," murmured Millie. "Imagine, killing a dragon!"

"They haven't fought it yet. I think we should reserve judgment until we see what they actually do."

"But those brave young men are going to risk their lives!"

"Maybe," I said, reaching for a piece of bread. I was torn in a way. I had friends back home who were dragons, so I knew they weren't all bad, but having a dragon live so close to the castle was bound to cause trouble. While I didn't want to see the dragon get hurt, I didn't want to see any of the princes get hurt, either, especially Eadric. But then they wouldn't have to fight at all if I could help it.

After dinner Eadric and the other princes left the Great Hall to collect their horses and weapons. I slipped away from Millie while she was talking to her parents and made my way to the garden. I'd thought about discussing my plans with Eadric, but he'd insist on going without me and handling it on his own, and that was the last thing I wanted.

Although Eadric was the bravest man I knew, he was more likely to wave his sword, Ferdy, in the dragon's face than he was to talk to him. Even after we'd become friends with a nice family of dragons, Eadric believed that they were the exception, and that most dragons were horrible monsters that deserved to be slain. We'd argued about it many times, but neither of us was willing to give in.

Once again I remembered Dyspepsia's warning, but since I'd already interfered when I chased away the harpies, I didn't think that getting rid of a dragon would be so bad. It wasn't like I'd be killing anyone. If all went well, I'd be saving lives, although I'd have to hurry to do it. If no one, human or dragon, was to get hurt, I'd have to be the one to confront the beast first. I was a witch and could use my magic if necessary. I also had a special salve with me that would protect me from the dragon's flames. Even more important, I was a Dragon Friend. In a tent at the Dragon Olympics, I'd been given the title after passing a test that could have taken away my magical powers. I hadn't had any need to verify it before, but I hoped the dragons had told me the truth when they said that the title would earn me the respect of dragonkind everywhere.

Wanting to be as inconspicuous as possible, I hid in a secluded spot in the maze and took out my farseeing ball, focusing it on all the places around the kingdom where I thought a dragon might lurk. A farseeing ball is a handy thing to have, although it does have its limitations. You can use it to keep an eye on someone who has recently touched it or to see places that you have visited. Getting it to do anything else isn't easy.

I decided to look where I had seen dragons in my own time. When I focused on the enchanted forest, I saw griffins skimming the treetops and unicorns butting heads, but no dragons. There were water sprites splashing in a stream, fairies dozing under flower petals and werewolf pups wrestling, but no dragons.

"Hmm," I said, and turned my attention to the

Purple Mountains. Deep in a cave where the Dragon King would one day keep his treasures, I saw nothing except bats hanging by their toes in the dark. I looked at a huge, high-sided arena, where the dragons would hold their Olympics in the future. There were no dragons yet.

When Eadric and I had been looking for a green dragon, I hadn't had enough experience or power to use a spell to find one. Now it was almost as easy as breathing. Cupping the farseeing ball in my hands, I said:

Sharp of tooth and fierce of claw,
With a gaping, hungry maw,
Find the dragon close to here,
Make the image very clear.
Show the path that I must take
To reach the beast; there's much at stake.

An image of a dragon took shape in the farseeing ball. Asleep in a cave, the dragon moved restlessly as it dreamed. There wasn't enough light to see its color or anything to compare it to that would indicate its size. While I watched, the image changed, pulling away from the dragon and leaving the cave. I saw a steep-sided ravine, a wooded slope and a path trampled flat by feet with claws long enough to gouge the ground. The path led through the forest until it dwindled away among the trees. The image continued however, showing me a break in the trees here, a deer trail there, until it met a road rutted by cart wheels. The image in the farseeing ball moved faster now, following the road where it passed between the trees and through farmers' fields, becoming wider and hard packed when it met another road. I recognized the area now; the slope of the hill and the outcropping of rocks hadn't changed much in a few hundred years.

As the image dissolved, I recited the spell to turn myself into a dove. It took just a moment, but even so, the first of the princes had appeared by the time that I was ready to go. Wearing a dented but serviceable suit of armor, Prince Jasper rode an older destrier, a huge warhorse bred for carrying the weight of a man clad in metal. What little I could see of the horse was golden brown. It, too, wore plain, undecorated armor and moved with a steady and purposeful gait.

I took to the air just as Prince Fenton arrived astride a more highly spirited horse that pranced rather than walked. Solid black, the horse wore armor that matched the prince's. Both sets were decorated with twin lions and an eagle and were so highly polished that it hurt my eyes to look at them.

I darted past Prince Jasper, following the road and leaving the armor-clad horses stirring up dust behind me. Anxious to deal with the dragon before the princes arrived, I flew as fast as I could and was exhausted before I reached the forest. The first tree I saw was an ancient oak, and I stopped to rest on one of its lower branches to let my pounding heart slow to a steadier pace. I took off again when I heard the clanking of the horses' armor and wondered how the princes ever thought they could catch a dragon unaware.

I found the deer trail right away and was approaching the break in the trees when I heard something snuffling. Wary, I slowed my pace and veered away from the trail while trying to keep it in sight. When I saw what was making the sound, I was glad I hadn't blundered ahead. A griffin as big as a small dragon stood over the carcass of a wild boar, tearing at the animal's hide with its wickedly curving beak. The griffin's wings were splattered with drops of blood and its lionlike sides heaved from exertion, but it wasn't too tired to look up when I flew through the far side of the clearing. Reaching the trees, I tried to put as much distance as possible between the eagle-eyed creature and myself. I was convinced that I was about to be plucked from the air, so I flew farther than I'd intended and didn't slow down until I nearly flew into a thorn-covered thicket. As I slowed my pace, I realized two things: the griffin wasn't following me, and I was lost.

It took me a while to get my bearings and locate the dragon's path. I wouldn't have found it at all if I hadn't stumbled across a charred tree trunk. There was another beyond it, and after that most of the trunks were scorched and scarred. Great furrows rent the ground as if huge creatures had scuffled there in the past, and a few pieces of partly melted armor told me that at least one of the battles had been between dragon and knight.

The damage grew more extensive as I continued on until the trees gave way to a gully twice as deep and three times as wide as a man is tall. I could see the opening of the dragon's cave on the far side of the gully. Unfortunately King Grunwald's forester must have been able to give good directions, because Jasper and Fenton had arrived as well. They sat astride their horses at the edge of the burned trees, their armor smudged with soot, looking down at the opening of the cave. While I was relieved that Eadric wasn't there, I hoped he hadn't gotten lost.

Jasper's horse stood his ground, but Fenton's steed was skittery, dancing aside and refusing to go on. When Fenton tried to urge him forward, the horse dug in his heels and threw up his head, rearing each time the prince yanked on the reins. "Blasted horse," muttered Fenton. Finally, with stiff movements and a lot of effort, Fenton backed his horse away from the gully and struggled to climb off.

I landed on the blackened branch of a nearby tree. Although it was too late to talk to the dragon before the princes arrived, I could still make sure that no one got hurt.

I'd been watching Fenton, so I hadn't noticed that Jasper had already dismounted and tied his horse's reins to a branch. "Come out, you cowardly worm!" Jasper shouted, and I turned to see him wielding his sword and shield at the edge of the ravine.

There was a strange whuffing sound from the cave, and a puff of pink smoke curled from the entrance.

"I'm not ready yet, Jasper!" yelled Fenton, still only halfway off his horse. "Wait for me! I just—"

A roar from the gully nearly knocked me from my perch. Fenton's horse took off, galloping through the forest with his master draped over his side, fighting to stay on. I saw Jasper step back a pace, then raise his sword above his head. Flying higher into the tree, I looked down into the gully. Scorching flame had burned away every twig and scrap of foliage, giving me an unimpeded view of the massive head that emerged a moment later.

I had seen many dragons before, and some of them bore scales as beautiful as precious gems, yet this dragon's scales were a particularly ugly color. A muddy, washed-out yellow, he looked even worse when he scuttled from his cave into the sunlight and raised his head to glare at Jasper. The dragon was smallish, with a patchy look, missing or damaged scales, and ragged wings. His legs were stiff when he ran, as if his joints hurt. He opened his mouth, and I saw that his teeth were crooked;

he was missing more than a few.

When the dragon sucked in air through his gaping mouth and pulled his wings back to his sides, I knew that he was about to flame. Without shield or armor to protect myself, I leapt into the air, rising high above the gully.

Holding his shield in front of his face, Jasper jumped to the side as the flame licked the ground at his feet. Although deadly, the flame wasn't very long and it dwindled at the end to a meager trickle of fire. My dragon friend, Grumble Belly, would have been embarrassed to call it his.

"Hold on!" shouted Fenton from the forest. "I'm coming! Dratted horse wouldn't stop!"

Seeing the prince still on his feet, the dragon started up the side of the gully, huffing pink steam as he ran with a shambling sort of gait. Jasper darted behind the closest tree as quickly as his armor would let him. I thought he was running away until he stopped and raised his sword. The trunk was singed nearly to the heartwood, the tree obviously dead, but since it was broad at the base and still standing, it made a fairly good shield.

The clank of metal came through the trees. "I'm almost there!" shouted Fenton, sounding out of breath even from a distance.

The dragon snorted, and flame curled from his nostrils.

"Come on, worm," taunted Jasper. "Is that all you can do?"

Even as he ran, I could hear the dragon sucking air into his lungs, and he began flaming while he was still too far to reach the tree. Shield up, Jasper crouched behind the trunk. The moment the dragon's flame shrank and died, the prince sprang to his feet and ran around the trunk, his sword aimed at the muddy-yellow head.

"Here I am!" shouted Fenton as he emerged panting from the trees, his sword and shield dangling uselessly from his hands.

Jerking his head up, the dragon spun around to face Fenton, his long tail whipping behind him. As Jasper ran at the dragon, the tail hit him with a clang, sending him sailing through the air. The prince hit the ground, his body rolling a few feet before lying motionless.

"Uh-oh," said Fenton, when the dragon lunged in his direction, his ribs expanding as he inhaled again.

The first hint of flame was just leaving the dragon's mouth when Fenton turned and ran. For a moment he looked like a shiny blur disappearing into the dark of the forest—and then he was gone.

Without an enemy to incinerate, the dragon's fire died down to a fizzling puff. He turned with a grumble and started back toward Jasper, whose body still lay where it had fallen. Alarmed, I flew lower to see what I could do. Jasper was defenseless; if he was alive, he wouldn't be for long. *This isn't right,* I thought. It was time for me to intervene.

As the dragon lowered its massive head to snuffle the injured knight, I darted down and pecked the creature on the back of his skull. The beast didn't notice me. Opening his jaws, he grasped an armor-clad leg and began to drag Jasper toward the edge of the gully. I tried to think of some magic spell I could use that wouldn't hurt either combatant, but then the dragon's ear flopped over. In the blink of a unicorn's eye, I darted toward the ear and pecked just inside its leathery opening. The dragon jerked his head up in alarm, dropping Jasper. I clung to his scales with my claws as he threw his head from side to side. When he calmed down again, I pecked once more to make sure I had his attention, then let go of his scales and took off. Since I didn't want him to lose sight of me, I stayed low to the ground, zigzagging so he wouldn't hit me if he flamed. The dragon roared and came after me, which was just what I wanted. I planned to lead him into the woods, then come back for Jasper, but someone else had different plans.

Both the dragon and I heard her voice at the same time. A girl was down in the gully, whimpering and calling out and making herself an irresistible target for an angry dragon. I tried to distract the beast, but the possibility of an easy meal was too tempting to ignore. When he scrambled down the steep slope, I flew past him and gasped. It was Millie, looking small and vulnerable in the burnt-out gully. At first sight of the dragon, she threw up her hand and pointed, a familiar gesture, but not one I would have expected her to use. Her voice rang out loud and clear as she recited a spell she must have made up herself.

Dragon, dragon in my sight,
You don't always have to fight.
Turn around and go back home.
Never more to want to roam.

I wasn't surprised when the dragon started spinning in circles since the spell had told him to turn around, although Millie's mouth dropped open and her eyes grew wide. I wondered how long it would take her to realize that she was standing between the dragon and the cave he currently considered his home, the very place she had just sent him. I was more surprised that Millie was a witch, although I really shouldn't have been. After all, she was a distant relative, and just because her sister had the talent didn't mean that it wouldn't show up in her as well.

I watched the dragon spin, moving one step closer to his cave each time he turned around. At that rate, it would take him ten minutes to reach the opening, giving me plenty of time.

I'd been circling in the sky over the gully, but now

that I'd made up my mind, I changed the angle of my wings and fluttered down to land beside Jasper. He was trying to get up, a difficult task for anyone wearing a suit of armor. From the way he was moving, I could tell that he was going to be all right. I would have stayed and tried to think of a way to help him without giving myself away, but I heard a shriek from down by the cave and knew that I had to hurry.

After making sure that Jasper couldn't see me and that the other princes were nowhere around, I said the spell that would turn me back into my human self and hurried to the edge of the gully. The dragon must have gone faster once he realized what was happening, because he had almost reached the cave. As the dragon spun nearer, Millie covered her mouth with her hand, stifling a scream. She had the look of a cat I'd once owned that had been too frightened to move when a dog came after her. I'd had to step in then, just as I'd have to step in now. The dragon was close enough that even his meager flame would engulf her.

I no longer cared if Millie saw me use magic because we shared a common secret. Pointing my finger at the dragon, I said a quick and easy binding spell. The dragon stopped in midspin, his mouth gaping as if he was about to flame. Hurrying down the slope of the gully, I shouted to Millie, "Go home! I'll handle this now."

"Emma, you're a witch!" Millie declared as if telling

me something I didn't know.

"And so are you, but I have more experience with dragons, so let me handle this. There is something you can do, though. Jasper needs your help getting back to the castle." I pointed up the slope. "You'll need to help him to his feet, then onto his horse."

"Jasper needs me?" Millie said, a faint blush coloring her cheeks. "I'd better go. Are you sure you'll be all right?"

"I'll be fine. Go help the prince," I said. "That's where you'll do the most good. By the way, do you have any idea what happened to Eadric?"

"I remembered what you'd said about using magic to protect the kingdom. I think it's a wonderful idea, but I didn't want anyone else around when I tried it on a dragon. When I saw Eadric and some of my father's knights starting out, I used a little magic to send them in the wrong direction. I would have sent Jasper and Fenton the wrong way, too, if they hadn't already left the castle."

"Good thinking, Millie," I said. "Any more men clanking around in suits of armor, and we might have had a real problem keeping this a secret. And we will keep the fact that we're both witches a secret, won't we?"

Millie nodded, and I thought she looked relieved. While I waited for her to climb out of the gully, I opened my pouch and found the vial Ralf had given me. Ralf was a young dragon who had become one of my best friends. Shortly after we met, he had taken Eadric and me to the Dragon Olympics and given us some salve to protect us from dragon flames. It was the same salve used on baby dragons until their sensitive skin became tougher. The salve had worked perfectly, so I was happy to accept when he offered to give me some to keep on hand just in case.

It didn't take much salve to cover my face and hands, but I went further than that, wiping it on my clothes and in my hair, on my neck and even on my eyelids. It made me feel greasy and disgusting, but at least it smelled nice, kind of like peppermint. Since I'd used most of the vial, I'd have to ask Ralf for more as soon as I got home.

When I thought I was ready, I tapped the dragon on his back and hurried out of the way. Even wearing the salve, I didn't want to stand too close.

"Hrumph!" grunted the dragon, shaking his head. Smoke billowed from his mouth as he looked about for his prey. "Where'd it go?" The dragon turned a half circle before spotting me. "A different one," he said, "but it should be just as tasty."

"Wait!" I said, but the dragon had already built up a good fire in his belly and was eager to use it. I shut my eyes as the flames washed over me. It felt hot, but no hotter than the sunshine on a summer's day. When it grew feeble and finally stopped, I opened my eyes and looked down. I looked wet and shiny from the salve, although the flames hadn't done a thing.

The dragon looked at me in surprise. "What happened?" he said. "It should be crispy. And that smell. . . ." He took a step toward me and sniffed. His gaze softened and he almost seemed to be smiling. "That smells like the salve my mother used when I was just a hatchling. How did a human get hold of it?"

"It is the same salve," I said. "A friend gave it to me."

"It knows the true tongue!" the dragon exclaimed, flicking his ears in agitation. "I didn't know humans were able to speak it."

"I'm a witch. I can do a lot of things most people can't."

"Why haven't I seen you before, human?" he asked, his eyes narrowing.

I didn't want to let him know that I was there for only a short time. If my plan worked and he left, I wouldn't want him to think he could come back. "I've been away," I said. "And I have a name. I'm Princess Emeralda, the Green Witch."

"Green Witch, you say? I've never heard of you."

"How could you, if you don't speak human?"

"You have a point," said the dragon, sitting back on his haunches. "Who was this friend who gave you the salve?"

"A young dragon named Ralf," I said.

"So what do you want with me?"

"I want you to move away from here. Find someplace to live where there aren't any humans around."

The dragon snorted a puff of pink smoke that smelled like boiling cabbage. "Why should I?" he said. "I like it here."

"Because I told you to and I'm the Green Witch, which means that it's my duty to protect the kingdom. If you stay here, I'll have to do something neither of us will like."

The dragon drew his brows together in a fearsome scowl. "Such as?"

I rubbed my chin and looked him over. "I could turn you into a newt and send you scurrying under a rock. I could extinguish your belly fire permanently so you'd never have another hot meal. I could bind a storm cloud to you so it rained on you every time you left your cave. I could shrink you and keep you as a pet. I could—"

"All right! And what's to keep me from eating you now? I know I can't cook you while you're wearing that salve, but I don't mind raw food."

"You wouldn't eat a Dragon Friend, now would you?"

"You're not a … OH!" he said, squinting at me. If a dragon looks at a Dragon Friend in a special way, he can see a certain kind of aura. I'd been told that Dragon Friends were very rare, and that all dragons were honorbound to treat them with respect. Of course that was in the future, and I had no idea what they'd been treated like in the past.

"Why didn't you tell me straightaway?" said the dragon, looking disappointed. "Now I'll have to find something else for dinner, and I was so looking forward to eating you! I don't get to eat an intelligent meal very often."

"Would you feel better if I told you that I know of a wonderful place not too far from here where there are no humans?"

"Not really. I'm giving up the nomad life. Going to settle down right here. I've just decided—no more roaming for me."

"That's because of Millie's spell. You can give up roaming once you've reached the place I mentioned. Going to a new permanent home isn't really roaming, especially since it isn't far from here. You'll be able to see it once you get above the treetops."

"Where is it?"

"I'll tell you if you swear on your honor as a dragon that you won't ever go near humans again."

The dragon rolled his eyes and sighed. "On my honor as a dragon. Now where is this place?"

"In the Purple Mountains," I said, pointing in their general direction. "You can't miss them. And if you look in the center of the mountains, you'll find a natural arena with a pool of lava where you can have a good, long soak."

When I mentioned lava, the dragon's face brightened noticeably. "Lava, you say? That would feel good."

I nodded. "And the arena would be the perfect spot for the Dragon Olympics."

The dragon shook his head. "The Dragon Olympics have been held on an island for centuries. No one is going to want to move it now."

"It won't hurt to look, will it?"

"I suppose not. But if it isn't just as you say, I'll be back."

"Fair enough." As the dragon raised his wings to begin his first downbeat, I added, "Before you go, I didn't catch your name."

"It's Bone Cruncher. You may have heard of me. My motto is: *Flame once and ask questions later.*"

Nine

I used my farseeing ball to watch Bone Cruncher fly to the Purple Mountains. When he didn't come back, I turned myself into a bird again and flew to the castle, arriving shortly after dark. Everyone had been hard at work getting ready for the party. Men had carried hogsheads of ale from the cellar under the kitchen. Maids had removed the old rushes and debris from years past before scrubbing the floor of the Great Hall. The new rushes they'd spread were scented with herbs, making the room smell wonderful. Torches had been cleaned or replaced, tables and benches set around the room and colorful banners hung from the ceiling. Additional guests had arrived, bringing their servants with them.

Hazel had been busy using her own special talent. A table in the buttery was piled high with everlasting bouquets of roses, lilies and some dainty white flowers I didn't recognize, all looking as fresh as if they'd just been picked. I wondered if she'd really made enough or if I should make extra myself. I remembered Dyspepsia's words, and I had to keep myself from making too many changes. Flowering vines spread across the walls of the Great Hall, dripping pink and lavender blossoms. Sturdy trees had sprouted in the corners of the room, arching to meet the ceiling in cascades of delicate leaves and pale yellow blooms. Even the herbs sprinkled throughout the rushes on the floor looked as if they had taken root and were growing.

I found Millie talking to Jasper, Fenton and Eadric. Of the other young men who had volunteered to kill the dragon, one had changed his mind and gone home, while a second had disappeared downriver, chasing a water nymph. Eadric admitted that he and another knight had continued on until they realized that they were lost. After wandering around for most of the afternoon, they'd stumbled into a woodcutter who had showed them the way back to the castle.

Millie seemed relieved to see me and couldn't wait to talk to me alone. "I know Jasper needed help, but I felt awful leaving you the way I did," she said. "I worried about you all the way home. Did everything go well?"

I nodded. "That dragon shouldn't bother anyone around here again."

"When Garrid came back from hunting, I asked if he'd seen you. He said he hadn't and offered to go look."

"Did you tell him why I was in the woods?"

She shook her head. "I said you went for a walk and hadn't returned yet. I'd better go tell him that you're back. He was going to the kitchen first to drop off some rabbits he'd killed."

"I'll go," I said. "I'd like to meet this mysterious prince."

Finding Garrid wasn't hard this time. Since Millie had told me about him, I knew he had to be the tall, young blond knight I'd found chatting with the head cook. What Millie hadn't mentioned was that he was the handsomest prince in the castle—with his chiseled features and broad shoulders—and that he made all the other visiting princes, including Eadric, look like little boys.

Although everyone in the kitchen was working long hours to prepare for the party, they'd taken the time to inspect the rabbits he'd brought, already bled and gutted. While the cook praised the rabbits, giggling kitchen helpers fawned over Garrid, but I had the feeling he wasn't listening to any of them.

"Prince Garrid," I said as he left the kitchen. "May I have a moment of your time?"

He raised an eyebrow and said, "Do I know you?"

"I'm Emma. Millie said that you had offered to go looking for me, so I came to tell you that I'm back now."

A spark of recognition lit his eyes. "So you're Emma. I've heard all about you."

"You have?" I said, wondering what Millie might have told him.

Garrid patted me on the shoulder and smiled. The moment he touched me, I knew there was something different about him. Once I wouldn't have noticed it, but since my power had increased, I was sensitive to all the magic around me. In some way I didn't recognize, Garrid had magic. "Don't worry," he said. "Your secret's safe with me." Stepping around me, he strode off down the hall.

I felt cold all over, as if someone had opened a door on winter. My secret? Which secret was that? In this time and place I had too many to keep track of easily, too many things I didn't want people to know. What had Millie told him? That I was a witch? That I wasn't Frederika's daughter? Or had someone finally figured out that I didn't belong there at all?

I hurried back to the Great Hall to see Millie, but it was crowded when I arrived and everyone was talking excitedly.

"Did you hear?" said one of Queen Angelica's ladies to another. "Jasper and Fenton fought the dragon. Fenton says they chased it off."

"I heard he dealt it a grievous wound. The monster will probably bleed to death."

I wandered through the Hall, looking for Millie and hearing snatches of conversation.

"Fenton says it was enormous, the biggest dragon he'd ever seen."

"Its teeth were strong enough to cut through stone! He said it can chew up rocks and spit them out again."

"Have you seen Prince Jasper's armor? You can see where the dragon bit him."

I nodded. That much was true.

I finally found Millie, gnawing on her lip as she tried not to say a word. I knew how she felt, because I would have liked to squash a few rumors myself. I ground my teeth and tried to keep a pleasant expression on my face. "I'm going to bed now, Millie," I said. "I have to get up early tomorrow morning—very early."

Meeting Garrid had only made me more interested in him. Of all the princes courting Hazel, I had a feeling that he was the one I'd really have to watch. Apparently the only way to do that was to follow him when he went hunting. Maybe I could learn why he always went alone. Could he be using magic? When I tried to find Eadric to ask if he wanted to go with me, a squire told me that he was meeting with King Grunwald to discuss the best way to deal with werewolves and probably wouldn't be back until late. I waited in the Great Hall for another hour or so and was about to give up and go to bed when Eadric entered, talking to one of the squires.

Running to Eadric's side, I told the squire, "Excuse us. We have something important to discuss."

"Really?" said Eadric. "Like what?"

"That depends," I said after the squire had taken his leave. "What are you doing tomorrow morning?"

"Sleeping," Eadric said. "I haven't gotten much rest since I started sharing a room with five other princes."

"How would you like to go hunting with me?" I asked.

Eadric raised an eyebrow. "Hunting? You were never interested in hunting before. What do you plan to hunt?"

"Answers. I think it's about time someone followed Garrid and found out what he's really doing. Don't you think it's a little suspicious that he goes off by himself every day?"

"You think he's up to no good?" asked Eadric.

"I think he's up to something," I said. "He's too secretive to be innocent. Do you want to go with me? We'd have to leave early."

Eadric sighed. "Of course I'll go with you. I'll just have to sleep late another day. Maybe in a week or two."

It was easy to get up before dawn the next morning since I tossed and turned all night. When I couldn't lie in bed staring at the ceiling any longer, I dressed as quietly as I could so I wouldn't wake Millie. I met Eadric as we'd agreed, and we slipped downstairs to the Great Hall together. The guards were dozing at their posts, so we tiptoed past them to stand beneath one of the windows. With one eye on the closest guard, I turned Eadric and myself into bats, and we fluttered through the opening. Being able to see in the dark meant that we didn't need to wait until dawn when the guards would lower the drawbridge, and we could be ready and waiting when Garrid arrived. Besides, being a bat was fun when no one was chasing you.

We flew to the maze and called for Li'l, but it seemed to take forever before she answered. While I perched on her rosebush, Eadric darted back and forth, catching his breakfast of mosquitoes. "Where have you been?" I asked Li'l when she finally appeared.

"With Bugsy," she said, with a faraway look in her eyes.

Eadric gulped, swallowing a mosquito, and asked, "Who's Bugsy?"

Li'l sighed. "He's the most wonderful bat in the world. He doesn't know it yet, but I've decided to stay here with him."

"You mean until we go home?" I said.

"No, I mean forever. I love him, Emma. Bugsy is the perfect bat for me! I've never met anyone like him before, and I probably never will again. He's sweet and funny and thoughtful. I hope you'll be as happy with Eadric as I know I'm going to be with Bugsy!"

"Are you sure, Li'l?" I asked. This seemed totally bizarre, but maybe I had been too focused on the human world, or myself. "Have you really thought about this? If you stay here when Eadric and I leave, you'll be stuck in the past forever. And you don't know a thing about Bugsy! You don't even know his real name. You made up the name Bugsy, remember?"

"Past, future, what difference does it make to me, Emma? I'll miss you and Eadric, but my life is here with Bugsy. I know he's wonderful, and that's enough for me."

The sound of rattling chains and groaning wood announced the lowering of the drawbridge. It was happening earlier than was normal in my day, perhaps at Prince Garrid's request. A figure crossed the bridge and started down the road toward the forest, a bow slung over his shoulder.

I'm glad we came early, I thought and took to the air. "I'll talk to you about this later, Li'l. This is a very big decision." Li'l was my friend and I didn't want to leave her behind in the past, but I didn't see what I could do about it.

"Don't wake me if I'm asleep," said the little bat, yawning broadly.

It was generally unheard of for a member of my own royal family to go hunting without a group of friends or servants, and I was sure it was just as unusual in Millie's. Even so, Garrid strode alone down the road with great confidence, acting as if he was used to walking in the predawn dark by himself. Eadric and I flew behind him, staying far enough back that we could see him but where,

I hoped, he wouldn't see us.

The black of night was graying to morning when Garrid entered the woods, although it was still dark under the trees. If we hadn't been bats, we would have lost him altogether because he could move through the woods as silently as a shadow. We hung back, watching him when he stopped and cocked his head, then took off running so fast that we had a hard time keeping up. We lost him for a moment when he disappeared into a scrub-lined ravine. Something hit the ground with a crash, and a creature thrashed the foliage. I flew toward the sound and found Garrid bent over an injured doe, its limbs scrabbling feebly. Garrid's back was to me, but I could see the creature shudder, then grow still. After a time, Garrid straightened and stood up, lifting the deer as if it weighed nothing. Cradling the lifeless body in his arms, he climbed out of the gully and picked his way through the woods.

Eadric had joined me, and we were both following Garrid when he suddenly disappeared. It wasn't until we reached the spot where he'd vanished that we saw the opening to the cave. It was pitch black inside, and I expected him to light a candle or torch. He didn't, though, and we had to use our special sounds to find him.

Garrid was walking purposefully to a large hook set into the stone, moving as if he could see perfectly well.

After tying the deer's hind legs together with a strip of leather, he hung the carcass up to drain, setting a wooden bowl under it to catch the blood. Then, taking off his cape, he turned toward a large box set on a broad stone platform. I wondered what could be in the box that had to be kept so secret. Weapons perhaps? Something magical? Secret messages about an invasion? Yet of all the things I imagined, nothing could have surprised me more than what happened next.

He must have kept the hinges well oiled, for he lifted the lid without making a sound. I craned my neck to see when he reached inside, but all he did was take out a pillow and plump it between his hands. After setting the pillow back in the box, he climbed in, lay down and yawned. Although his two front teeth had looked normal when I spoke to him in the castle, they were now long, pointed and tipped with blood. I gasped when I realized what it meant. Handsome Prince Garrid, suitor to the future Green Witch of Greater Greensward and possibly my own ancestor, was a vampire!

Garrid must have heard me because he blinked and looked in our direction. He began to sit up, but we didn't wait to see what he'd do next. Beating our wings as fast as they could carry us, Eadric and I darted out of the cave and zipped between the trees. I didn't even try to talk to Eadric until the trees thinned and we could fly side by side.

"He's a vampire!" I said. "We'd better hurry back and tell Millie. I was sure he had some kind of secret, but I never thought it could be this bad." I didn't have anything against vampires as long as they kept to themselves, but I certainly didn't want Hazel to marry one. Not only did vampires exist on the blood of others, but they were known to carry all kinds of diseases, keep terrible hours and spend most of their time trying to convert everyone they met.

"I guess that explains where he goes every night," said Eadric. "And I thought he wasn't feeling well."

"He won't be," I said. "Not if he tries to marry into my family."

We were out of the forest, speeding back to the castle, when we heard the nicker of horses and saw three men at the edge of a pond. We wouldn't have paid them any heed if we hadn't noticed that one was Fenton. He was arguing with two men I didn't know, a hulking man with a neck as big as his oversized biceps and a smaller man with a narrow face and pointed chin.

"Let's see what that's all about," I said to Eadric.

"I thought you were in a hurry to get back to the castle."

"I am, but Millie asked me to find out what I could about all the princes. We won't stay long."

We flew closer, hoping to hear their conversation. Circling the pond, we landed in the grass at the edge.

"I'm tired of your excuses!" said the shorter man. "You've owed me this money for a fortnight, and if I don't get it today, Georgie here will make you wish your ancestors had never been born." The big man grunted and narrowed his eyes until he looked fierce.

"I told you, you'll get it," said Fenton. "Once Princess Hazel chooses me, I'll push up the wedding date. Greensward's coffers have never been fuller. There's plenty there to pay off my debts and finance my return to the tournament circuit. I'm at the peak of my jousting career. The crowds love me, and so does the princess."

"What makes you think she'll choose you?"

"Because I'm her best choice, and she knows it. Some suitors have left already, scared off by the princess or that blasted dragon her father wanted us to kill. I'm the most attentive, as well as the best looking. She'll choose me; I'm sure of it."

"You'd better be right," said the smaller man. "Georgie doesn't like to be kept waiting."

As Prince Fenton mounted his horse and started back to the castle, we took to the air once again. I had a mission ahead of me. I had promised myself I would find out what I could about Millie's sister's suitors and I had plenty to tell, regardless of Dyspepsia's warning.

Ten

We reached the castle just as a small whirlwind landed at the foot of the drawbridge, depositing a plump, little witch with blue-tinged hair. It was only midday, yet some of the guests were already arriving. We landed in the garden and stayed there only long enough to become humans again before hurrying into the castle. I found Millie watching servants place tankards on tables set against the walls of the Great Hall.

"There you are, Emma," said Millie. "I've been looking for you all morning."

Someone opened a door leading into one of the corridors, and the scent of roasting meat wafted past us. Eadric sniffed the air like a hound and turned toward the kitchen. I almost expected to see him drool. "If you'll excuse me," he said, "I think a leg of mutton and a loaf of fresh bread are calling me. Do you need me now, Emma?"

I smiled and patted his arm. "Go ahead. I can tell her

by myself."

"Tell me what?" Millie asked as Eadric strode down the hall.

I led Millie away from the listening servants to a corner made private by the foliage of one of Hazel's trees. "I told you I had to get up early," I said. "I followed Garrid when he went hunting, and I learned his secret. Then I overheard Fenton talking, and I know what he's up to as well."

"I knew they were hiding things! What were they?"

I told her about Fenton first. She nodded and said she wasn't surprised. When I told her about Garrid, her eyes grew wide and she looked as horrified as I'd felt.

"A vampire here in our castle? We have to tell my father!" Millie gasped. "And Hazel! We have to tell her, too!"

"Shh!" I said. "Not so loud! We don't want to ruin the party."

"Ruin the party? I'm afraid she might ruin her life!" When Millie ducked under a branch and headed from the Hall, I hurried after her, concerned about what she might do.

Although we found Hazel right away, we weren't able to see her. She had locked herself in her room with her maids and seamstress and refused to let anyone else in.

"Hazel!" shouted Millie as she pounded on the door. "I need to talk to you!"

"Go away!" said her sister's muffled voice. "I'm busy! Ouch! Be careful, you wretch," she said to her seamstress. "You poke me with a needle again and I'll have you thrown into the moat."

"But Hazel," said Millie, "this is important! Open the door so I can talk to you."

"If it's that important, you can tell me from there," Hazel replied. "Otherwise go away!"

Since Millie didn't want to shout the news through the heavy wooden door, she decided to go looking for her father instead. Unfortunately, after searching the castle, we learned that King Grunwald had insisted that Eadric show him how to place escape-proof werewolf traps the way they did in Upper Montevista. No one knew exactly where Eadric and the king had gone.

We were still hoping to talk to Hazel and had gone back to wait outside her door when her mother saw us. Like most of the ladies of the castle, she had been primping since early morning and was already dressed for the party. Her gown of shimmering silver seemed to glow in the dimly lit corridor. "Ladies," she said, eyeing our everyday clothes, "I know you both have gowns more appropriate for tonight. Don't you think it's time you got ready?"

"Actually," said Millie, "we want to talk to Hazel first, but she won't let us in. Are you going to see her now?"

"I am, but you're not. You're to go to your chamber

immediately to change. Emma, see if you can do something with your hair. It looks like a bird has been nesting in it."

"But Mother," Millie wailed, "this is important! We learned something about Garrid that Hazel needs to know. If we can talk to her for just a minute—"

"You'll do no such thing, young lady. The last thing we need is for you to upset your sister. This is a very big day for her, and we don't need you ruining it. Now off to your room and that's an order!"

"We'll go, but would you please tell her for us? We found out that Garrid—"

"I said *now*!"

Millie ducked her head like an obedient daughter, but I could see the anger flash in her eyes. "Yes, Mother," she said, curtsying to the queen.

"Don't worry," I said as we hurried to her room. "We can tell Hazel at the party."

Millie nodded. "We'll think of something. I'm not giving up yet!"

We were near a window when something flew past, and I darted to the windowsill to look out. An old wizard seated on a battered door was spiraling down to land in front of the castle. As I watched, a half-dozen witches arrived on their brooms while several swooped in, seated on chairs laden with cushions. I stepped back when an enormous eagle with golden feathers stared at me through the window on his way to drop off the small, wizened woman he carried.

"Did you see all those witches?" I asked Millie, who had stopped beside me.

She nodded. "We'd better hurry and get dressed. I think the party is about to start. Your clothes are waiting for you. Mother sent them this afternoon."

I'd never been interested in fancy gowns, but for Millie's sake I tried to look excited. When we reached her chamber, I found a rust-colored tunic with a crimson surcoat lying on her bed.

"Tell me," said Millie as I wiped the last of the dragon salve off and slipped the tunic over my head. "After Hazel hears about Garrid, do you think she'll choose Jasper?"

"Probably," I said, glancing at Millie as soon as my head was free of the fabric. She looked distressed, making me wish I hadn't said anything.

When we were ready, Millie looked wonderful and far older than her thirteen years. Her hair was laced with a silver cord that glistened when she moved her head. Her tunic was the blue of a summer sky over which she wore a darker blue surcoat trimmed with silver. My clothes were plainer, but Millie had twisted my hair and looped it on top of my head in a way I thought was so flattering that I resolved to wear it that way when I got home. We were about to go out of the door when Millie took a delicate golden circlet out of a trunk by her bed. "I almost forgot Hazel's present," she said.

"Oh, no!" I said. "I was going to make one, but I've been so busy.... Give me a minute and let me think." I wanted to give her something she'd like, but I couldn't give her an obviously magical gift since I didn't want everyone to know that I was a witch. That didn't mean that I couldn't use magic to make it, however. If only I had something....

While Millie waited patiently by the door, I found the pouch I'd worn when I arrived and took out the candle stub. It was small, but it was enough. Only a few minutes later, Millie was in the Great Hall setting her golden circlet on the table set aside for gifts, leaving room for my wax replica of the castle, complete with miniature flowers.

It wasn't until we finally joined the party that I realized how difficult it might be to find Hazel. The Great Hall was crowded with guests of every shape and size. I saw hovering fairies no bigger than my thumb talking to hulking knights dressed in silk and leather. Other fairies were the size of the average human, but had a sparkle to their hair or a lilt in their voices that set them apart. Although none of the fairies was dressed like another, they all wore clothes derived from nature. Tunics of leaves or grass and gowns of flower petals or moonbeams clothed the dancers twirling across the floor to the melodies of human musicians.

The wizards were also dressed in fantastic clothes, having tried to outdo each other by using magic to make them. One wizard was dressed in a black robe that bore constantly changing numbers and symbols drawn in chalky white. Another wore a blue robe bedecked with floating clouds. A third, and the one that demanded the most attention, wore a mirrored robe and a tall, peaked hat that shot sparkling dust out of its pointed crown.

Although the wizards' clothes were interesting enough, it was the witches' clothes that made me catch my breath. I saw a gown that shimmered from one color to the next, encompassing the entire rainbow. A second was covered with splashing raindrops that seemed so real I almost expected to find water on the floor. My favorite, however, was a gown of moss green that smelled like the forest after a cleansing rain. It reminded me of my aunt Grassina and the kind of gowns she wore before the curse changed her.

There were normal people as well: relatives of Hazel's, inhabitants of the castle and the nobility from the surrounding area. Even though they were dressed in their finest clothes, they seemed drab and uninteresting when standing beside the magical guests.

"What color is Hazel wearing?" I asked Millie, craning my neck to search for her sister in the crowd.

"I don't know. She wouldn't tell me anything about it

except that it was much better than mine," Millie replied.

Human musicians played their instruments on a balcony above the Great Hall while dancers paraded below in the center of the room. Although most of the guests stayed at ground level, nearly half the fairy dancers cavorted in the air above them, creating a multihued spectacle with their fluttering wings. I stopped to watch the fairies for a moment, wondering if one of them would pronounce the curse that would do so much damage to my family.

A table had been set up at one end of the Hall. Laden with delicate, eggshell cups filled with dandelion wine and large, pewter tankards brimming with ale, it was the most crowded place in the room. A short distance away, another table stood covered with platters of hummingbird eggs, sugared violets and the herbed wings of some tiny bird. A third table supported platters of roasted pheasants and peacocks with reinserted feathers; suckling pigs glazed with honey, their mouths filled with sweet, red apples; and tureens of baked eels floating in a thick cream sauce. Eadric stood between a tall, thin man with jutting cheekbones and a handsome fairy dressed in hose and a tunic the color of new spring buds.

An already heaping plate in his hand, Eadric was reaching for one of the herbed wings when I stepped between him and the table, forcing him to look at me. "Emma," he said, "you look lovely."

"Thanks," I said, craning my neck to watch the people entering the room. "Have you seen Hazel?"

"Not since yesterday."

Millie squeezed between two heavyset witches and a long-haired warlock with a dragon emblazoned on the back of his robe. "Here, try this," Millie said, thrusting an eggshell cup into my hands.

The cup was so delicate that I was afraid to use it, but Millie and Eadric had no reservations. Common in the land of the fairies, the cups were sturdier than they looked. I followed their example and took a long sip, then started coughing when the sweet liquid burned my throat. This was no ordinary dandelion wine.

"The fairies brought the cups and the wine," Millie said, wiping her watering eyes.

"I believe it," I said, my voice a hoarse whisper.

Carrying our drinks with us, Eadric joined us in our search for Hazel. We were skirting the dancers in the middle of the room when I spotted Millie's mother approaching a group of witches in the far corner. A light breeze seemed to come from that part of the hall, stirring the banners hanging from the walls and the leaves of Hazel's trees.

Millie glanced at me. "You can tell that the witch Windifer is here. She can't go anywhere without her breezes. I forgot to warn you that some of Hazel's guests are a little unconventional."

"I didn't know there were so many witches in the area."

"They've come from all over," said Millie. "Hazel meets them at witches' gatherings. Let me introduce you to the ladies over there." Turning toward a cluster of witches, Millie led the way across the floor.

Four witches stood talking by the trunk of one of Hazel's trees. They all looked up when we approached, their eyes suspicious until they recognized Millie.

"Hello, princess," said a beautiful witch with hair and eyelashes of real gold and impossibly large, amber eyes. She wore a gown of brilliant red with tiny golden specks that gave off its own kind of heat. "It's a lovely party," she added in a deep, throaty voice.

Eadric's eyes seemed to glaze over when he saw her. I stumbled and stepped on his instep, which seemed to bring him back to the real world.

"I'm glad you're enjoying it," Millie said to the witch in red. Placing her hand on my back, she gave me a small nudge forward. "This is Emma, one of my cousins, and this," she said, "is her friend Eadric."

"How nice," said the golden-haired witch, dismissing us with a flick of her eyes.

I learned the names of all four witches, although I doubt they remembered mine. Scarletta, the witch dressed in red, was the only one who spoke to us.

I was trying to think of something polite to say when

the witches turned to stare past Millie at another witch who had come up behind her. Middle-aged, with dull, brown hair, everything about her was thin, from her thin face to her thin body to her thin, whiny voice. Unlike the other witches, she didn't look as if she had dressed for the occasion since she wore a faded, gray gown with a straggly, unraveling hem.

Scarletta sneered and said, "If it isn't Scrofula, looking as scrawny as ever. You'd best stay where you are or Windifer's breeze might blow you right out the door."

Scrofula's eyes narrowed. "Oh, I won't be the one to get blown away. We all know how full of hot air you are, Scarletta. It comes from puffing yourself up over your appearance every time you make yourself look twenty years younger, sister dear."

"Why," said Scarletta, "if we weren't guests in this castle, I'd—"

"You'd what?" said Scrofula, tilting her chin defiantly.

Millie whispered in my ear, "Emma, we have to do something. Those sisters are known to have the most awful fights."

Fights between witches often involved magic, putting everyone at risk. I shoved my cup at Scarletta and said, "Have you tried the dandelion wine?"

"What?" she asked, distracted for the moment.

"It's very good," I said. Taking a step toward her, I

did something I'd never done before; I pretended to trip. The dandelion wine sloshed out of the cup and down the front of Scarletta's gown, making the heated fabric sizzle.

"You clumsy girl!" said the witch, her voice suddenly shrill. "Why, I ought to—"

"Leave her alone, Scarletta," said her sister. "It's just a little wine. You aren't going to melt."

The golden-haired witch glared at Scrofula, then, with a crackle and a snap, Scarletta disappeared.

"How very rude!" said one of the other witches. Even I knew that it was impolite to vanish so abruptly at a social gathering.

"You were brilliant!" Millie told me as we continued our search for Hazel. "And pretending to be clumsy…."

"I've had a lot of practice with the real thing," I replied.

I was beginning to wonder if we'd ever find Hazel. Could she have decided to stay away from her own party? I was thinking of sending a page to look for her when a fairy I was passing fluttered her wings, slapping the side of my head with one.

"Oops," said the fairy, waving a nearly empty tankard of ale in my face. I backed away when the fairy burped, her ale-soaked breath strong even a few feet away. "This is good stuff!" she said, putting the tankard to her lips and draining it dry.

"The Swamp Fairy," said Millie.

I caught my breath with a gasp. Glancing at Eadric, I saw that his eyebrows were raised in surprise. We had met the Swamp Fairy once when we'd been frogs back in our own time. She'd been older then, yet when I looked at her more closely, I knew she hadn't changed much. Her blue hair didn't have the gray streaks it would have later on, and her flower-petal skirt looked fresher, but it was definitely the same fairy. Unlike witches, who are mortal, fairies live forever.

"Oh dear." The Swamp Fairy turned her empty mug upside down. "It's all gone. Better get more!" she said in a cheery voice. Fluttering her wings, she rose straight into the air, nearly colliding with a dancing couple. "Watch where you're going!" she declared.

We circled the room, studying the mingling guests, when a bell chimed, light and sweet. "Attention, everyone!" called a voice as the volume in the room dwindled.

"There she is," Eadric said, gesturing toward the raised dais. Flanked by her mother's ladies-in-waiting, Hazel stood facing the dance floor. Her clothes were magnificent; both her tunic and her surcoat had been made from cloth of gold, and diamonds sparkled in her hair.

"I have to get up there," Millie whispered as she looked for a way to reach her sister. Seeing an opening between two knights, she squeezed past them while I followed close on her heels.

"Thank you for coming," said Hazel. She was so loud it sounded as if her voice was magically amplified. "I'm happy to celebrate my birthday with all my closest friends."

"Who is that?" asked a fairy with spiky green hair, pointing at Hazel.

"Shh!" hissed the people around him. I saw another gap between two groups of witches and hurried to get through.

"I'm about to open my presents," Hazel said. "And I'd like to thank you all now."

"She does that so she doesn't have to thank anyone afterward," whispered Millie.

It took some time for Hazel to open all the gifts because there were so many, but it gave me the opportunity to work my way closer to the dais. The presents from her relatives were fairly boring—clothes mostly and a few pieces of jewelry. The princes had given her cups embedded with gems, bolts of rare fabrics and boxes with lids of hammered gold. The witches gave her gifts such as a farseeing ball, a ring for carrying secret potions and a new broom. The membership in the Apple of the Month Society—one plain and one poisoned apple per month—was more original, although it earned the gift giver scowls from the people around her.

When Hazel unwrapped a hand mirror, she held it up

so everyone could see it, then asked the traditional question, "Mirror, mirror in my hand. Who's the fairest in the land?"

A light shimmered over the mirror's surface. "Not you, missy," it said. "You cheat at dice!"

Blushing, Hazel handed the mirror to one of her mother's ladies-in-waiting. "This mirror doesn't work right. Put it with the others we need to get fixed."

We had almost reached Hazel when she began to open the presents from the fairies. Suddenly even the most bored guests were taking an interest. Everyone had already seen the cups and the dandelion wine, but the silver flute that played itself and asked for requests after each selection was new. So was the pink flower-petal skirt that came with directions. "Water twice a week," read Hazel from the attached leaf.

There were other musical gifts and a few that were meant to make the wearer more beautiful, like the crown that made her glow with a golden light. A tiny gilded cage held a hummingbird that laid golden eggs. "Stingy," said a lavender-haired fairy near me when the fairy who'd given the gift beamed smugly. "She could have given the princess a bigger bird."

Another gift, and the most exciting one as far as I was concerned, was from an elderly fairy dressed in willow leaves. Everyone waited quietly as she climbed onto the dais. When she reached Hazel's side, she showed her a ring, the very same ring I would wear many years later on my finger, and spoke in a loud, clear voice that carried throughout the hall. "My gift to you, sweet Princess Hazel, will last for all generations. From this day on, the nicest and most powerful witch in your kingdom will be the Green Witch. With this gift comes greater power as well as greater responsibility, for the Green Witch must be the kingdom's protector, using her magic to ensure the safety of its inhabitants, whether human- or fairy-kind." Taking the princess's hand in hers, the fairy slipped the ring on Hazel's finger and said, "I name you the first Green Witch."

A ripple of applause ran through the room. Smiling, Hazel curtsied to the fairy and thanked her. As the elderly fairy climbed down from the dais, I watched the first Green Witch turn her hand this way and that to admire the ring on her finger.

"Look at her," whispered Millie. "She likes the ring, but I doubt she paid any attention to the part about taking care of the kingdom."

"Now it's my turn," called out the green-haired fairy who hadn't known Hazel. "I didn't know what to bring you—" he said, striding toward the dais.

"Since he crashed the party and didn't know anyone here," said a fairy no taller than my knee whom I hadn't noticed, even though he was standing beside me. His broad red cap dotted with white spots made him look like a mushroom, and he had an earthy kind of smell.

"—so I decided to wait for inspiration before choosing a gift," continued the green-haired fairy. "That last gift inspired me!" Flourishing his hand in the air, he presented Hazel with a tapestry that seemed to appear out of nowhere.

"What is he, a wizard or a fairy?" asked the mushroom.

Hazel glanced at the tapestry and frowned. "Let us see," called someone from the back, so she turned it around and held it up.

It was one of the tapestries that hung in my tower room and showed the Green Witch from behind as she watched a retreating enemy from the battlements. Only now the Green Witch had long blond hair instead of auburn like mine.

"What is it?" someone shouted.

The fairy's grin slipped when he saw the puzzled expressions. "It's the Green Witch defending the castle, of course," he said, pointing at the picture. "It will always show the current Green Witch, no matter who she is."

"It's very nice, I'm sure," said Hazel, but it was clear that she was disappointed. When the deflated-looking fairy had rejoined the other guests, the princess smiled again. "And now for the announcement that you've all been waiting to hear."

"Oh, no!" said Millie. "I'm too late!"

"Wait!" shouted a voice, and Prince Jasper pushed his way to the front. "Before you tell us who you plan to marry, I have something to say that I'd hoped to say in private."

You too? I thought.

"I owe it to you to be honest," said the prince. "I am not worthy of you. I have fallen in love with another and can never give you the love that you deserve."

"Forget it," Hazel said, brushing him off with a wave of her hand. "I wasn't going to choose you anyway."

"You weren't?" Millie squeaked.

"I'm going to marry Prince Garrid! We've made our plans. We'll be married within the month."

"You can't marry him!" Millie said, pushing past the little mushroom fairy. "Garrid is a vampire!"

Hazel glanced at her and shrugged. "So?" she said. "Nobody's perfect!"

The crowd had begun to get restless when they realized that Hazel had received her last present. Hazel must have noticed this, because she held up her hand and called out, "One last thing! Make sure you see me before you go. I have gifts for each of you!"

Even the dour-faced witches looked happy after hearing this. Since she hadn't let me help, I'd just have to hope that she had enough for everyone.

Eleven

The party went on until dawn, but by the time the faint light of a rainy day had crept through the windows high on the wall of the Great Hall, nearly all of the guests had gone home. The normal, human guests—including the relatives and the unsuccessful suitors—had already gone to bed, even though they wouldn't leave until the next day. After staying up with us all night, Eadric had wandered off to the kitchen in search of breakfast. Only Hazel, Millie and I were still in the Great Hall waiting to say farewell to the last of the guests.

A trestle table had been set up to hold the everlasting bouquets. When the final guest came to claim her present, I was delighted to note that there were still two bouquets left, even though some guests had taken more than their share. It looked as though Hazel had enough bouquets for everyone.

"You're sure she's the last one?" I said, gesturing toward the table where Scrofula was chatting with Hazel.

"I'm positive," said Millie. "We had the pages look everywhere, just as you suggested. They found her in the garden and brought her here to get her gift."

"Good," I said. "Then maybe it really is over."

When Millie and I went to the table to say good-bye to Scrofula, she was reaching for a second bouquet. "My sister left early. I'll give it to her the next time I see her."

"So we still had enough," I said, watching Scrofula leave.

"I don't know why you're so worried," said Millie. "If we'd run out, Hazel could have made more."

"Made more what?" asked Garrid.

I hadn't noticed him come into the room, and apparently neither had Hazel. "Where have you been?" she asked, her gaze frosty. "I've been looking everywhere for you."

"I had things to take care of so I could concentrate on you this morning," he said, putting his arms around her. "We still have a lot to talk about."

I turned away when they started to kiss, and that's when I noticed something small and black fly in through a window and land in one of Hazel's trees. I slipped away to investigate. "Li'l, is that you?" I whispered.

A little head popped up from behind a branch. "Why didn't you tell me there were trees in this castle?" Li'l asked. "I could have stayed in one of these."

"They weren't here before," I said. "Hazel grew them

for the party. I'm glad you came. I was just about to go look for you. I'll be leaving as soon as I say good-bye to Millie and Hazel. The party is over. Most of the guests have left. Since there were enough gifts for everyone, no one cast a curse."

Li'l crawled around the branch until she was hanging upside down. "I didn't come to say good-bye now. I was looking for Bugsy. He was late coming to see me, and then he acted funny. I was worried about him, so I followed him after he took me home. He came to the castle. He has to be around here somewhere."

"I haven't noticed any other bats, but then I haven't been looking. Maybe I should go—"

Someone groaned on the other side of the tree, loudly enough that even Millie heard it. "Emma, was that you?" she asked from halfway across the Hall.

"No," I whispered, tiptoeing around the trunk. "It was. . . ."

The Swamp Fairy sat up and looked at me, rubbing her eyes with her knuckles. "What day is it?" she asked.

"The day after my birthday party," said Hazel, joining us by the tree. "Everyone else has gone home. I thought you'd left already."

Li'l pulled her wings closer to her sides, trying to make herself look smaller and less conspicuous. "Is that a bat?" asked Hazel, backing away from the tree. "What is a bat doing in my castle?" She looked around frantically, spotting a dirty tankard on a table. "Get out of here!" she hollered, snatching up the tankard and hurling it at Li'l.

The tankard missed Li'l by inches, but was close enough to frighten her. Releasing her hold on the trunk, she fell a few feet, then began flapping frantically. Hazel reached for another tankard and was about to throw it, when Garrid leapt in front of her and shouted, "No! Don't hurt her. That's Li'l!"

Frightened, Li'l blundered onto the table where the ale had been served. "Oh my, oh my!" she cried, knocking over an empty eggshell cup and dragging her wing in a puddle of spilled ale.

I ran over to the table to help her, but Garrid was there first. He caught her in his hands, then cupped her gently and said, "Don't be afraid, Li'l. It's me, Bugsy!"

"What do you mean, *Bugsy*?" demanded Hazel, her face turning a deep red. "Why are you acting like you know that bat? What's going on, Garrid?"

Garrid looked up. "Hazel, I—"

With Garrid distracted, it was easy for Li'l to wriggle free. She slipped out of his hands and darted toward the window.

"Li'l! No!" Garrid called after her.

"Pardon me," said the Swamp Fairy, massaging her temples with her fingertips. "If you'll just give me my guest gift, I'll be on my way."

"Li'l!" shouted Garrid, more loudly than before. A shadow passed over him, there was a puff of cool, dank air and Garrid turned into a bat. Hazel shrieked when he followed Li'l out the window.

"Now do you believe me?" Millie asked. "Vampires do that kind of thing."

"About that gift—" the Swamp Fairy began.

Red faced, Hazel turned on the fairy. "Stop pestering me!" she screamed. "Can't you see that I'm in the midst of a crisis! I don't have any more of those bouquets, anyway, so just go away and leave me alone!"

I bit my lip as the Swamp Fairy's eyes grew hard and her tired face turned angry. "I can't believe you said that to me!" she said to Hazel. "No one talks to the Swamp Fairy like that and gets away with it!" The air around the fairy began to shimmer. Raising her arms to the ceiling, the fairy called out in a loud voice,

For being rude to fairy-kind,
There is a price to pay, you'll find.
From those who could not be polite,
We do not soon forget a slight.

If, after your fifteenth year,
You should touch a flower, dear,
All your prettiness shall fade
Leaving you an ugly maid.

Your beauty gone, your sweetness, too,
No one will want to be with you.
A nasty spirit, ugly face,
You won't be welcome anyplace.

Daughters of your family, too,
Will become nasty just like you.
If after the fated hour,
They should touch a single flower.

This curse shall last until the day
A true love's kiss can help convey
That he looks past her nasty ways
To see her true self in her gaze.

Thunder boomed and green lightning flashed through the window as the fairy left the Hall. When Millie cried out, Hazel turned on her and said, "Don't be stupid! I'm a witch! My magic is more powerful than anything a fairy can throw at me."

I staggered, shocked by what had just happened. I'd come to their time to hear the curse, but had begun to hope that the fairy might not pronounce it after all. Although I'd worried about changing history, I'd meddled where I probably shouldn't have. It didn't seem to have had any real effect, however, since the curse had been cast anyway, making me feel like a failure even though I'd done what I'd originally set out to do.

Millie and Hazel were arguing when I went outside to find Li'l and Garrid. *Li'l's heart must be broken,* I thought, dashing past the guards and into the garden. It was pouring rain, and I stepped in a puddle the moment I left the drawbridge, soaking my shoes and the hem of my gown.

I found the two bats in the spot where I usually met Li'l. Perched on a rosebush beside Garrid, she was so agitated that she couldn't sit still. "You were one of the princess's suitors, weren't you?" she asked Garrid. "What did you plan to do? Were you going to marry her and never tell me? It's not going to work."

"I'm sorry, Li'l," he said. "I didn't mean for this to happen. I never wanted to hurt you. I think you're wonderful. I'd choose you if I could, but I'd already offered my hand to Hazel. If only you and I had met sooner."

"Well, we didn't, and now you're going to marry *her*. And to think I wanted to stay here with you after Emma went home. Emma," she said, turning to face me. "When are you leaving?"

"As soon as I change my clothes and say good-bye. I heard the curse, so I know what needs to be done."

"Then I'm going to the castle with you. The sooner we get back where we belong, the happier I'll be!"

I sneaked Li'l into the castle inside my sleeve, which was just as well since the rooms were bustling with people clearing off the tables and hauling away the trash.

After I'd changed back into my own clothes, I gathered my pouch and farseeing ball and went downstairs to the Great Hall to say good-bye. We heard the sound of wailing before we reached the door. Millie was gone, but Queen Angelica and her ladies-in-waiting were there, tears streaming down their faces.

"This is terrible," the queen wailed. "You've offended a fairy! We've tried so hard to get along with the fairies, and now this!"

Hazel rolled her eyes. "Don't be ridiculous, Mother. It doesn't mean a thing. I'm a witch. Fairies can't cast curses on witches!"

"Is that true?" Li'l whispered.

"No," I whispered back.

"Look. I'll prove it to you," Hazel said, "and you'll see that you're being silly."

"Don't!" screamed her mother as the princess reached for an enormous blossom dangling from a vine on the wall. There was an audible gasp in the room when Hazel buried her face in the flower.

"Princess Hazel," said Garrid, standing by the door, a man once again. His eyes were sad, and he looked more dejected than a hound left behind from the hunt. "I must apologize for what just happened. I will marry you, if you'll still have me."

"Of course I'll have you," said Hazel, taking her face out of the flower. But she had changed already, and the difference was shocking. No longer lovely, her eyes were small and beady, her nose and chin so long and pointed that they nearly met in front of her mouth. Bumpy warts had sprouted on her cheek, and her once-lustrous hair was thin and straggly.

After one glance at her elder daughter, the queen shrieked and fled the room while two of her ladies-in-waiting fainted. Garrid's face turned ashen, but he stood his ground without flinching.

"But you're going to have to change your ways, bat boy," said Hazel. "No going out at night with your friends. No more all-day hunting trips. You'll stay home with me and do what I tell you. Your taste in clothes is pitiful, so I'll pick out what you'll wear. Starting tomorrow, you'll. . . ."

Garrid looked horrified. With each new pronouncement, he stepped backward, away from his future bride. She was still listing the changes she would make in his life when he reached the doorway.

"I know you have an eye for the ladies, so I can't trust you. I'll need to know where you are every minute of the day. You'll report to me and—"

"Never!" shouted Garrid before he turned and bolted out the door.

"You're not getting away that easily, mister!" shrieked Hazel. She had a gleam in her eye when she passed me at a run. Even after they left the room, I could hear their feet pounding the stone floor. When I felt a cool, dank puff of air, I knew that Garrid had turned back into a bat.

"Well," said Li'l. "I guess he changed his mind. But I haven't changed mine. Emma, can we go home now?"

Twelve

The castle was in an uproar after Hazel disappeared, and Eadric, Li'l and I couldn't wait to go home. Relatives afraid of the curse were throwing their belongings into wagons and onto the backs of packhorses as they rushed to leave early. Prince Fenton was already gone, having taken one of the ladies-in-waiting with him. The queen had retreated to her chamber along with the rest of her ladies. No one went near King Grunwald, who was bellowing that he'd find the fairy and force her at sword point to change his daughter back.

Eadric wanted to leave right away, but I insisted that we find Millie before we go. We finally located her in a quiet antechamber, far from the chaos in the rest of the castle. She was talking to Jasper, and I could tell from her expression that something wonderful had happened. Jasper was holding both of her hands, and he didn't look as if he planned to let go.

"Emma, I want you to be the first to hear the news," Millie said. "Jasper told me that I'm the one he loves. He wants to ask my father for my hand in marriage."

"And what did you say?" I asked her, although I was sure I already knew the answer.

"I told him yes," she said, blushing, "as long as he can get Father's permission. We won't actually get married for a few more years, though. Hazel was waiting until she turned sixteen to choose a suitor, and I'm sure Father will expect me to wait as well."

"Did you tell him about … you know?" I asked.

"If you mean my magic, yes, I told him that I'm a witch," said Millie.

"She told me," said Jasper. "It doesn't make a difference one way or the other. I'd want to marry her no matter what. I'm just glad she's willing to marry someone as ordinary as me."

"I know what you mean. That's how I feel about Emma," said Eadric, giving me a quick kiss on the cheek.

"I see you already have the ring," I said to Millie, pointing at her hand.

Millie looked down and saw the green ring on her finger. "How did that get there?"

"That ring belongs to the Green Witch," I said. Millie opened her mouth to protest, until I held up my hand. "No, I don't think you took it from Hazel. She's no longer the Green Witch. You are."

"How is that possible?" Millie asked. "She received the title yesterday."

"Think about what the fairy who gave it to her said. The nicest and most powerful witch in Greater Greensward will be the Green Witch. I never thought Hazel was very nice, but that fairy must have thought so and the ring must have been waiting to see for sure. Anyway, Hazel didn't believe in the fairy's curse, so she touched a flower to prove she was right. The curse took effect, turning Hazel nasty—certainly nastier than she used to be. That means that you're the nicest, so. . . ."

"I'm the Green Witch? But you're much more powerful than I am, so why didn't you get the title? And what about those other witches at the party? Surely they were more qualified, too."

"The Green Witch has to be from Greater Greensward, so that eliminates a lot of witches. I already am the Green Witch, back where I came from. There can be only one at a time, and this is not my time."

Millie's hand flew to her mouth. "I think I understand now. You aren't really my cousin, are you?"

"No," I said, "but we are related." If Millie was the first real Green Witch, she and Jasper were probably my ancestors. Somehow, I found that thought very comforting.

"I'm never going to see you again, am I?" Millie

asked, her eyes welling up with tears.

"No, I'm afraid not. But in a way, you'll always be with me."

"I guess so," she said, glancing at Jasper. He raised one eyebrow, but she just patted his arm reassuringly and turned to Eadric. "It was nice meeting you, Eadric. Take good care of Emma."

"I always do," he said. I don't think he understood why Millie and I grinned at each other.

Since I hate long good-byes, we left as quickly as we could. I knew how to end the curse, although it wasn't going to be easy, and I was anxious to get home and try it.

The oubliette was empty when we got there, which meant that we didn't have to disguise ourselves. Since we knew what to expect, Eadric held on to Li'l with one hand and put his arms around me while I released a little of the dragon's breath from the bottle.

I needed to come up with an event to mark the time of our return, but all I could think of was the tournament that my father had planned to start the day before my birthday.

> I need to go to the future now,
> To the time from which I came,

Before the day of the tournament
And the start of the very first game.

We were in the dark tunnel almost instantly. The wind tumbled us around like drunken jesters. *This won't last forever,* I promised myself, as the air began to grow thicker. When the roar died down enough so that I could hear Li'l moan, I noticed that the air smelled sour again. Then the high-pitched whine started, and something shoved us through the cloying layer.

This time we hit the floor rolling and didn't stop until we bumped into something solid. Hard objects rained on my head as I tried to get my bearings.

"Help!"

"Watch out!"

"Oh, nooooooo!"

When something landed on my back and bit me, I knew right away what had happened. I'd bumped into the pile of skulls, dislodging the top layer. I rolled over, trying to get away from the skulls, and ended up on my side.

"Mmph," said Li'l in a muffled voice. "Get off me!"

"Sorry!" I said, struggling to sit up. I opened my eyes and closed them again right away. The room was bright, or seemed that way to eyes grown used to the tunnel. I saw the reason when I opened them to little slits, glanced toward the ceiling and saw the witches' light I'd left behind.

While Li'l shook the dust from her wings, I looked around the oubliette. Grandfather was gone and the pile of skulls was in disarray, but otherwise it looked much the same as it had when we left.

"Wouldn't you know it," said one of the skulls that I'd knocked to the floor. "It's that clumsy girl and her suitor again."

"Don't be rude," said a skull still on the pile. A hand raised up from the mound of bones and waggled its fingers at me. "Hello," said the skull. "Nice to see you again. Did you have a nice trip?"

"Very funny," said the first skull. "And you said *I* was rude."

"It was fine, thank you," I said, picking up a skull and setting it back on the pile.

"Here, Emma," said Eadric. "I'll do that." Ignoring the grumbling from the skulls, Eadric restacked the pile, making it neater than it had been before.

As Eadric set the last skull on the pile, I reached into my purse and said, "I have Hubert's medallion. Thanks for letting me use it."

"Hubert, come get your medallion," shouted one of the skulls.

The pile of bones shuddered while a hand rose up and twiddled its fingers. I handed it the medallion. The fingers fumbled until they had a good grip, then the hand sank back into the heap.

"Can we go yet?" asked Li'l.

"Before you go," said one of the skulls, "we wondered if you could leave that ball of light here. It's nice having light in the old place, even if there isn't much to see."

"All right," I said. "If you really want it."

"What about us?" said Eadric. "How are we supposed to see in the dark?"

"Don't worry," I said. "I know what I'm doing."

I said the spell that changed Eadric and me into bats.

"Very nice!" said a skull, and a scattering of hands in the bone pile turned to each other and applauded.

"Bats again?" said Eadric. "Couldn't we try something else?"

"Not if we're flying in the dark," I said, testing my wings.

When we flew out of the oubliette, we found that the dungeon had changed again. The magic loose in the dungeon was always rearranging the walls. A new wall blocked the passage we'd used before, so we had to take a different way that twisted and turned in all sorts of strange angles. We ran into magic fog only once, and that was such a small patch that I had scarcely noticed it before we were out of it again.

We were passing through the guardroom when we came upon a trio of ghosts. "How do you plan to scare people tonight?" asked a hollow-voiced specter. "I'll wait until they sit down to supper, then scream whenever someone sticks his knife in his meat."

"I'll haunt the bedchambers," said another. "A bloody ax at midnight always gets a good reaction."

A ghost with a purplish tinge to his aura spoke next. "I can top both of you. I'm going to dress like a guard and haunt the privy. I'll hide in the hole and when anyone sits down I'll wail, 'Who goes there? State your business!'"

The other ghosts snickered, but I was too angry to think anything was funny. Most of the castle ghosts were friendly; the few who weren't stayed in the dungeon and never bothered anyone upstairs. Yet these ghosts were plotting to terrorize the castle's inhabitants, and I didn't think this would be their first night to do so. I was sure that they couldn't have changed so much unless someone had influenced them, and I had a good idea who that someone might be.

When we finally reached Grassina's room, I turned us back into humans before I knocked on the door. I had a lot to say to Grassina, and it would have a bigger impact if I didn't say it as a bat. No one answered when I knocked, so I opened the door and peeked inside, hoping to find her anyway. Grassina wasn't there, but Blister the rat was sitting on her moldy blanket, gnawing an old melon rind.

"You're back," he said, twitching his pointy, little

nose at me. "Too bad you made it. If you're looking for Grassina, she isn't here."

"Where is she?" I asked.

The rat smirked. "How would I know? I'm stuck down here all day, although I have been thinking about taking a trip upstairs."

"Go right ahead," I said. "And I'll have the biggest, meanest cat that you've ever seen waiting for you."

Blister snarled, baring his teeth. "Maybe I'll wait."

Eadric and Li'l had been poking around on Grassina's workbench, examining water-filled jars containing a baby octopus, a baby shark and a tiny crab. A small cage held a tiny hamster covered with long, flowing fur.

"What's this?" Eadric asked, lifting the lid off my aunt's cauldron. "It smells like rotting cabbage."

Snatching the lid from his hand, I said, "Don't touch anything! You never know what she's cooking up." I sneaked a peek into the cauldron, where a lavender substance bubbled and seethed.

"Put that down," squealed Blister. The mangy rat scurried across the floor and up the leg of Grassina's workbench. "Ooh, Grassina's going to be so mad! No one's supposed to touch that except her!" He chattered his teeth and tried to knock the lid from my hand.

"Watch out!" I said, stepping back a pace.

Blister rose up on his hind legs and reached for the lid.

A large bubble popped, splattering glowing droplets, and a few landed on the agitated rat. Blister squealed and fell onto the table, rolling back and forth as if his fur was on fire. When he started to shrink, I thought my eyes were tricking me; but when his fur began to grow, I was sure it was because of Grassina's concoction. His once-patchy fur became long and luxurious. No longer a muddy brown, it was a deep, velvety color. Even as I watched, his fur grew until it was so long that his face and limbs were hidden in a thick, brown mat. "I told you not to touch it!" he whined, his voice muffled by fur. "You stupid nitwits are always prying into other people's business. A gnat has more brains than you three put together!"

Another bubble rose to the top, and I clapped the lid on before it could pop. Some lavender dust had been left on the rim of the cauldron, but the lid dislodged it and it drifted down, settling on the ranting rat, coating him with a thin layer. "You're morons," the rat continued. "You must be the stupidest, clumsiest creatures I've ever seen. If I was half as clumsy as you, I'd—"

"That's enough out of you," I said. "If you can't say anything nice, don't say anything at all!" It was something I'd heard the cook tell gossiping scullery maids and it had always made them stop. Even so, I was surprised when Blister's mouth closed with a snap.

Li'l blinked and glanced up at me. "Do you suppose the dust did that, too?"

"Maybe," I said. "Too bad we didn't find it sooner."

I thought about leaving a note for my aunt saying that I wanted to talk to her, then decided that she probably wouldn't read it. When we went upstairs, Li'l flew to the tower to take a nap while Eadric left to check on Bright Country and I went to talk to Grassina about the ghosts.

I stopped to ask a maid if she'd seen my aunt. The girl had a strange, panicky look in her eyes, although I didn't think much of it until she spoke. Her mouth opened and her lips moved, yet nothing came out except a shiny bubble that grew bigger the longer she talked. When she closed her mouth, the bubble floated free and drifted up to the ceiling.

I tried to say, *What's wrong with you?* but I couldn't make any sort of sound no matter how hard I tried. Instead I felt a bubble form between my own lips. The more I tried to talk, the bigger the bubble grew. I gestured, trying to tell the maid that I didn't understand what was happening, but I couldn't make her understand *me.* The maid shrugged and pointed at the ceiling. I looked up, and my jaw dropped. The ceiling was covered with hundreds of shiny bubbles.

Grassina, I thought, grinding my teeth.

I went to the Great Hall, determined to find my aunt, but I found my mother instead. When she saw me, she handed me a long pin and held up one of her own. I was confused. “Mother,” I said, “what’s going on?” or at least that’s what I tried to say. A large bubble floated from my lips, but before it had gone far, my mother stabbed it with her pin. The bubble popped and my words came out as clearly as I had intended.

Then it was my mother’s turn. She pointed at my pin and opened her mouth, letting loose one bubble after another. Although I tried to pop them and listen to what they said, Mother was talking so fast that it came out in a crazy jumble.

“Eadric’s parents will arrive this afternoon,” said one bubble.

“You’ll wear them whether you like them or not,” said another.

“This is all Grassina’s fault.”

“Where have you been?”

“I’ve had three gowns made for you.”

“The tournament starts tomorrow.”

“We had to order additional tents.”

“You never sat for your fittings.”

“I can’t get anything done.”

“She’s driving us mad.”

Although I probably missed more bubbles than I popped, I did learn that Eadric’s parents would be arriving that afternoon and that the spell had brought me back the day prior to the beginning of the tournament, which meant that I didn’t have much time. Before I did anything else, I had to locate Grassina and make her do something about the bubble spell.

I searched the castle, questioning everyone I met, but no one had seen my aunt. It took longer than it should have since everyone spoke in bubbles. When no one inside the castle seemed to be able to tell me where she might be, I decided to look outside the castle walls and finally found my aunt kneeling at the edge of the moat trying to coax a slime monster out of the water. The monster, a large transparent sac filled with dozens of eyes floating in pale green goo, left a slimy sheen on anything it touched. It moved by pulling its boneless body on dripping, shapeless feelers.

"What's this all about, Grassina?" I said, surprised that words came out of my mouth and that I was no longer making bubbles. "You confined the voice-bubble spell to the upper floors of the castle, didn't you? It doesn't work outside the walls or in the dungeon."

Grassina patted the slime monster, then wiped her hand on her gown. "Good for you, lady genius. How long did it take you to figure out that one?"

Gurgling softly, the slime monster slipped back into the moat.

"We're having company soon," I said, "and we can't have your voice-bubble spell working when they get here."

Grassina made a face at me that would have been

frightening if I hadn't known her. "Why not?" she asked. "I like bubbles. Don't you?"

"Of course I like bubbles, but I think you like them too much. And if that's the case. . . ." The spell was simple and I'd said half of it before she even figured out that it was a spell.

Since you like the bubbles so,
In a bubble you must go.
In that bubble you will stay
Till your bubbles go away.

Sound can't pass from inside out
Even if you scream or shout.
If you want to be set free,
End your own spell, that's the key.

Grassina threw up her hand to ward off the spell, but it was too late. A giant, shimmering bubble formed around my aunt, who let out an anguished wail that was cut off when the bubble was complete. Although I couldn't hear her, I could see her quite clearly and I could tell that she was furious. Her face contorted with anger, she pounded on the bubble with her fists. Nothing happened until, very slowly, the bubble began to roll in the direction she was pounding. I could tell she was shouting at me, but I still couldn't hear anything she said.

The bubble fell into the water with a splash that drenched my gown and swept the slime monster halfway across the moat. Grassina thrust her hands against the side when the bubble wobbled and bounced. She tried to keep her balance as it floated across the water, but something big must have rammed the bubble from below, because it suddenly shot into the air, then slammed back farther down the moat. Grassina fell to her knees, and I could see her staring into the water. Her lips were moving when the monster surfaced. A cross between a fish and some sort of lizard, it had long, sharp teeth, jagged fins and a serrated tail. Whatever spell she'd said didn't seem to have any effect, but neither did the monster's teeth when it tried to bite the bubble. While I couldn't hear Grassina, the screech of the monster's teeth scraping the bubble made me cringe.

The bubble continued to float, nudged by the monster's butting snout. Grassina's face turned red, and little veins stood out in her forehead. She glared at me until the monster hit the bubble again, knocking it across the water. Apparently the monster had made her angry enough that revenge had become more important than her bubbles. After glancing at me one last time, she nodded and recited a spell. When she'd finished, the bubble shimmered more brightly than before, then burst with a loud POP.

Grassina screamed as she fell into the water, but the

sound from the castle was even louder. All the words that had been trapped in bubbles since the moment she had cast the spell were suddenly let loose. I was delighted until I noticed that my aunt had disappeared beneath the surface and had yet to come up. Although I knew she could swim, only Grassina knew what kinds of monsters she'd let loose in the moat. I was trying to decide what I could do to help her when her head broke the surface and she gasped for breath.

"Do you need a hand?" I asked.

She shook her head and turned around just as the monster rose up out of the water and eyed her hungrily. It was huge, nearly as long as the moat was wide, and it certainly frightened me. I heard Grassina mutter something, although I couldn't hear what she said, but then I wasn't really paying attention because the monster had started to move. Sweeping its tail from side to side, it bore down on my aunt, who was still bobbing in the water. Before I could warn her, she disappeared with a bright yellow flash, and the biggest shark I'd ever seen was swimming in her place. The monster swerved and turned tail, speeding away from my aunt. Snapping her jaws, Grassina took off after it, diving below the surface as they disappeared around the curve in the moat. And to think I'd been worried about her!

Thirteen

I found Eadric in the stable brushing Bright Country. "Your parents are supposed to arrive this afternoon," I told him. "I need to go now if I'm to be back before then."

"What do you intend to do?" he asked.

"Go see the Swamp Fairy, of course. I'll ask her to remove the curse. It was laid so long ago, I can't imagine that she'd still hold a grudge against our family. She's probably forgotten all about it."

Eadric nodded. "Just give me a minute to get ready."

"There's no need—"

He sighed and rubbed his forehead as if it ached. "We've been through this before. I don't want you going alone if there's even the chance that it might be dangerous. I'm going with you and that's all there is to it. Where do you want to look? We could start by the river where we first met her when we were frogs."

"That's what I thought," I said. "We'll just have to

hope she's there, because I wouldn't know where else to look."

I sat behind Eadric on Bright Country when we left a short time later. We tried to make our plans on the way, which was difficult since we really didn't know what to expect.

"So we're just going to ask the fairy to end the curse, is that right?" Eadric asked.

"That's the first thing we'll try," I said.

"What will you do if she refuses? She will, you know. She's that kind of fairy."

"I hadn't really thought that far."

"Then here's what I suggest. Think of a spell ahead of time, and when she isn't looking, do something that will make her remove the curse."

"Even if I wanted to do something like that, it wouldn't work on a fairy. Witches' magic never does."

"Have you ever tried it?" Eadric asked.

"No, but—"

"Then how do you know it wouldn't work?"

"Because Grassina taught me a long time ago that fairies aren't affected by ordinary magic. Their magic is completely different from ours." I usually enjoyed Eadric's company, but sometimes he could be so annoying.

Eadric grunted and said, "Do you have another plan?"

"Yes, but it's not nearly as good as the first one."

"We are in trouble, then, aren't we?"

"I sincerely hope not," I said, but I had a feeling that he was right.

The last time we'd gone to the river, Eadric and I had been frogs and Aunt Grassina had carried us. The trip was much faster this time, partly because we were on horseback, partly because we knew where we were going. It wasn't long before we saw the river through the trees ahead, although it took a bit of hunting to find the place where we'd met the fairy. When we found a clearing that looked promising, Eadric jumped down, then helped me off Bright Country's back.

Cupping my hands around my mouth, I called, "Swamp Fairy! We need to talk to you."

"Don't you have a better name for her than Swamp Fairy?" Eadric asked. "Like Petunia or some typical fairy name?"

I shook my head. "I don't know any other name for her. Tell me if you learn of one."

"Huh," said Eadric. "It just sounds stupid, calling '*Swamp Fairy*' like that."

"Sorry," I said, getting even more exasperated with his unhelpful advice. Turning my back to him, I tried calling again. "Swamp Fairy, are you there?"

When there was no answer, I gritted my teeth and said, "Maybe we're in the wrong spot. Let's try down by the river."

We left the clearing, forcing our way through patches of wildflowers and scrubby-looking bushes. Thorns caught at my skirts, slowing me down, while Eadric forged on past me and reached the river first, even though he was leading Bright Country. I was about to start calling to the Swamp Fairy again when I noticed something that hadn't been there before. Someone had built a small hut beside the water only a short distance downriver. It was a cozy-looking hut, fairly new with a freshly thatched roof and a door woven out of still-green reeds.

"You don't think the Swamp Fairy lives there, do you?" Eadric asked.

I shrugged. "I suppose it's possible."

We were approaching the hut, looking for some hint of who might live in it, when Bright Country nickered, and the door to the hut flew open. A man stepped out, shading his eyes against the afternoon sun. It was Haywood.

"Hello!" he called. "Is that you, Emma, Eadric?"

"Haywood," I replied. "What are you doing here?"

"I live here now," he said, gesturing to the hut. "How do you like it? This is the house I told you about. I built it myself."

"Very nice," I said.

"Isn't this where you lived when you were an otter?" asked Eadric.

"The exact spot. I was living in town until my landlord kicked me out. My magic kept blowing holes in his thatched roof. I had a lot of fond memories of this place, and I didn't know where else to go."

"You could have come back to my parents' castle."

"Not the way Grassina acts around me. Besides I didn't want to impose any more than I had already. Would you like to come in? It's roomy inside."

I followed him through the door while Eadric tied Bright Country's reins to a tree. "It's very nice of you to—oh my!"

It was obvious that Haywood's magic had improved. The hut that had seemed so small from the outside was spacious within and reminded me of Grassina's former room in the tower. While I knew the walls were some kind of plaster, the roof was thatched and the floor was pounded dirt, it didn't look like that to me—they all seemed to be made of stone. A large workbench stood against one wall, while a bed with a wooden frame rested in the corner. A fire burned in the fireplace, although I'd seen no sign of either a chimney or smoke from the outside. A dog lay in front of the hearth, and it wagged its tail when it saw me.

"Olefat's visiting," said Haywood. "He can stand your grandmother for only a few days at a time. I told him he could stay here when he needs to get away."

I nodded, having recognized the animal. Olefat, the

former wizard, looked healthy and well fed.

Haywood offered us seats on his only bench. When we were settled, he sat down beside us and asked, "What brings you out this way?"

"I found out who pronounced the curse on my family," I said. "I came to ask her to remove it. You haven't seen the Swamp Fairy, have you?"

Haywood jumped to his feet. "She's the one who did it?"

Eadric nodded. "The curse said that a true love's kiss would also break the spell."

Haywood looked doubtful. "A kiss? You mean someone would have to kiss—"

"Grassina," said Eadric. "And if you still love her, that someone would have to be you. You do still love her, don't you Haywood?"

"Well," Haywood said reluctantly, "I love the sweet person she used to be, but she isn't that person anymore, is she? You know that Grassina doesn't like me. Even if I wanted to kiss her, I don't think she'd let me get close enough, although I suppose I could try it while she's sleeping."

"The curse mentioned seeing her true self in her gaze," said Eadric. "Doesn't that mean that her eyes have to be open?"

"Probably," I said. "I think the cure is about love, not whether or not you can sneak up on someone. That's why we need to see the Swamp Fairy. You haven't seen her recently, have you?"

"She takes a nap under the old willow in the afternoons. But if she's the one who cursed your ancestor, I don't think it would do you any good to talk to her. I don't know her very well, but from what I've heard about her, she's more likely to put another curse on you than she is to be of help. You might consider turning around and going home. As bad as the curse may be, there are some things that are much worse."

"I can't give up, Haywood. Grassina's always playing tricks on people and making our lives miserable. I don't think we can stand her much longer, but she has no intention of leaving. The only way I can make the castle livable again is if I change Grassina back to the way she used to be."

Haywood shook his head. "All I can say is, 'Good luck,' because you're going to need it. The old willow isn't far from here. I can show you the way, if you'd like."

Accompanied by Olefat, who had to stop and sniff all the interesting scents, Haywood led Eadric and me to a steep slope, then stopped and pointed. The slope ran down to the river, and at its base grew a willow so old that its roots seemed to be the only things holding the edge of the crumbling bank in place. Haywood left after trying to dissuade us one more time. Olefat had already scampered off, following some animal's trail.

Eadric and I climbed down the slope to the willow, but we didn't see any sign of the fairy. Wary of the insects that make willows their homes, I pushed aside the long, trailing leaves and looked again. At first glance there didn't seem to be anyone in the green-tinted world beneath the tree.

"Is that her?" asked Eadric. He gestured to a glowing dot attached to one of the gently swaying leaves.

"Swamp Fairy," I called, trying to keep my voice soft so I wouldn't startle her. "Swamp Fairy, we need to talk to you."

The dot shivered, and suddenly the full-sized Swamp Fairy was standing in front of us, rubbing her eyes and yawning. Her blue hair was disheveled and streaked with more gray than I remembered, and her flower-petal skirt was rumpled and creased. She patted her mouth when she yawned again, then said, "What do you want? Hasn't anyone ever told you to let sleeping fairies lie?"

"I thought that was sleeping dogs," said Eadric.

"Doesn't matter." After studying our faces through narrowed eyes, she said, "Say, don't I know you from somewhere?"

This was encouraging. At least she remembered us. "We met at a party a long time ago," I said.

"It must have been a long time. I don't go to parties anymore."

"It was a birthday party," said Eadric. "They served

great food."

"Really?" said the fairy, her eyes brightening.

"And excellent ale," I said.

"Oh, that party," said the Swamp Fairy. "Yes, that was a while ago. How did you get there?"

"I'm a witch," I said. "And a relative of Hazel's. That's why we're here. You laid a curse on my family when you were leaving."

The Swamp Fairy's eyes narrowed. "I remember," she said. "Your relative was very rude."

"I know, and I'm sorry. I didn't like her much, either. But it's been a long time, and we were wondering if you could remove the curse now."

The fairy shook her head. "I never remove a curse I've cast. It's admitting that you were wrong, and I'm never wrong."

"But it's been hundreds of years! Generations of my family have suffered because of your curse. Isn't that enough?"

"No, I told you. She was very rude."

"What if we gave you something in exchange?" asked Eadric. "Emma has some dragon's breath."

"Eadric, I don't think—"

"No thanks. I already have a vial full. Got it from some dumb-looking frogs awhile back."

"Dumb-looking?" Eadric said. When I saw the muscles of his jaw tightening, I knew we were in trouble.

"If you want to know what dumb-looking is, try looking in a mirror."

"Uh, Eadric...," I began.

"How dare you?" exclaimed the fairy. The air around her began to shimmer, but before she could raise her arms, Olefat the dog tore down the slope, barking at a rabbit he was chasing. Darting this away and that, the rabbit veered away from the fairy, only to have Olefat drive him back. The fairy shrieked when the rabbit ran across her feet, leaving dirty paw prints on her toes.

Grabbing hold of Eadric's belt, I hustled him away from the willow. "What are you doing?" he said after we'd scrambled up the steep embankment. "She didn't do anything about the curse yet."

"And she won't, either, not after you insulted her," I said, pulling his arm to keep him moving. "In case you didn't notice, she was about to turn you into a slug or something equally repulsive. We have to get away from here. I don't know how far a fairy can cast a curse."

Eadric and I hurried back the way we'd come, heading toward Haywood's hut. When the willow was a good distance behind us, Eadric turned to me and said, "You should have used your magic and made her remove the curse while you had the chance."

"I told you, my magic doesn't work on fairies," I snapped. "If I'd tried it, we'd *both* be slugs. We're going to have to go see Haywood again."

"What's the point?" grumbled Eadric. "He already refused to help us."

We had nearly reached Haywood's hut when Olefat trotted up beside me, a satisfied look on his doggy face. "And that," he said, "was number two!" Wagging his tail, Olefat disappeared into the underbrush.

We stopped to watch a patch of wildflowers rustle with the dog's passage. "What did he mean by that?" Eadric asked.

"I don't think he intends to be a dog for much longer. I think he's trying to do favors for strangers so he can break the spell and become human again."

"And distracting the fairy was the second one? What do you suppose the first one might have been?"

"He saved me from a cat," I said. "He was a lousy human, but he makes a very nice dog."

Haywood wasn't surprised when we told him that the fairy had refused to remove the curse. He nodded and said, "I hate to say I told you so."

"We were hoping you could help us," I said.

Haywood frowned. "I can't. Even getting Grassina to talk to me would be nearly impossible."

"You could try, couldn't you?" I asked. "If you kiss her, she'll turn back into the sweet Grassina she used to be, and you already said that she was the one you love."

"Think about it, Emma," said Haywood. "Grassina

doesn't want to have a thing to do with me and threatens me if I go anywhere near her. Who knows what she'll do if I try to force a kiss on her? She could do something to make all of us miserable, and I'd never forgive myself if something happened to you two. You'll just have to learn to live with her the way she is or find some way to get her to move."

"Please?" I asked. "It isn't just about Grassina. There's Eadric and me, too."

"Huh?" said Eadric. "What are you talking about?"

"I want to marry you, Eadric, but if we don't end the curse one way or another, I can't marry you or anyone else."

"Emma, you can't mean that! You know how much I want to marry you. I love you!"

"And I love you, too, which is why I can't marry you with the curse hanging over us. I don't want the same thing to happen to you that happened to my grandfather. I don't want you to end up married to someone so nasty that living in the dungeon is preferable to living with her."

"Just because that happened to them doesn't mean it will happen to us. We won't have any flowers near the castle and you can—"

"Eadric, it wouldn't work. There will always be the chance that I might come in contact with some by accident. Look at what happened to Grassina when my grandmother sent all those magical flowers to fall on her."

"Then we'll have to do whatever it takes to end the curse, won't we?" said Eadric. "What do you say, Haywood? Will you try?"

Haywood sighed. "If it means that there's a chance that I could get my Grassina back and that you two can get married, yes, I'll try. But I can't guarantee anything."

"We don't expect you to, do we, Eadric?"

"Well, it would be nice," Eadric muttered under his breath.

"I'll be there tomorrow," said Haywood. "I have a few things to do first."

It was dusk when Eadric and I returned to the castle, and I half expected to see Li'l out hunting for insects. The area around the castle was curiously quiet, however, and I learned why when Bright Country suddenly reared up, nearly dumping us off his back.

"What happened?" Eadric asked Bright Country, patting his neck as the horse danced nervously to the side of the road.

"Didn't you see it?" said the horse. "A huge, scaly beast just ran in front of me. It looked right at me and stuck out its tongue!"

"That was probably Grassina," I said. "She must have gone out for the evening."

"Grassina is a scaly beast now?" asked Bright Country.

I nodded. "She likes turning into a lizard. A few weeks ago, she tried being a wolf. Who knows what she'll try next."

As we'd missed supper, Eadric and I went straight to the kitchen to find something to eat. He had befriended everyone on the kitchen staff during his frequent visits there, so they were delighted to see him. After they spent a few minutes reminiscing about his last stay, the cook said, "We know where you got your appetite. Your father can eat even more than you can!"

"My parents are here?" Eadric asked.

"They arrived right before supper. 'Good timing,' I said, when I heard how hungry His Majesty was. I had to cook extra eels just for him."

Eadric grinned. "My father likes eels, but they give him awful indigestion."

"You do take after him, don't you?" I said, kissing him on the cheek. "Come on, you can introduce me."

Eadric gazed at the platters of leftovers with great longing. "All right," he said, "as long as Cook saves us some supper."

Cook laughed. "Don't worry, we'll save plenty of food. It will even be enough for you!"

We were leaving the kitchen when Eadric said to me, "I'd better warn you. My parents aren't anything like yours."

"You mean your mother is sweet and friendly?"

"I wouldn't go that far," he said, grinning again.

"Eadric, my boy!" called a deep voice, and I looked up to see a short, heavyset man with a well-rounded belly coming toward us. A tall, thin woman with frizzy, brown hair turning to gray followed at his heels.

Eadric greeted the couple, then said, "Father, Mother, this is Princess Emeralda, the girl I'm going to marry."

"This is your Emma?" said Eadric's father. "Why, she's lovely, my boy. You've found yourself a good one."

"Emma," said Eadric, "this is my father, King Bodamin, and my mother, Queen Frazzela."

"Delighted to meet you, my dear," said the queen, in a high, thin voice.

Even through the formalities of royal greetings, I noticed that the queen's nails were nibbled short, and she had permanent worry creases on her forehead. *Eadric was right,* I thought. *They aren't anything like my parents.*

Later, when Eadric and I finally had a minute alone, I said, "Your father is the first person to tell me that I'm lovely who seemed to mean it. The only people who've told me that before were ones who think they're supposed to flatter a princess."

"I think you're lovely," murmured Eadric.

"Only because you love me," I said.

"Hmm," he said, kissing me before I could say anything else.

Fourteen

The next day was overcast, with a heavy blanket of clouds blocking the sun. The tournament to celebrate my birthday was to be held in the field where Father and his knights usually practiced with their swords and lances. Carpenters had taken over the field weeks before, building stands for the crowd that would come to watch and setting up tents for the competing knights. The wooden barrier that ran the length of the tilting field and divided the field in two was also ready, its frame draped with colorful fabric.

Since I hadn't seen Eadric in the castle, I assumed he was getting ready for his first run against someone called the Black Knight. It had become fashionable for a knight to choose a color for his armor, then claim that color for his name during the tournament. Eadric's color was silver, which looked wonderful when he was on his white horse. Although I had met most of the competing knights, I didn't know which colors they had chosen.

With their helmets closed and their faces covered, I had no way of telling until after they'd competed and removed their helmets.

I was on my way to the field, hoping to see Eadric before the games began, when I saw my grandmother chatting with Oculura and her sister, Dyspepsia. Olefat the dog was also there, sniffing the hems of their gowns. As I approached the tents closest to the castle, I spotted Grassina scurrying toward the moat. She was carrying something in her arms, but I couldn't tell what it was from a distance.

The herald's trumpet blared just as I started toward my aunt. "King Limelyn has declared that all lances must be blunted for this tournament," announced the herald. "Any knight using a pointed lance will be disqualified."

My father always ordered the blunting of lances, though even blunted lances could deliver powerful blows. I'd been so preoccupied with the curse that I hadn't thought about Eadric's safety, and suddenly I was worried. The competition was dangerous, and so was the threat of the unknown magic that my grandmother and Oculura had mentioned. I decided to do something about it—nothing that would help Eadric win, because I knew he wouldn't stand for that, just something that would keep him from getting hurt.

I found a quiet spot behind two of the tents where no one could see what I was doing and reached into my purse. There wasn't much inside that was suitable, but I found a small coin that would do. Holding the coin in one hand, I recited a health-and-safety charm.

Keep the wearer of this charm
Safe from any kind of harm.
Keep the wearer healthy, too.
Bring him back as good as new.

The coin glowed bright orange for a second, then faded to its original copper. When it was dull again, I took a scarf I'd intended to give to Eadric as a token of my favor and tied the coin in one of the corners. I'd give it to him as soon as I saw him.

The festive atmosphere surrounding tournaments always attracted people from all over. Some came to compete, some to watch and others to make money. Wandering minstrels, jugglers and merchants selling food and trinkets all vied for the attention of anyone passing by. This tournament seemed to be especially popular, with commoners and nobles traveling all the way from Eadric's kingdom of Upper Montevista.

I wandered through the growing crowd looking for Eadric. Instead I ran into Haywood, who was listening to a minstrel's song about an enchanted prince.

"It's not like that at all," Haywood said when he saw me. "But you would know what I mean, having been a frog. Everyone thinks that when you're turned into an animal, you pine away for your human life. You don't, though. You get used to being an animal pretty quickly. It takes a lot longer to remember how to be a human when you turn back. I still don't have it mastered, and it's been more than a year."

"You were an otter for so long," I said.

"That's true. I'm sure it'll just take time. Let's go see Grassina and finish this. I don't like being around crowds anymore."

We found Grassina by the moat near where I'd seen her before. She was staring down into the water, muttering to herself, with her long, straggly hair hanging down around her face. Her cloak lay on the ground beside her, covering something large and lumpy.

"Aunt Grassina," I said. "There's someone here to see you."

She turned her head abruptly and peered up at Haywood through her curtain of hair. "What does he want?" she growled.

"He just wants to talk to you."

"Well, I don't want to talk to him."

Haywood cleared his throat and said, "Hello, Grassina. How have you been?"

"Good, since you left. Why don't you leave again so I can be even better?"

"There's no need to be like that, Grassina," he said.

"We haven't really talked in a long time and—"

"Not nearly long enough. Can't you see I'm busy with matters more important than talking to a brainless nit like you?"

"What are you doing, Aunt Grassina?" I asked.

"Nothing," she snarled. "Now, go away and let me do it some more."

"What is that?" If anyone was going to ill-use magic at the tournament, it was bound to be Grassina. I reached for her cloak, but she slapped my hand aside.

"Keep your hands to yourself if you don't want to lose them," she said, spitting out the words.

"Aunt Grassina," I tried one more time. "I found out how to end the curse."

"What curse? You mean being cursed with rotten relatives who won't leave you alone? Or cursed with nincompoops who have smaller brains than fleas do and don't know when to quit? What do I have to do to get rid of you two? I'd turn into a lizard and eat you both if I wasn't so busy. Now, leave me alone before I turn you into worms and toss you into the moat. I'm not too busy for that!"

"But Aunt Grassina!"

"Now!" she barked, pointing a finger at us as she began to mutter a spell.

I could have counteracted any spell she tried on me, but that wouldn't make her any nicer. Remembering the wording of the curse, I was sure a forced kiss wouldn't do any good. The way Grassina was acting, there wouldn't be any other kind. "Let's go, Haywood," I said, hustling him away from my aunt. "We'll come back when she's in a better mood."

"I'm in a wonderful mood now, you ninny!" my aunt shouted as we hurried toward the tilting field, "because you two are leaving!"

We didn't stop until we reached the first of the tents, and Haywood turned to me to say, "It's no use, Emma. I wouldn't be able to get close enough to that woman to kiss her even if I wanted to. The only reason I was willing to try was to help you and Eadric, and that probably wasn't enough to break the curse, anyway. I'm sorry, Emma. I'm going home."

I was feeling desperate. After everything I had gone through, the curse was as strong as ever. "Are you sure, Haywood? You know she acts like that because of the curse. That wasn't the real Grassina back there. Maybe it would be different next time."

Haywood shook his head. "She seemed real enough to me. You know she's not going to change. Good-bye, Emma. You and Eadric should come visit me sometime."

I headed toward the stands, feeling more dejected than I'd ever felt before. I dreaded having to tell Eadric that I couldn't marry him after all. Even worse, I was going to have to live with an aunt who was getting nastier by the day. If only Grassina could have been nice for just a few minutes!

I glanced back and saw my aunt bending down, pouring something from a big jug into the water. *She's up to something,* I thought, and turned around. By the time I reached the moat, however, Grassina had already gathered her cloak and jug and scuttled off toward the drawbridge.

Kneeling beside the water, I tried to peer into its depths, but all I saw were green bubbles rising to the surface. I was considering using a spell to call up whatever Grassina had put in there when I heard the strident notes of the heralds' trumpets above the clamor of the crowd. I sighed and brushed off my skirts, knowing that I'd have to figure out what Grassina had done later. The tournament was about to start, and Eadric was in the first round.

I found my seat in the stands between my mother and Queen Frazzela. Mother nodded approvingly at the yellow gown I wore, one of the new ones she'd had the seamstress make while I was in the past. Queen Frazzela gave me a halfhearted smile, but she seemed too worried to be enjoying herself.

"I hate tournaments," she said. "Someone always gets hurt. At least Bodi no longer competes." She patted her husband's hand where it rested on the arm of his chair beside her. I wondered how the portly, little man had ever fit into a suit of armor. He smiled at his wife reassuringly, then turned back to the approaching knights. Dressed in silver armor, Eadric rode Bright Country, who pranced alongside the Black Knight's all-black charger as if he was having a wonderful time.

"If only Eadric would stop competing," said his mother.

"There, there, my dear," said King Bodamin. "It's good for the boy. And before you know it, Bradston here will be ready." The king patted the head of a boy about ten years old seated at his other side. "Princess Emeralda," said the king, "this is our younger son, Bradston." The boy smiled at his father, but the king had already looked away so he didn't notice that the smile dissolved into a scowl as Bradston smoothed his hair back into place. Sticking his tongue out at me, he rolled his eyes up in his head and shoved back the tip of his nose with one finger so he looked like a pig.

I'd heard about Eadric's younger brother. It was because of Bradston that Eadric had met the witch who'd turned him into a frog.

"It's nice to meet you, Prince Bradston," I said. For the first time in my life, I was glad that I was an only child.

"You'll have to excuse Brad the Brat," said a voice, and I looked up to see Eadric smiling at me from Bright

Country's back. "He usually falls asleep during the lessons on courtly manners."

I smiled and reached into my purse for the scarf. "This is for you," I said, handing it to Eadric.

He grinned and tucked it under the neck of his armor. "Thank you, my lady. I shall wear your token by my heart." Bradston made a rude noise, which we all pretended not to hear.

Wondering who Eadric was competing against, I glanced at the Black Knight, but his visor covered his face. After saluting both royal couples, the knights turned their horses and trotted down the field, taking up their positions at opposite ends of the tilting barrier.

I sat up straighter when trumpets blared and the herald announced, "The Silver Knight shall ride against the Black Knight!" then held my breath when they lowered their lances and charged.

I'd never seen Eadric joust before, although I had seen him fight a monstrous spider with his sword. He had told me that he was good with a lance as well, but I didn't know how good until he charged down that field. His back straight, his lance poised, his horse's hooves pounding the turf, Eadric looked like the kind of knight in shining armor that every princess dreams about. He was perfect for me, so perfect that he made my heart ache. I'd still have to tell him that I couldn't marry him.

I gasped when the knights' lances slammed into their

opponents' armor. Both lances splintered and the knights rode on, unharmed. They rode again with fresh lances in their hands. Once again, the lances splintered, the sound of the impacts making me wince. On the third round, the Black Knight's lance splintered and broke while Eadric's held firm, knocking his opponent off his saddle. The Black Knight landed on his back with a thud that shook the ground and made my heart skip a beat. Although I was rooting for Eadric, I bit my lip until the Black Knight stirred and some eager squires helped him to his feet. I hated seeing anyone get hurt.

I glanced at Queen Frazzela. Her face was pale, and beads of perspiration had formed on her upper lip. "Eadric will be fine," I said, thinking of my health-and-safety charm.

"If only I knew that for certain!" said his mother.

Although I was tempted to tell her about the charm, I didn't dare because I didn't know how much Eadric had told her about me. Given a choice, I'd rather not be the one to inform her that I was a witch.

While Eadric trotted off to wait for his next turn, the Red Knight rode up to take his place. To everyone's surprise, another knight in silver armor forced his way past the milling squires, taking up the opposite position. When the herald approached, the noise of the crowd died away.

"You may announce me as the Silver Knight," said

the new arrival.

"You can't be the Silver Knight," said the herald. "We already have one. There's only one of a color allowed per tournament, so you'll have to go."

"And if I come back in another color?" asked the knight, his voice muffled by his lowered visor.

"That would be fine," said the herald.

Turning his gray charger back the way he'd come, the knight rode off the field just as the Blue Knight arrived. A large man, he looked imposing in his deep blue armor astride his chestnut steed. However, after the second round he, too, lay flat on his back staring up at the sky.

The Blue Knight had scarcely been helped from the field when the knight on the gray charger was back. Armored in black, he rode into position and waited for the herald to announce him. Once again the crowd fell silent as the herald approached the knight.

"You can't wear that color, either," said the herald. "We've already had a Black Knight. You're going to have to find a color no one else has claimed."

"But I don't have any other armor with me," protested the knight.

The herald shrugged. "The court armorer might have something you can borrow."

The knight leaned forward and tried to speak in a confidential tone, although I could still hear him. "Are you sure I can't wear this?" he asked the herald. "I hate wearing borrowed armor. You never know who's worn it or if it's been properly cleaned."

"Sorry, Sir Knight," said the herald. "Rules are rules. I'm sure one of the young lads would be happy to show you the way."

"If I must," grumbled the knight, yanking the reins so his horse reared up and the herald was forced to jump aside.

When it was time for Eadric to ride again, Bright Country pranced to his place at the end of the tilting barrier, obviously enjoying himself. I was expecting the Gold Knight when the knight on the gray horse returned. His armor was an unusual color, a mix of brown and purple. This time an expectant murmur ran through the crowd as the herald approached him.

"Now, that's a different color," said the herald, smiling broadly. "How do you want me to announce you?"

"As the Purple Knight, of course," said the knight.

"But that's not purple," offered a squire standing nearby.

"This is ridiculous!" said the knight. "I don't care what you call it! Just announce me."

The herald grinned. "Whatever you say, Sir Knight." The herald sounded his trumpet once more, then shouted, "Lords and ladies, gentlemen and gentlewomen. The Puce Knight!"

Shouts of laughter rocked the stands. Pennants

waved in the air as the squires holding them chortled and guffawed. Apparently this angered the Puce Knight. He spurred his horse until the silk covering its flanks tore and blood trickled. Rounding the end of the tilt barrier, he took up his position and waited, his lance aimed and ready.

Once again I held my breath as Eadric rode into position. When the trumpet sounded, the two horses charged, their hooves thundering in unison. The lances hit with resounding thwacks and both knights flew off their horses, landing on their backs in the dust.

I jumped to my feet, but I couldn't see through the press of bodies that had quickly surrounded Eadric. Some men helped the Puce Knight stand, and I began to worry when Eadric didn't stand as well.

"Sit down, Emeralda," said my mother. "The men will see to him."

"But why isn't he standing yet?" I said. "He should be up by now."

With a sigh and a soft thump, Eadric's mother fainted. Everyone rushed to help her, so no one noticed when I slipped under the railing and ran to Eadric. I was nearly there when the Puce Knight reached him.

Eadric lay on his back, the Puce Knight's lance protruding from his armor. Someone had already removed Eadric's helmet and I could see the pallor of his face beneath his sweat-matted hair. The crowd was muttering about pointed lances when the Puce Knight grabbed hold of the lance and pulled it free.

Eadric groaned and lifted his head. "What happened?" he asked.

The Puce Knight raised his lance and slammed it into Eadric's armor. We heard a strange twanging sound, and the lance bounced back. Eadric looked bewildered, but he didn't seem the least bit hurt.

Two of the men standing nearby restrained the Puce Knight while others helped Eadric to his feet. "Let me see that!" Eadric said, grabbing the lance from the Puce Knight's hands. "Emma!" he called, looking for me in the crowd. When people turned and saw me, they moved aside and let me through. "What do you make of this?" he asked, showing me the lance.

It was sharpened, just as I'd thought, but that wasn't all. Holding my hand over the lance, I could feel the magic surrounding it. "Someone has strengthened the point with a spell."

"The point, huh?" said Eadric. "Then let's see what this does." Taking the lance in both hands, he slammed the shaft against his armor-clad knee, breaking it neatly in two. "Now let's see who's hiding behind this helmet."

The Puce Knight struggled to get away, but two burly men held him tightly as Eadric lifted the helmet from the knight's head. I gasped when I saw his face. It was Prince Jorge, the son of the king who had led the invasion of

Greater Greensward the previous summer and the man my mother had wanted me to marry before I met Eadric.

"Jorge!" I said. "Why did you do this?"

Jorge looked from Eadric to me, his eyes hard and angry. "You two humiliated the royal house of East Aridia. It was time you learned a lesson."

"So you tried to kill Eadric?" I said. "What kind of lesson was that?"

"A good one," said Jorge, looking smug. "I thought of it myself."

I hadn't noticed that the crowd had parted for my father until I heard him say, "Arrest that man!" The captain of the guard led the way as three of his men hustled Prince Jorge off the field.

While the men-at-arms herded the crowd back to the stands, Eadric turned to me. "What just happened? Why didn't that lance kill me?"

"Remember that token I gave you?" I asked. "I put a health-and-safety charm on it. The air was knocked out of you when you fell, but Jorge couldn't do any real damage to you as long as you carried that scarf."

Eadric frowned. "I thought it might be something like that. Here, take it back," he said, reaching into his armor. "It isn't a fair fight if I have an advantage."

"But Eadric, Jorge wasn't trying to fight fairly. He wanted to kill you!"

"And now he's under arrest and we don't have to

worry about him, do we? Promise me you won't ever do anything like that again. I don't want you to use magic for me unless you ask me first. Do you promise?"

"If I have to," I said. "But I don't think it's right. I was only trying to keep you safe."

"I know," he said, kissing me on the tip of my nose. "And that's why I'm not really mad. Just don't do it again. Understand?"

"Yes," I grumbled.

Eadric's fall had shaken his mother so badly that she insisted he quit the field for the day, nagging him until he agreed. Then, complaining of a headache, she went back to the castle to rest, taking Bradston with her. Since he was no longer participating in the jousting contest, Eadric removed his armor and took his mother's place in the seat beside me.

The jousting contest was far from over, although the rest felt like an anticlimax to me. Before any more knights met on the tilting field, my father had them all come before him with their helmets off. "Just so we know who's here," he said.

The only surprise was the Black Knight. When he took off his helmet, he was a stranger to everyone except Eadric and me. It was Prince Garrid, the vampire we'd met in Hazel's time.

I gasped and sat forward in my seat. "Garrid, what are you doing here?" I asked.

He smiled. "Hello, Emma. You don't know how relieved I am that I finally found you. I've been waiting for you for years."

"For me?" I asked, confused.

"Actually, I've been waiting for Li'l, but I knew I'd find her only if I could find you. She told me about a lot of things, including this tournament. That's how I knew when to look for you."

"But why?" I knew that vampires were immortal, yet trying to find a particular bat after all those years didn't seem to make much sense.

"Because I realized that Li'l was my one true love. I never married Hazel or anyone else. No one could compare with my Li'l."

"Li'l? Who's that?" asked my mother.

"A friend of mine," I replied. "I met her shortly after I met Eadric."

Mother frowned, her expression changing to one of astonishment when she realized what kind of friend Li'l might be. I'd made a number of friends when I was a frog, and they'd all been animals. "Does she live around here?" she asked, looking at me suspiciously.

"Up in my tower," I said. "Garrid, if you'd like to go see her, she's taking a nap in the storage room right now."

"In the storage room?" Mother echoed, her face turning pale.

I pointed at the castle. "It's the tall tower on the

right," I told the prince.

Grinning, Garrid saluted me and left, his armor clanking all the way across the field.

My mother tugged on my sleeve. "How will he get into the tower chamber? You always keep that door locked."

"He'll find a way," I said, glancing at the tower windows. It wouldn't be any problem for a bat.

Fifteen

I'd begun to relax, certain that Jorge's lance had been the magical threat Oculura and my grandmother had warned me about, when Eadric leaned toward me and said, "I saw Grassina when I was coming out of my tent. Why is your aunt strewing pieces of raw chicken on the ground? She was making a lot of dogs happy until she chased them away with her broom."

I jumped to my feet and looked toward Eadric's tent. "Where was she headed?"

"I don't know," he said. "I—"

A woman shrieked. At first I thought it might be a peacock, but when the ground shook and other people started screaming, I knew I'd let my guard down too soon.

While I tried to see what was going on, Eadric hurdled the railing. "You stay here," he said.

I slipped under the railing and started running. "I'm the Green Witch, remember?" I shouted over my shoulder. "I don't stay out of trouble; I take care of it."

Eadric yanked Ferdy from his scabbard and ran to catch up with me. "How could I forget?" he yelled.

I was still in front of the viewing stand when the tent at the end shivered. Looking up, I saw an enormous gray tentacle rise above the green roof, then smack down its peak, squashing the tent flat. A few people—unlucky enough to have been caught inside—squirmed out from under the fabric walls. I hoped that there was no one left behind.

Eadric had always been the faster runner, so he reached the pavilion first. This time when the tentacle swept down out of the sky, he was ready for it and grabbed hold with one arm, twisting his body so he could wrap his legs around it. Hanging on with all his strength, Eadric rode it up into the sky, where it thrashed back and forth, trying to shake him off.

I couldn't make up a spell to fight it until I knew exactly what I was fighting, so I ran around the flattened pavilion, hoping to get a better look at the creature. There was a whoosh of air above me and I heard Eadric shout. Looking up, I saw him riding the tentacle as if it was a wild, bucking horse. I was so close that I could hear Ferdy singing as Eadric hacked at his ghastly, gray steed.

> Slash, hack, chop and whack.
> Cut down the foe, he'll not come back.

Slash, hack, chop and whack.
No monster shall hurt my master.

Pieces of its flesh dropped from the sky, but the tentacle kept flailing, smashing tents and flinging tent poles and cart wheels through the air. People screamed and scattered as the creature moved toward the tilting field.

"Emma," called Eadric from somewhere above my head, "let me have that token."

"Are you sure?" I hollered. "You made me promise."

"Forget the promise," he yelled. "Just send it to me!"

"Fine," I said to myself. "And they say women can't make up their minds."

Taking the coin and scarf in one hand, I sent it to Eadric with a flick of my fingers and a few whispered words. The scarf shivered, then spread out like the wings of a bird and began to flap, carrying the coin up to Eadric. It took a while for it to reach him because the tentacle kept moving, but he finally saw the scarf coming and grabbed it as he whipped past.

Hearing a loud hiss, I dashed around one of the few tents that was still standing, past a fleeing troop of jugglers headed the other way and found what I was looking for. The enormous creature carrying Eadric lurched across the ground, dragged by tentacles that had never been intended for dry land. Half again as wide as the biggest tent, the monster had the hard-shelled body of a crab, the sharp-faced head of a shark and the tentacles of an enormous octopus. It was a composite of three different creatures. Now I knew what I had to do; I just had to find a way to do it.

Two knights were trying to drive the monster back with their lances, but the shell-covered body was too hard to penetrate and the shark's head too fierce to approach. When it snapped at them, its shark's teeth clanged against their already dented armor. Shattered lances littered the ground, and the hafts of their broken swords jutted uselessly from the monster's mouth.

Eadric must have seen this as he tore through the sky, for the next time the tentacle carried him over the monster's body he let go and leapt onto its back. The shark's jaws gaped as the body shook, trying to dislodge Eadric.

A horse screamed, and I turned to see another knight spur his destrier straight at the lurching monster. When the shark's head turned and lunged, the poor warhorse reared up, nearly dumping the knight onto the ground. The horse whirled, and the last thing we saw of the knight was the back of his armor, bouncing wildly as his steed galloped between the remaining tents and out of sight.

Unlike the monsters Grassina had created before, this was a composite monster created out of three innocent creatures. Leaving them in this form would not only make them miserable for the rest of their lives, but would introduce a new, more horrible beast into the world of monsters. I needed a spell that would separate the monster into its individual forms.

While Eadric tried to drag himself onto the back of the monster's head, I pointed at it and said,

> Take this monster. Make it three
> Separate creatures. You will see
> They'll be happy once again
> When they live in their own skins.

The monster lurched again and the spell missed its mark. I was trying to think of a way to get the spell where I wanted it to go when Eadric threw himself forward and landed on the shark's head. The monster snapped at him, but Eadric ducked, jamming Ferdy into the spot where the shark's head joined the shell. He was trying to drive Ferdy in farther when one of the monster's tentacles wrapped itself around his waist, plucked him off and tossed him aside like a broken doll. I cried out as he flew through the air, his arms and legs flailing.

Eadric was yelling when he hit the ground, but instead of a solid thump, he hit with a squishy kind of sound and immediately bounced back onto his feet.

"Wow!" he said, when I ran to make sure he was all right. "That was incredible!"

"Eadric, I know what we need to do—" I began.

"Yeah, but did you see that? I was flying, and then I hit the ground, and I bounced and then—"

"Eadric, are you listening to me? That's a composite monster. I can render it harmless if I can break it up into its individual parts again, but I need you to help me deliver the spell."

"I can handle that," said Eadric.

"I'll put the spell in a ball like the ones we used when we fought King Beltran and turned his soldiers into frogs and mice. You'll need to aim for a spot where you'll hit parts of all three creatures. Do you think you can do that?"

"With the charm you gave me, I think I can do anything."

"Then here goes," I said. Shaping a ball with my hands, I repeated the spell that would break the monster apart. The whole time I was working, I could hear two knights fighting the beast. I was almost finished when the monster flung them into the sides of a tent. The tent broke their fall as they flattened it to the ground. They were wallowing in the fabric when I handed Eadric the spell-filled ball.

"How sturdy is this thing?" he asked, taking it from my hands.

"Strong enough," I said. "Just don't drop it."

A high-pitched cackle grated on my nerves. Glancing

toward the tents, I spotted Grassina peeking out from behind a shattered cart, watching her creation with a mother's pride. When the monster noticed Eadric's approach, it turned its head to snap at him. Grassina chortled and rubbed her hands together. When Eadric dodged aside and tried again, she fairly danced with joy. But when he ran straight at the monster's head and tossed the ball with all the strength he could muster, she stopped laughing, her eyes clouded over and she began to mutter a spell of her own.

"Oh, no you don't!" I said and recited a binding spell.

Grassina's hand froze in mid-gesture. Her face turned nearly purple as she realized what I'd done. The only things she could move were her eyes, but she glared at me with a fierceness that said everything. The binding spell was an old one that I was sure Grassina knew, but it would take her a minute or two to break it, giving my own spell enough time to work.

The ball hit the monster, bursting with a shower of green droplets. Eadric tried to jump out of the way, but he'd underestimated the monster's reach, and the daggerlike teeth closed over his back and shoulder. Then, between one breath and the next, the monster shivered and dissolved in a lavender puddle.

Eadric stumbled and nearly fell while Ferdy clattered to the ground. Grassina howled wordlessly, the binding spell not fully broken.

The monster was gone, leaving a tiny crab, a baby octopus and a miniature shark floundering on the hard-packed dirt. They would die if we left them on the ground, so I sent them home with a quick spell. They disappeared in a green haze smelling strongly of salt water.

"How dare you?" screamed Grassina, finally getting her voice back. "That was the best monster I'd ever made! You ruined it! Now I'm going to have to start again and—"

"No, you're not," I said, glaring back at her. "Your monster-making days are over."

Grassina sneered at me. "Oh, really? And I suppose you're the one who's going to stop me?"

"If she doesn't, I will," said my grandmother, who suddenly appeared beside me. "Why did you have to ruin this tournament, you good-for-nothing, spoiled brat? You know how much I love tournaments! I used to watch your father joust before you were even a twinkle in his eye. You did this just to spite me."

"Maybe I don't like tournaments and all the noise and partying. Did you ever think of that? Or maybe I wanted to see your expression when my monster ate those precious knights."

"Or maybe you're just so cantankerous you can't stand to see anyone enjoying herself," I muttered under my breath.

"Mind your own business," Grassina said, scowling at me. Once again I'd forgotten how good Grassina's hearing could be. "Did you invite the old hag so she could help you spoil my fun? It won't do either of you any good. The feeble, old bag of bones hasn't helped anyone in years. Her magic is so pitiful that—"

"Who are you calling a feeble bag of bones, you low-life fleck of pond scum," growled my grandmother. "I'll teach you to mess with me. My magic is stronger than yours any day!" Pointing at the ground beneath Grassina's feet, my grandmother muttered a few obscure words. The ground began to rumble, and a small crack opened up.

Eadric had come up beside me when I wasn't looking. "I don't think Grassina was really thinking of your grandmother when she—"

I clapped my hand over his mouth before he could say another word. "Shh, Eadric! Not now." The last thing I wanted was for two fighting witches to turn their attention to him.

Looking back at my aunt, I saw that the crack had widened, forcing her to stumble out of the way. "Is that all you can do?" she taunted, waggling her finger almost playfully. Grassina raised her arms to the sky and began to spin in place, slowly at first, then faster and faster until she was a whirling blur. A wind began to blow, bringing dancing snowflakes with it. The snow grew thicker, swirling out in a horizontal blizzard.

I turned my head to keep the snow from blinding me and saw my grandmother stomp her feet and gesture. Suddenly there was another kind of blizzard that made us back away. A swarm of insects had formed between Grandmother's hands, pouring forth in a stinging, biting, hopping, crawling, flying cloud that roiled and swirled toward my aunt.

The snowstorm grew fiercer, freezing insects in the air and on the ground, but when a few made it past her snowy barrier, Grassina slapped at them and called up another weapon, letting her snowstorm die down to a few drifting flakes. Birds of every shape and size flocked to her, dropping out of the sky from miles around to devour the insects before turning their beady eyes on my grandmother.

"So that's how you want to play," said my grandmother, and within moments an army of cats descended on us. Snarling, screeching, stalking cats—from stable cats to lions with shaggy manes—seemed to appear out of nowhere, batting at the birds as they flew and pouncing on them when they landed.

Nearly everyone had been scared off the field by Grassina's monster. When the big cats ran out of birds to chase, they began to stalk the few humans who were still around. A tawny-coated cat with irregular spots stared at me and licked its lips. I had to do something, and I had to do it fast before things got even more out of hand. I thought of turning myself into a huge dog to chase the cats away, but Grassina beat me to it by calling up a pack of enormous wolves, exactly the kind I'd chased out of the kingdom only a few weeks before. The wolves ignored Grassina, my grandmother and me, but I knew it wouldn't be long before they turned on us as well, and if we weren't there to stop them, they'd go after anyone who stepped outside the castle walls.

"Stop it!" I shouted at my aunt and my grandmother, trying to make myself heard over the fighting. Neither paid me any attention.

I had to do something to get them to stop fighting, something they couldn't ignore. There was only one creature that I knew they both respected. I'd never turned into one before, but then I'd never tried.

Dragons big and dragons small,
Fiercest creatures of them all,
Change me into one of these.
Do it quickly, if you please.

When my skin began to burn, I wondered if I'd made a horrible mistake. Maybe people were never meant to turn into dragons. When my stomach felt like it was on fire, I was convinced that my mistake was going to be fatal. Why couldn't I have chosen a nonmagical creature?

Instead of the tingling or bubbly feeling that I usually felt when I changed, turning into a dragon was painful. Everything about me hurt: my skin, my stomach, my head, my muscles, even my bones. The pain grew worse until I felt as though I'd been dipped in molten lava. I was lying on the ground, writhing in agony, when the pain ended as abruptly as it had begun. *I must be dead,* I thought, opening my eyes, but I was still on the field between the moat and the tents. The fight had stopped for the moment, and everyone was staring at me.

I looked down and saw why. I was a dragon just as I wanted to be, but I wasn't quite like any dragon I'd ever seen. From the tip of my pointed snout to the end of my ridged tail, my body was an iridescent peridot green. My finger-length claws were a dark emerald color, and my pale green wings were translucent. As I'd learned months before, there were no green dragons, yet that was exactly what I had become. I was nearly twelve feet long and covered with scales, but for the first time in my life, I felt beautiful.

While everyone stared at me, I raised my wings and flexed them to see if they really worked. I didn't move them very much, but I still created a wind strong enough to send some of the smaller cats flying and blow away the last of the insects.

"Emma, is that you?" asked my aunt.

"Yes," I said, my voice sounding like a hiss.

Grandmother scratched her head. "That's not possible," she said. "No witch has ever been able to turn herself into a dragon. It must be an illusion."

"Does this feel like an illusion to you?" I asked, spreading my wings again and beating them one, two, three times. Grandmother's gown streamed out behind her, and she had to brace her feet to keep from being blown over.

"I guess not," she said, blinking at the dust I'd blown into her eyes.

Grassina sneezed, then blew her nose on her sleeve. "How is it possible?" she asked.

"It's magic," I told her. I didn't really know, either, but I suspected that it had something to do with my being a Dragon Friend.

Neither Grassina nor Grandmother protested when I herded them together and said, "No more fighting with magic. If you don't agree about something, you're going to have to learn to talk about it. Do you understand?" They nodded, their heads wobbling as if pulled by cords. "Now go to the castle and stay there until you can work this out."

They stumbled off together, glancing back at me now and then to make sure I was still behind them. I followed them as far as the drawbridge, then sat down and watched them trudge inside. "Go get started," I called after them. "I'll be right there."

My voice must have been loud in the enclosed space, because they flinched when I spoke, then scuttled away like pages caught stealing tarts from the kitchen. I flexed my wings once more, enjoying the supple way they stretched. Unfortunately I didn't have time to try them out, but I promised myself that I would turn back into a dragon as soon as I had the time to experiment.

When my aunt and my grandmother were out of sight, I repeated the spell to turn myself back into my human form. Eadric had stayed behind, but now that I was myself again, he joined me at the drawbridge. "That was easier than I expected," I said. "Did you see how they listened to me?"

Eadric licked his lips and tried to smile. "Anyone would have listened to you when you looked like that. You scared them so badly that they couldn't do otherwise. To be honest, you scared me, too!"

"Sorry about that. I just wanted them to stop fighting. It seems that's the only way those two can relate to each other anymore. I wish I could order Grassina to kiss Haywood, but I doubt it would help now. She wouldn't really mean it, and I think it has to be heartfelt to work. We'd better go see what Grassina and my grandmother are up to," I said, kissing Eadric on the cheek.

I could hear them arguing long before I reached the Great Hall. Their voices were shrill and carried well. When I entered the room, I saw that I wasn't the only one they'd attracted. Oculura and Dyspepsia were seated on a bench at the back of the room, sharing a trencher of roast goose and onions while listening to the argument. My parents were also there along with Queen Frazzela and King Bodamin, both of whom were dressed for travel.

"A forest of stinging nettles," said my grandmother. "That's what I would have tried next if Emma hadn't been there."

Grassina snorted. "You are so old-fashioned. Stinging nettles went out of style years ago! I would have tried quicksand or maybe a fog so dense that—"

"Not around my castle, you wouldn't," said a hollow-sounding voice as my grandfather materialized in the center of the room. "This isn't a testing ground for new spells. It's a home and a seat of government, which you two seem to forget. Grassina, I found out about that dust you've been using on the ghosts in the dungeon. I'm acting on behalf of the Council of Ghosts when I say that you may no longer use it under penalty of personal haunting. I've sent the affected ghosts to be purged of the dust. There will be no more tomfoolery like that around here again. It's time you and your mother grew up and started to help Emma instead of making things harder for her. Curse or no curse, you're still family."

Everyone turned their heads when Queen Frazzela groaned on the other side of the room. Her face was pale and she had her hand pressed to her throat, but that didn't stop her from speaking her mind. "This is a horrid family!" she said, her voice turning as shrill as my aunt's and grandmother's. "When I came inside to lie down, I heard the commotion, so I climbed up to the battlements. I saw everything that's gone on here today. Witches for relatives, monsters in the moat and ghosts in the castle! Even that girl is a witch," she said, pointing an accusing finger at me. "After meeting all of you, I will never give my son permission to marry into such a horrid family, regardless of how much he says he loves your princess."

My grandfather's color deepened to a rich blue as he floated toward Eadric's mother. "You have no idea what you're talking about," he said with more feeling in his voice than I'd heard in a long time. "This family may be unique, but it's not horrid." Raising his transparent arm, Grandfather pointed at my grandmother. "This woman was the best wife any man could ever have, king or not. She loved me with all her heart, but I was too busy to notice. We argued over something inconsequential, and I thought I'd make up for it with a silly bouquet of flowers. It was my fault that she fell prey to the awful curse that changed her life. If I'd known her better, it would never have happened. I loved that woman then, and I love her still. If there is such a thing as a soul mate, then this woman is mine. Any man could count himself fortunate if he could marry into this family, and he'd be a fool to think otherwise."

"Aldrid?" said my grandmother.

Grandfather turned to face her, floating back across the room until his aura nearly touched her. "I should have told you how I felt years ago, but other things always seemed to get in the way. However nasty you might have been, I've always known it was the curse talking and not you. I love you, Olivene. I always have, and I always will."

Grandfather moved toward her again, the blue of his aura engulfing her as his arms seemed to wrap around her body. Although we could see through him, we could also see when he kissed her full on the lips, and she responded, trying to kiss him back.

Tears pricked my eyes, and I was wiping them away when Eadric nudged me and said, "Will you look at that!"

A hole seemed to have opened in the ceiling, and through it streamed a shower of flower petals of every description. They fell around us, drifting onto our faces, our clothing and down to the floor. My mother shrieked and hid her face in my father's shoulder, but for the first time in centuries flower petals had no power to change the women of the royal family of Greater Greensward.

Someone laughed, a light tinkling sound that

brought a smile to everyone's lips. It was my grandmother, her face restored to her former beauty—older, sadder, but still the face that my grandfather had loved. I looked at my aunt and she had changed as well, her face the one that I had missed so much. Hearing the laughter, my mother looked up, and I saw her face transform. Years seemed to drop away from her as she realized the truth. The family curse was over.

Everyone started to laugh, a joyous sound that hadn't been heard in the castle for far too long. Still laughing, I turned to Eadric, the words I'd wanted to say already on my tongue.

Something thudded by the door, and I heard a voice cry out, "Stop it! Let go of me!" A moment later Olefat the dog backed into the room, his teeth clenching someone's sleeve. Instead of letting go, Olefat snarled and shook his head, then braced his feet and pulled even harder. With one last yank, Haywood popped through the door. When he saw everyone, he looked around sheepishly and said, "I didn't mean to intrude. The dog—" And then his eyes fell on Grassina. The astonishment on his face lasted but an instant, chased away by a look of such longing that I felt as if we were the ones who were intruding. "Grassina?" he asked. "Is that really you?"

"Oh, Haywood," she said, and suddenly they were holding each other. Olefat yipped and hopped up onto an empty bench. "And that," he said, "makes three!"

"What does he mean by.... Oh!" said Haywood as a tiny whirlwind danced around Olefat the dog, leaving Olefat the wizard in his place.

"Awk!" said Metoo the parrot, perched on the old man's shoulder. "It's about time!"

"Why are you complaining?" demanded Olefat. "I was the one who did all the work. You were just my flea!"

Taking Eadric's hand in mine, I led him to an empty corner of the room where we could have a little privacy. "The curse is over," I said before wrapping my arms around him.

"Mmm," he said. "Does that mean that we can get married now?"

I nodded. "Nothing would make me happier."

"Nothing?" he asked.

"Well," I said, "I would like to hold the ceremony in the swamp. We'll have to invite all our friends. You know who I mean. There's Li'l, of course, and Garrid if they're still together and some of the ghosts in the dungeon. Then there's Fang and—"

"What about my parents?" he asked.

"We'll have to invite them, too," I said. "They may not like me now, but you know they'll love me after they get to know me a little better."

"Of course they will," he said, kissing me on the forehead. "People always do."